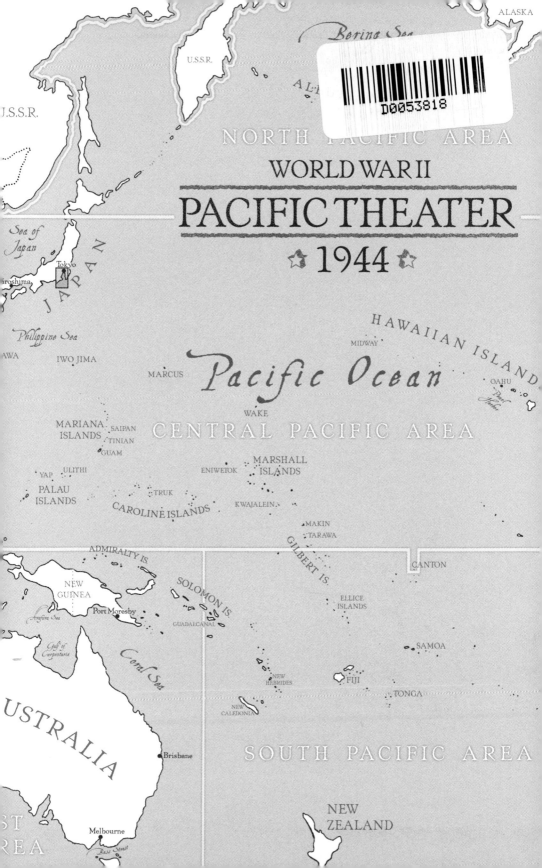

ALASKA

Bering Sea

U.S.S.R.

AL...

U.S.S.R.

NORTH PACIFIC AREA

WORLD WAR II

PACIFIC THEATER

★ 1944 ★

Sea of Japan

Tokyo

JAPAN

...iroshima

Philippine Sea

...AWA

IWO JIMA

MARCUS

MIDWAY

HAWAIIAN ISLAND...

Pacific Ocean

OAHU
Pearl Harbor

WAKE

MARIANA ISLANDS

SAIPAN

TINIAN

GUAM

CENTRAL PACIFIC AREA

YAP

ULITHI

ENIWETOK

MARSHALL ISLANDS

PALAU ISLANDS

TRUK

KWAJALEIN

CAROLINE ISLANDS

MAKIN

TARAWA

ADMIRALTY IS.

GILBERT IS.

CANTON

NEW GUINEA

SOLOMON IS.

ELLICE ISLANDS

Port Moresby

Arafura Sea

GUADALCANAL

Gulf of Carpentaria

Coral Sea

SAMOA

NEW HEBRIDES

FIJI

TONGA

NEW CALEDONIA

AUSTRALIA

Brisbane

SOUTH PACIFIC AREA

...ST ...REA

Melbourne

Bass Strait

NEW ZEALAND

I'LL BE
SEEING
YOU

OTHER BOOKS AND AUDIO BOOKS
BY JERRY BORROWMAN:

Three Against Hitler (with Rudi Wobbe)

A Distant Prayer (with Joseph Banks)

'Til the Boys Come Home

I'LL BE SEEING YOU

A WORLD WAR II NOVEL
PACIFIC THEATER

JERRY BORROWMAN

Covenant Communications, Inc.

Published by Covenant Communications, Inc.
American Fork, Utah

Printed in Canada
First Printing: April 2006

12 11 10 09 08 07 06   10 9 8 7 6 5 4 3 2 1

ISBN 1-59811-108-6

DEDICATION

Carl Ned Allen
1920–1980

Ned was my father-in-law and an Army veteran who served with distinction in some of the most grueling campaigns of the South Pacific, including the liberation of the Philippines and as part of the army of occupation in Japan. With permission, I've included a tribute that appeared in the *Church News* that tells of his loyalty to the Church and the unusual step he took to engrave it in metal when his life was threatened in the jungles. In my experience, it is the most eloquent expression of personal testimony and an enduring legacy of his faith.

Reed Park Borrowman
1917–2001

My father was a veteran of the navy, serving as a fire control director on the aircraft carrier USS *Lake Champlain*. His ship was commissioned too late to see active service in combat, although they ferried troops from Europe. Dad played trumpet in a jazz band when he was young, and his lifelong love of music was the inspiration for an important part of this story.

ACKNOWLEDGMENTS

I owe a great deal of thanks to a group of readers who were kind enough to review my manuscript in advance of submitting it to the publisher. The story always benefits from the insights and suggestions of my wife, Marcella, a natural-born editor. I particularly appreciate the help I received on the story line and line-by-line edit from Val Johnson, a professional editor, writer, and personal friend, as well as Eden Borrowman and Dr. Andy Borrowman. Others who contributed include Evan Rowley, Kelissa Borrowman, Dan Pendleton, Jeff Haber, Hilary Borrowman, Ryan Morganegg, and Analia Funke. Special thanks to Cindi Schmidt, who illustrated the end sheet; Robert Poll, Tabernacle organ technician, for his technical insights; and World War II submarine veteran Merrill Paskins, whose insights were invaluable to telling the story. Finally, my sincere appreciation to my editor, Christian Sorensen, and the staff and designers at Covenant Communications.

PREFACE

I've often puzzled why I should be so intrigued by such an ominous subject as war. It started when I was very young, watching the old black-and-white movies about World War II. Even then, I sensed that this conflict was about great causes: evil versus good; freedom versus tyranny and oppression; men and women who made heroic sacrifices in behalf of country and liberty.

Since then, I've read tens of thousands of pages in hundreds of books, as well as coauthoring a number of biographies that tell the story of some of those heroes. I've been blessed to tour the battlefields of Europe and England to see firsthand the obstacles that had to be overcome to liberate Europe. I've traveled in Japan and learned from my son, who served a mission there, the unique relationship the Japanese feel for America in that we were the first conquering power in their history to actually invest in their society at the end of the war rather than demanding war reparations and inflicting humiliations on their proud and ancient society. It is a humbling experience to go through the museums scattered across England, France, and Germany that bear witness to the utter desolation that was rained down on the people who suffered through this ordeal. It's almost beyond the ability of words to speak of the intensely spiritual and emotional feelings I experienced when walking on the sacred ground of the military cemeteries where the soldiers who made the ultimate sacrifice for the United States found their final peace. Even writing about it today leaves me weak and heartbroken at the price they had to pay so that I can live the blessed life that has been my birthright. A birthright paid for in blood.

And so, at the end of all the study and writing, my opinion is unchanged from when I was a boy. World War II *was* about the perpetual struggle between freedom and tyranny. America and our allies *did* fight in a noble cause, and the world *is* irrevocably better because of that heroic effort. It was a triumph of both political and military strength and determination, and I am grateful to pay tribute to the men and women who earned the right to our veneration.

Prologue

"O'Brian! Get your men ready. We're going over the top!"

Over the top! He can't be serious—it's suicide to go into no-man's-land in broad daylight! "But, sir!" Dan said desperately. "There's been no infantry barrage to soften up the Germans. Shouldn't we call for a supporting bombardment to keep their heads down while we launch the attack?"

He was startled by the look on his commanding officer's face—a wild-eyed look that betrayed the insanity behind the order. His mind struggled to make sense of what was happening. It wasn't Lieutenant Stennis, his regular CO who looked back at him. In fact, Dan didn't recognize this person at all. But he was clearly in charge.

The stranger screamed at him, "I ordered you over the top. How dare you question my order!" Dan didn't know whether to obey the order or shoot the officer. It seemed madness, sheer unadulterated madness to go up in these conditions—broad daylight without a cloud in the sky and the Germans sitting safely in their trenches, ready to open fire with their machine guns while the Americans struggled to cross through the barbed-wire maze of the open space between the Allied and German trenches. They'd be sitting ducks with nothing to protect them.

Dan was about to question the order a second time when he heard a familiar voice whisper quietly in his ear, "Don't fight him on this, Dan. He's likely to bring you up on charges of insubordination."

"Jody? Is that you?" Dan's heart leaped inside his chest at the sound of his friend's voice. How he'd longed to hear Jody's voice since he had died. *Since he died—he died in this very trench, saving my life!* Now Dan felt a new kind of panic. He remembered Jody being killed. Yet he was talking to him. *Am I dead?*

Before he could ponder the question, there was a shout up and down the American line, and, his training asserting itself, he was up and running while firing his rifle as he went. In the back of his mind, he heard the sounds of the German machine guns, felt the ground being churned up all around him as their shells plowed into the mud and dirt. He heard the pathetic cries of men as they were hit. Still he kept running. Then, he heard something new—the sound of an airplane. Hitting the ground, he looked up to see a German Fokker roar overhead, guns blazing as it strafed the Americans on the ground. This was worse than anything he could have imagined. Being fired on by the Germans in the trenches ahead and by an airplane overhead meant that there was no safe place to find cover. They were absolutely vulnerable, and the cries of the men being hit on every side were a perfect witness to the hopelessness of their situation.

Instinctively, he ducked his head as he heard the sound of the aircraft again. Glancing up he saw not one, but two aircraft approaching. "We're done for now," he shouted to Jody. But for some reason, the lead aircraft wasn't firing. In fact it was making some incredible maneuvers to avoid being shot out of the sky by the airplane that was following it.

"It's an American airplane!" someone shouted. "He's got the Germans on the run!"

Dan strained to see the second aircraft. As he watched it drawing closer, there was something familiar about it. As recognition dawned on him, he felt a great shout come up and out of his throat. "It's Trevor! It's Trevor Richards! Oh, Jody, it's Trevor—he's come to save us!"

Dan felt happier than he'd felt since the war broke out. Straining his eyes, he was sure he could see Trevor's face. Then he saw the German sweep up in a maneuver that brought him directly behind the American aircraft, his machine gun blazing away. In an instant, Dan's joy turned to horror as the American aircraft burst into flames.

"No!" he shouted at the top of his lungs. "No! This can't be happening!" He jumped up and started running to where the aircraft had crashed, heedless of the danger. "Not Trevor—oh, please, make it not Trevor!" Hot tears streaked down his cheeks.

As he ran, he felt a searing pain in his side, and he fell to the ground in agony. Then he heard someone call out his name, "Dan! Dan!" and he felt Jody shaking him.

"Dan, wake up. It's alright."

Sitting up, Dan realized with a start that it wasn't Jody's voice; it was Sarah's. As he awoke in the darkness, he let out a sob as he gasped for air, his chest heaving in rapid succession.

"Danny, it's alright. It's a dream. It's just one of the old dreams. You're here with me. You're safe."

Dan winced as his wife turned on the lamp by their night-stand. He struggled to slow his breathing. As his eyes focused, he glanced at the doorway and saw four frightened little eyes looking at him.

"Are you alright, Daddy?" The terrified sound in his little boy's voice caused Dan to take a long, deep breath, which he held for a moment. He let it out slowly while tipping his head back so he could mask the expression on his face.

"Daddy's alright, Cory," Sarah said evenly. "He just had a bad dream."

Dan licked his lips and gratefully took Sarah's hand into his. Finally, he was able to look back at Cory and Kathy. He smiled at them. "Why don't you two come climb in bed with Mommy and Daddy for a few minutes," he said with as much cheer in his voice as possible. The two young children scurried across the linoleum floor and jumped up into the bed. They snuggled under the covers, as close as possible to their mother, obviously still a bit frightened by their father.

"Did I shout out?" Dan asked tentatively.

Sarah smiled. "A few words . . . It wasn't as bad as other times."

"It was about Trevor, wasn't it?"

Her smile faded a bit. "I think I heard his name . . ."

Dan shook his head slowly from side to side. "It's been so long since I've had a war nightmare. I thought they were over." He hated the feeling of tears on his cheeks, but Sarah simply wiped them away with her warm hand. "I hoped they were over," he said miserably.

"Maybe something happened during the day that you didn't even realize at the time that reminded you . . ."

Dan shook his head. "No, it's August." He tried to smile as he turned and rubbed Cory's hair affectionately. The little boy smiled back at him, still a bit tentative, but clearly happy that his father could smile. "It's just not a very friendly month, at least to me. It was August when I was wounded and," he struggled to control his breath again, "when Trevor's plane was shot down."

Sarah reached her hand behind his neck and stroked it gently. "I know," she said. "It's a hard month with too many memories. It's no wonder they come spilling out once in awhile."

Dan settled down further in the covers and tickled Kathy, which made her giggle and snuggle closer to her mother. That would be enough for her, but he worried about the effect his dream would have on Cory.

"Have you ever had a scary dream, Cory?" Dan asked him with as confident a voice as he could muster in the circumstance. Of course he knew the answer. Cory often had disturbing dreams. It seemed an unfair burden for such a little person to bear.

"Sometimes," Cory replied in his high-pitched little voice.

"What do you do to feel better when it happens?"

"When I get scared, I like to come in here and snuggle you and Mommy."

Dan smiled. "I think that's a great idea, Cory. It's such a good idea that it's why I like to snuggle you and Mommy and Kathy when I get a bad dream. It's awfully nice of you to come in here to help me tonight."

Now it was Cory who smiled. "What was your dream about that scared you so much?"

That set Dan back. For just a moment, he closed his eyes, hoping perhaps that the images of Jody, Trevor, and all the others who had been killed in the war had left. But they were still there. He opened his eyes and sighed. "It's an old dream, Cory."

"About when you were in the war?" It sounded odd to hear such a small voice talk about something so serious as the war. Dan looked at Sarah, who gave him a wan smile. Dan regretted that his son had to even think about things like war, but there was no use denying it. It was part of who Dan was.

"Yes, about the war." Then he smiled. "But it wasn't all bad, Cory. I got to remember some very good friends of mine. People who I loved very much. So, maybe it was worth it, after all, to get to visit them in my memory."

In his childlike way, that satisfied Cory, and he snuggled close to Dan. That was the best feeling in the world. Dan turned and gave Sarah a look of gratitude.

"I love you, Dan," she said simply.

"And I love you. Thanks for putting up with me."

Sarah rubbed her hand through his hair and then pulled Kathy close. The little girl was already asleep. Sarah turned out the light, and Dan settled back on his pillow again. He wanted to close his eyes and go back to sleep, but he was afraid, afraid that he'd find himself in France in 1918 instead of Salt Lake City in 1927. "Please, God," he mouthed in silent prayer.

"Please help me to sleep . . . and to have better dreams." In spite of the prayer, he was still afraid to close his eyes. But in time, his eyelids fluttered closed, and he drifted back to sleep. Fortunately, on this particular night, God heard and answered his prayer with dreams that were warm and pleasant, dreams of Sarah and their children.

Chapter One

FROM THE CROSSROADS
OF THE WEST

Salt Lake City, Utah
July 1935

Dan O'Brian looked up from his desk in the dispatcher's office of the Union Pacific Railroad. Even though he was struggling to decipher the handwriting on the work order he'd just received, the familiar sound of a particular British accent broke through his concentration. Sure enough, Jonathon Richards caught his eye and gave him a discrete salute from the front counter before disappearing into the chief dispatcher's office. As the superintendent of the Las Vegas line, Jonathon didn't often make his way over to their office, but he always managed to brighten people's day when he did. Today was no different, as evidenced by the hearty laughs that came through the open door of the dispatcher's office.

"It never ceases to amaze me how cheerful he is."

Dan turned at the sound of Bill Reynolds's voice. Since Dan had moved to Salt Lake City nearly ten years earlier, Bill had been Dan's best friend in the department, helping him to learn the ropes when he was new and even volunteering to split his hours with Dan when Dan was threatened with unemployment in late 1930. Bill understood Dan's relationship to Jonathon Richards and his wife and accepted it without resentment, even though some of their coworkers were suspicious of Jonathon in the early days, since he had used his influence to get Dan his job. Bill enjoyed so much respect in the department that his acceptance helped smooth Dan's transition into the closed world of the dispatcher's office. Since then, they'd weathered a lot of storms together, including the cuts in pay and reduction of hours that resulted from the loss of business caused by the Great Depression.

"Yes, he's pretty much always like that. No matter what's going on in the world, he always seems to find a way to put a good face on it. He loves people and somehow manages to be cheerful . . ." Dan was thoughtful for a moment, trying to decide if he ought to give Bill a more complete picture.

"But . . ."

"There have only been two times that I saw him really down. The first was when he and Margaret lost their son in the war; the other was five years ago at the beginning of the Depression. Jonathon lost a lot of money in the stock market crash, and it was a real blow to both his finances and his self-confidence."

Bill was quiet for a moment. "I never knew that about him. I remember the panic that followed the market collapse, yet I never saw anything in Mr. Richards's reactions that indicated he was troubled by it."

Dan reflected back on the agitated look on Jonathon's face when Dan happened to run into him the day after the market crash. Jonathon and Dan regarded each other almost as father and son, and it had unnerved Dan to see Jonathon so frightened. Like most people at the time, Dan had no money in the market, so he failed to appreciate the serious weaknesses in the American economy that the Crash foreshadowed. As he became aware of the magnitude of Jonathon's losses, he felt terrible for him.

"The reason he didn't show it publicly is that he feels it's the responsibility of a leader to inspire confidence. Behind the scenes, he's had to work long and hard to pay down the debts that he incurred buying stock on margin. Before the Crash, he worked here mostly because it interested him—he was close to being independently wealthy. Since then, he's depended on the job to get him through. I think that's why he's still working instead of retiring. I get the feeling they're about out of debt, but he's still working to build something for retirement."

Bill nodded. Lots of people had their plans changed by the Crash. The prosperity of the post-war period had evaporated almost overnight, leading into the stagnation that left people feeling desperate, even when they were fortunate enough to have a job. Five years into the Depression, the American economy was still languishing with more than twenty percent unemployment. And that was only part of the story, since most of the people who were lucky enough to still have a job had taken multiple pay cuts along the way, sometimes even having their working hours reduced so that two people could share what had once been a single job.

Working as a clerk for the Union Pacific, Dan had not been immune to these adjustments since fewer goods being shipped meant fewer rail cars to track and route. He probably would have been laid off altogether if it hadn't been for the union, which had negotiated a series of pay cuts and reduced hours. It had been a discouraging and frightening struggle to support his family. Eventually, the only thing that had saved them was that Sarah had gone back to work part-time as a nurse while Dan picked up some extra money playing piano in a dance band. At least that had been a positive experience, since it gave him the chance to enjoy the music.

Another bright spot in his life had been the invitation to serve as a substitute organist in the Tabernacle on Temple Square. Dan enjoyed playing the great organ on special occasions or when one of the regular organists was unavailable.

In fact, as the summer reached its peak, he was looking forward to playing an organ solo at an evening concert the Friday before repeating one of the numbers on the Sunday broadcast, so he was anxious to get in some practice time.

Unfortunately, the weeks leading up to the broadcast were rather frantic, which made it difficult to find time to practice. The problem was that a crew was coming in from New York City to help the technicians from the Church-owned radio station, KZN, install new broadcast equipment and microphones that would replace the already out-of-date equipment that had been considered state-of-the-art just five years earlier. Apparently the specialists were needed to help determine the placement of the dynamic microphones that would best capture the full sound of the choir. All access to the Tabernacle was temporarily suspended when they arrived.

Because Dan wrote his own arrangements, he needed time at the keyboard to refine the various stops he planned to use, and it was worrisome not to have access. He was relieved when he finally got a call indicating he could come in on Tuesday afternoon. That forced him to arrange for some extra time off from work, which was difficult in the highly structured environment of the railroad. Fortunately, he had a friend who normally worked weekends and nights who was pleased to trade for an afternoon shift. Dan would have to work Saturday to make up for it, but it was worth it to play at the Tabernacle.

On Tuesday afternoon, just before he was to leave for the Tabernacle, Dan's boss asked him to send just one more teletype. By this time, Morse code had been replaced by a repeating machine that allowed one to "type" characters on a keyboard that connected via wire with each of the other hubs in the system. Perhaps it was his skill at the organ that enabled him to be the fastest typist in the clerk pool.

Dan hurried to get the message off, nervous that his boss had chosen to look over his shoulder.

"I just love to watch you do that. My eyes have trouble keeping up with the rhythmic movement of your fingers. I don't know how your brain can think fast enough to remember which key comes next."

Dan smiled. His boss was from the old school where orders were handwritten and trains ran on a strict schedule to avoid any possibility of a conflict on the tracks. Now, there was "flexible" scheduling that allowed rerouting based on up-to-the minute reports of the movement of trains to the dispatchers' office where Dan worked. The complexity of the new system eluded his boss. "The truth is, I don't ever think about which key is coming next . . . I just think of the word and my fingers do the rest. It's like playing the piano—you see the notes on the page and the music comes out. If I ever stopped to think about it, I'd probably get all tied up and forget what comes next."

"Well, it's all a mystery to me. I just hope there's not a major collision out on the tracks somewhere because all these wires get mixed up. Or, heaven forbid, the precious machines go down and the whole system grinds to a halt . . ."

Dan and the other clerks had heard all this before, of course, so he quickly finished the teletype and pleaded that he'd be late for his practice window if he didn't hurry. "The folks from KZN are scheduled to dominate most of the afternoon setting up the new broadcasting equipment," he added casually.

He recognized his mistake too late to prevent his boss's new tirade against the sheer madness of sending electric waves out through the air where they collided into people's bodies and so forth. "We'll all be electrocuted someday," was his favorite launching-off point. Fortunately, Bill Reynolds sensed the problem and interrupted the conversation so Dan could make his escape. Dan cast him a grateful glance and slipped out the door into the magnificent four-story open lobby of the Union Pacific depot with its larger-than-life panoramas sparkling in the afternoon sun. Dan loved the feeling of life and vigor that permeated the depot, in a sense the very heart of the city, and he felt energized as he stepped out onto the busy street for the two-block walk to Temple Square.

While he usually preferred to enter the Tabernacle from the east so he could take in the view of the pipe organ from the back of the hall, this time he took the direct route through the west gates and into the private entrance that brought him up under the massive beams that supported the choir area and the organ. As he turned the corner to mount the steps to the platform, lost in thought as he was, he bumped into Henry Jones, nearly knocking him over.

"Sorry," Dan said, as he recovered from the collision.

Brother Jones was not the most cheerful of fellows and on this occasion simply muttered under his breath as he forced his way past Dan toward the basement where the electric blowers that gave air to the organ were mounted. Henry was one of the tuners who would spend hours adjusting the major pipes to make certain all was in order when the choir went live across the nation.

As Dan reached the Austin console, he saw a small crew of men unpacking some heavily padded steamer trunks in the center of the platform. The public never saw the disordered chaos that was ever-present prior to a major concert, and they'd probably be shocked to see the jumble of wires snaking their way across the floor directly in front of the podium where the prophet and apostles spoke to them during the seven sessions of each quarterly conference.

As he settled himself on the seat of the organ console, John Fisher caught his eye and came over to chat.

"Sorry for all this just as you're getting ready for a recital, but we're all pretty excited about the new equipment."

"I just hope everything turns out alright. What if something goes wrong with hundreds of thousands of people tuning in?"

"Everything will go fine, I'm sure of it. Brother Kimball and Brother Lund are old pros, and these folks from New York really seem to know what they're doing."

"Did I hear someone talking about me?"

Dan turned to see a trim, good-looking man in his late thirties approaching. Dan was a bit startled because he had the distinct impression that he'd seen the man before, although he couldn't figure out where.

"No gossip," Dan said quickly, "just curiosity about all the new equipment and what it's going to do for the program."

"Well, I'll tell you. The very best radio in 1929, when the original equipment was installed here for the first Tabernacle Choir broadcast, had just one tiny speaker that could produce most of the treble tones, at best. Now there are some truly remarkable sets out there that can actually reproduce some of the deeper tones that this organ can produce. Trouble is, it takes an extraordinarily high-quality microphone to pick that up. So that's why we're here. Of course, we could have just shipped the equipment, but we've got to justify our expense accounts somehow." The fellow smiled in a way that increased Dan's sense of knowing him.

"Well, as much as I'd like to talk, I don't have a lot of time to get in the practice I need, so if you'll excuse me . . ."

"Practice?"

"Yes, Brother O'Brian is giving a concert on Friday evening and accompanying the choir on Sunday's broadcast. I'm sure we mentioned that to you," John explained.

"Oh, right, you're the organist. I meant to talk to you about it. We were wondering if we could have our equipment active on Friday night to test it. It wouldn't interfere with the performance, but it would give us a chance to make sure all our affiliates get a good signal."

Dan looked a little alarmed. "Your affiliates?"

"Don't worry, you won't be broadcast. We'll just send a feed out at a frequency they can tune in to. Then on Sunday, they'll rebroadcast our feed on their own frequency. One way or another we'll do a test, but I thought it might be good to broadcast an actual performance to simulate what we'll experience on Sunday. But if you find it distracting . . ."

Dan thought for a moment, then replied, "It's fine with me. Being distracted is the least of my worries. My biggest problem is that I sometimes get so lost in the music that I forget there's anyone out there. One time I actually stopped in the middle of a song to experiment with another stop. It was very embarrassing." He smiled. "Maybe you could wire me up to one of your electrical cables and give me a shock if my mind starts wandering."

They all laughed, then the conversation fell into a heavy silence as Dan and the stranger stared uneasily at each other. Finally, after John glanced back and forth between the two several times trying to figure out what was going on, he extended his hand and introduced himself to the stranger.

"Pleased to meet you. I'm Josh Brown from New York City."

Dan felt a shock go through his system, and his stomach lurched at the unexpected sound of the stranger's name. He felt his knees go weak, and he had to struggle to steady himself. The change in his face must have been apparent because Josh said, "I have the feeling we've met somewhere before, but I can't place you."

Dan replied, almost inaudibly, "We met in France. You came to see me with some bad news at a field hospital in 1918."

Josh blanched. "O'Brian. You were Trevor Richards's best friend—the sniper."

Dan could only nod in reply.

After a few moments, Josh continued, "I'm sorry I didn't recognize you, but the truth is you didn't look very well back then, and I certainly wasn't expecting to meet you here."

Dan tried to smile. "At least then most of my face was covered in a bandage and probably looked a lot better." The joke fell flat. "I guess I wasn't prepared to have all that come back up in memory. Sorry." He paused for a few moments. "At any rate, I'm glad to see you again. I've felt bad through the years that I wasn't more appreciative of your coming to see me that day. I know it must have been hard on you."

At this point, they both realized that John was looking at them with a mixture of curiosity and concern. "Lieutenant Brown here flew a fighter aircraft and roomed with my best friend from high school, who was killed in an air battle on the day we were supposed to get together for a little reunion. It was also the day I regained consciousness in a hospital and learned that I'd been gassed and wounded. Not my best day, to be sure." Dan struggled to maintain his composure before continuing, "Lieutenant Brown was kind enough to come down a couple of days later and tell me about our friend himself so I wouldn't be left to wonder. I took Trevor's death pretty hard, and, well . . ." His voice trailed off.

"I didn't know . . ." John said quietly. "You've never talked about being in the Great War." Suddenly, Dan felt them looking at his face, which still had scars from the burning mustard gas that had also ruined his lungs and ended his dreams of being a professional singer. He'd gotten over being self-conscious about his appearance years earlier, but now his face flushed to have such a tangible reminder. John continued, hesitantly, "I was too old to serve, but my younger brother was killed near St. Mihiel in the trenches. It's still hard to think about."

"That's exactly where our friend lost his life," Josh broke into the conversation. "It's actually a very beautiful spot, where your brother died. Belgium, Luxembourg, and France . . . three of the most beautiful places in the world, except for the ugly scars of no-man's-land. It almost seems unreal now." After a pause, he turned to look squarely at Dan. "At any rate, I'm glad to see that you're doing well. I've actually thought of you quite often and wondered if things turned out alright."

By now, Dan had managed to partially contain the panic that he thought he had long since put behind him. It had been at least half a dozen years since he experienced uncontrollable panic, but it was clear from his reaction to Josh Brown that the old memories were not as far below the surface as he thought they were. He replied, as cheerfully as possible, "Well, I can't imagine meeting again under more favorable circumstances. And, in spite of my initial surprise, I really am glad to see you again so I can properly thank you. Perhaps you could join my wife and me for dinner some evening while you're here?"

Josh smiled. "I'd like that. I'd like it very much. Now, then, perhaps you can talk me through the acoustics of this place, Mr. Fisher. This is one of the most remarkable buildings I've ever been in, and I suspect that the gigantic dome overhead is going to present some challenges for us."

"Challenges and opportunities," John said excitedly. "This room has some of the most astonishing sound effects you'll ever encounter. Without a single supporting beam, it's a great shell that gives perfect visibility from every seat. And the acoustics are even more amazing. I'll walk you to the back of the hall after Brother O'Brian's practice is over and have someone drop a pin on the podium. Because of the curved surface of the ceiling, you'll hear it as clearly back there as if you were standing right next to it. Imagine a room that holds eight thousand people with no need for artificial amplification!"

"I'm not sure I like that," Josh said wryly, "speaking as a sound reinforcement engineer, of course. Your tabernacle could put us all out of business." That brought the expected chuckle and provided a transition so that he and John could drift out into the auditorium while Dan settled onto the seat of the organ bench.

It's back. Dan's lips were dry, and he licked them to try to provide moisture. "The war is back," he said softly to the keyboard. He leaned forward and rested his head on the upper edge of the console while his stomach churned at the flood of memories that he was powerless to control. As he closed his eyes, the colors of France sprang into view—the lush green of the countryside, the beauty of the wildflowers, the filthy mud and grime and stench of the trenches, the color of blood on his buddies' brown uniforms. In an impossible way, he heard the sound of an artillery barrage in his mind, and he recoiled at the terror he'd felt at the early-morning bombardments when it was clear that the enemy was going to come up and out of the trenches. The great dread he felt then, and visualized now, was how many men he would have to kill before the battle settled down. *How many men have to die so we can force them back to their own lines?* "Oh, my," he said quietly. "How can I face this again?" Without even activating the console, he quickly stood up and left the Tabernacle to go walking—a dazed sort of walk up State Street toward the Capitol Building. He was glad when his lungs started to hurt because it gave him something else to think about. When the inevitable coughing started, with the tinge of blood on his handkerchief, the anxiety over his memories subsided, replaced by a real and present danger. Odd as it sounded, the latter was better.

Chapter Two

SOMEONE WHO WAS THERE

After dinner, Josh and Dan went out to the front porch to get some relief from the July heat. Just as they started talking, Josh reached anxiously for a handkerchief that he put up to his nose. "Tip your head back and squeeze," Dan said helpfully. Then he called out to Sarah, who was a registered nurse. As soon as she saw the bloody nose, she retrieved some ice from the icebox, wrapped it in a small towel, and had Josh hold the cold compress against his nose.

"This is very embarrassing," Josh said. "I haven't had a bloody nose since I was a boy."

"It's not your fault," Sarah said. "You're four thousand feet above sea level with practically zero humidity in the air. This often happens to visitors from the South and East. Dan got them often when he first came home from England." Finally, after a little prompting from Sarah, Josh blew his nose gently and was relieved to find that the bleeding had stopped. Sarah took the towel and went out to the old hand pump in the backyard to rinse it clean. Then, kindly, she went into the house through the back door so that Josh and Dan could be alone. The kids had already run off to play with the neighbors.

"Your wife is very kind. I hope she gets a chance to meet my wife, Barbara, and our son, Nate, someday." Before Dan could reply, Josh continued, "Do you mind if I ask you a question? As I remember our visit in the hospital, your lungs were seared from a mustard gas attack. I would think that this dry, thin air would be difficult on them. Of course, if it's something you don't like to talk about, you don't need to."

Dan took a deep breath. After his hike up Capitol Hill, he'd gone home and told Sarah what had happened. Since they met at his father's bedside in 1919, she'd been his best friend and ally in learning to control the anxiety that had dogged him since the end of the war. As their relationship developed into romance, the unhappy memories faded, allowing Dan to put the war behind him. That was nearly sixteen years ago. Now, with Josh's return, it had all come back. Fortunately, Sarah had not lost her touch and was able to calm him down and reassure him that he could handle it. In fact, she'd even convinced him that it might be good to talk with Josh, since he had actually been there where his struggle had begun.

With a great leap of faith, he replied as evenly as possible to Josh's question, "It's alright. Usually I don't like to talk about the war or what happened to me because there's just too much to explain for people to understand what it was really like. Plus, they almost always start talking about what a great patriotic thing it was and how we made the world safe for democracy, and I simply don't have the energy to deal with it. So I've given up trying." There was an edge of bitterness in his voice.

"So you're not one of those who march proudly in the Decoration Day parade each year?" Josh said this with a smile, as if to indicate he understood.

"I'm afraid not."

"That's fine, then . . ."

"No, actually, I'd like to talk with you. You were there, so you can understand what we went through." Then more quietly, "Plus, you knew Trevor, and I don't really have anyone to talk with who knew him as a pilot. His parents have sort of adopted Sarah and me and look on our children as their grandchildren, but we don't talk about Trevor. He was their only child, so it's even harder for them." He smiled weakly.

"Sometimes I think it's best if I never think about him, because then I don't get that awful ache inside. But other times I realize that if I don't think about him, then he's gone for good and all the things I liked about him really have died. That's even worse." Wisely, Josh didn't say anything. With a stronger voice, Dan continued, "The truth is, there are a few questions I'd like to know about his days in the army, what his plans were for after the war, and things like that. I thought maybe you'd know."

"I'll be glad to tell you anything I know. I think I told you at the hospital that Trevor was one of our favorites, including my commanding officer, who usually didn't get close to anyone. I personally loved the guy. The day he didn't come back was the worst day of my life. I've always wondered why he was able to get past our defenses, so I have a few questions of my own about what made him so unique."

For the next hour, Josh and Dan talked earnestly with each other, sometimes quite animated, other times in low tones. Together, they relived some of the memories of France in 1918, although their service had been radically different with Dan in the trenches and Josh fighting the air war.

Finally, as the stars began to shine through the dusk, Dan summed it up, "I'm smart enough to know that life would have separated Trevor and me as adults. He would undoubtedly have moved to California and I'd be here—that's just the way life is. So it's not that I miss him in the sense of having him around like when we were kids. But I also know that there would have been times when we could get together and talk about our lives and our families, and then I get awfully lonely for him. It seems such a waste that he doesn't get to have a life, since I don't know anyone who deserved it more."

Josh broke the ensuing silence. "It seemed to me that Trevor wasn't from Salt Lake City."

"Actually, he was born here, but his family moved to Pocatello, Idaho, when we were fifteen years old. That's when I got to know him. His father is an officer of the Union Pacific Railroad, and my father worked as a fireman and union representative." Dan smiled. "That caused a lot of friction." Josh waited while Dan processed the memory. It was obvious he was trying to decide whether to say something more, so Josh simply waited. "My father and I had a troubled relationship. Life was pretty bleak until the Richardses moved to town. My life changed in amazing ways after they arrived. Trevor's father, Jonathon, is suave and debonair and perfectly at home with adults. Yet when he was called as our youth leader at church he took all of us in the group into his heart and home. Trevor's mother shares my love of music and actually became my piano teacher." He looked up at the handful of stars that had started to shine. "That's why I grew so close to Trevor—it wasn't just him, it was the whole family. They took me in and treated me like I was one of them."

"So that's why your son and daughter think of them as grandparents?"

"It is. After the war, Jonathon and Margaret moved back here to Salt Lake to be close to their families. After my father died, Sarah and I courted and married, and I tried to make it as a music teacher there, but my heart wasn't in it. I wanted to be a singer, but it just wasn't to be. So I contacted Jonathon and he helped me get my current job. We had Cory and then Kathy and now here we are." He smiled. While he had some great friends at work and in the music community, he hadn't opened up to anyone like this in years.

"Well, I better be going. Thank you for bringing me into your home. There's a good feeling here in Salt Lake City and in your family." Dan smiled again, then Josh went in to bid Sarah good night and to tell her that he hoped she'd have the chance to meet his wife and their son someday. Then he set off to walk the six or seven blocks to the Hotel Utah next to Temple Square.

* * *

Dan always enjoyed wearing a tuxedo. Afer living in the squalor of the trenches, where one was never free of the mud and filth, he enjoyed the crisp, clean feeling of a well-tailored tuxedo. He'd resisted buying one when he was first invited to give a formal concert at the Idaho State Academy on the grounds that it was too expensive, but Sarah had insisted. "I want everyone to take my husband seriously as an artist," she said simply. Then with a glint in her eye, she had added, "Besides, I find it hard to resist a tall, trim man in a tuxedo . . ." He'd gone out the next day and used part of his inheritance to order a coal-black formal suit with tails. He hated lifting the tails as he sat down on the organ bench, but Sarah said it added "panache" to his presentation.

His recital at the console of the Tabernacle organ was everything he could have hoped for. There were approximately one thousand people in attendance, which was a large crowd for a summer concert, even though it left most of the seats unoccupied. At first, he played some traditional music written specifically for the organ, including classical works. Then he played a contemporary song with his own adaptation. The crowd's applause indicated that they liked the lighter feeling of nonclassical music. Sensing the sound they liked, he made a few mental adjustments for his final number and quickly flipped the various stop keys on the console to create just the right sound for one of his favorite hymns, "Come Thou Fount of Every Blessing." It had a peculiarly American feel to it, having been particularly popular during the Civil War. As the final verse approached, he thrilled the audience by adding the "celestial pipes" at the rear of the auditorium. Suddenly, they were surrounded by sound, and it washed over the crowd like a warm wave of the Spirit. As Dan brought the song to its magnificent conclusion, he made full use of the great pedals to fill the hall with the thunderous voice of the bass pipes.

Following the concert, as Dan and Sarah started to descend the stairwell out into the hall with Cory and Kathy, they saw Josh Brown approach them from the area that had been reserved for Sunday's broadcast.

"So how do you think it went?"

"I think it's amazing. I'm not familiar with many of the songs, but that last one was absolutely stunning. As good as they are, I'm afraid that even our new microphones, which are the best in the world, won't do justice to the bass notes."

"So there's still some advantage to listening to music live?" Dan said mischievously.

"Currently there is, but give us enough time and we'll make recorded and broadcast music the equal of live."

Dan raised an eyebrow and was about to respond when he looked up to see Margaret Richards approaching him.

"You were wonderful, Daniel," she said while giving him a hug. "I wept on that last song. And then I smiled when I thought of you playing that pathetic little organ in the basement of our church in Pocatello."

Dan laughed. "There is a bit of a difference, isn't there?" Then, leaning close to her ear, he whispered, "It's all because of you and my music lessons. You're the reason I'm here. Thank you." She pulled him close and wiped a new tear from her cheek.

Turning to Jonathon Richards, he gave him a hug as well, and then said, "Josh Brown, I'd like to introduce you to Jonathon and Margaret Richards. They're my unofficial parents . . . and the natural parents of a mutual friend." Jonathon looked startled and then clouded up when Dan explained how he knew Josh.

"Even though it's been a long time since the war, I still think of your son often, Mr. Richards. He was a true and good friend. I was proud to know him. Please accept my belated condolences for your loss."

"Thank you," Jonathon said. He struggled a bit. "I didn't expect to think of Trevor tonight . . . I'm afraid it's caught me off guard."

Dan jumped into the conversation. "Sorry to surprise you, but I've been so busy with work and rehearsals, I haven't taken time to stop by and introduce you properly. Now, perhaps I can change the subject. Since I didn't commit any heinous mistakes tonight, I hope we can all agree that this is a cheerful occasion. I'm glad you were here to give me moral support."

"On the off chance that you'd do well, Margaret has some cake and ice cream waiting at the house. We hoped you might all come over." Cory, who had immediately moved to stand by Jonathon when he saw him, let out the delighted yelp one would expect from a teenager who got to experience ice cream infrequently. "Of course, we'd like you and your friends to join us, Mr. Brown."

"Thank you very much, sir, but we discovered some problems with our equipment during the trial broadcast. I'm afraid we'll be here long into the night working to solve them. But perhaps I could have a rain check."

"We'd be delighted," Margaret said. "I remember Trevor mentioning you in his letters. I'm very glad to put a face to your name. He clearly thought of you as a friend." She smiled to control a tremble in her lip and then reached out and gave Josh a small hug. "Perhaps you would consider supper on Sunday after your broadcast?"

"I think that would work. I'd appreciate the chance for another good meal like the one Sarah was kind enough to prepare for me."

With that, the Richardses and O'Brians prepared to depart. As they turned to leave, Josh called out to Cory, "By the way, I couldn't help but notice you eyeing our equipment. Are you interested in radio?"

"Yes, sir, very much," Cory said. "All those glowing tubes and dials."

"If your mother and father feel alright about it, perhaps you'd like to join me at the control console on Sunday."

Cory looked up with unrestrained excitement. "Can I, Mom?"

Sarah looked at Cory searchingly, then spoke in an even tone of voice, "You can sit with Mr. Brown, as long as you promise not to touch anything. Wouldn't it be something if you interfered with the broadcast?"

"I'll make certain that doesn't happen," Josh said pleasantly. "See you at 8:30 A.M. sharp on Sunday then?"

"Yes, sir, I'll be there!"

Chapter Three

GERMANY'S VIOLENT TURN TO ANTI-SEMITISM

As the choir filed out of their seats, Dan went over to the broadcast booth to retrieve Cory. "He wasn't any trouble, I hope."

"None at all. In fact he's the one who flipped the switch that opened the transmission to all the other stations across the country." Josh pointed to the appropriate switch while Cory beamed.

"Think this is something you'd like to do when you grow up, son?"

"I don't know, Dad. It's pretty fascinating. It's kind of exciting to think that people all across America heard you play today."

Dan smiled. "I find that satisfying myself. Fortunately, I didn't make any obvious mistakes."

By this point, Sarah and Kathy had joined them. "Margaret and Jonathon have invited us to come over for a late lunch." Turning to Josh, Sarah added, "They're hoping you can make it today."

"Let's see, a homemade meal or lunch at the hotel . . . What time should I meet you?" They made arrangements to pick him up at the Hotel Utah, then returned home so they could make it to Sunday School. Dan had missed priesthood meeting earlier that morning, but his quorum was used to his occasional absences on behalf of the choir.

* * *

Dinner with the Richardses was always an interesting affair. Food was prepared in abundance, with more than enough leftovers for at least one or two meals later in the week. Margaret couldn't stand the thought of people going away hungry, and Jonathon couldn't stand the thought of a limited offering on the menu. So they always put out far more dishes than were really needed to satisfy their hunger, but the tastes were delicious and the presentation tasteful. Even when Dan and Sarah's children were little, Margaret had used her best china, asserting that everyone should have at least one formal meal per week and that the children would behave properly if they grew up with it.

Just as abundant as the menu was the number of turns in the conversation. Over time, the discussions tended to follow a pattern. First, a chat about the weather. No matter what time of year it was, Jonathon would find something "splendid" about it, whether it be how much he liked the brisk feeling of fall, the beauty of snow in winter, the return to life of spring, or the heat—at last—of summer. Because he was responsible for the Las Vegas line, he always had some kind of interesting story to tell about the mountain passes near Scipio and Fillmore in central Utah and how the weather there contrasted with the perpetual warmth of St. George and Las Vegas.

Next up would be a discussion of the food, a review of the week's activities for everyone in the family, a sampling of some of the cultural activities Margaret had participated in, and finally a turn to politics. It was here that Jonathon and Dan most often found reason to disagree, but always in an agreeable way. Even though he related personally to Jonathon, Dan still worked for the union and tended to support the Democrats, while Jonathon was clearly management and favored the laissez-faire, hands-off-of-business approach of the Republicans. With the discrediting of Herbert Hoover, the

Democrats were in ascendance with their massive public works projects, which Jonathon maintained would bankrupt the government and destroy individual initiative, while Dan just as passionately maintained that the economy needed stimulation that would create more jobs, agreeing with President Roosevelt that federal debt was just "money that we owe each other," so why not get men working productively so they can support their families?

The only place where they sometimes had serious differences of opinion was in international affairs. Dan was a confirmed isolationist, while Jonathon read everything he could about the international scene. He longed for the days of the first President Roosevelt when America was expansionist in nature and anxious to actively engage the world community.

On this occasion, Jonathon brought up one of his favorite topics, perhaps hoping to goad some new discussion since they had Josh as a first-time guest. "Speaking of Winston Churchill . . ."

"Pardon me, sir, but we weren't speaking of Winston Churchill."

"Ah, yes, Dan, but we should have been." Jonathon grinned broadly. "So speaking of Winston Churchill, he's written a new article about recent ugly events in Germany. It seems that Chancellor Hitler has declared a national boycott of Jewish business establishments, yet again."

"Here we go again," Dan said to Josh. "You're in for quite a ride if you show him the slightest sign of encouragement. Ever since he heard Churchill speak while on his American tour in 1932, Jonathon has become a disciple."

"Actually, I'd like to hear what he has to say," Josh said a bit somberly.

"A very wise man. Do you read much of what Churchill writes?"

"No, sir. But I am interested in what's happening in Germany."

"Well, as you know, last year, the Nazis declared a national boycott against all small Jewish-owned establishments. Now, it seems that they've extended it to even large corporations that have Jewish officers or owners. In fact, it's taking such a toll on Jewish business that the Ullstein Press, the largest publisher of newspapers, books, and magazines in Germany, has been forced to sell at a loss because their sales were off so much. I think it's despicable."

"I do too," Dan said, "but I don't see what it has to do with us."

"That's what everybody says. Who cares what happens in Germany, as long as it doesn't spill over to America? But it seems to me that when any human being is harmed, no matter where it occurs, it should be of concern to everyone else. John Donne's famous, 'No man is an island,' seems to apply, don't you think?" Then not giving anyone time to respond, "The truth is, the Allies have every right under the Treaty of Versailles to intervene in German affairs when they become undemocratic—and what could be more undemocratic than suppressing one of the most successful segments of your own citizenry? I agree with Churchill that we should go in and assert our rights and bring some kind of order to the place."

"And just how are we supposed to do that? Do you really think we should send American troops back into that quagmire?" Dan asked.

Alarmed at Dan's tone of voice, Sarah tried to divert the conversation. "Why does the German government have such hostility toward the Jews anyway? And what do they hope to accomplish with these boycotts?"

Jonathon started to answer her, but Dan cut in with a very well reasoned response that showed he was aware of the issue. "Mr. Hitler is actually a student of history. A sloppy student, in my estimation, but he's read about efforts here in America after the Civil War to make life so unpleasant for the freed negroes that they would give up in despair of living here in America and want to return to Africa. He's actually a great admirer of the worst in American society."

"So he wants the Jews to become so unhappy that they choose to leave Germany?" Margaret responded.

"That's my understanding. From what I gather, life is getting ever more vicious, with placards in many restaurants declaring, *Jews not admitted.*"

Sarah looked ashen. "But what purpose does it serve? Certainly, with all the other troubles the nations are facing, the presence of Jews can't make any real difference in the success of the German republic."

"It's not going to be a republic for long, if you ask me," Jonathon interjected. "Hitler is consolidating his power, and in my opinion, he'll find some excuse to take complete control before too long."

Dan agreed with Jonathon, then continued, "What he hopes to gain is national unity. Germany has suffered the most from the Depression, even more so than America, and far worse than either England or France. If you're in charge, then people will blame you. But if you can transfer guilt to a minority element inside the population, then you can turn all the anger and despair against them. By making Jews the scapegoat, Hitler gets off scot-free."

At this point, Jonathon turned serious. "Dan, I had no idea you've been paying this much attention. In view of that, I don't understand how you can see what's happening so clearly, yet believe that we shouldn't get involved. Somebody has to help those people."

Dan shook his head as he struggled to compose an answer. It was a complex question, not easily answered. Finally, he replied, "It's just that it's hopeless. Europe has been fighting with one another for the past two thousand years. Power shifts from one kingdom to the other, then back again. In 1918 it was Germany who lost. In 1870 it was France. In 1800 France was triumphant under Napoleon until defeated by the Russian winter in 1812.

No matter how many men fight and die, the wars go on. In 1917, we tried to go to their rescue, and to what end? Our men died—men I knew and cherished—and now they're at it again. I just have this sense that if we go back into it, we'll be drawn into yet another war. That would simply be a catastrophe."

By now the cheerful mood of the day was gone. In saying what he did, Dan knew that it had to hurt Jonathon because no one had paid a higher price than he and Margaret. Yet, for his part, he couldn't understand how Jonathon would want anyone to go back into war.

"I'm really not advocating war. I agree that it would be a disaster. But with all his insight and wisdom from nearly thirty years in the government, Churchill feels that this is the time to set things right—that the Allies could do it without the loss of a single life. Germany is still militarily weak, while France has the largest standing army in the world. Hitler is acting in defiance of the treaty and could be brought to heel with very little cost or effort. I believe I'm advocating a course that will avert war, not cause it." There was a pleading sound to Jonathon's voice. "Besides, think of those people—those good Jewish people—who have lost their jobs in government, who can't go to public parks or swimming pools. In some cities, they can't even ride public transit. As bad as the Depression has been here, imagine what it would be like to be one of those people? What kind of chance do they have?"

Although Jonathon was pressing him, Dan wasn't angry. "I'm not disagreeing with what you're saying, but I just feel it's up to the Europeans to police their own backyard, not America. We have enough troubles of our own."

Jonathon didn't reply, but it was clear that he was stressed by the conversation.

Finally, Dan turned to Josh. "What do you think of all this? Certainly you don't want America to go back to France."

Josh was very quiet, his gaze fixed on his plate. After an unusually long pause, Dan was tempted to ask him again, although it was obvious he'd heard the question the first time. Finally, with a slight quiver in his voice that betrayed some kind of deep and almost malignant anger, he said, "The Allies have both the right and the responsibility to supervise Germany, and they are failing miserably in the task. England is too preoccupied and timid, and France is too selfish and vacillating to act, even though they have the most to lose. America doesn't seem to care about anything beyond our borders, even though fifty thousand of us died in the Great War. You'd think we'd want something in return, yet we allow Germany to turn on its own citizens while we stand by and do nothing. We speak of democracy and what a grand thing it was that we freed Germany from the kaiser, yet now we watch the Nazis make a mockery of everything that democracy represents." He looked up, his face dark and foreboding. "The truth is that there is anti-Semitism throughout Europe, and many are willing to step back and let the Germans have their ways with the Jews. Small store owners are being dragged into the street by gangs of Brown Shirt thugs, their stores demolished, their inventory stolen, their bodies kicked and beaten. Citizens are being coerced into abandoning Jewish doctors and lawyers. The Jews are told they can leave, but with no property and no place to go. How do you emigrate when no one wants to take you? And yet the world turns its gaze and pretends it's none of their concern."

Dan was so surprised by the intensity of these remarks that he was momentarily speechless. Finally, Jonathon stepped into the silence. "It seems that you follow events in Germany very closely, Josh."

"I have family there. Family members who, like me, are Jewish."

Chapter Four

ADJUSTING TO A NEW REALITY

It was Margaret Richards who first broke the stunned silence. "I had no idea. You must be worried sick about your family. Do you know if they're in present danger?"

Josh shook his head, as if clearing it from an unpleasant nightmare. "I'm sorry, I shouldn't have blurted out like that." He looked up, abashed. "Please forgive me."

"Nonsense," Margaret said. "It's only natural to react emotionally to something so close and personal like that. What an awful thing to have the people you love threatened. Is there anything that can be done to help them?"

Josh inhaled slowly. The anger was gone, replaced by embarrassment and fear. "I've written to my relatives and urged them to emigrate. Barbara and I would be happy to sponsor them. But they think they can make a difference by staying there and resisting through legal means."

Very quietly, Dan said, "I hope they're not making a huge mistake. The stakes are pretty high, and the Germans are a very focused people. If they're committed to driving the Jews out, I'm not sure that anything will stop them."

Another silence followed. "I didn't associate the name Brown as one of Jewish origin." Jonathon's sincere tone made it clear that he really was interested and not simply trying to make conversation.

"It's not. My mother is Jewish, my father a German Protestant. My mother was as devout as she could be, given that I grew up in the Midwest where there was a very small Jewish population. My father wasn't very interested in religion. But my grandparents in Boston were very involved in the Jewish community. They did their best to include me in the culture when I visited there each summer." He looked up and smiled. "It was there that I met Barbara when we were children. Her grandparents lived down the street from mine, and we ended up going to activities together. She was from New York, and I grew to love her with each passing year. She has such a vivacious and outgoing personality."

"I hope to meet her someday," Margaret said, causing Dan to marvel at how she always seemed to know the right thing to say.

"At any rate, we ended up getting married right after the war, and now Barbara does her best to raise Nate in the faith."

"I take it you're not as devout as she is?" Once again, Jonathon said this without guile.

"I love our tradition and culture, but I'm afraid religion simply isn't that important to me. If anything, I've enjoyed my experience here because it seems much less complicated."

Jonathon laughed. "Perhaps that's because you haven't been called to work with the young men, as I have so often been." Josh finally smiled.

"I really am sorry for dropping that little revelation on you. I usually find a way to prepare people, given that many have strong feelings about the Jews."

"I have strong feelings," Jonathon said simply. "I think we owe much that is good and right in our culture to the heritage that your people have carried through the ages. We, in our church, believe that the blessings of Abraham flow through the house of Israel, and we actually seek to learn individually which of the tribes that we are to receive the Lord's blessings through. So in many ways, we feel something of a kinship with you."

Josh smiled again. "I'm pleased to hear that. Of course, most devout Jews would not recognize it as you do, preferring to keep their culture unique, but I appreciate it." Then looking around, "Well, that was pretty heavy. Perhaps we could find something a bit more cheerful to talk about. After all, we're here to celebrate another successful broadcast, with Dan doing his very best to overwhelm my microphones with the air he set in motion from all those pipes."

Dan laughed. "I hope we taxed them right to the limit, but not beyond." At that, the conversation turned to other topics, but once again the problems of Europe seemed closer than they had before, leaving everyone unsettled, particularly Dan when he looked out the window and saw Cory tossing a baseball to a friend. The thought of Cory in a uniform was deeply unsettling.

* * *

It was nearly two weeks before Dan and Sarah saw Josh again. The regular organists had returned, and so Dan had no reason to go to the Tabernacle where Josh was busy with the final installation and adjustments to the new equipment. Finally, on a Tuesday afternoon, Josh stopped by the railroad and asked if he could drop by that evening. Dan was relieved that he did, because he worried that Josh's experience at Jonathon and Margaret's had put something of a block between them.

"Why not come to dinner?" Dan asked.

"It wouldn't be fair—all I seem to do is eat when I'm with you or the Richardses. How about if I take you and Sarah out to dinner?"

"Out to dinner? We haven't been out to a restaurant in ages. You don't need to do that."

"I'd like to. Can you call Sarah and arrange it?"

Dan laughed. "Oh, I think she'll find the time."

"You can bring the kids, if you like."

"I'm sure they'd like that, but let's make it the adults' night out. I think Sarah would love it."

"Great—let's say seven."

* * *

As dessert was being served at Lamb's Restaurant, Josh looked up expectantly as the waiter brought out Lamb's famous rice pudding. He'd fallen in love with it since coming to Salt Lake City.

"So what are you going to do when you go back to New York, now that your project here is completed?" Dan asked.

"That's up in the air a bit. In fact, it's one of the reasons I invited you out tonight, aside from wanting to express my appreciation for your hospitality." Josh continued, tentatively, "Actually, I probably shouldn't be discussing this with you since I haven't had time to talk with Barbara." He got a determined look on his face. "The truth is, KZN has offered me a full-time job as an audio engineer. The program is doing very well, and the Church is interested in expanding its interest and experience in radio. After all the years I've spent doing contract work, it sounds so inviting to have something permanent and reliable. Plus, I'm just so taken with the beauty of the place. It seems like it might be a good idea for at least a few years."

Dan couldn't suppress the delight he felt. "Josh, this is great news. I think you'd love it here, and we'd love to have you close by. I know we haven't known each other all that long, but somehow you just seem to fit into the family." He laughed. "As you know from my situation, the Richardses have an expansive definition of family, and I guess I inherited some of that."

"I hoped you'd be pleased . . ."

"I should warn you, though, that one of my other friends, Philip Carlyle, accompanied me back from England, and he ended up living here for eight years. So who can predict how long you'd decide to stay?"

"Carlyle. For some reason that name sounds familiar."

"He was the British chaplain who saved my life in France. He got wounded for his generosity and was in the bed next to mine when you came to see me. When it became clear I needed to recover in a humid environment, he was kind enough to take me to London to recover. I still wasn't in great shape to travel, so he volunteered to come with me to Pocatello when I received the telegram about my father's illness. After that, he moved to Salt Lake and eventually married an American girl. He and his family lived here until two years ago, when he learned that his father had died and he'd inherited the estate. At any rate, he loves Salt Lake City and keeps writing that they want to come back someday."

Dan noticed that Josh was still acting a bit tentative, as if he wanted to say more, so he quieted down.

"You and your family would be welcome to stay with us for as long as it took to get settled," Sarah said. "I'd love to meet your wife and son."

Josh shifted uncomfortably.

A look of understanding dawned on Sarah's face. "Perhaps you're worried about how Barbara will react."

"She's never been outside of New York and Boston. I think it might be a real challenge to get her interested. Particularly since . . ."

"Particularly since she's Jewish and this is an LDS community?"

"Exactly."

Dan joined in, "I'm afraid I don't know much about the Jewish community here, although I do know they have a synagogue for the Congregation Montefiore on Third East. I've actually played at a number of their events. I think most of the Jewish people like living here."

"There's usually a lot of hostility in a mostly Christian community."

"I don't think you'll get that here. As Jonathon explained the other day, the Mormons feel a special connection with the Jews. One of the people I played for told me that when the synagogue was built at the turn of the century, the President of the LDS Church, Joseph F. Smith, gave one of the dedicatory addresses in recognition of the fact that our church made a large contribution to the cost of its construction. And, just before the war, Utah elected a Jewish governor, Simon Bamberger—one of the few states to do that." Dan was thoughtful. "One other thing is that years ago, one of our Apostles, Orson Hyde, actually went to Israel and dedicated the land for the return of the Jews. We believe that will happen, even though it seems impossible right now."

"I've heard that story. Still, it's usually in the context of our people eventually converting to Mormonism, and I know that's simply unthinkable for Barbara."

Sarah smiled. "Of course we don't have an answer for you. After our talk the other day, I understand why Jewish people are so cautious. But I'm pretty sure that you wouldn't face anything like the kind of prejudice here that there is in Europe or on the East Coast. I think people would be glad to have you. I know we would." Then, as an afterthought, she added, "Perhaps you could take the job on a trial basis. You can come out and live with us for a time and see if it works out."

"Maybe that would work. At least I can give it a try. I think I'd like living here. It would be good to get Nate out of the city. I think this is a better environment to grow up in."

"I hope it works out," Dan replied. "I really do. Even if it doesn't, though, it's got to feel good to be asked. Jobs are so hard to come by these days, and good jobs are almost impossible. Congratulations."

"Thanks. I'll see what comes of it when I get home." In spite of his efforts to appear cheerful, Josh still had a strained look on his face. "It is a lot to ask of her . . ."

Sarah saw the turmoil in Josh's thoughts—the anxiety he felt as a provider who finally had a chance at something stable, the concern of a husband who worried about displacing his wife.

Chapter Five

CORY, NATE, AND KATHY

Sarah had no idea of the intensity of the storm that was about to break when she matter-of-factly announced that Cory would have to temporarily move out of his bedroom into the attic so the Browns would have a place to stay.

"I have to do what?"

"You have to move to the attic for a few weeks while the Browns find a place to live."

"But it's cold in the attic—not that my room is warm. But it's freezing up there!"

"Then we'll leave the door open so that it can warm up. Heat rises, you know."

"But why do I have to move? Why not Kathy? Her room's nicer, anyway, and I'm sure these people want a nice room."

"Cory, ever since turning fifteen, you have done nothing but complain—about everything. You know perfectly well that your room is larger than Kathy's, and the Browns will need the space. Besides, they have a sixteen-year-old son who needs a place to sleep, and it makes sense for the two of you to share the attic."

"They have a what?" His mouth dropped open and his eyes bulged. "They have a son that is going to live here too?" He was so astonished at this news that he started pacing. "You can't be serious! There is no way—just no way—that I am going to sleep with a stranger. It's out of the question." He continued circling the kitchen. "This is just too much to ask. No one should have to put up with this sort of thing."

"Cory, calm down—"

"I'll move out. That's what I'll do. This New York kid can have the whole darned attic to himself, and I'll move over to Paul's house. You can invite the whole East Coast to move in if you want, but I won't be here. I'll just move out."

Sarah could see that he was close to hyperventilating, and she was irritated that he was being so selfish, but the words that were pouring out of her son's mouth were just so amazing that she couldn't help but laugh. "What if the Ebbers don't want you? Then where will you sleep?"

He turned and looked at her furiously. "Oh, they'll want me. They wouldn't expect Paul to take in a stranger—you can count on that. They'd never do this to their kids!"

Sarah started to respond, but Cory didn't let her. "Mom, this is the craziest thing you've ever come up with. How can you even think about it?"

"Cory, sit down and talk to me. Sit down!" The look on her face was threatening enough that he slumped into a chair.

"First, of all, this man is a friend of your father's, and they need a place to stay for a few weeks while they find a house or an apartment. They happen to have a son who also needs a place to sleep. You'll have separate beds, for goodness' sake. Besides, you liked Mr. Brown when he was out here in July."

"Yeah, but that was a one-hour meeting. Having a guy be nice to you for a couple of hours is a lot different than having him move into your house."

"Cory, he's coming out to a job, so they're not moving in forever. Second, if we had to move to New York City for a job, I'm sure they'd welcome us into their home; it's just what people do for one another. Stop being selfish, and help me get things ready."

"I'm not being selfish. What if he's a jerk? What if he's some big bully? What if he's some kind of lunatic killer?"

"Cory, I have no idea where your imagination comes from. You can tell the best stories I've ever heard, and you've thought up a great one this time." He started to protest, but she continued, "What if it turns out that he's this great guy who loves baseball, hates math, and has always hoped he could learn how to ski and will finally get the chance. What if he's just like you?"

"Yeah, right. A New Yorker who wants to ski. This is just unbelievable. It is just too much. Why did he want to come out here for a job anyway? Why would anybody want to leave New York City for Salt Lake?"

"Mr. Brown is just like the rest of us. It was hard to find regular work there. KZN liked the work he did while he was out and offered him a full-time job as one of their engineers, so he decided to move out here and take the job. It's really that simple. So we need to help them while they look for a house."

Cory sat staring sullenly at the floor for a few moments. "Fine. If that's the way it is, then I'll just have to put up with it. But I don't have to like it, and I don't have to be nice to this guy, whoever he is. So just don't ask me to be nice."

"Of course not, dear. I think it makes perfect sense that a boy should move into a new city that's totally different than the one he's used to without anyone being nice to him. I'm sure that is how you'd like to be treated if the situation were reversed. So you just plan to ignore him, and I'm sure it will be fine."

"Oh, Mom. It's impossible to talk to you. I'll help move all my stuff, but do you mind if I go over to Paul's for awhile first? I need a break."

"So do I, dear. So do I . . ."

* * *

As Cory stormed out the door, the screen door slamming behind him, Sarah reflected on her son. He was such a great young man, yet clearly a typical teenager. He had an easy smile and pleasant face, good-looking with brown hair and green eyes, but not particularly handsome. Cory had always been about an inch or two shorter than his classmates—not a lot, but enough to make him self-conscious. More than once in the past year she'd found him sliding up to the measuring post his father had marked off on one of the hall closets to see if he was gaining on them. But after a fairly pronounced growth spurt at age twelve, his progress had slowed to almost a standstill. He would be lucky to reach five-foot-nine when fully grown, which was a bit surprising since Dan was fairly tall at six-foot-one. The thing that people loved about Cory was his gentle humor, tinged with just a bit of sarcasm. He was clever, but in a quiet sort of way. Not one to tell jokes, but rather to find the irony in a situation. People instinctively liked him, and he was friendly with everyone, but chose to stick close to a fairly small group of friends.

Kathy was quite a different story from her brother. With her red hair and green eyes, her father's Irish heritage had found its full flower. Bright and energetic, she was top in her class, active in drama, a good athlete, and just fun to be around. People were drawn to her like a magnet, and she was happy to make room for whoever wanted to be nearby. At this age, she was silly, but underneath had a cool competence that allowed her to easily manage and organize any size group. Even though they didn't look much like each other, many people commented that Kathy had Sarah's common sense and intelligence.

Sarah was proud of her children. Not in a boastful way, but in a satisfied way. She knew they would grow up to be responsible adults who were capable of caring and providing for their families, and that thought gave her enormous satisfaction.

* * *

Cory stood off to the side of the front window so he could look out without being seen by the car as it drove up. First out was Mr. Brown, whom he recognized from his earlier visit.

Next, he helped his wife out, and Cory was surprised at how small a woman could be. Her head was covered with a scarf, but some dark brown hair showed at the edges. At barely five feet tall and less than a hundred pounds, Barbara Brown was indeed diminutive, but as she started organizing things, it was obvious that she was a bundle of energy. Finally, from the other side, the boy stood up and came around to help his dad. He was taller than either of his parents, but just as slender. Cory winced when he saw how tall he was—a good three inches taller than Cory. He had the same dark hair as his parents, but his complexion was deeper than either of theirs, almost like he had a really dark suntan. Cory was so intent on watching the boy and Mr. Brown that he was startled by the sound of the door. Kathy bounded through with her irritating smile and meaningless chatter, absolutely ruining his escape plan. He'd intended to duck out the back door and over to Paul's before he had to meet these folks—anything to postpone the stupid compliments and inevitable questions like, "Oh, what a handsome young man!" and "Do you like sports?" and all the other things people said at times like this. Unfortunately, his only route out of the living room was directly across the front door, and Sarah and the lady were already coming through the door. He braced for the inevitable.

"Oh, Cory, there you are. We wondered where you were. Please come introduce yourself to Mrs. Brown and then help her carry these things to their room."

"Yes, ma'am," his voice squeaked. He heard Kathy laugh, but the withering glare he turned on her quieted that down in a hurry. He scowled at his mother.

"Cory, this is Mrs. Brown. Mrs. Brown, Cory—he's fifteen."

"Pleased to meet you, ma'am." At least this time his voice sounded normal.

"My, what a handsome young man. You must be an athlete—do you have a favorite sport?"

Through incredible self-discipline, Cory was able to limit the distance his head covered as he shook it from side to side.

"I like baseball and skiing, Mrs. Brown."

At that, her face lit up like someone had turned on a light switch. "Nathan loves baseball and skiing too. Can you imagine that?" she said brightly. Her strong accent was unlike anything Cory had ever heard in his life. He later learned it was common to Brooklyn. Her words were delivered so rapidly in this strange brogue that he had difficulty understanding her, and he found himself leaning forward every time she talked in an attempt to concentrate better. "By the way, you should call me Barbara if it's alright with your parents. I hate being called Mrs. Brown—it makes me sound so old and stuffy."

His resolve to not like these people was shaken by her excitement. Her wiry little body was electrified, and he was unable to hold down a small smile. He looked up at his mother, who said simply, "If that's what Barbara wants us to call her, then that's what we'll do."

Just then he heard a noise on the stairs, which meant his dad and the others were coming in, so he quickly said, "Why don't you let me take your bags, Mrs. Brown, um, I mean, Barbara." But once again his escape was blocked.

"Not until you meet Nathan. He's almost your age, you know. And it's just amazing that you both like the same sports. Nathan, come here and meet the O'Brians' son, Cory. He likes baseball and skiing—can you believe that?"

Reluctantly, Cory turned to look at the stranger who was invading his space. Halfway through the turn, he was startled by the look of sheer awe on his sister's face. It was enough to make him pause for a moment, wondering if something was wrong. In response to his curious glance, she mouthed the words, "He is so handsome!"

"Cory, this is Nathan Brown," his dad introduced him.

Cory obediently put out his hand. "Pleased to meet you." He took some comfort from the fact that it looked like Nathan was just as uncomfortable as he was.

"Pleased to meet you too. People call me Nate." Cory saw Nate flash a glance at his mother, who obviously preferred his more formal name.

They stood awkwardly for a moment before Nate's dad said, "Cory, it's good to see you again. I think you've grown a bit. Still like radio?"

"Uh, yes, sir." He was caught off guard. Of course, Josh was asking because Cory had sat with him at the controls of the broadcast, and it was the only thing they had in common. Still, not knowing what to say, Cory let the conversation drop to an awful silence.

"Well, why don't we get all the luggage into the rooms, and then Sarah has some lunch ready." Cory was relieved that his dad had stepped in. But then he was thrown another curveball when Dan continued, "We can get the Browns' things, Cory, so why don't you help Nate carry his stuff upstairs?"

"Sure. The stairs are this way." They both reached for one of Nate's suitcases at the same time, which Cory found embarrassing. They finally figured it out and started up the stairs in silence. Once in the room, Cory pointed to a bed, and Nate moved over close to it. The silence was killing him, but it seemed like Nate could take it longer than he could. "So your mom says you like skiing. I didn't know they skied in New York."

Nate turned, and it was obvious why Cory's sister had been taken with him. With sharp, well-defined cheekbones, his face came to a distinct point at his chin, and his dark brown eyes seemed almost penetrating. He was just one of those guys that girls were bound to look at. But instead of saying something witty and profound, Nate rolled his eyes. "My mother exaggerates everything. I've actually been skiing just once in Vermont, and that was four or five years ago. I spent most of the day falling down. I'd probably kill myself in your mountains. Do you ski a lot?"

"Not as much as I'd like. It's real expensive. My grandfather's brother owns a car dealership that sponsors a ski team, so I get to go up with them once in awhile. It's really fun. I'm sure you'd figure it out in no time."

"Where do you go?"

"Park City, usually. It's a mining town east of here." He walked over to one of the small windows at the end of the attic and pointed toward the mountains. "It's up that canyon."

Nate came over and leaned into the window cove to see it. "Those are some mountains. Vermont's are like little hills by comparison. I still think I'd kill myself."

"I've also been up to Brighton one time. You need horses to get up the canyon, but once you get there, they have a towrope that pulls you up the ski hill. It makes it a lot easier since the mountains are actually a lot steeper there than in Park City."

Nate nodded appreciatively but didn't say anything.

"Well, maybe we can go sometime. The guys on the ski team are really nice, and they could teach you in no time."

"Maybe. I'll have to see what my dad thinks. He's been skiing a couple of times, so he might like it. Does your dad go?"

Cory shook his head. "My dad can't do anything too physical. His lungs got burned in the war, and he starts coughing whenever he has to breathe too hard. About the only thing we can do together is play catch. Still, he's a good baseball coach, and all the guys like him. He's gone a lot, though."

"Gone? How does he coach you if he's gone?"

"He used to do it a lot more. Then he started playing piano in a jazz band, so he's gone most weekends. He doesn't coach that much anymore."

There was a moment of silence, so Nate moved over to his bed and started arranging things. Cory was about to leave when Nate said, "So what position do you play?"

The question took a moment to register. "Shortstop. I like covering the holes. What about you?"

"First base. I'm pretty tall, so I can get in the runners' way pretty easily. I try to scare 'em." They laughed. "Too bad it's winter, or we could play some."

"Oh, we can still play. We have a street game almost every Saturday, unless the snow is too deep to find the ball. The weather isn't bad for February, so maybe you could play on Saturday."

"I'd like that."

"Well, guess I'll go downstairs and let you unpack. Mom has sandwiches if you're hungry."

"Thanks."

Cory started to walk down the first stairs.

"Hey, I gotta know," Nate said. "How old are you, and what grade are you in?"

Cory turned, a little embarrassed. "I turned fifteen in November." Then more quietly, "I'm in tenth grade." The time had arrived for the question he dreaded. "What about you?"

"I'm sixteen and a junior. So we're pretty close."

"You'll be with a different group of kids at school. But we're in the same quorum at church." Then almost as soon as the words were out, his face turned red. "Oh, wait, you're not a member of our church, are you? My mom told me that."

"What did she tell you?"

"That you belong to some other church that I don't know much about, Hindu or something."

Nate laughed. "We're Jewish, actually. My dad already told us that you're Mormons. It's going to be kind of weird having him work for a church. But he also said there's a synagogue here, so we won't be too out of place." He seemed uncomfortable disclosing this personal information.

"Jewish. I don't know anybody who's Jewish. But I'm sure you can find your church pretty easily. My dad can probably help."

"So it doesn't bother you that we're Jews?"

"No. Why should it?"

"Well, back east, there can be a lot of prejudice against the Jews. We sort of stand out."

"I think that's true about Mormons too. Apparently a lot of people think we're kind of strange, although I've only ever lived here in Salt Lake where it's pretty normal."

"Are Mormons Christian?"

"Of course. We believe in Christ, don't you?"

Nate was still tentative. He didn't really want to have this conversation, but he also really needed to know how the local people would feel about him, so he decided to go ahead with his questions. He was glad that Cory was being so open about it. "Like many Jews, I was taught that Jesus was a great prophet, but we don't accept that He was the promised Messiah. That's why a lot of Christian churches have given us trouble through the years."

Cory was thoughtful. "We've actually talked about this in church. Jesus was a Jew and was put to death because the Jews didn't like what he was teaching. But we have a book called the Book of Mormon that talks a lot about the children of Israel. At any rate, I think we really like Jewish people." He shrugged his shoulders. "At least that's what I remember. Sorry, I don't know more."

Nate looked thoughtfully at Cory. It was obvious that Cory was quite naïve, at least compared to the people Nate knew. But it was also apparent that he was absolutely sincere. In New York, people had an opinion the moment they discovered that someone was Jewish. It instantly defined their place and role in society, and there was no negotiation about it. It was something of a puzzle to Nate to hear Cory talking as if he were unaware of all this. Finally, Nate felt himself relax a little, since it didn't look like he'd face the same kind of prejudice in Salt Lake City that he'd grown up with in New York City.

"Where were we?" Cory asked. "I kind of forgot what we started talking about."

Nate smiled. "We were talking about going to different high schools and churches."

"Oh, yeah. Well, at any rate, I don't know where you'll end up going, but I don't think you'll have any trouble making friends. Most people here are pretty friendly."

"I'm glad to hear that. Where I come from, you usually stick to the people in your own neighborhood, although I had some friends who were Catholic. I'm pretty open about things."

Cory shook his head. "I hardly know anybody but Mormons. Salt Lake City must be pretty small and dreary compared to New York."

"It's small, no question about that. But it's anything but dreary. The streets here are huge! And everything's so clean. You can't imagine how bad New York smells sometimes. I didn't even realize it until today. The air here is so fresh by comparison. This is amazing!"

"Well, I'd like you to tell me about New York sometime. I've always dreamed of traveling—I love it when my dad tells stories about the places he's been."

Nate smiled. "I'll tell you about New York if you'll promise to take me skiing. I guess if I'm gonna die, that's as good a place as any."

Cory laughed, then turned and started down the stairs again.

Nate interrupted his exit a second time. "By the way, thanks . . ."

"For what?"

"For talking to me. I was as nervous as a rat in a rainstorm that I'd hate it here. I threatened to stay with friends in New York until my dad laid down the law to me."

"I was pretty nervous too. But it turned out okay. I think you'll really like it here. There's a lot to do." Then rather awkwardly, he stuck out his hand. Nate shook it and smiled, then turned back to his things.

* * *

"So what's he like?" Kathy asked breathlessly.

"What's who like?"

"You know who—Nate Brown! What's he like?"

"I see no reason in the world why you should care what he's like. He's sixteen, you're thirteen, so what does it matter?"

"He's handsome." She rolled her eyes as if that explained everything.

"Well, I didn't notice. But if you must know, he seems like a nice guy. Different, of course, growing up in New York City. But nice."

"He'll probably be bored to death here. There's never anything to do."

"How would you know? You're always talking to your stupid friends. You don't have time to do anything."

"Cory," she said plaintively, "you've got to tell me about him. *Nice* doesn't mean anything."

"Look, we talked for maybe five or ten minutes. He's interested in skiing, plays some sports, and is embarrassed that his mother talks so much. In other words, he's a regular guy." He looked thoughtful for a moment. "He's kind of quiet actually . . . at least he's not a jerk, which is a good thing. But that's all I know. So leave me alone."

"His eyes are amazing," she said as her gaze drifted to some distant place.

"What did you say?" Cory said with a start.

"Nothing. I didn't say anything."

"Yes, you did. You said his eyes are amazing. Which is about the stupidest thing I've ever heard come out of your mouth. You're only thirteen years old, so stop looking at him."

"I've got to look at somebody—why not him?"

"Oh, Kathy. Don't you talk like that ever again. That's the last thing he needs to hear. He's a stranger in town, and he doesn't need to be hounded by a lovesick thirteen year old. So just stay out of things, do you understand?" He grabbed her arm and gave it a twist.

"Ow—you leave me alone. I won't say anything, but you're the jerk." Then once she had twisted free, "But still . . ."

Cory rolled his eyes and strode out the front door to go over to Paul's. "What did I do wrong in the preexistence to deserve a sister?"

Left by herself, Kathy went over and took up her favorite spot by the oil stove where she spent hours reading when she wasn't with one of her many girlfriends.

"I see you've positioned yourself in the perfect spot to see Nate when he comes down."

"Oh, Mother, don't be ridiculous." Kathy picked up a book with a huff and buried her face in the pages. Every so often, she'd glance around the side, hopeful that he'd see her and strike up a conversation. But it wasn't to be. An hour before dinner, the Browns announced that they had an appointment with a realtor and would probably be gone for the evening. Kathy watched as the three of them breezed past and out the front door to where a real estate agent—a profession Kathy had never really paid attention to before tonight, but one she now resented bitterly—was waiting in a car. She'd gone to bed before they returned home late that night.

Chapter Six

PLAYING THE BLUES

Dan glanced up to see Josh and Nate waving at him. The railroad car with their household possessions had arrived, and they'd backed a truck up to the siding. It was hard to believe that a month had already passed. The Browns had purchased a nice home in the Avenues, near where Jonathon's parents lived before they passed away. Josh had explained that moving from the New York real estate market to Salt Lake City was extremely favorable because of lower prices in the West. Dan made his way to the car and picked up a box, which turned out to be heavier than he expected. He stumbled a bit and was embarrassed when Josh reached out to steady him.

"Let one of the professional movers get that, Dan. It's way too heavy for one person."

It wasn't, but Dan settled it back down on its spot. His inability to do heavy work had turned him into something of a weakling.

"Why don't you help over here?"

Dan turned and saw that Josh was pointing at the bedding. He sighed. It was the old decision—play manly and risk a coughing attack or stick to the sheets and blankets and underwear. The early spring weather, with its wildly fluctuating temperatures, had been murder on his lungs.

"Sounds good. The nice thing about bedding is you can make a big pile of it so it looks like you're doing more work than everybody else."

Josh smiled and looked relieved. They never talked about Dan's condition, but he knew that Josh was sensitive to it.

"So how are things going at KZN? Settling in alright?"

"Pretty easy, actually. I think people are afraid of me—they're all so concerned about not offending me because I'm Jewish that they fall all over themselves to show how tolerant they are." He laughed. "Give it a couple of weeks and one of them will blow up over something stupid I do, and then we'll settle into a normal routine."

Dan lifted a couple of pillows high up on top of a dresser that had previously been transferred to the van and then asked Josh as matter-of-factly as he could, "Now that you're here, I have to tell you that it still seems a little odd that you'd choose to leave the East Coast to come to Salt Lake City. Although I don't know a lot about broadcasting, it seems like most people in your industry are trying to get to New York City, not leave it. Of course it offers steady employment—"

Josh shook his head quickly from side to side, and when he saw that Nate had gone down the platform to get some water, he replied quietly, "It's a good job. The weekly choir broadcast is actually turning into one of our most popular programs. Plus, I like it here in the West—it's clean and uncrowded. But one of the main reasons is Nate. We lived in a rough neighborhood, and he was getting pretty hard. He had two groups of friends, one that we really liked and another that was leading to trouble. Manhattan is just a hard place to be a teenager. He started smoking last year and came home with alcohol on his breath a couple of times. As you know, I'm just not into that sort of thing. At any rate, we talked about it and decided I should try to find something else. I think Barbara is still in shock that it's here in Utah, because she was so nervous about coming into a place that . . ." He stumbled.

"That's so Mormon? Did it turn out to be as big a deal as you thought it might?"

"Actually, yes. She'd heard all the stories about polygamous wives and strange clothing, and it really frightened her. I tried to tell her it isn't that way, but she's still nervous. It's helped a lot to live with your family the past month and to go to synagogue. She's already picking up some friends, and I think she'll settle in fine."

"What are you going to do to help Nate make the adjustment?"

"We've got him enrolled at East High School, and we've joined the Jewish Community Center. That should give him a place to go after school and on weekends. I think he'll be fine."

Just then, Nate came back, so Josh and Dan rather naturally turned the conversation back to work. After another load or two, Cory and his friend Paul showed up and helped with some of the heavy living room pieces. Nate immediately went to join Cory, and it appeared that the two of them were comfortable with each other. With Nate at East High and Cory going to West, it wasn't likely that they'd spend a lot of time together, but it was good that they were on friendly terms, since it would make it easier to have occasional family get-togethers. When they were finished, Josh gave the boys some money for ice cream, and they hurried off to Snelgroves. There was something luxurious about ice cream, even in the mushy days of March.

"Once we get unpacked and settled in, we'd like to have you over to dinner. We can never repay your kindness for a month's worth of boarding, but we'd at least like to say thanks."

"We'd be glad to come. We love this neighborhood because of Eliot Richards. We had some wonderful times at his home before he passed away."

* * *

The era of the big bands was born at the Palomar Dance Hall in Los Angeles on August 21, 1935, when Benny Goodman finally let loose and gave his band its head. It was an astonishing performance that forever changed the way the country understood music. In the era of the Great Depression, people wanted something exciting and driving that could force them to their feet in a flurry of increasingly complex rhythms and steps that left one exhausted but exhilarated. Jazz, and its darker cousin the blues, expressed both sides of the times—the yearning for fun and excitement and the deep emotional struggles of people attempting to cope with economic forces that were beyond them.

For his part, Dan loved the incredibly tight harmonies of Duke Ellington and Ben Pollack. The ability of jazz to allow the musicians to improvise on one another's themes created an endless variety of musical points and counterpoints that fascinated his mind and liberated his emotions. If he had his way, he'd play true jazz at all their performances. But fortunately Howie, the bandleader, had a better sense of the audience and called for easier dance tunes most of the time, with just a little sprinkling of avant-garde jazz thrown in to keep the musicians happy. While Dan loved playing the traditional and stirring hymns on Sunday, he also loved letting loose on Fridays and Saturdays. He loved music in all its colors and shades. Unfortunately, it was the one thing he couldn't share with his wife, and that left an empty pit that he couldn't figure out how to fill.

* * *

"That was really great, Dan! I had no idea you were so accomplished," Josh raved.

Dan laughed easily. "No one ever says that about pianists. It's the trumpets, saxophones, and drums that get all the glory. The pianist is there to start the set and provide the fill." While there were a lot of things he could get uptight about, Dan was perfectly at ease in the world of music and humble about his talent. He just loved being part of it.

"Rant on, but I've been to Harlem where jazz was born. And tonight was great jazz—starting with the piano."

"Well, thanks. I may not be the best in the world, but no one loves it more than I do."

"Besides, why don't you tell Count Basie, Fats Waller, and Freddy Johnson that pianists can't lead the band? They seem to be doing alright."

"Okay, okay, I surrender. Still, it's the trumpets that get the audience cheering."

"Agreed." Josh and Dan sat quietly as the custodians swept the floor around them. "So how long have you guys been together?"

"You know bands—the side men are coming and going all the time. But Howie and I have been together for nearly six years now, from before the days of swing. Back then, we played mostly sentimental songs that were fairly boring to the band, but now it's getting pretty fun." Dan sighed. "The travel is exhausting, though. Sometimes we travel to southeastern Idaho and Wyoming to play in the small venues there. But even when we stay in Salt Lake City, the hours are terrible, and Sarah doesn't like that. Sometimes I get home so late on Sunday mornings that I miss morning church service."

Josh looked at his watch. "It's after two."

Dan took a long sip on his lime soda. "Exactly."

Josh saw how exhausted Dan looked. "She's probably right. You really put yourself through it tonight."

"I just don't know what to do to make it better. The clubs like to rotate bands so they get a new sound periodically, and that means we have to be flexible. I should probably give it up. It's just too irregular. Besides, Howie's getting anxious to try his luck in bigger venues, so he's talking about breaking up the band anyway." Dan lapsed into silence.

Josh sat quietly for a few minutes. The silence was actually pretty nice after the incredible noise of the crowded club earlier that evening.

Dan started to get up and excuse himself.

"Before you leave, could I ask you a question?"

"Sure. What is it?"

"Does anyone in this area have a regular radio show—I mean a dance show?"

"No, nobody that I know of. We get Benny Goodman on the Camel Caravan, and the late night remotes pick up Jan Savitt and Bob Bou out of Atlantic City. And, of course, Artie Shaw from New York City. Why?"

"You probably didn't know this, but I actually helped set up Artie's broadcast from the Hotel Lincoln."

"You're kidding." Dan looked at Josh skeptically at first, but then he realized that he wasn't kidding. "You're telling me that you know Artie Shaw?"

"I do. Great guy. Amazing music."

"Oh, that's something. You've gone from Artie Shaw in Manhattan to Howie Holmgren and the boys from Utah. That's about as big a fall as a person could experience."

"Don't be so hard on yourself, Dan. You guys really did make some terrific music tonight. And it's obvious the crowd loves you." He sat brooding for another moment or two, while Dan sat by with nothing to say. "Here's the deal. I need something more than the daily ritual of KZN and the weekly choir broadcast. I love it here, and I feel good about the work we do. But we need to involve more people in our broadcasts. Plus, we want to extend our playing hours to attract more advertisers. Why don't you and I start a regular weekly broadcast? Instead of driving to Idaho and Wyoming, you can get there by radio."

Dan's mouth dropped open.

"I'm serious, Dan. I know how to do radio, and you know how to do music. People are crying for good entertainment, and the kind of music you make isn't inconsistent with what the people in this area prefer to listen to. I think they'd love it."

"But the band is breaking up," Dan stammered. "And I don't know anything about playing for a microphone."

"You don't play for a microphone—you have a regular performance each week that goes for two hours. You have a crowd that dances to the music and then goes home, or another band follows you and you get to go home. You could do it from ten to midnight on Friday night and be home in time to get a good night's sleep." He looked at Dan earnestly. "I'm dead serious about this. I think you could make a show."

"But the band—"

"The band needs to be reorganized with you in charge. Tell Howie you want to take over. If he gives you trouble, tell him I'll give him some names of guys in New York that he can get in touch with."

"But what would we call ourselves?"

"What does it matter?"

"It matters a lot . . . A band's got to have a name."

At this, Josh burst into a grin. The seed hadn't taken very long at all to sprout. "You were in the infantry, right?"

"What? What has my being in the infantry got to do with a band?"

"Were any of the other band members in the war?"

Dan looked surprised, cocked his head to the right as he thought about it, and Josh watched as Dan's eyes darted back and forth. "As a matter of fact, a lot of us were. Maybe that's why we came together."

"Then you should be called Danny O'Brian and the Soldat Ordinaires!"

"The Soldat Ordinaires?"

"Sure, French for soldiers—ordinary soldiers. It has a nice ring to it."

"Dan O'Brian and the Soldat Ordinaires . . ."

"Not Dan—that has no rhythm to it. Danny. It's time to get the old name out and dust it off." Josh was so excited he was almost dancing in his chair.

"Oh, wow. This is too much."

"Sarah will love it. She gets her husband back, you get to play the kind of music you love, and I get a new program that's fun to produce. Will you think about it?"

"Uh, sure, I'll think about it." Then Dan burst into a grin. "But I won't think too hard. If you're serious, I think we should give it a try."

"Well, then, it sounds like we're in business. This calls for a drink." Turning to the bartender he shouted, "Two more Shirley Temples for me and my partner, my good man!"

Chapter Seven

LADIES' NIGHT

May 1936

Sarah turned and admired the beautiful front porch of the Browns' home while waiting for Barbara to answer the door. She had always been one to notice flowers, and it was obvious that gardening was Barbara's passion. Sarah turned as she heard the bolt turn in the door. "All ready?" she said brightly when Barbara's face appeared around the corner of the door.

"Almost. Could you come in for just a moment? I think it's still cool enough that I'd like to get a shawl."

Stepping inside, Sarah reflected on the fact that in the past year and a half they'd only been to the Browns' once, for a holiday gathering. With all her boundless energy, Barbara had quickly gotten involved in her church auxiliaries and as a volunteer at her son's high school, and they simply hadn't seen each other very much.

The house itself was not ostentatious, but it was well furnished by Salt Lake City standards, and it was obvious that Barbara was a meticulous housekeeper. Sarah could imagine that everything was in tip-top shape by ten each morning.

"All ready," Barbara said brightly. But there was also a distinct edge of anxiety to her voice. She fumbled with the door. "It is so kind of you to take me out today. But I really don't see why I should be the one being celebrated since it is Nathan who has graduated from high school."

Sarah smiled. "Events like graduation are always so mixed up, emotionally. On the one hand, I'm sure you're thrilled for Nate that he's reached this important point in his life, but I can't help but think it's also poignant for you to think that he's almost fully grown. At least, that's what Margaret said when she suggested our outing."

Barbara's face clouded up just a bit, for a moment. "She only had one child too, didn't she?"

"She did . . . perhaps that's why she thought of you. At any rate, we decided that you could use an afternoon and evening out on the town to celebrate the occasion. We'll pick Margaret up next, and then your friend Beverly."

By this time, they'd slid into the front seat of the O'Brians' Buick. "Oh, Sarah, I'm so sorry we don't get together more often. This is just so nice of you and Mrs. Richards."

"It's good for us too—a nice break in the routine." As they pulled up in front of the Richardses' home, which was grand by comparison to either the Browns' or the O'Brians', Margaret came out the glass-paneled front door and started down the steps before Sarah could even set the parking brake. She hurried out of the car to help her down the steps.

"Isn't this a beautiful day?" Margaret said brightly. "You look lovely in that dress, Barbara. I'm so glad you can spend the day with us." It was almost impossible not to be charmed by Margaret Richards, who carried herself with a grace and dignity that bespoke her love of culture. Barbara and she chatted politely as Sarah drove to Thirteenth East and down to Seventh South to pick up Beverly. Sarah had met Beverly at the holiday party and could see why she and Barbara were such good friends. Beverly was a no-nonsense sort of person who had helped keep things organized at the party, even though she was an invited guest.

After Beverly had gotten in the car, Margaret asserted control. "Ladies, with no husbands or children to worry about, let's get started. We thought we'd first go to the Tiffin Room at ZCMI for lunch, and then take a walk down Main Street for a little surprise I have in mind, and then, if all goes according to plan, we'll wind up at the Hotel Newhouse for High Tea at four. After that, it's off to the theatre for a musical variety show. How does that sound?"

"It sounds like a delightful afternoon," Barbara replied. Sarah had observed the puzzled glance exchanged between Barbara and Beverly when Margaret mentioned tea, but decided to wait until the moment to clear up their confusion.

"Then off to South Temple and Main Street," Sarah said cheerfully, and she started the steep descent down Seventh South to the valley floor.

The Tiffin Room was celebrated for its homemade pies and for the ice cream bar that served endless varieties of homemade ice cream, banana splits, and milk shakes. The ladies ate a light lunch so they could enjoy dessert. Then, stepping out into the afternoon sun, they started strolling south on the east side of Main Street. When they reached the Anglin Gallery, Margaret suggested they step in. Once inside, the proprietor smiled brightly and greeted Margaret warmly. It was obvious they knew each other well.

"So what do you think, Barbara?" Margaret asked.

"Oh, these painting are simply wonderful." She couldn't seem to decide where to put her focus, with oil paintings of every variety on the different walls.

"Why don't you and Beverly walk around and see which style you like best? I need to talk with Mr. Anglin for a few moments, and then we'll compare notes."

In one of the alcoves, Barbara and Beverly found some natural landscapes of Utah and the western desert; in another, paintings in the French impressionist style; and in yet another, a gallery of portraits. But the section that seemed to capture Barbara's imagination the most was an area devoted to flowers—flowers in vases, flowers in gardens, and wildflowers set against mountain hillsides. Sarah was pleased to hear her quiet exclamations of wonder as she discovered the various paintings.

"So which ones do you like best?" Margaret asked quietly as she came up behind them.

"I like them all," Barbara replied. "The colors are so bright and cheerful."

"But still, some must stand out as especially inviting? What about you, Beverly?"

"Oh, I'm a realist. I like the landscapes that actually look like a landscape—none of this impressionism for me. I think those artists must have needed glasses, and so they saw the world as all blurry."

Margaret laughed easily. "I can understand that—it's exactly what my husband says whenever I bring yet another one home. Of course, what I see in impressionism is the essence of the scene—the colors, the light, the textures that create the special mood we feel in a setting like that. By stripping a bit of the reality away, you feel the scene, rather than just see it."

Beverly tipped her head. "I've never thought of it that way. Maybe I'll look at those pictures differently from now on."

"What about you, Sarah?"

"Oh, you know me. I like the people pictures. I particularly love that one of the mother with her children on a picnic. I can almost feel the warmth of the afternoon and hear the sounds of the children laughing as they play near the water. For me, that's what life is about . . ."

Margaret nodded, not at all surprised by her answer.

"Alright, Barbara, it's down to you. Which are your favorites?"

"Well, the flowers of course. I love this small one with the bouquet of roses."

"If you were buying a painting today, is that the one you'd get?"

"What? Oh, no. I mean, it's too expensive. Josh indulges me, but we've never been much for original art."

"I understand your love of flowers, but I personally thought you'd be attracted to that painting of Central Park in New York City with the trees and buildings mixed together."

Barbara turned. "Well, of course I love that. Who wouldn't?" Her voice tightened up. "I mean, I remember standing in the very spot where it was painted. I used to love going into Central Park in the afternoon after taking a leisurely stroll up Fifth Avenue, looking in the elegant store windows. Then to walk through the fields of the park, watching the people playing sports, taking a boat out on the lake, or flying kites in the stiff spring breezes." Her voice took on a distant quality, as if lost in memory. "I particularly loved the sound of the city coming through the trees—the cars rushing down the street, their horns and brakes screeching, and people everywhere talking and laughing. It was always such a delightful contrast—the serenity of the park with the vitality of the city."

Sarah smiled at the thought that Margaret had touched such a nerve. Barbara, usually so plain spoken, was almost poetic.

"Well, then, you have a real problem on your hands," Margaret said seriously.

"What? What do you mean, a problem?"

"The problem is that I've told Mr. Anglin that I intend to buy you a painting today in honor of Nathan's graduation— something that you'll have to remind you of this wonderful time in your lives. But now, I'm afraid, you have to choose between the flowers and Central Park. Which is it going to be?"

Barbara's face flushed. "Oh, Mrs. Richards, you can't do that. I could never let you spend so much money on something like that—"

"It's not your money to worry about, dear. Besides, I've waited a long time to remember a high school graduation, and I frankly can't wait to do something special for it." Then very softly, "I received a painting from Jonathon when our son graduated, and to this day it always makes me smile and think of our boy. I want you to have something special as well."

"I'm told that he was a wonderful young man," Barbara said hesitantly.

Margaret's voice trembled. "Yes, he was. A bright and cheerful boy who meant the world to me. Just like Nathan is to you. So won't you please let me do this for you?"

Barbara hesitated again.

"Besides, I'd like to support this young artist. I think he shows real promise."

"Oh, thank you," Barbara said as she hugged Margaret. "This will be a special memory forever. I really can't believe this is happening. Thank you."

Releasing their embrace, Margaret regained her composure and said, "So I assume it will be Central Park?"

"Oh, that would be nice, but I really love the flowers—they're so bright and cheerful." Those were the words Barbara said, but her gaze stole over to the New York City scene.

"It's true that the flowers are less expensive—but not likely to elicit such happy memories. Why not get the one you really like?"

At that, Barbara started weeping with the peculiar sound of a Brooklyn accent as part of the sob. Beverly hugged her as Barbara pulled out a handkerchief. "This is just the sweetest thing that's ever happened to me. Thank you."

Margaret smiled broadly and went to give the news to Mr. Anglin, along with instructions on where to deliver the painting.

* * *

High Tea at the Hotel Newhouse was a tradition loved by the non-Mormons in Salt Lake City since they could savor the sandwiches, cheese, and fresh fruit while sipping wonderful tea. It soon became clear to Barbara and Beverly that Margaret was an old hand at this, because she simply ordered some herbal tea for her and Sarah while allowing the others to choose their favorite. The bonbons were of the finest chocolate and melted in their mouths. About midway through the event, the conversation turned to Dan and Josh.

"So how does Joshua like his job here in Salt Lake City?"

"Oh, I think he likes it a great deal. He always comes home happy, and he speaks so highly of the people he works with. He particularly enjoys managing the broadcast of Dan's band."

"Oh, yes," Margaret said. "How are Dan and his band doing?"

"He loves it," Sarah replied. "Even though he comes home exhausted, he is always happy and relaxed on Saturday morning."

"And it's better for you than before the radio program . . ."

"Much better. Now it's just one night a week, plus one or two nights for rehearsal. It's still quite a time commitment, but at least he's not in those awful clubs anymore, and I don't think it takes the same toll on his health. Now that he's working full-time at the railroad again, that's important."

"Do you like jazz, Mrs. Richards?" Beverly said tentatively. "Barbara told me that you were Dan's piano teacher when he was a boy."

Margaret laughed. "I was. But I mostly taught Dan classics, although I insisted he always play some of the contemporary songs of the day so that he wouldn't get bored. Of course, those songs from the turn of the century sound very dated now."

"So you don't like jazz?"

"Oh, I wouldn't say that. I suppose I'm a lot like Dan in that I enjoy all music. It's like the paintings we saw at the gallery. Church music is like the portraits—it tells a story and inspires people. Classical music is like the great landscapes—grand and sweeping in their scope. And jazz is like the impressionists—all feeling and emotion with very little emphasis on structure." She looked thoughtful for a moment. "Still, I suppose I like impressionist paintings more than I like impressionist music." She laughed. "But Dan always did have his own tastes. And is the broadcast being well received?"

"Oh, yes," Barbara said enthusiastically. "They have a wonderful audience here in Salt Lake City, and they're even being broadcast in Nevada, Wyoming, and Idaho. The band is making quite a name for itself, and KZN has picked up a much younger audience. Josh thinks it's quite a success."

"I'm so glad to hear that. When Dan lost his singing voice he thought it was the end of the world. As much as we tried to convince him there were other ways to express his music, he struggled. So now he has an outlet." Margaret smiled with great satisfaction.

"And it is so good for him," Sarah said. "He always wanted to make something of a mark—perhaps this is one of the ways he can do it."

The conversation was quiet for a few minutes as they each nibbled on a small sandwich.

"By the way, did you hear that Cory sang with the band last weekend?" Sarah said.

"What? Cory sang for his father's band?" Margaret asked.

"Yes—and he was wonderful. He has a young voice, but somehow he really understands the syncopation of the music, and everyone was delighted with his performance."

"Sarah, why didn't you tell me so I could come down and hear him? I think I ought to scold all of you."

"Yes, I'm sorry about that. It was actually a last-minute sort of thing. Their regular singer came down sick, and so Dan was going to cancel the number. That's when Kathy suggested that Cory sing it. When Dan looked surprised, she said, 'Oh, for heaven's sake, Daddy. Cory's always singing your songs around the house. He knows all of them!' As always, Cory pretended to be upset with Kathy, but he was actually quite flattered. Dan had him try out, and the band was unanimous that he should sing with them. It was a wonderful experience."

"Well, next time this happens, you better have a place set aside for Jonathon and me or there will be serious repercussions, I can assure you!"

"We will, I promise."

Then turning to Barbara, Margaret said, "And what about Nathan. What are his plans?"

"Oh, I don't know exactly. We want him to go to the university—he's got a very good head for mathematics, you know. But he thinks he wants to take a year off to go work somewhere. He's tired of school. I think he should go back to New York because there are so few eligible girls here—" Barbara caught herself. "I mean, he hasn't found anyone at school, girls who are—" She stumbled again, but caught herself.

"But he doesn't want to go back east?" Margaret said.

"No, no. He thinks he wants to take off a semester or two to work and then maybe go to the university here. I'd really like him to go to an eastern school. But Josh likes the idea of him staying here, so I find myself the odd person out."

"Ah, life is often confusing, isn't it? Particularly since our children form opinions of their own that don't necessarily match ours."

"Yes," Barbara said reflectively. "It was hard for him to come here at first, but now I think he likes it even more than the city—the skiing and outdoor sports are so accessible." She was quiet for a few moments. "In some ways, I think it's much easier for young people to adjust than it is for older ones."

Both Sarah and Margaret heard the trace of tension in her voice.

"Well, if we're going to make the late matinee we better hurry to the theatre. They're calling this a Broadway revue, and it has all the contemporary songs that are popular in New York City. It should be the perfect way to end the day."

"The perfect way to end a perfect day," Barbara replied.

* * *

Because of where their houses were located, Sarah dropped Barbara off first, then Margaret, and finally Beverly. As they pulled up to Beverly's house, Beverly said, "This was one of the best days I've ever had. Thank you."

"You're very welcome. I'm awfully glad you could come—I think it made it easier for Barbara to have a close friend along."

Beverly hesitated. "You mean, a non-Mormon friend?"

"Yes, I suppose that's what I mean. Josh has adapted very easily to Salt Lake City, but I get the feeling it's been harder for Barbara."

"It's kind of hard for all of us, Sarah. I have to admit that my experience with you and Mrs. Richards has changed me and the way I look at things. Do you mind if I say something about living here?"

"Not at all. I'd like to know what you think."

"Well, the Mormons are wonderful people. My neighbors are very friendly. But your church is so complete that a lot of times people don't even think about us. And it seems like there's a lot of misunderstanding about the Jewish community—" Sarah started to interrupt, but Beverly continued, "Please, we've all heard about the 'convincing of the Jew and Gentile' that your missionaries talk about. The truth is, I've always pushed away my Mormon neighbors, taking refuge in my own kind of prejudice—maybe like if I'm standoffish first, then they can't hurt me." She paused. "The point is that what you and Mrs. Richards did for Barbara today is simply wonderful. Your friend is such a kind person. It makes me think I may have been wrong in some of my opinions." She smiled. "Perhaps we could all be friends after all."

Sarah reached across the seat and gave Beverly a hug. "I feel exactly the same way. It was a wonderful day, and you and Barbara are wonderful people."

Chapter Eight

KRISTALLNACHT

November 1938

Josh was not usually one to act rattled, but when Dan saw him at the Tabernacle on Sunday morning, he was startled by his appearance. It looked as if he hadn't slept in days, and he was far more fussy at the controls than usual. Jonathon, who had been invited to share a short message during the broadcast, noticed it as well. They didn't really have time to talk with Josh before the broadcast, so when it was finished, the two men moved as quickly as possible to where he was locking down the equipment and securing the area.

Dan was first to get there. "Are you alright, Josh? You seem a little distracted."

"I'm alright. I just have a lot on my mind right now."

At this point, Jonathon had joined them. "Does it have anything to do with what happened in Germany?"

Josh looked up. "It has everything to do with what happened in Germany. I've sent cables to family members in three different cities, but not a single response. I think that because they're addressed to Jews, the company must not be delivering them." Josh's lower lip trembled.

"I'm sorry," Dan said, "but I haven't read the newspaper for the last couple of days. What happened?"

Josh shook his head and tried to respond, but found he was unable to speak. So Jonathon explained. "They're calling it

Kristallnacht in the newspaper—the Night of Shattered Glass. It seems that on November ninth and again on the tenth, over seventy-five hundred Jewish shops were destroyed and more than four hundred synagogues burned to the ground. The S.A., or Brown Shirts, was utterly ruthless in the destruction, beating and maiming Jewish citizens, including women and children. It's a horrible event and frankly a stain on all humanity."

Josh looked up and corrected Jonathon. "You've got the details mostly correct, except that you called them Jewish citizens. Since the Nuremberg Laws on citizenship and race, no one of Jewish ancestry has been considered a citizen . . . no voting rights, no right to own property, not even basic civil liberties. Dogs have more rights in modern Germany than Jews do." His voice was choked with emotion. "Jews can't even marry one of the infamous Aryans that Hitler is so proud of. It's against the law."

"In fact," Jonathon added with disgust, "the only members of the S.A. to be arrested so far are those who raped Jewish women and girls—not because they committed the act of rape, but because they violated the Nuremberg law regarding sexual intercourse between Aryans and Jews."

Dan felt the anger rising in his throat. He'd been aware of the Nuremberg Laws but had assumed that most Jews had emigrated. "So your family is still there?"

"Hard to believe, isn't it? I've pleaded with them to come. I've promised them that they could find a job here, that there's an active Jewish community, that Barbara and I would welcome them into our home. But my family can be stubborn. Now, who knows what's happened?"

"I know that Hitler justifies all this as 'social Darwinism,' but I just don't see how the everyday, ordinary citizens go along with it. Do they really accept the thought that they're so innately superior as a race that they can harm an entire people like this?" Dan was so perplexed that his voice trembled.

"Who knows what they think," Josh replied. "My father was a first-generation immigrant, and he's as stubborn a human being as has ever lived. My feeling is that many of the German people are shocked by it all but too weak or cowardly to do anything, while many others actually accept that humanity would be better off without the Jews. After all, we 'killed Christ' and are supposed to suffer in all our generations because of it!" He looked up at Jonathon and Dan, who were quiet at this. "I'm not sure either of you realize just how different the Mormons are from other Christians in your affinity with the Jews. Europe has kicked us around for centuries, and now no one is doing a thing about it."

"I know that some very brave Christian ministers have spoken out in Germany and paid a terrible price themselves for doing so." Jonathon's voice was very subdued.

"I know," Josh sighed. "It does me no good to be angry at people. I'm just so frightened for what might have happened—and what will happen. It seems like insanity has taken over an entire country."

"Churchill saw all this," Jonathon said, shaking his head. "He tried to warn people, but no one would listen. For twenty years, he's been wandering in the political wilderness. If England would have taken his advice just four years ago, they could have disarmed Hitler without a single shot being fired. Now, he's rearmed the army, built great naval surface ships, and created a submarine corps, and all under our noses while vacillating politicians shake their heads and scold him." Jonathon turned to Dan. "I know you don't want to hear this, but I honestly don't see how a war can be avoided. I just don't see how this can go on unchecked."

Dan sighed. He didn't either. The politicians would undoubtedly file their protests against Hitler, extracting a promise that he'd be better, but then events would move on unchecked by any real authority. "What does it all mean, and how will it all end?" he asked no one in particular. The pit in his stomach made it clear that the answer was not one he'd like to hear.

Chapter Nine

A SKI TRIP TO BRIGHTON

March 1941

"Hey, Cory!"

Cory turned and brightened as he saw Nate Brown waving from across the room. "Hey, buddy. What are you doing here? It's been a long time."

"I'm helping my dad with the broadcast. I convinced my professors at the University of Utah to give me an internship to study radio—not a bad way to get credit, listening to dance bands and playing with equipment I like anyway. What about you?"

"I'm actually one of the guys you'll be broadcasting. I'm one of the singers in Dad's orchestra. It's kind of weird working with your dad, but I really like it. I'd probably never get a chance like this if it weren't for him."

"I had no idea—Bing Crosby, Frank Sinatra, and Cory O'Brian!"

"Probably not this week. I'm pretty sure the California and New York audiences aren't in the habit of tuning into the Utah-Wyoming network on a regular basis."

"You'd actually be surprised. Dad says that with KZN's 50,000-watt clear channel, people in really odd places tune in from all around the country when they get a good skip in the night. Apparently there's a spot in Oklahoma that almost always gets us. And I know there are some places in southern

California that can pick us up once in awhile. In other words, your dad's band has more followers than you might think." Then he laughed, "At least that's what we tell the sponsors!"

Cory laughed, then, looking up at the clock said, "Uh, oh—I've got to get dressed. It's good to see you, Nate, and to have you working on the show. It'll be nice to have somebody close to my age on the crew." He turned to leave. "By the way, do you ever go skiing anymore?"

"All the time. You want to go sometime?"

"I would. I haven't been in awhile, so I'd probably make a fool of myself on the slopes. But it would give us a chance to catch up with each other."

"How about a week from Saturday? I'm going up to Brighton with some friends. You're welcome to come along."

"Sure. We'll figure out a meeting place at next week's show." They shook hands and Cory turned to leave, then paused again. "Darn, I forgot that I promised to do something with Kathy next week—she's always nagging me for not spending time with her anymore."

"Bring her along. She skis too, I assume."

"Not really, but she thinks she does. She's just a kid—your friends probably wouldn't like her hanging around."

"She can't be too young anymore."

"Hmm . . . guess not. She's nineteen. Still, she's a kid to me."

"That's not so young. At least ask her. She's welcome to come."

"Alright, I'll ask. Maybe if I'm lucky, she'll turn it down but let me out of my commitment." He laughed and went back-stage to the dressing room.

* * *

Cory had set his alarm for eight so he could meet Nate and his friends at nine at the entrance to Big Cottonwood Canyon. Even though the radio show ended at midnight, his dad always kept playing for at least another hour for the locals who came to support them: "We owe it to them since they give the applause the radio audience hears in the background." Cory knew the band actually liked the last hour best, since they could cut loose and fool around more than when the microphones were on. But getting home at two in the morning, eight was prime sleeping time. Which is why he was so overwhelmingly annoyed when Kathy woke him at seven-thirty. Particularly since she went straight to yelling, "Get out of bed right now, Cory, or we'll be late!" bypassing the more traditional and customarily gentle first call.

Even though he covered his head with his pillow, he knew it was a losing battle. Finally, he rolled over and threw the pillow at her as she closed the door to protect herself.

He sat up to convince her he was awake, but she had to come back fifteen minutes later to shake him into consciousness. "Alright, alright. I'm up."

He wanted to be grouchy over breakfast, but he was too excited about the chance to go skiing again. His mother had a long list of instructions about how he needed to watch out for Kathy and such. "If she's so helpless, Mom, then tell her to stay home. I'm going out there to have fun, not to watch my little sister. Besides, Nate has been skiing for years now, and I'm going to have to work hard just to not look like a fool."

"He's right, Mom. He doesn't have to take care of me—I can do fine all by myself."

Sarah sighed and worked on the lunch she was packing for them.

Dan stumbled into the kitchen, rubbing his eyes and yawning. "What's all the noise? I thought Saturday was supposed to be a morning of rest around here." Then, seeing their parkas and skis, "Oh, that's right. You're going out with Nate Brown. Is Josh going along?"

Cory shook his head. "Just a bunch of Nate's friends. And Kathy."

"Well, take care of her, Cory," Dan said.

Cory rolled his eyes as Sarah arched her brow in an "I told you so" sort of way. Jumping up from the table, he said, "Well, let's go, squirt. I don't want to be late!"

Kathy was indignant, since she was the one who had been pressing him to get going, but he simply brushed her off.

"Cory, for heaven's sake, brush your teeth before you leave, and comb your hair!"

"Can't, Mom. Gotta go. Thanks for lunch. We should be home around six tonight. Any chance for chili and hot chocolate?" He didn't wait for her answer as he hurried Kathy out the door.

* * *

As Cory and Kathy got out of the car and stretched, he looked up in wonder at the sight before his eyes. There was no sight in the world quite like the Wasatch Mountains covered in snow, the sharply angled morning sun casting a golden glow on the northern slopes. The dark shadows gave definition to the jagged granite peaks and turned the evergreen pine into a wintry jade that stood out in stark contrast to the beautiful snow. "God must have a special love for this place to make it so beautiful," he said to no one in particular.

Kathy thought he was talking to her. "It smells wonderful too, doesn't it?" she said breathlessly. "I love it when you see your breath and feel the bite of the morning air in your nostrils."

Cory agreed with her, but she was always so overly enthusiastic that he simply grunted and proceeded to start unloading their skis so they could get on the bus to take them up the narrow canyon road. Just then, a low-riding Mercury pulled up next to them and gave a couple of light toots on the horn. Cory turned to see that there were just two people in Nate's car. Nate parked and then bounded out cheerfully. "The other

guys turned coward, so it's just Jake and me." He then introduced Jake Holden.

Kathy came around from the side of the car, and Cory was
about to introduce her to Jake when he saw a strange look
come over Nate's face. He turned and saw the same look on
Kathy's face. It was one of the unmistakable moments when
something is going on that's hard to define, yet you know it's
happening. He started to say, "You remember Kathy . . ." But
Nate had stepped around him and straight toward Kathy.
Quite suddenly, Cory felt like the odd man out, and he
turned to see Jake looking at Nate with the same puzzled
expression.

Talking like he and Jake weren't even there, Nate said
earnestly, "But this can't be right—you were just a little girl."

"I'm not a little girl, Nate. I'll be twenty next month," she
said shyly.

"Well, then, I see you two remember each other . . ." but
Cory's sarcasm didn't get through. Pretending to cough, he
said, "Should anybody be interested, this is my sister, Kathy,
and this is Nate's friend Jake Holden."

"What?" Kathy said distractedly. Cory put his hand on her
arm. She turned with a startled look and replied, "Oh, yes,
Jake. Pleased to meet you." Nate had turned to look at them
too, and somehow it didn't look like he was feeling well.

"Are you okay?" Jake asked him.

"Fine. I'm fine. We had better hurry and get on the bus." It
wasn't scheduled to leave for ten minutes, but it was a conve-
nient way to cover the silence that followed whatever had just
happened. On the way up the canyon, Kathy and Nate tried to
act uninterested in each other, but Cory could plainly see that
his sister's cheeks flushed periodically, and she always seemed to
laugh just a little too hard at Nate's jokes. That was bad
enough, but even worse, Nate seemed just as smitten with
Kathy, which, in Cory's opinion, was just not natural. She was
a sister, not someone who his good friend should look at. Cory

spent most of his time trying to talk to Jake, who was also a little put out that his friend was ignoring him. It made for a rather awkward bus ride.

Cory was relieved when they got up to the parking lot and disembarked. At the appropriate moment, he pulled Kathy aside and asked, not very kindly, just what she thought she was doing, to which she replied that she was doing nothing and that he should stop fantasizing and mind his own business. He was pleased that she hadn't entirely lost her ability to infuriate him.

The first ride up the towrope was a little disconcerting as he got used to it again, but he made it without falling. He was shocked at how easily Kathy seemed to make it. But then, she had Nate holding her and helping her at every turn. Cory was surprised at his own irritation, particularly since it felt a little bit like jealousy. The phrase, "protect your sister," came into his thoughts, though he doubted this is what his parents had in mind. Fortunately, they reached the top of the run before his thoughts drove him completely crazy.

"You going to be okay?" Cory called out to Kathy.

"Don't worry," Nate called back. "I'll make sure she gets down okay. You and Jake go ahead, and we'll see you at the bottom."

Cory shook his head in disbelief and turned to cast an irritated glance at Jake. "Alright, then, I guess we're on our own. Last one down buys hot chocolate?"

"You're on!" And with that, the two skiers tore down the mountain.

Downhill skiing was undoubtedly one of the most thrilling sports in the world. While Cory wasn't really gifted at basketball or football, particularly because he was shorter than most young men his age, his natural sense of equilibrium and timing allowed him to display particular grace when negotiating the twists and turns of the mountainside. He was pleased to find that even though it had been a year since he'd been in the mountains, it took very little time for him to regain his sense of control. Jake was a worthy opponent, and the two of them had a great time cutting and crossing each other's path as they worked their way to the base. In the end, it would have been something of a photo finish if Cory hadn't had an inexperienced skier cross his path. As he picked himself up from the small mountain of debris he created in the fall, Jake skied over to offer him a hand.

"Okay, guess the chocolate's on me," Cory said, wiping the snow from his face and brushing his trousers.

"Oh, I think it's only fair that I pick up the tab," Jake said pleasantly. "You could've knocked that kid senseless and won, but you chose the path of valor. Hurt anything?"

Cory shook his head to clear some snow out of his ear. "I don't think so. I forgot just how rough snow can be on your skin, particularly when the sun has melted the surface into an icy glaze. What happened to the kid, anyway—did he even know he caused me to crash?"

"Oh, I think so," Jake replied, "particularly when his dad got there. He was yelling something about 'I told you to stay on the learner's hill' loud enough for nearly everyone in the canyon to hear. I doubt he'll cause any more trouble today.'"

They skied over to the small shack where hot drinks, sandwiches, and candy bars were sold and munched down a Baby Ruth candy bar while sipping some hot chocolate. "So do you wonder where my sister and Nate are?"

Jake smiled. "Probably stuck in some trees with a broken ski."

Cory's face blanched. "She's just a kid."

"Don't worry. Nate's an honorable person. Maybe she's having trouble with her skis." At that, Jake attempted to change the subject, but Cory wasn't very talkative.

In just a few minutes, Nate and Kathy came skiing into view, Kathy with a big grin on her face and Nate acting like a protective knight-errant. Kathy had a little trouble stopping, knocking down a ski instructor in the process, which Nate thought was the funniest thing he'd ever seen. Cory wasn't nearly as amused.

"Had enough?" he asked Kathy. "We could catch the early bus back."

"What?" Nate said. "We're just getting started, aren't we, Kathy?"

She looked at him reverently and nodded.

"Oh, good grief," Cory muttered. "Well, I'm going to head up the hill then. You ready?" he called to Jake.

Jake swallowed down a sandwich and started working his way to the bottom of the towrope line.

"We'll catch up to you guys later," Nate said as he handed Kathy the cup of chocolate he'd bought her.

"Yeah, whatever." Cory grabbed hold of the line that started pulling him up the hill. He couldn't really say why he was angry, but he was. And it irritated him. This was supposed to be his day with an old friend, and it was obvious that Nate had forgotten about him and Jake. "Stupid world," was all he could get out, and he found himself almost falling down as it came time to dismount from the towrope.

It was hard to keep his anger up for long, however. First, it wasn't in his nature to be angry. Second, the day was absolutely spectacular at this point. The sky was a brilliant blue and crystal clear. With all the coal furnaces and gasoline refineries in the valley, the air was never clear down there, so this offered a refreshing contrast. Plus, the snow had acquired a crystalline sheen from the morning sun that made it glisten like thousands of small diamonds. The day was too beautiful for anyone not to appreciate the simple fact of being alive, so he started down the hill for the second time. After a short pause at the bottom, he and Jake ascended for a third trip, which was also fun. With each run his confidence grew stronger until he was tackling the moguls straight on and doing some simple acrobatics. He was also really learning to like Jake's company.

After the fourth run, the sun was coming from the west, and Cory decided that they really should catch the next bus if they were to get home by six as he had promised his mother. So he settled down on one of the few available benches to wait for Nate and Kathy. At first, there were dozens of skiers who came down, most of whom started heading for the bus line. In time, fewer and fewer came in, and none of them included his sister. After a half hour, he was getting really irritated. After forty-five minutes, his anger was moderated by a twinge of fear. After an hour, he was up pacing, debating with Jake as to whether or not they should start up the hill. It was at that point that the towrope shut down, and now Cory was beside himself with worry. He finally went over to one of the members of the volunteer ski patrol to see if he knew what might have happened to them. "Don't worry, we always send a team of skiers to the top before we shut down the tow so they'll be last to come down and make sure everyone's off the mountain. We'll hold the bus until they get down."

"And, if something major is wrong?" Cory asked.

"If something's wrong, they'll fire a flare, and the rest of us will go up to help bring anyone down who might be hurt or injured."

At this point, Cory felt a deep ache in the pit of his stomach. After another ten minutes, he was almost frantic. It was then that he saw a group of skiers come into view, pulling something behind them. He started in their direction and quickly saw that Kathy wasn't skiing with them, but Nate was. Then he saw that the members of the ski patrol were skiing behind a sled, easing it down the mountain. Kathy was lying on the sled with her right leg propped up at an odd angle. He jerked so suddenly as he attempted to ski over to her that he lost his balance and fell into a heap on the side of the mountain. Normally he'd be mortified, but he was too worried to even care.

"What's wrong? What's happened?" he shouted to Nate.

"She lost control and skied into a grove of trees. Fortunately, she was smart enough to sit down before she clobbered herself, but she twisted her leg in the process. It looks like it's broken." Nate's face was ashen, which tempered Cory's initial impulse to hit him or yell at him. "I tried to help her, but the pain is just too intense. Fortunately, these guys came along and were able to help."

By this time, Cory had reached the sled. "Are you alright?" he asked Kathy. "Is there anything I can do?"

Tears welled up in her eyes. "I'm okay, Cory. I'm sorry I ruined your day."

Any anger he'd felt earlier simply added to his grief at her pain. "It's okay. You shouldn't worry about me. Let me help you." Tenderly he reached down and helped the men of the ski patrol ease her into a standing position on her good leg. He put her arm over his shoulder, thanking Jake for taking their skis.

"Can I help?" Nate asked cautiously. Cory wanted to say, *Oh, you've helped enough,* but instead replied, "Maybe you could help her support the injured leg while we get her on the bus."

"You don't need to go down by bus," one of the ski patrol members said. "We've got a station wagon that will let her stretch her leg out in the back. We really need to get her to a hospital."

"Alright," Cory said. "I'll come with her."

"Why don't you give me the keys to your car?" Nate said quietly. "Jake can follow me to the hospital, and I'll drop it off."

"Thanks," Cory said, handing him the keys. He quickly slid inside the wood-paneled Ford station wagon, then took Kathy's hand. "I'm sorry this happened to you, sis. You get on my nerves sometimes, but I love you more than anything. Is your leg in a lot of pain?"

"It really hurts bad, Cory," she said, gripping his hand, tears streaming down her cheeks. "I don't think I can stand it."

When they arrived at LDS Hospital, they went straight into the emergency room, where the doctors determined that she had two fractures. They gave her a mild dose of ether to calm her down so they could work on her leg. Cory couldn't stand it, so he stepped out into the hallway for a moment.

Almost the instant he stepped into the hallway, he was startled by the sound of his mother's voice. "Cory, what are you doing here?"

Cory suddenly realized that his mother was working today. The shocked look on his face instantly conveyed the nature, if not the fact, of his being there.

Looking around quickly, Sarah cried, "Where's Kathy?"

Cory pointed toward the emergency room.

"Oh, no! What happened?"

Cory explained as quickly as he could, then stood aside as his mother forced her way past him. While Cory paced in the waiting room, Nate and Jake arrived and asked about her condition.

"I don't know. They've been in there for a half hour, and no one has come out to tell me anything." He was too miserable to yell at Nate or even ask what happened. He wasn't so far out of it that he didn't notice how agitated Nate was.

Finally, Nate said, "It's my fault. I was supposed to take care of her and this happened. It just happened so fast. We were skiing and laughing, just having a great time, and suddenly she missed a turn and was off into the trees before I could get to her." He sat down and put his elbows on his knees and held his head while looking down at the floor. "This is just the worst."

Cory didn't like being put in the position of comforting him, but somebody had to say something. "It's alright, Nate. Skiing is dangerous. I'm sure it's nobody's fault—that's why they call it an accident." It was a strange sensation to hear his own voice speaking his father's words.

"It's not alright . . ." Nate looked up a bit desperately. "I like her, Cory. I really like her."

Cory felt like somebody had hit him in the stomach. "But, Nate, you really just met her for the first time. I mean, I know we've done a few things together through the years, but you two have never really talked to each other."

"I know it sounds stupid, and maybe it doesn't mean anything, but I want to see her again."

"But, Nate, your mom . . ." Cory hadn't heard all of his parents' discussions through the years, but he had overheard enough to know that Barbara Brown desperately wanted her son to leave Salt Lake City so he could find a "good Jewish girl" and that any romance between Nate and Kathy was bound to provoke a confrontation. He started to say something, but when he saw the miserable look on Nate's face, he decided this wasn't the time. Besides, Dan arrived about this time, and they had to give him the details of what happened. It was obvious that he was irritated with Cory for not skiing with her personally, but he avoided a direct confrontation in front of the other two boys, which simply postponed Cory's distress.

After another half hour, Sarah came out to the waiting room and announced that they'd been able to set the leg in a way that would hopefully avoid the most obvious scarring and disfigurement.

"Can we see her?" Nate asked.

"Not now," Sarah said quietly. "She's been sedated. Her father can go in, but it will probably be at least tomorrow before she's ready to see anyone else. Why don't you boys go get something to eat?"

"I'm so sorry," Nate said, his voice trailing off. "It happened so fast . . ."

Dan didn't say anything, so Cory chimed in, "Thanks for helping with the car. I'll call you if anything else changes." After Nate and Jake left, Dan turned to Cory and said, "We'll talk more about this tonight," then he turned and headed for Kathy's room.

Chapter Ten

BLACK SUNDAY

September 1941

Nate was fairly quiet as they wrapped up the jazz broadcast, but Josh was unusually cheerful. It was apparent to Dan that Josh had no idea of Nate's interest in Kathy. In the six months since the ski accident, Nate had spent a great deal of time at the O'Brians', but there was still nothing definitive to indicate a long-term romance. Since Nate hadn't brought it up, Dan decided it didn't make sense for him to raise the subject. *Who knows? Maybe the initial passion is fading . . .* He felt that was wishful thinking, but what else was there to do?

"So, tell me about your part in Sunday's broadcast. You're playing an organ solo?"

"Actually, I'm playing a duet with Kyle Byland, one of the technicians who maintains the Tabernacle organ. He's an accomplished musician in his own right."

"Ah, four hands at the keyboard."

"No," Dan replied. "I'm not being very helpful. Kyle is going to play the organ while I play the concert grand piano. We're doing a duet called 'Ere You Left Your Room This Morning.' We worked together on the arrangement. In my opinion, the combination of piano and organ allows the best of both instruments to shine through—the deep, sustained tones of the organ and the lighter, percussive touch of the piano."

"Still, it's got to feel pretty good to be on the air twice in the same week."

Dan smiled. "It's been good. With the world in such a miserable state, I'm glad there's something to be happy about."

"I know," Josh replied. "I'm so frustrated about the war in Europe. It's been two years now since Germany invaded Poland, and it's just been one defeat after the next for the Allies. The Germans are triumphant on nearly every front. It's like everything we went through was for nothing—all we did was give the Europeans a twenty-year interlude to build up even stronger armies and navies. I just can't see how the world can escape from this without even more carnage than in our war."

The images of the trenches of World War I came vividly into Dan's mind. "I just hope Roosevelt's serious about keeping us out of the war." Dan caught himself, knowing Josh's deep feelings about the war, particularly since he hadn't heard from his relatives since the outbreak of war in 1939. "Still, with Lend-Lease and all the other things he's doing to help Britain, there may be a chance for victory. Our only hope is that by taking on both Russia and England, Hitler will have over-reached and the Wehrmacht will be forced to withdraw. If not, our boys . . ." Dan shook his head in despair.

"I know. Our boys are likely to be drawn in." They stared sullenly at their sodas for a few moments. "Well, I better get home to Barbara. We're looking forward to Sunday. Are you sure it's alright to have the luncheon at your house?"

"Of course. We'll see you bright and early for the broadcast and then lunch in the afternoon."

* * *

The broadcast went well. Dan and Kyle performed their number with no miscues, the plaintive melody of the song inviting all who knew its words to consider if they had properly invited God to be part of their day by seeking Him in prayer each morning.

Since the broadcast was a special occasion, the Richardses were joining them for lunch. Although he couldn't point to any one thing, Dan felt like there was electricity in the air from the moment their guests started arriving. Sarah attributed it to their own nervousness, but Dan felt there was something more. After dessert, the reason became clear.

"We have an announcement," Jonathon Richards said hesitantly. When everyone quieted down, he continued, "We had an unusual call this week from the First Presidency of the Church. On Friday, we met with President Grant and his counselors personally."

While that didn't mean much to the Browns, the O'Brians were duly impressed and excited.

"And?" Sarah said.

"They've issued a call to us—one that we could turn down if we were concerned about it. But we've decided to accept."

It was highly unusual to be given a call that the Brethren would clearly specify could be turned down, and Dan suddenly felt overwhelmed by a sense of dread. He instinctively reached under the table and took Sarah's hand. The quick way she responded told him that she'd felt the same thing.

"It seems that they'd like us to go to England to serve as a mission president."

Sarah gasped, and Dan sat back in his seat as he reeled from what he'd heard. "But I thought there were no missionaries being called anymore. They stopped issuing calls nearly three years ago!"

"I know, but they still need someone over there to preside over the branches and to ensure that there are services for the increasing number of Americans who are involved in transporting goods to the island. They think that because of my English citizenship and my experience living here in Salt Lake City these many years, I'm uniquely qualified to be one of their on-the-spot representatives. I see it as quite an honor and an opportunity to serve."

Everyone sat in stunned silence for a few moments. "But with all the bombing and attacks on the cities . . . I mean the Germans are showing no mercy to the civilian population . . ."

"I know, Dan. It certainly has its dangers. That's why they gave us the chance to opt out if we wanted." Then, leaning forward, Jonathon said earnestly, "But it's our brothers and sisters in the gospel—and my countrymen—who are facing all this, and they shouldn't have to face it alone. We have to go. If the king and queen can stay in spite of the danger, who am I to resist the call to serve?"

"But, can you afford it?" Dan asked. "I mean with the Depression and all."

"We can afford it—we'd make ourselves afford it, no matter what. But Providence actually intervened to help us." He laughed. "Who would have thought that my surly old brother Tom would stand in for Providence?" Everybody looked at him quizzically. "I shouldn't laugh. Tom was actually great about it. When he heard that we'd been asked to go to England, he approached me and asked if he could buy out my interest in the car dealership. When my father died, I inherited part of the stock, which really wasn't fair since I haven't ever worked in the business. Tom is one of the few businessmen to manage his affairs so carefully that he's actually done pretty well in spite of the sad state of the economy, so he offered to cash me out. Probably glad not to have to share his affairs with me." When he saw Margaret's disapproving glance at even this modest criticism of his brother, Jonathon continued, "At any rate, it was a very decent thing of him to do, and it means that we can afford to support ourselves there for as long as it takes."

"Oh, my," Dan said with resignation. "I suppose you'll see Philip?"

"He's actually consented to be one of my counselors. We'll move in with the Carlyles until the family that's been occupying the London mission home moves out."

"Then you'll be in London itself?" Sarah said, tears welling up in spite of her best efforts.

"That's where we're needed," Margaret replied. Then as if to reassure everyone, "I know it sounds awful, but my heart tells me that this is just what we're supposed to do. We sat by helplessly during the last war as all you boys went off to fight. I don't think I can stand it a second time, not when one of the two countries I love most in the world is under such vicious attack. We hope you'll understand . . ."

Of course, most everyone in the room felt both the inspiration and the peril associated with their words. Sarah was crying in spite of herself, Dan was ashen, Cory looked defiant, like he thought this was the best thing that anyone could possibly do, and Kathy was obviously distressed. The Browns had their heads down, as if they were intruding on a family discussion that should be private. The silence was deafening.

"When do you leave?" Sarah asked softly.

"In January," Jonathon replied with a forced attempt at cheer. "So we've got time to get things in order." There was another silence.

"I'm proud of you for going," Cory said. He felt his father's gaze turn on him. "I think that America should do more to help England. It's obvious that the Germans have gone mad with power, and somebody's got to stand up to them."

"Cory," Dan said as evenly as he could, "with all due respect for your motives, you really don't know what you're talking about. Standing up to the Germans is a lot more than guts and glory." No matter how hard he tried, he couldn't keep his voice from trembling.

"I know you disagree with me, Dad, and I know that I didn't go through what you did. But freedom is worth fighting for, and the French, Austrians, Poles, Norwegians, and Belgians have all lost their freedom. How long are we supposed to stand by and watch the massacre take place without doing anything?"

Dan started to rise from his chair, but Sarah's grip tightened on his hand until he sat down. "This really isn't the time to debate the merits of the war," Sarah said smoothly. Then, turning to the Richardses, "Of course we're pleased for you. You've received a call from the Lord through the prophet, and so you'll go with His blessing and our goodwill. We'll miss you, but we're proud of you."

"Thank you," Jonathon replied. "Our thoughts will be with all of you every single day."

Cory cleared his throat. "I know this probably isn't the time to talk about it, Dad, but you need to know that I've been thinking about signing up with the British Royal Air Force for pilot training. And now that Grandma and Grandpa are going over there, it makes it seem like an even better idea."

"Oh, Cory," Sarah said. "Please, not now!"

"If not now, when? There will never be a good time. I'm not a child anymore, and I'm not uninformed. I've been studying this, and I'm convinced that if the English are unsuccessful, it's the beginning of the end of freedom everywhere. This Hitler and his Nazis are like anti-Christs—they're against everything we believe in."

Dan stood up, his face flushed, and started shouting at Cory: he had no idea what he was talking about; it was absolutely ridiculous for him to sign up for service overseas when America wasn't even involved; he'd forbid it; did he realize the life expectancy of an English pilot; why did he want to put them through that kind of agony . . . Finally, he heard Sarah saying repeatedly, "Danny, Danny," and he felt foolish and frightened and excused himself to get some air. Cory looked thunderstruck but defiant, and the Browns stood up to make their exit.

Sarah couldn't imagine how anything could be worse than this until she heard Barbara cry out, "Nathan, what are you doing holding that girl's hand?"

Sarah turned to see that Nate had taken Kathy's hand into his while the fight had raged.

Now it was Nate who looked up defiantly. "I'm holding the hand of a person I care a great deal about, Mother."

"What are you talking about?" Barbara cried. Then looking around the room she read the concern on Sarah's and Cory's face. "What has been going on here? Tell me what's been going on here!"

"Barbara—" Sarah began.

Before she could continue, Barbara grabbed at Nate's sleeve. "You get up this moment, young man, and come home with us. You're going to New York City to live with your cousins." Then, turning to Josh, "And I may go with him!"

She pulled, but Nate didn't budge. She turned on him in a fury. "You get up this moment!" she shrieked.

"I will not get up, Mother. I will not leave this house, and I will not go to New York. I like Kathy!" Realizing what he'd said, he turned to Kathy, "I don't know how you feel, but I want to start dating you." He turned a defiant glance at his mother before returning his gaze to Kathy. "I've wanted to ask you out for a long time now, but I've been afraid of this."

Kathy leaned forward and took his hand. "Of course I want to date you, Nate. I always have."

"This can't be happening," Barbara cried. Turning to Josh, she shouted, "This is your fault. You made us move to this forsaken place, and now he thinks he's in love. With a Gentile!" Barbara stormed out of the house.

Josh stood up, apologized, and turned to follow his wife. On the way out, he said to Nate, "Come home as soon as you can. It won't get any easier by waiting."

Sarah slumped down into her chair and started sobbing. Margaret came around and put her arms around her while Nate and Kathy beamed at each other. Jonathon went outside to find Dan and tell him of this new development.

Chapter Eleven

HOPELESS HOPES

After three days of pointedly ignoring each other, Cory finally decided to confront his father. "Dad, I know you don't want to talk about it, but ignoring me isn't going to make it go away. Can't we talk about my future?"

Dan took a few moments to look up from his newspaper. "Do you really want to talk about it or simply announce what you intend to do?"

"That's not fair, Dad. I've always listened to you, and you know it."

"We've never talked about something like this." Dan could hear the cold edge to his voice but did nothing to soften it.

"It's my life—I should have some say in it." Cory had to work to suppress his rising anger.

Dan looked at him as evenly as he could. "It's your life that could very easily be lost—and for nothing. What kind of parent would let a four year old play in the street? As I see it, I have the same responsibility now. You may think you know what it's like, but you don't."

Cory shook his head, his face flushing. "But you have to agree that what's happening over there is evil. How can we sit here and not do something about it?"

"It is evil, Cory. It's very evil. I've seen it face-to-face. But the Europeans have been fighting each other like this for literally thousands of years, and with millions already in combat,

I'm not sure that your being there is going to change any of that. They're a people who seem crazed with war, and we shouldn't indulge them."

Dan's voice was steady, but Cory felt something in it that he'd never experienced before. It was cold and calculated. It frightened him. But he was resolved to see this out. "But it might. One thing's for sure, if England runs out of pilots, they will fail. And then the Nazis will control all of Europe. How long can America be secure if that happens?"

"Cory, you can talk to me all day about this, but I'm not changing my mind. War makes you do unspeakable things. And unspeakable things happen to you and others you care about. I don't think you should be there—certainly not unless you're compelled to."

Cory noticed that his father's hands were clenched, the blood drained from the knuckles, leaving them white and stretched.

"But you're an adult, and I can't stop you. Just don't ask me to endorse it." Then he added, "Only a fool would go into a war voluntarily. Only a stupid, naïve fool!"

Cory had tried to be civil, but this was too much. Almost by instinct he fired back where he knew he'd cause the deepest hurt. "Trevor volunteered—Grandpa Richards told me about it. And you were on his side. Now you're calling me a fool! Does that mean he was a fool?"

"Don't you dare lecture me about Trevor or anybody else. We were all fools. How dare you bring him up—you know nothing about it!"

The fury in Dan's eyes was unbelievable, and for a moment Cory thought he was going to jump up and physically assault him. But then Dan slumped back in his chair, his face drained of color. The silence was almost worse than the interchange.

It was infuriating to Cory that his dad simply set down these platitudes without explaining himself, yet heartbreaking to see how troubling it was for him. "Dad, I'm sorry. I know it's something that you never talk about. But I need to know. I'm sorry, but I have dreams. I want to fly, and I want to make a difference. We're taught that agency means everything, but how is it fair for us to have it and for all those people to lose it? If you don't want me to go to war because of what happened to you and the other people you knew, then talk to me about it—don't just lecture me and call me a fool."

Dan shook his head slowly, as if to clear his thoughts. Finally, he looked up and smiled weakly. "I've heard the first part of that argument before—long ago in Pocatello." Then he was lost in thought.

"Did you try to talk him out of it?"

"What?"

"Did you try to talk Trevor out of going?"

"No—it wouldn't have made any difference. Once his mind was made up, that was it. He was so headstrong. Plus, we were young and immortal. We knew that millions were dying, but it wasn't going to be us. After all, we were special . . ." He laughed a humorless laugh. "Interesting that we all think we're special, that through some divine grace or merit we'll be spared while others aren't." He went silent again.

Very tentatively, Cory asked, "What was he like? I've seen his pictures, but nobody ever talks about him. Grandpa tried once, but he became too emotional." Then, seeing the look of clear distress on Dan's face, "But if you don't want to talk about it . . ."

Dan took a deep breath and then exhaled slowly. "I should have told you about him long ago. He was my best friend. I loved him, and you would too. It's just so hard when you lose somebody . . ."

Cory felt bad to see the tears come into his dad's eyes. "It's okay, let's not talk about it."

"No, no. We need to talk. I need to tell you about Trevor." Then softly, "You'd have liked him a lot. Everybody did. Trevor wasn't exactly like you—you're more serious and steady—but like you, he wanted to do things fast. He was a daredevil who was always telling us he had things in control and that we were silly to worry." He smiled as the good memories returned, and for the next thirty minutes he shared the wonderful and troubled days of growing up with a kid like Trevor Richards.

When the stories came to an end, there was a silence. But it wasn't a bad silence. Cory realized that nothing had been decided about him, but he knew he'd put his father through an ordeal and so decided not to pursue it any further that day.

As he stood up to leave, Dan asked him to sit down. "Here's the deal, Cory. Trevor was going to go to Europe no matter what anyone said. Fortunately, Jonathon and Margaret allowed it to be his decision, even though it broke their hearts. I know that you have to make this decision, and I don't want it to come between us, no matter what you decide. But it's worse than you can ever imagine, and I'm sincere when I say that whether you go now, later, or even never, it isn't going to directly change things. The scale of it all is just too grand. So if I could plan things, I'd do this: If America isn't drawn into the war, and that's looking increasingly less likely, then you stay out. Learn to fly in commercial aviation. They're starting mail service in a lot of places, there are crop dusting services for farmers, and there's even some opportunity for passenger service. Wait it out and spend a long and happy life doing this, if it's what you want."

Cory started to interrupt.

"Wait a moment. If America does enter the war, then go and immediately enlist in the service of your choice. I won't fight you on it. If it comes down to our own country's interest, then you should serve. Is that something you would consider?"

Cory took a deep breath. "It's not what I want to hear. I really want to get over there and be part of it." He paused. "The problem is that what you're asking is reasonable and fair. I don't know that you've ever given me bad advice." He shook his head quickly from side to side, as if it was all too much. "I'll have to think about it, Dad, but I guess I can hold off for awhile . . ."

Dan's face darkened again. "We thought it was over . . . We thought that all the blood and terror would end these insane wars. America had fifty thousand men killed in that war so that all this would end. Eighteen million people died! But now it's back with even more fury. What an incredible waste." And with that, he lapsed into silence again.

Finally, Cory stood up to leave, and instinctively Dan stood and embraced him. "I love you, son—and I'm proud that you want to do the right thing. I just don't want to lose you." He choked up and held Cory even tighter. Then, backing up to look at him, "I'm proud . . ."

* * *

November 1941

Shortly after Nate started dating Kathy in September, Barbara returned to New York City, alone. At first, she went to clear her head, but the passing days turned into weeks, and still she didn't come home. Josh made a trip back to the city, but nothing was decided. "I think she's considering divorce," he said dejectedly when Dan asked him how she was. "I may have to give up my job here and try to find something back in the city." He looked wistful. "We've had our struggles, and there have been times I've wondered if it's really worth it, but I love her, and I don't want to lose her."

"What about Nate? Isn't he worried about driving a permanent wedge between them?"

"He feels terrible about it, but he's also being quite stubborn. He can't understand why his mother is putting him in such a bind."

"What about you? How do you feel about their dating?"

"I've worked with LDS people every day for the past four and half years, and I have no problems with Nate dating a girl from another faith, particularly Kathy. But to Barbara, it's a rejection of everything she believes. Even though I think it's foolish, she feels betrayed. Plus, since it's the one thing she's dreaded most since moving out here, it's like her pride is tied up in it as well. Her heart is broken, and I'm not sure she can ever accept it. I honestly don't know if she'll ever reconcile with Nate. When a Jewish boy leaves the faith, it's as if he ceases to exist. It's the hardest thing I've ever had to deal with."

"But he hasn't left the faith," Dan said with some alarm. "He's simply dating . . ."

Josh was silent for a few moments. "He's started investigating your church, Dan. He didn't want me to say anything to you, but he's been meeting with a set of stake missionaries."

Dan's face registered the shock. "Oh . . . I see. So, perhaps that's the real reason Barbara left."

"That's the real reason."

"What does Barbara hope will come out of this?"

"She hopes that Nate will abandon Kathy and move back to New York. With everything that's happening to the Jews in Europe, she thinks it's more important than ever to build up their community here in America." Josh shook his head and then said in a bewildered tone, "How do you choose between your wife and your son? How can a man possibly make that choice?"

It was a rhetorical question, but Dan addressed it anyway. "You can't, Josh. At least I don't know how you could. You have to love them both. Hopefully it will never come down to a choice, but if it does, it seems to me that they'll each have to agree to let you love the other one."

"It's just that the culture means so much to Barbara. This kind of anger is beyond anything in my family."

Dan's gaze took on a faraway look. "I've had experience with it. There was a lot of anger in my family. It made no sense to me either, but it was real. There's no winning—only losing. Oh, Josh, I hope it doesn't come to that."

* * *

The more Kathy got to know Nate, the more she both liked and loved him. Clearly she had a romantic interest in him—she actually trembled at times when she looked at him. She loved his dark hair, his penetrating eyes, and his bright smile that filled his whole face when he laughed. He was taller than anyone in her family, which gave him a powerful sense of presence, but his personality was anything but dominating. In many regards, he had the easygoing personality of his father, unassuming and unpretentious. Probably the biggest difference between Nate and Kathy's family was that he had the mind of an engineer—precise, generally unemotional, and logical. Her father's and brother's musical skills made them more temperamental. Nate and Kathy's private conversations focused on his dreams of going to engineering school for a master's degree, perhaps in civil engineering, to design bridges and transportation systems. He was such a stark contrast to the other people in her life that Kathy found herself endlessly fascinated.

As Nate's investigation of the Church continued, he found it difficult to talk with Kathy about it—not that she wasn't willing and enthusiastic that he was doing it. The problem was that she held back, probably because she didn't want him to ever feel that he'd been coerced into joining.

It was actually in this area that he found common ground with Dan. After Josh confessed to telling Dan about Nate's investigation of the LDS Church, he was able to discuss Church principles with Dan in a nondoctrinaire way. It was obvious that Dan could see the world from more than one point of view, and so he was able to somehow step into Nate's shoes and see what it would be like for someone raised Jewish to deal with the remarkably different story of the restored gospel. He was never judgmental, even when Nate was critical or skeptical of some element of the Church, which Dan usually ascribed to social custom rather than to Church doctrine.

"I guess one of the things that puzzles me is the idea that there is one true way," Nate said on one occasion. "There are so many good people in the world—why restrict the truth to such a small number? That's always been something troubling to me about Judaism—why would God make the chosen people such a small number?"

"I suppose that's where I see things differently than some in my church. Some see membership as a clear-cut decision of good versus evil. I was fortunate to have a very good friend who was a minister for another church who took me into his home when I was at the lowest point in my life. It was in England, and there were no LDS services nearby, so I went to his church for more than a year. What I discovered is that there are wonderful people who sincerely love God and who have great spiritual insights that are authentic and real. So for me, it isn't nearly so important to define the Church in terms of right versus wrong, but rather incomplete versus complete and whole."

"I'm not sure I understand."

"In my estimation, the LDS Church has the most complete and full understanding of the purpose of life and of our relationship to God of any religious denomination in the world. But that doesn't mean it is the only church that has elements of truth. Nearly all do in that they teach people to lead moral lives, to seek and worship God, and to be kind and generous with other people. But in this church, one has the added dimension of modern revelation and authority to give credibility to our acts. The prophets have answered many of the questions that have divided religions over the centuries. So the question a person needs to ask is, 'Am I satisfied to live in partial light, or do I want all of the available light and truth?'"

"Maybe I've been asking the wrong question," Nate said thoughtfully. "In my mind accepting your church was rejecting mine." He dropped his gaze. "That's certainly how my mother sees it."

"It's not that kind of choice. It's simply an invitation to add more and to act under priesthood authority. The things you give up pale in significance to the additional light and spirit you'll feel." Dan smiled. "And, in spite of all the goodness that comes into our lives because of our affiliation with the Church, there are still problems that threaten to overwhelm us. Jonathon and Margaret are still going into harm's way and may die. Families are still troubled by unemployment, anger, and rebellious children. The Church doesn't give you a pass on those challenges. It just gives you context to understand them and to move forward with more confidence."

"You're a good man, aren't you, Dan?"

"I'm a man who is gaining confidence, but it's hard for me. There was a time when I seriously doubted that God even existed. It was a time when I struggled to hold on to even the smallest faith in Him. And, whatever faith I had in God, I had none in myself. So my faith was as immature as anyone's has ever been. But I believe in the goodness of people, and I see in them the elements of godliness that whispers that their existence is not an accident, but rather part of a plan. Eventually, I surrendered to the Spirit and now find joy in my Church affiliation." He looked up and smiled wistfully.

Nate stood up. "Thank you, Mr. O'Brian—Dan. I'm glad to get to know you better."

"I hope it helps you in your search. You know that we'll love you no matter what you decide."

Nate smiled. "I've already decided. I've had the spiritual feelings you spoke of on several occasions. You helped settle a few questions today that I needed answers to." He smiled. "Would you be willing to baptize me?"

"Nate, are you sure? What about your parents?"

"Dad already expects it. I think he's actually happy about it. He sincerely admires you and the other people he works with. As for mother, she'll never accept it." His voice broke. "She may never talk to me again."

"I hope that's not the case."

"Me too. But even if it is, I have to do what's right for me. And," he added shyly, "perhaps for Kathy." He dropped his gaze.

"I'd be honored, Nate."

The young man looked up. "I feel sorry for my mother, because this is so different than what she's hoping for."

Chapter Twelve

DECEMBER 7, 1941

In some ways the news on December 7 should have surprised no one. For more than a year, the United States had imposed an ever-tightening economic noose around Japan's neck trying to force them to withdraw from their hostile and viciously cruel occupation of mainland China. The trade embargo was slowly starving Japan of the oil and natural resources it needed to survive. Almost everyone who followed the situation felt that the Japanese would soon strike at the Philippines, where the United States had an important but difficult-to-defend outpost. Still, right up to the last moment, including an official dispatch on December 5, the Roosevelt administration continued to make peace overtures and everyone hoped for a change that could help America avoid a conflict. The O'Brians were just returning home from Sunday School with the radio tuned to the newly renamed KSL when the news was announced that Pearl Harbor was under attack. Dan had to pull to the side of the road while he tried to stop trembling. He finally asked Cory to take over the wheel to get them home.

Lunch was eaten mostly in silence, because everyone knew that this war would be different from the last. In World War I, America had made its entrance long after the battles had started, making the decisive gesture in the end, but most of the troops had endured less than a year of fighting. This war was barely two years old, and with the fleet destroyed in Hawaii, there was no telling how long it would be before the navy could effectively fight Japan.

Shortly after lunch, Dan sought out Cory. "Any chance you'll stay with the band until you find out if you're going to be drafted?" He knew the request was hopeless almost as soon as he completed the question. The fire in his son's eyes showed that he was ready to go off on the grand adventure of war to once again save democracy. Dan had seen that look before—in the eyes of his childhood friends who had wanted to serve in the first Great War. Rather than force a discussion, he allowed Cory to dart out the door and over to Paul's and, presumably, his other friends' to find out what they all intended to do. Kathy was with Nate and Josh, so it was just Sarah and Dan as the afternoon faded and the early winter darkness deepened into gloom. They sat and read with few words spoken.

Later that night, as they retired to their bedroom, Sarah expressed surprise that Dan had said so little when the news was received.

"What is there to say? This war is going to be far more destructive than the last one. We'll end up fighting in both Europe and Asia, and our commitment of troops is going to be unlike anything ever imagined. It's inevitable that Cory will be drafted, so why try to throw cold water on his ambitions now when he'll end up going anyway?"

"What about his goal of being a pilot? Should we try to talk him out of that?"

Dan shook his head slowly. "And into what? Even if we were successful in getting him into something that wasn't on the front lines, he'd end up hating himself for the rest of his life. Eventually he'd despise us for doing it to him. Besides, I don't know what would be worse—imagining him in an airplane or knowing what he's going through in the infantry, which is where he'll wind up if he gets drafted. It simply has to be his choice."

Sarah started crying, and Dan tried to hold her, but he didn't know how to comfort her when all he could feel was the cold, clammy hand of dread reaching around his throat and constricting his own airway. "I don't know if I can take it," he said quietly.

Sarah looked up at him through her puffy eyes and pulled him as close as she could. His skin was cold and his breathing shallow. "You'll make it, dear, because this time you have me. We'll make it together." She started weeping, and they held each other close as the darkness tried to engulf them in fear.

* * *

The declaration of war proved the impetus for a number of important decisions—paramount of which was Nate's proposal of marriage to Kathy. While they had talked about it before, it had always been in the context of waiting until he finished college and found a job that could support them. But once it was clear that everything was about to change, they decided to face the uncertainty of the future with each other. In that decision, they were like millions of other young couples who hastened their wedding plans in preparation for full-scale mobilization.

Usually, an engagement would last nine months to a year—six months at a minimum. But that no longer made sense, so they set the date for mid-March. In fact, the time selected was the one-year anniversary of Kathy breaking her leg. "That's truly the day I fell in love with you," Nate had said. Kathy had accused him of being a romantic, a charge which he didn't take trouble to deny.

The Richardses had to leave in January. Kathy cried at the thought that they couldn't be there for the wedding. Prior to leaving, Jonathon and Margaret asked Dan and Sarah to move into their home to take care of it while they were gone. "We plan for you to have it someday anyway, so why not enjoy it now?"

"But we already have a home," Sarah said simply. The fact that the two houses weren't really comparable didn't matter to her. "Besides, what would we do with our house? You'll be coming back someday."

"We thought you might let Kathy and Nate live in it," Margaret replied.

"That's the perfect thought . . . Kathy and Nate can take care of your home while you're gone so they can save up money to buy their own house when you return." The thought of giving newlyweds a grand house in the Avenues probably seemed a bit absurd to everyone but Sarah. But it was clear that her mind was made up, and so that was that.

When the day of the Richardses' departure arrived, the family went to Union Station to bid them farewell. Going into Europe in the most desperate days of the war made it a particularly difficult experience.

Dan tried to smile. "You know, it's supposed to be the children and grandchildren who leave, not the grandparents."

"I know," Jonathon said, "but it actually feels good to be needed. And right now, the English Saints need all the help they can get."

"We understand," Dan replied, "but it's just really hard to imagine what Sunday afternoons will be like without you." He smiled ruefully.

"And I feel bad that you'll miss my wedding. But I know you're doing a good thing." Kathy tried to smile, but the tears started streaming from her eyes again.

"Oh, Kathy. Your wedding will be lovely. And I've arranged a little something with your mother so it will be more like I'm here. And your grandfather has set up a special arrangement with Western Union so that a telegram will be sent the moment you say yes so we'll be able to celebrate there in England. We'd pay for a telephone call, but with the war as it is, the lines are all reserved for official business." Margaret hugged her. "I'll think of you every single day, and I'll write to you even when you don't have time to write back."

"Thank you, Grandma, but you know I'll write. And we're going to be happy. I hope we're as happy as you and Grandpa have been, because that will mean we're succeeding. Thank you for loving me."

Margaret started weeping, and the men all rolled their eyes, even though they were close to tears themselves. Margaret didn't care what they thought, nor did she feel guilty for her tears.

Jonathon smiled at Kathy. "Be happy, sweetheart. And always keep God as a partner in your marriage. That's the real key to success. People can't always be there, but He is."

"Thanks, Grandpa—and promise me that you'll be safe. I just can't stand the thought of never seeing you again."

"I'll promise to do my best, because that's the only promise I can keep." He pulled her into an embrace. "My, what a beautiful woman you've become. Nate is fortunate, and so are you. You two deserve each other." Jonathon swallowed hard.

After giving everyone on the platform a hug, including Josh, the Richardses turned to get on the train. Looking back at Dan, Jonathon returned and embraced him, whispering in his ear, "A man could never ask for more from a son than I've received from you. I'm glad to have shared you with your parents. No matter what happens, live or die, I'll always be nearby. And we'll always love you."

Dan took a deep breath. "Thank you." And then he said something he'd never said before, even though he'd felt it. "Thank you, Dad. Thank you."

* * *

When the date of the wedding arrived, Barbara was still in New York, brokenhearted. Josh waited until right after the wedding ceremony and then got ready to run and catch a train back to New York City so he could be with his wife again.

"Tell Mom that I love her," Nate said as Josh came up to say good-bye.

"I promise. Maybe someday . . ."

Nate smiled. "I know she doesn't agree, but I'll be forever grateful that you brought us to Salt Lake City. This is where I was supposed to be, so thank you."

Josh, not an emotionally demonstrative person, just hugged his son with a warm embrace to cover his feelings.

When Kathy and Nate lingered to receive the well-wishes of the crowd, Cory grabbed them and said, "Come on, we have a deal with Grandma and Grandpa. You can come back to the reception in a few minutes."

"Alright," Kathy laughed. "Let's go." So with Cory as their chauffeur, the newlyweds and Dan and Sarah headed straight for the Western Union office where Dan's friend was waiting.

"Is it official?" he asked. Kathy held up her ring finger and gave Nate a kiss.

"That's official enough for me." He started tapping out the telegram that would work its way to England. Normally, it would take up to a day to receive a response, but he'd greased the skids so that repeaters in New York were instantly ready to forward the message across the transatlantic cable. It took just ten minutes for the teletype machine to start clattering a response.

```
Congratulations and welcome to the family
STOP Hugs and cheers in London from a
tearful grandmother STOP Make that happy
tears from Grandma and Grandpa STOP
Philip and Marilyn send their regards
STOP Our prayers for a long and happy
life together STOP Love Grandma and
Grandpa Richards STOP
```

Kathy wiped a tear from her eye, and Nate drew her head to his chest while he stroked her hair.

"You used to be the one she turned to for comfort," Sarah whispered quietly in Dan's ear.

"And you used to turn to your mother before I came along. I'm glad you gave your heart to me, so how can I be sad that she wants Nate now?"

"I love you, Danny O'Brian."

"And I love you back, Sarah O'Brian." Then very quietly, "More than I can ever fully put into words."

Finally, Kathy looked up at Nate and laughed. "It's just that I'm happy, you know."

"Of course, dear."

Then to the crowd of puzzled onlookers who had never seen a wedding party at a Western Union station before, Dan said in as loud a voice as he could muster, "Ladies and gentlemen, may I please present the bride and groom, Mr. and Mrs. Nathan Brown!" The crowd of both strangers and friends applauded and then cheered as Nate and Kathy embraced with a long and lingering kiss.

Their gift from the Richardses was a night in the Grand Suite of the Hotel Utah. For their gift, Dan had arranged complimentary travel on the Denver & Rio Grande Railroad from Salt Lake City to Glenwood Springs, Colorado, through the magnificent canyons of the Wasatch up to the high mountain desert of eastern Utah. Nate was fascinated by the great S-curve during the crawl-out through Provo Canyon where the first cars in the train traveled in the opposite direction of the last cars. Later, when they entered the red cliffs of the Colorado River Canyon, the train often seemed to hang precipitously over the river, and Kathy occasionally had to fight vertigo while looking down the dramatic drop-offs just below the train. Arriving in Glenwood Springs late in the afternoon, they settled in to spend two nights at the historic Hotel Colorado as Dan and Sarah's wedding present, enjoying the hot springs, hiking in the granite mountains, and sightseeing along the Colorado River. They wished it could have lasted forever, but even two nights was expensive. When they returned to Salt Lake City, they had become a couple, deeply in love and thrilled to have their lives before them.

* * *

February 1942

"Are you going to finish this semester before you sign up, Cory? I'm surprised you've waited this long to enlist."

Cory looked at Nate and framed his response carefully. "I wanted to sign up in December, but my mother pleaded with me to finish college, saying it made a lot more sense for me to go into the service with a degree. It will be easier to become an officer. It's frustrating, but I'm going to finish out this term. I am going to go in and talk to the recruiters about it this week. I think they can get me signed up but defer my enlistment until after I finish in the spring."

"I think your parents are right. Are you going to go for the army or the navy?"

Cory got a puzzled look. "Guess I hadn't really thought about it. I've always thought of the army. Why the navy?"

"Oh, I don't know. I've just always thought that if I had to go into the service, I'd sooner be in the navy than the army. I don't like the thought of getting too close to the enemy like your dad had to do in the trenches."

"Your dad was a pilot, wasn't he?" Cory asked.

"He was. A pretty good one too. He was just one kill short of becoming an ace when the war ended. He says that the aircraft the military has today is so far advanced from what he had that it's like comparing a musket to a machine gun."

Cory was thoughtful. "Have you considered being a pilot?"

"No. I don't have fast enough reflexes to deal with air combat. When my dad tells stories about the maneuvers they had to make, I almost get dizzy. You know me well enough by now to know that I'm a deliberate thinker, not a fast thinker. But you'll be perfect."

Cory laughed. "I hope so. I'm worried about some of the math tests I have to take to get into flight school. I wish you could help me with those."

Nate laughed. "I would if I could. At any rate, I hope you get where you want to go." Nate went quiet. "And I hope you make it out alive." He looked up and smiled. "It took my marriage to Kathy to get a brother, and it just wouldn't be right to lose that as soon as I got you."

Cory smiled broadly. "I'm not going into this to lose my life—it's the Japanese who need to worry." Then thinking about what he'd said, "Hmm . . . I guess that means I need to consider the navy. The only way to get airplanes near Japan is on an aircraft carrier." He nodded, almost unconsciously. "What do you know?" He smiled again. "I'm going to join the navy." Then he pursed his lips as he thought about it. "Why not? I've always liked the idea of being on a ship. Besides, just think how great I'll look in blue! The women will go crazy!" He looked at his watch and gasped, "Uh, oh, I'm not dressed, and the show starts in ten minutes. Dad will be having a heart attack." He stood up. "Thanks, Nate. I needed to talk this through with somebody. I'm going to be a Navy man." With that, he walked off with a swagger that Nate hadn't seen before.

"I hope I did you a favor . . ."

* * *

Cory attended a recruiting seminar where each of the three branches of the service made a play for him. The Marines appealed to his vanity, the Army to his loyalty, and the Navy to his sense of adventure. In the end, it came down to which service gave him the greatest chance of getting into the air, and the Navy proved the one most anxious to get him. He easily passed the basic physical, but the battery of tests that followed was far harder than he'd imagined.

"So how did you do?" Nate asked him later that week.

"I thought I'd messed up completely. The math stuff was really tough—I barely passed the calculus test. And the physical exams were pretty rigorous. The one I hated the most was the spinning chair, where they blindfolded me, spun me around, then told me to point to various points on the compass. Somehow I was able to keep track of location, but I almost panicked when I felt myself starting to get dizzy. The smell in the room told me that others had it a lot worse than I did. At any rate, when I came out of there, I had no idea as to whether I passed or not." Then, he burst into a grin. "But the recruiter called me yesterday and said that if I don't wash out of basic training, I'm on track to enter pilot training school."

"Good for you, Cory. I'm convinced that aircraft will be much more of a deciding factor in this war than the last one."

Cory looked around to see if anyone was listening. He and Nate were sitting on the front porch of the Richardses' house since Kathy had wanted to prepare Sunday dinner for the family. At this point, Cory had avoided talking to his father about the tests other than to say that they seemed to have gone well. He'd have to tell him in the next day or two, but he dreaded the conversation.

"So what about you, Nate? Are you going to sign up for anything?"

Nate's face fell, and he leaned forward so he could speak very quietly. "I want to—I think I should be part of it. But . . ." He stumbled a bit on the words.

"What?"

"Kathy and I are going to make an announcement after dessert—we're going to have a baby."

"That's great! Congratulations!"

Nate shushed him, and Cory quieted down. "As it stands, I don't want to leave Kathy to deal with all that alone. And the last thing I want to do is make our child an orphan." His face flushed with embarrassment. "It sounds so strange to say 'our child.' I don't feel like I'm really done with childhood myself, and now I'm going to be a father."

Cory was thoughtful. "Maybe you can find a stateside job in the military where you won't face combat. I've heard that more than two-thirds of all military personnel serve away from the front lines, so that should help."

"I hope so," Nate said wistfully. "Still, a man should serve his country at times like this . . ." They were interrupted by Kathy calling out for everyone to come in for dessert. "Wish me luck in the announcement," he said. "It's kind of scary."

"Do you think my mom won't be the happiest person in the world?"

"It's my mother that I feel bad about. I don't think she'll be happy when she gets the letter."

"Still not talking to you?"

"Not a word. Dad says he tries to bring our marriage up, but she's not ready to talk yet." Nate's face darkened. "It's not like we committed a crime or anything. She acts like we're criminals." Then he sighed. "Still, I hope that we can figure out some way to reconcile."

* * *

Getting accepted into the Navy and going to basic training were two different things. Cory waited nearly six months before receiving the telegram ordering him to active duty in July of 1942. As the war had heated up in Europe, the services had seen a dramatic increase in peacetime enlistments, and the training facilities and staff simply weren't prepared to handle the huge influx of new personnel that the declaration of war itself had brought. It was frustrating as the days passed, and Cory found himself worrying that all the action would be over before he even got a chance to train. But inevitably the months rolled by, and too soon for his parents—the day of his transfer to San Diego drew near.

In the interim, Cory and his dad continued to make music each Friday night. Dan had become quiet, except when he was playing jazz. There was a new passion to his playing that astonished even some of the best musicians in the state. He drove the band to improve their musicianship, and it was paying off in ever higher ratings. Their show was now being played in most of southern California, including Los Angeles, as well as being a hit in Las Vegas and the rest of Nevada.

Cory would generally sing two or three songs in the two hours of the show. One of the innovations that Dan implemented was to invite a guest singer every week. It was a way to provide a little diversity to the program as well as to give a young singer a chance to step into the spotlight. Occasionally, when one of the nationally recognized big bands were playing in Salt Lake City, some of the musicians would come on Dan's show and play a set or two, which always thrilled the crowd. Cory was surprised at how at ease Dan was with these famous people and that they seemed to genuinely enjoy swinging with the Soldat Ordinaires. It was obvious that there was some kind of informal music fraternity and that his dad was a natural member. For his part, Cory enjoyed the singing and the music, but the part he liked best was going out on the floor and dancing with the girls when he wasn't performing. Even though he had the voice and style to really succeed in music, it just wasn't the passion for him that it was for his father.

"Your voice is getting better and better," Dan said one night as Cory stepped away from the microphone.

"Thanks," Cory said suspiciously. His dad wasn't usually one to compliment.

"The audience is going to miss you."

Cory wondered if this were some last-minute attempt to thwart his enlistment, but his next comment told Cory that it was just Dan's way of trying to tell him thanks.

"I probably didn't pay you enough. Somehow I always thought of you as temporary, even though you've become as much a part of the band as any of us." He looked up and smiled. "At any rate, you're one of the best crooners in the country. Your voice is rich and soothing, and people love your style. I appreciate you stepping in to help us out. We wouldn't be where we are today without you."

Cory stumbled a bit but recovered and started to say, "Thanks, Dad—" when he was interrupted by the countdown at the end of the commercial break.

Normally, Dan didn't do a lot of the talking during a performance, even though it was his band. He let Jim Chatterton, one of the trombonists, do most of the announcing—primarily because he loved it and was really glib at the microphone, but also because Dan was always self-conscious about his voice. That's why Cory was so surprised when the spotlight swung to Dan.

"Ladies and gentlemen, this is Danny O'Brian. Usually we end our set each night with something hot so you can dance us off the air. But tonight's kind of special to the band because our vocalist, Cory O'Brian, is shipping off to basic training on Tuesday, and we don't really know how long it will be before we get to hear him again." There was a gasp from the audience, then applause. "He wants to be a Navy pilot—you know, the guys who learn to take off from the deck of a flattop propelled by a slingshot. You talk about hot—that's got to be the thrill of a life-time." The crowd cheered as the spotlight swung to Cory, who, though embarrassed, took a little bow and waved his hand.

"At any rate," Dan said quietly, "we're going to miss him a lot. I'm his dad, and his mother and I will miss him more than anybody." Of course the room was totally silent now. "So I wanted to do something that I don't think anyone, including Cory, has heard since before the last war—the one we hoped would be the war to end all wars." He looked up and smiled at Cory. "I'm going to sing a song for my boy. My voice isn't what it used to be, so don't expect too much. And the song is anything but swing. At any rate, Cory, this is for you and for all the other young men who are going off to defend our country and put down tyranny. Hopefully this time the world will get it right . . ."

Then with a simple lead in on the keys, Dan started to sing in his raspy, but still melodic voice.

God be with you till we meet again;
By his counsels guide, uphold you;
With his sheep securely fold you.
God be with you till we meet again.

Then with a little more strength,

Till we meet, till we meet,
Till we meet at Jesus' feet,
Till we meet, till we meet,
God be with you till we meet again.

Smiling through his tears, Dan leaned into the microphone situated above his keyboard and said, "God be with you, son. We love you." At that, the crowd went crazy as Cory stepped forward and lifted his dad off the piano bench and into his arms.

Chapter Thirteen

REPORT TO NAVAL TRAINING STATION, SAN DIEGO

Along with perhaps a dozen other young men in uniforms, Cory leaned out the window of the Union Pacific rail car and waved good-bye to the small crowd that had assembled to see him off to San Diego. Sitting back in his seat, he sighed to himself, "Thank heavens that's over."

"Thank heavens what's over?" Cory turned and looked at the fellow sitting next to him. Brown hair, blue eyes, moderate build. But, as was so often the case, a bit taller than Cory.

"Oh, uh, that probably wasn't the best way to say it. I'm just glad I got through the good-byes so I can finally concentrate on getting through basic training and qualifying for flight school."

"Tearful mom, huh?"

Cory laughed. "Tearful mom, dad, and sister. Jealous brother-in-law. You name it, they were crying."

"What about you?"

"Yeah, me too." Then, looking away from the stranger, "Which is why I'm glad it's over." When the other fellow didn't say anything, he added, "I'm Cory O'Brian, Navy Seaman Second Class, but on my way to flight training."

The stranger smiled back. "I'm Spencer Tolman, from Portland, Oregon. Navy, I don't even know my rank."

Cory couldn't help but laugh. "The Navy's got its work cut out with guys like us, doesn't it?" They shook hands and settled back in the seat.

"Flight school?"

"I want to be a pilot. My dad was in the infantry in World War I, and the few times he talked about it is enough to convince me that I don't want any of that hand-to-hand stuff if I can avoid it."

"But why an airplane instead of serving on a ship?"

Cory thought about that. "I suppose it's because you'd feel like a sitting duck on a ship—no matter what the enemy was throwing at you, you are powerless as an individual to get out of the way." Then, with a grin, "Unless you're the captain, I suppose. But they're not likely to turn a battle cruiser over to a twenty-three-year-old, are they? Which is why I like the idea of being a pilot—out there, you are the captain of your own little ship and have at least some ability to maneuver." He was thoughtful again. "Truth is, it's just something I want to do. What about you?"

"I don't know. I'd like to be involved with airplanes, I guess. My father thinks there's a lot of opportunity in aviation, and I'm good mechanically. But I don't think I'd like to be a pilot. I'm a deliberate thinker, and it seems to me that pilots have to be more spontaneous. If they give me a choice, I guess I'll try for something like ship's navigation."

"Why not be a radioman or gunner on an airplane? Depending on the type of aircraft, that puts you in a fairly senior position, even though you're young. And usually the radio guy does most of the navigation."

"Radioman? I hadn't ever thought about that. Still, there's that business about falling out of the sky if something goes wrong. You don't have to worry about that on a ship."

Cory laughed. He liked this guy, and the thoughts about leaving home were temporarily forgotten as they learned about each other's lives.

* * *

The furthest Cory had ever traveled prior to this was to southeastern Idaho and Las Vegas to do an occasional show with his dad, mostly at the urging of Josh Brown, who had always pushed them to get outside of Salt Lake City to build their audience. As the troop train passed through southern Nevada he remembered one particular trip that he'd especially enjoyed when the band performed in Las Vegas. As usual, his mother and sister had traveled with them, and his mom had arranged for them to spend an extra day without telling them what she had in mind.

It turned out that she'd arranged a bus to take the band out to see the new Boulder Dam. Cory loved it because of the amazing technology involved—the two giant intake towers situated out in the lake where water from various depths could be mixed together to keep the output below the dam the proper temperature. He also thrilled at the tour of the generator room, where the giant turbines turned at a constant speed, the eighteen-inch shaft between the turbine and the generator shining as it turned. Of course none of that mattered to his mom. She was thrilled with the beauty of the sandstone canyon, filled with the sapphire blue water of Lake Mead. And Kathy smiled at the desert flowers while Dan unconsciously tapped his fingers to the tune of some song he was hearing in his brain. They were all so different, yet happy together. It was at moments like that when Cory realized how much he loved his family.

To fight off the wave of homesickness that threatened to engulf him, he asked Spencer if he'd like to go into the club car to play a game of chess. Spencer readily agreed, and in just a few minutes, Cory figured out why. "I don't think I've ever lost a game of chess quite so fast," he said, abashed.

"Chess is a blood sport in the Tolman family. We play at least three or four times per week, and no one shows any mercy whatsoever."

Cory didn't look encouraged.

"If it helps," Spencer said, "I was president of my high school's chess club, and we were ranked best in the state of Oregon based on tournament play."

"So I was set up? Is that what you're telling me?"

"You invited me, not the other way around."

"Well, I thought we could pass a couple of hours this way, but if you're going to beat me in ten minutes each time we play, we're going to have a long trip."

"How about if I show you some strategies I've picked up through the years instead?"

"I'm not proud—teach away."

It was in that way that the final hours passed as the train worked its way south to Union Station in Los Angeles, with its elegant, polished, wood-paneled ceiling, and then onto the Coast Rails to San Diego. Even though Spencer was more than willing to keep playing chess, Cory finally broke it off so he could watch the various California beaches as they made their way south. The bougainvillea was still in full bloom, with different bushes aflame in pink, purple, and even yellow, and the palm trees reminded him of all the movies he'd seen set in this part of the country. "Just look at how big it is," he said under his breath.

"What's big?"

"The ocean. It just goes on forever and ever."

"You've never seen the ocean before?" Then seeing the embarrassment in Cory's eyes, Spencer continued, "We used to go out to the Oregon coast nearly every year for a week or more. I love the ocean—particularly the sound of the surf crashing into the rocks."

"Salt Lake City's a long way from the coast," Cory said quietly.

"I didn't mean to hurt your feelings. It's just that I figured a person would have to love the ocean before signing up for the Navy. It took me by surprise to think that you'd join without ever having seen it."

Cory nodded. "It's probably crazy. For all I know, I'll get seasick and wash out. My dad told me that the voyage from New York to France about killed him. He has this theory that musicians are more susceptible to motion sickness, which doesn't bode well for my career in airplanes either."

"So I take it you've never been in an airplane before either?"

"No, but I did fine on all the qualifications tests, so I hope I'll be okay."

"Well, my experience is that nearly everybody gets seasick at some point or another. It's just too hard to cope with all that movement. But the good news is that after a couple of days, you get your sea legs, and then the problem is getting used to being back on the land once you reach port. At least that's the way it is for the fishermen in my dad's family."

Cory started to reply, then caught his breath as he saw an extended view of the beach near La Jolla. There were bathers out in the surf, and somehow he knew that this was where he wanted to spend his life. Sun, palms, sand—this is what he was meant for. Now, more than ever, he hoped he'd get an assignment to the South Pacific.

After perhaps another twenty minutes in which Cory lost sight of the ocean, San Diego came into view. There weren't a lot of buildings, but he could see the harbor and understood for the first time why this was such an important port for the Navy. The area protected by Coronado Island was enormous, and he gazed in wonder at the seemingly endless row of Navy ships extending along the wharf and out of sight. As the train pulled into the Spanish-style Santa Fe Railroad Station, right in the heart of downtown, he felt his heart rise in his throat as he realized he was about to really enter the military. It was the most thrilling moment of his life.

But, typical of Cory, just as soon as he and Spencer and the hundreds of other recruits they'd been traveling with descended from the train and were ordered into lines for transport to the Recruit Training Command, he got a sick feeling in his stomach. The people getting them on the bus were not gentle or polite, and he had this overwhelming sense that life as he knew it before the war was officially over.

Chapter Fourteen

CLASSIFICATION 1-A

Nate looked at the envelope with mixed emotions. Kathy was obviously frightened. "Maybe they're going to take into account the fact that you've just graduated in industrial engineering and could be of real help in war production," she said hopefully.

He looked at her and sighed. Part of him wanted that—wanted it desperately. It was now just two months before the baby was to be born, and Kathy was reduced to wearing a rather limited wardrobe. She was extremely self-conscious about the size of her stomach, which did seem much larger by comparison to most women who were seven months along. Nate loved it—she looked so beautiful that he could seldom resist the temptation to periodically rub his hand over her tummy. More than once in public she'd had to swat his hand away.

"You're so beautiful," he said in a disconnected response.

"My looks have nothing to do with your classification," she said anxiously.

"I know. I'm scared too. I told them about the baby, and I told them about my degree. But now is the moment of truth." With a gulp, he reached for a knife and slit open the envelope. Pulling the paper from inside he looked down to see *Classification 1-A.* In what had to be the oddest feeling of his life, his heart jumped with fear, sorrow, and elation all at the same moment.

"It's bad news, isn't it?"

"I'm classified 1-A," he said flatly.

"Oh, no," she cried, melting into his arms.

He pulled her head tight against his chest and rubbed her hair gently as he felt his shirt grow wet from her tears. That was enough to make his eyes water, and for a few moments, he simply stood there quietly holding the person he loved most while the weight of the news sunk in.

"It's got to be a mistake. They must not have received your letter in time before making a decision. We can try again, can't we?" The *can't we* was said with an almost hysterical tone to it, and rather than respond immediately, Nate simply pulled her even closer.

"There's no mistake. I've been talking with my friends, and nearly everybody is getting a 1-A. John Van Hazelin has two kids and another on the way, and he actually received his draft notice, not just his classification."

"But there must be something . . . If Grandpa Richards were here, he could get you a position at the railroad. It's considered essential to the war effort."

"Kathy, you know as well as I do that it wouldn't matter. The railroad will get along just fine with older men." He dreaded what he was about to say next, but the subject had to be broached sometime. "Kathy, I don't want to wait to be drafted. I want to have a choice in where they send me."

"What?"

He felt her stiffen and then pull away from him.

"You want to go in now? But it may be months before they get around to drafting you. Look how long it took before they had a spot for Cory!"

"The point is that they found a place for Cory, and they'll find a place for me. I don't want to be in the infantry. I don't want to be in the Army. But if I wait until I get drafted, that's where they'll put me." Swallowing hard, he finished, "I want to join the Navy."

Kathy stumbled backward and grabbed the top of a kitchen chair to steady herself. "The Navy? But why the Navy? Look at what happened to all those poor men at Pearl Harbor."

The look of terror on her face startled him. He wanted to promise her that it would be all right, but he couldn't. "Kathy, I'm an engineer. I need to help out where my particular set of skills can do the most good. And I believe that's in the Navy. If I have to go to war, I want to go somewhere that will make the biggest difference."

"But what would you do in the Navy?" Then, brightening a bit, "Maybe you could serve stateside, helping in supply."

"Maybe. I honestly don't know. But I have this feeling that my chances will be better if I sign up than wait to be drafted."

Kathy paused to consider Nate's comment. The thing that had surprised her most about her husband's conversion was the remarkable way that he could feel inspiration. Nate had often commented that he'd been indifferent to religion most of his life, even though he liked going to synagogue. But he always viewed religion as optional, much like his father. Then when he became interested in Kathy, he'd started studying and praying in earnest and in time had come to relish the things that he was learning about God and about what it means to be a Christian. Where before there had been apathy, suddenly he spoke with confidence about feeling the Spirit of the Lord and about receiving answers to prayer. She'd seen it a number of times, particularly when he'd helped her father in giving someone a blessing. So while she hated the words she was hearing from him, it somehow calmed her immensely to think that he was being prompted and that perhaps this was a way for him to make it through the war alive. At least that's what she hoped it meant. Inspiration, even when it was valid, didn't always assure that things would work out the way one hoped. "So you feel like this is what the Lord wants you to do?"

"I do. I don't know why, but since I figured this would be the classification I'd get, even though we tried to make our case,

I've been pondering and praying as to what course to follow. I've tried to sort through my feelings, since the Navy would be my first choice for purely selfish reasons, so I've tried really hard to make sure that I'm not just putting words into the Lord's mouth, so to speak. But I honestly feel that this is what I should do." He smiled and lifted her chin. Seeing her sad eyes, he smiled a bit broader, only to have his hand swiped away.

Finally, he smiled warmly and was relieved to see his wife wipe the tears from her cheek and smile back. "How about if I give your legs and feet a good rub," he said. "Right now you're the one doing all the work on our . . . project."

"Okay." Her smile brightened momentarily, then her lower lip trembled again, and a tear started its way down her cheek.

"Come on. Off to the couch where you can put your legs up over my lap." He felt Kathy relax as he massaged her calves and feet. Even so, it surprised him when she drifted off to sleep. He kept rubbing, because every now and then he'd feel her whole body jerk. "Bad dreams. There will be a lot of those before the war is over. I just hope they don't come true," he whispered quietly to himself. And then he felt a warmth flood his body from head to toe. It helped him find a bit of serenity in the midst of all this anxiety. "Thank you, God," he mouthed quietly as he gazed with love on the girl who had stolen his heart. "Please help her feel it too."

* * *

Kathy had counted on it taking at least six months before Nate was called up, just like it did with Cory. That way he could be there for the birth of their baby and they would have a few months to spend as a family. But fate had a different plan, and within a month of his trip to the enlistment office, Nate was standing on the platform of a train destined for Seattle. His father and the O'Brians were there, as much to support Kathy as to say good-bye to Nate.

Sarah was the first to break—Sarah who was usually so strong and upbeat in even the worst of moments. Hugging her son-in-law, she whispered, "I'm sorry. I didn't want to cry—you need me to be strong." He started to protest, but she shushed him and continued, "But you don't need to worry about Kathy and the baby. She'll be fine, and you'll be proud of them when you come home to see her."

"The thing I'll never understand is why people make jokes about mothers-in-law." Nate smiled as Sarah acted surprised. "I love you like my own mother. And I love you for giving me your daughter."

Now Sarah did weep and gave him a mock slap for making her cry.

Turning to Dan, he said, "Sometimes it feels like you have the wisdom of the ages locked up inside your head. I've never known anyone so sensitive, yet strong."

Dan sighed. "I'm afraid that some of that strength came from the very experience you're about to have, and it really isn't something I'd wish on anybody."

"When I hear and see you play music, I'm just amazed at the creative energy you have. It makes me feel like I have this small insight as to how God must have felt when He was creating the world. I hope someday I can create something as wonderful as that."

"Thank you, Nate. There are a lot of ways to create, and I have this feeling you'll do great things. Heck, look at what you've already done—the life that you and Kathy have started is about the most important creative act anyone can do."

Nate smiled. "Thank you, sir. Take good care of them for me."

Giving him a hug, Dan finished, "Keep your humanity, son, and come home in one piece to live a long and happy life. It's hard for me to imagine this, but I'm standing in the shoes that Jonathon Richards once filled for me. His parting advice was to simply study the scriptures and to make certain that whatever I did in war I did it without guile. It's alright to fight the enemy, but not out of anger and certainly not out of revenge. He promised me that if I did that, I could come home and still be clean. It will be hard, but you can do that too." He quietly slipped a serviceman's miniature edition of the Book of Mormon into Nate's pocket. "We'll pray for you to come home both clean and strong."

Finally, turning to his father, Nate gave him a crisp hug. "Oh, Dad, what have I got myself into?"

Josh smiled. "A mess, I'm afraid. But it's not a mess of your making. I'm proud that you're going to help clean it up, though." Looking at the man who had been his little boy, he added, "You're a good person, Nate. Sometimes I'm simply astonished at your goodness. You're up to this challenge, and I know that you will be one of the people who can be depended on. That's not to say that tough things won't happen, but you can count on yourself. Remember that, because it means a lot in battle. I'll be praying for you." Smiling, he added, "And since I trouble God so infrequently with prayers, perhaps these will stand out."

Nate's laugh was what was needed to break the emotional tension. "Will you be here when I get leave to come home to see the baby?"

"Probably not. Now that you're gone, I've given my notice to KSL. There's a job at CBS headquarters that I've got a good shot at, and I want to be with your mother. She's a stubborn woman, but I love her."

"I love her too. Will you tell her that?" Nate's voice tightened at the thought of his mother, so noticeably missing. He and Josh hugged one last time, and then Nate turned to Kathy.

"So, darlin', it looks like I have to go for awhile. But I'll be back soon . . ."

By now the old Kathy had returned—the confident, sassy one. "You better, Mr. Brown—'cause even the South Pacific isn't big enough to hide you if you try to run out on us now."

He laughed and pulled her close, which wasn't particularly easy with her being eight months pregnant.

"I don't know why this had to happen, Kathy, but I promise we'll make the best of it. Once I know where my permanent assignment is, you and the baby can come to live with me for as long as possible. With my college degree, I'll be an officer, and that makes it easier to find housing."

"Oh, sure. Take me away from all of this," she said with a sweeping gesture to the dusty streets surrounding the depot. "Move me off to some forsaken place like Washington or California where I'll have to put up with lush trees and beaches and sunshine. You've got some nerve, Mr. Brown."

He laughed, buoyed by her cheerful banter, but he also recognized that her eyes told a different story. "Guess I'll have to trust God—and your mother—to help with the baby. But that's not such a bad team, is it?"

With that, they hugged and kissed, Kathy holding on until the last possible moment before he'd miss the train. Then, with a wave, Nate bolted to the slowly accelerating train and swung up onto the landing where he stood looking back until the train pulled out of sight.

Chapter Fifteen

FLIGHT TRAINING AT SAN DIEGO

The biggest surprise of boot camp was beans for breakfast. The first day, it was a novelty. The second, a reason for a joke. By the end of six weeks of calisthenics, endless runs, and forced marches in the foothills near Point Loma, all driven by drill instructors shouting aggravating orders in their face, the new recruits were sick of it all. But the beans most of all. The jokes that accompanied the natural processing of the unappealing legumes were a continual source of amusement. Not that one could actually laugh out loud. Cory figured he'd done more push-ups in the past six weeks than in the previous twenty years. At night he'd fall into bed so exhausted that on more than one occasion he forgot to even pull a blanket up to cover himself.

The second most disconcerting element of basic training was the absolute lack of respect. The title *mister* was a sign of deference and regard. Not in basic training. When it was being shouted by one of the innumerable host of noncommissioned officers, it carried more contempt and sarcasm than it seemed possible to put into a voice. "Are you slow, Mr. O'Brian—is this a little too complex for your feeble mind to comprehend? Is an about-face really that hard to grasp?" Then to add to the humiliation, "Well, sailors, it seems that Mr. O'Brian has a different interpretation of which way we should turn than the rest of you. And, since he was a *college man,* he must be right and all of you must be wrong. So let's have everyone but Mr. O'Brian give me thirty push-ups." The groan from the group was far worse than if Cory had been made to do the push-ups himself.

Nearly everything about the experience was humiliating—and often infuriating. But the difference in the men's bodies at the end of six weeks was noticeable, and Cory was surprised that the sleeves of his shirt were tight, even though he knew he'd lost weight overall. Fortunately, given how grueling it was, at least he was in fairly good shape when he arrived at camp because of the sports he'd played. Some of the men really suffered from the workouts, and he thought one poor fellow was actually going to die of heatstroke on the drill field. He'd been hospitalized for a couple of days before being returned to the unit. Cory had expected that the rest of the guys would torment the man, but instead most just shrugged and expressed envy that he got to have a few days out of the sun.

In the course of the training, no one really became that close, since they knew they'd be sent to different schools once boot camp was over. But Cory did spend a lot of time talking with Spencer, whom he decided was a really good guy with a terrific sense of humor. It was that droll kind of humor that would pop up at the least expected moments—not like a joke teller, but rather like a wry commentator on what other people said. He could always be counted on to break the tension as soon as the men were left alone in their barracks. In a lot of ways, he reminded Cory of Nate. The fact that Spencer indicated an interest in engineering was no surprise. Cory decided that he was destined to be surrounded by the analytical type and was surprised that he didn't mind the idea.

Graduation from the naval training center was one of the happiest days of the young men's lives. It was the necessary precursor to military service since it formed men into cohesive units rather than a collection of strong-willed, self-indulgent individuals. As graduations go, this was far better than high school, since it meant a relative end to the torture. Now, even though they were still on the lowest rung in the Navy, they could advance into the first phase of flight training that held out the promise of ensign for those who passed. Cory was determined as never before to be part of the successful group, even if it meant doing homework.

* * *

In ground school, Cory and Spencer and all those interested in aviation were still together. It would only be after the initial round that they'd break up and go to separate schools for advanced training. Ground school consisted of classes in navigation, Morse code, theory of flight, and meteorology. One fellow in the class, Seaman Winton, was brave enough to ask all the questions the others wondered about but were afraid to look foolish by asking. Consequently, he had to endure the mocking of his classmates, even though they were secretly relieved when he'd ask what they pretended were dumb questions. He might have fared better in their estimation if such a high percentage of his questions didn't actually turn out to be genuinely stupid.

On one particular occasion, everyone wondered why they had to learn Morse code when radio was seemingly so much easier to use and more effective. When Winton asked the question, the instructor looked at him like he was fresh off the bayou—which, in fact, he was—and replied, "It's for navigation purposes mainly. As your classmates are likely to learn, when they get to fly, Morse code is used to signal your position relative to a stationary beacon, such as the flight deck of your ship. When you're making an accurate approach, you'll hear a constant signal. Deviate to the left, and you start to hear the Morse code for the letter *N*—da-dit. Drift to the right, and you hear the letter *A*—dit-da."

Winton should have left it alone. "What if you can't tell the difference between a dit and da, sir?" The class busted up laughing, more because of how long it took him to draw out the sounds with his strong Southern accent.

"Well, Mr. Winton, that tells you why I said your class-mates. I'm afraid that a man who can't tell his dit from his da is simply unfit for aviation."

The class laughed.

"Said another way, Mr. Winton, if you sent a signal at the same pace you speak it, the war would be over and your aircraft carrier would have been retired and turned into scrap metal before you ever found your way home."

If Winton was humiliated, however, he didn't show it, and his grades at the end of the course showed him to be anything but dumb. In fact, he got the highest score in theory of flight, and second highest score in aviation, which pretty much ended the taunting—even from the instructor.

"There's a lot of math in ground school," Cory muttered to Spencer on their way back to the barracks one night.

"Not nearly as much as I hear there'll be in navigation," Spencer replied enthusiastically.

That infuriated Cory, of course, which Spencer had antici-pated. "You're doing fine, O'Brian—you think just like all the other pilots. Soon enough you'll go off and learn to be a pilot so you can stick some underappreciated gunner/radioman with the real work of flying. Whoever the poor guy is, he'll pull you through."

Without cracking a smile, Cory replied drolly, "If he's anything like you, it would be a stroke of good luck if his Gosport malfunctioned so I don't have to listen to him prattle."

"Fine. Then you won't want my help on your homework assignment tonight," Spencer said with mock hurt.

Cory shook his head sadly. "You know I'm not the only potential pilot having trouble with navigation—I'm just the one having the most trouble. So what have I got to do so you don't let me fail?"

"Oh, so hotshot pilot really does need mouthy radioman with math skills?"

"Yes." Cory was tightlipped.

"That's all? Just yes, with no pithy comments?"

"Yes, that's all."

"I've been thinking about it, actually."

Cory looked at him suspiciously.

"I don't need anything. Helping you is actually good for my patience."

* * *

Phase three of his training saw Cory walking out to the flight line one sunny afternoon for his first flight in a Yellow Peril, the infamous N2S-3 bi-wing, a two-cockpit trainer aircraft built by the Stearman Aircraft Company. "Just like flying a World War I fighter, only a little harder to handle" was the way his commanding officer explained it to the group. "It weighs more, you see, but it also has more power, and the wings don't tend to shed their fabric skin as much, so it's a good trade-off on balance." When the CO saw the look of anxiety on the men's faces, he scoffed at them, "Oh, for pity's sake, an old yellow dog could fly this thing. All you have to do is point it toward the end of the field, run the throttle up, and pull back on the joystick when you're about to hit the palm trees. She'll jump up like a startled duck in the swamp, and you'll be flying before you even have time to worry about it." Of course, he didn't mention that the harder part was getting it to land properly.

Cory was lucky enough to get assigned to Lieutenant Carter for his first flight. "Just sit back and enjoy the ride," the lieutenant called through the Gosport. "Go ahead and rest your right hand lightly on the joystick so you can feel the motions I put it through as we take off and land. Your stick moves in tandem with mine, so you'll feel everything I do. Plus, I'll try to talk to you through the whole flight so you understand the mechanics involved. Any questions?"

"No, sir!" Cory then felt his heart speed up as Lieutenant Carter spoke his way through each step of the preflight checklist. At the appropriate moment, he told Cory to prime the engine and engage the starter. Cory thrilled as he felt the powerful battery crank the engine, then looked with joy at the cloud of black smoke that belched from the exhaust manifold as the powerful engine caught and then roared to life.

"Not quite so much gas," Carter shouted. "We're not ready yet." Cory backed off the throttle and listened as Carter ran the engine up and down a couple of times to warm it up and to test that it was running smoothly. Once satisfied, he instructed Cory to give a thumbs-up to the ground controller, who signaled for them to move out onto the tarmac. With an increase in rpms, the aircraft lunged forward. Cory felt his feet move as the lieutenant manipulated the brakes to steer the aircraft.

As they approached the runway, they received an All Clear from the flagman, and the lieutenant pushed the throttle forward even before he completed the turn onto the runway. The little aircraft lurched a bit as he brought it into line with the runway, and Cory's heart pounded as he felt the engine run up to maximum rpms. They lunged forward in the most amazing acceleration he'd ever felt. "You shout out to me when you think I should pull back on the stick to let her take off," Carter yelled at him.

That shook Cory, because he'd never even been in an aircraft—how was he to know when it was ready? But an order was an order, so he kept his hand resting on the stick. As they approached the midpoint of the runway, he could feel the lift on the wings attempting to pull the aircraft into the air, but somehow he sensed it was still too early. By two-thirds of the way the stick was actually shaking, and he shouted, "Now?"

Without responding verbally, Lieutenant Carter pulled back on the stick and the aircraft lifted off the ground, but then settled back for a moment before lifting again.

"Not bad, Seaman. You were about two seconds early is all, and we were far enough along that it turned out okay. What made you think that was the moment?"

Cory thought about it. "It's just the way the aircraft felt, sir. It's like we hit some breakthrough moment when flight was the more natural thing to do than staying on the ground."

The rest of the flight was a bit disorienting. Cory felt how each of the movements of the stick affected the aircraft. Pull to the right and the ailerons on the starboard side of the aircraft elevated while those on the port wings depressed and the aircraft banked into a right-hand turn. Push it to the left, and the opposite occurred. "That's a banking turn," Carter yelled. "Now push the left pedal and feel the difference." As Cory pushed the pedal slightly, he felt the aircraft turn, but without the same tipping of the aircraft. He knew that he'd moved the tail flap and understood that this helped maintain level flight through the turn.

Eventually, Carter demonstrated all the various maneuvers, then told Cory to take control of the stick and maintain level flight. It turned out to be more difficult than he'd imagined. He had to concentrate on the horizon indicator because his natural tendency was to let the aircraft tip forward and lose altitude. Carter then told him to pull back on the stick while simultaneously adding power, which caused them to immediately gain altitude. Cory started to level off without being instructed, but Carter told him to hold it until they stalled.

As the aircraft started to climb almost vertically, without enough power to do a loop, they eventually lost airflow over the wing and started to fall forward, creating the same feeling Cory had experienced at the amusement park Lagoon in Utah when the roller coaster came to the top of an incline and started down the steep hill. "It's okay," Carter shouted. "Let her fall for a few moments, then take control of the stick and bring it to level flight. Add a little power to increase your control."

By the end of the flight, Cory was hooked and knew that he wanted to do this more than anything in the world. Carter landed the aircraft and taxied over to the hangar, then instructed Cory to shut it down. Dismounting after the lieutenant, Cory stood at attention and saluted. He did his very best to suppress a smile, because it didn't feel very military.

"So, Seaman, what do you think?"

"I loved it, sir!" Then failing himself, he grinned, "I really loved it."

"Well, don't get too excited, because you're very much like the toddler who just took his first steps. It's a long way to being combat ready. But it was a good first flight."

"Thank you, sir." Then dismissed, he went to lunch, where he gossiped cheerfully with the others in his class who had also gone up for their first flight.

* * *

Two things characterized the next few weeks of Cory's life: washing airplanes and scrambling to get as much flight time with an instructor as possible. The washing business was supposedly about helping the young students learn the nomenclature of the airplane, since they had to wash, wipe, and polish every fin and surface on the aircraft. In positive moments, it seemed like an excellent way to learn the aircraft. On about the fifth or sixth aircraft of the day, however, there was the temptation to think of it as more like slave labor than a learning exercise. But the students were so fierce in their desire to get past this first phase of training that no one dared gripe about it.

The second goal was to learn as much as possible in the ten hours of joint flight time they had with an instructor, because at ten hours, a student had to successfully solo or wash out of the school. With about a fifty percent washout rate, the pressure was intense. Cory had something of a natural sense of the aircraft and its controls, which worked to his advantage, but he occasionally had to fight feelings of nausea as they did the twisting and turning of maneuvers. That really scared him— not from a fear of flying, but a fear of being found out. He didn't dare talk to his instructor about it, but the lieutenant must have suspected, because one day he spent an unusually long time talking about how to focus on the instruments to keep one's orientation, rather than relying on external visual cues. With time, it started to get better. But ten hours went by pretty quickly, and before he knew it, it was time to make his solo attempt. Once again, it was Lieutenant Carter who supervised the exercise.

"Alright, O'Brian, I want you to take it real easy to the east end of the runway, then take her up at full acceleration when the flagman signals. Once you're airborne, continue to increase altitude while starting to execute an easy turn to port. Circle the field twice and then bring the aircraft into position for landing. I'll be tuned in to your radio channel, so if you have any problems or questions, just talk to me. Any questions?"

"No, sir!"

"Then mount your aircraft, Seaman."

"It's now or never," Cory said quietly as he climbed into the cockpit. He quickly but methodically went through the preflight checklist. It wasn't a complicated aircraft, but there was still a lot to remember. He finally gave the clear signal to the ground crew and received permission to turn the engine over. Once it was running smoothly, he taxied rather smartly to the takeoff point: *Trim Tabs set; fuel pressure steady; engine rpms checked; controls free.* The flagman waved the flag, and Cory added power until the engine was singing and the aircraft was straining to move forward. Releasing the brakes, he felt the little plane lunge forward confidently. He kept it centered on the field while approaching takeoff velocity. Clearing the ground was the greatest feeling in the world. He kept the power steady as he climbed to the appointed altitude and then gently pulled the stick to the left to start a banking turn. He lost a bit of altitude and so added more power. The aircraft quickly responded to his correction, and he executed the first of the two required loops. As he reached the halfway point of the second loop, he broadened it out a bit to come into position for landing.

This time everything happened in reverse. He backed off the throttle, holding the nose up and into the wind. He could feel the aircraft start to descend even before it registered on the instruments. The field was clearly in sight, and he centered himself on the runway. His speed was a little hot, so he backed off a bit further and felt the aircraft settle. He experienced the standard twisting caused by the crosscurrent on the runway but didn't let it rattle him. He simply kept enough power to control the descent. Finally, after passing above the leading end of the runway, he let the aircraft settle and felt the port wheel touch. The aircraft bounced a bit, and then both wheels hit. He decreased power so the plane would come down evenly, then gently applied the brakes until he was firmly enough on the ground where he could decrease speed a little more authoritatively. With a silent yelp of joy—it wouldn't be good to say anything out loud, just in case the radio was on—he exited the runway and taxied back to his starting point on the tarmac. Shutting down the engine, he secured the aircraft, then climbed out on the wing.

"My report will be posted tomorrow morning, Seaman. Dismissed."

Cory had hoped for an immediate indication of success, but he wasn't going to get it. He kept telling himself that he must have passed—after all, both he and the airplane were back on the ground in good condition—but he didn't know if there were any mistakes or errors that would be written up. So he was a little nervous that night, but he felt pretty confident. The next morning, he and all the other pilots in his group looked at the posting. In what had to be the most important test score of his life, he saw the simple word *Cleared* in the column next to his name. He and the other pilots who passed couldn't help but cheer, even though they felt bad for the guys who hadn't done as well.

Cory now moved on to the four elements of basic flight training: small-field landings, aerobatics, landings and takeoffs, and landings without power. At the end of each segment, he had to do a "check ride" with an instructor and be certified for that particular element. Cory failed the aerobatics check the first time and had to fly an extra five hours with an instructor. While that was embarrassing, he didn't really care because it was so important that he get past it. On his second attempt, the check-ride instructor told him that he was marginal but signed the paper anyway. It was all he needed at this point to remain as part of the group. Still, he wasn't able to brag like some of the guys.

On the night he passed his final check, Cory and the other men in his unit sat around the mess table, talking about what kind of aircraft they were going to apply for in advanced training. It was a joyful occasion. Cory knew that his scores weren't high enough to qualify him for fighters, and, in view of the trouble he had with aerobatics, he didn't want to be a fighter pilot anyway. Fortunately, the choices were pretty diverse.

One of his roommates wanted to fly heavy aircraft so he'd gain experience for commercial aviation. Another, Jack Wilson, was into fighters. He'd scored great in aerobatics, and he had just the aggressive sort of personality for fighters. Another choice was a patrol/bomber aircraft that flew out over the battle scene to send back reconnaissance information and to ferry people to where they needed to go. For some reason, the idea of serving as an air taxi to officers didn't appeal too much to Cory.

The only thing he absolutely knew was that he wanted to fly off aircraft carriers. He wanted to be out front where the action was. That left dive-bomber and torpedo planes as his options. Both relied on heavier airplanes than fighters and required either a two- or three-man crew. The major skill required for these operations was steady nerves and the ability to hold a course—even when under attack—so that the bomb or torpedo could be released at precisely the right moment to strike its target. Somehow, Cory knew that he could do that.

"How do you know?" Spencer asked later that night.

"I don't know. It's just that I think I can. In fact, I'm sure of it. I'm not as fast with my reactions as the fighter guys, but I'm patient. I think that's what's needed in a dive-bomber—waiting for the right moment, then following the flight path until the ordnance is delivered."

"It seems like it would be pretty nerve-racking to me with all those Japanese fighters scrambling to take you out."

Cory grinned. "That's why we have you gunners sitting in the backseat. You take care of the fighters!"

"You're right," Spencer sighed. "We're probably even more crazy than you pilots—looking backward as an aircraft goes into a high-speed dive. Still, at least we get to see the enemy and try to do something about it."

"Besides," Cory added, "just think of the fireworks I can cause. You never heard of a fighter pilot sinking a battleship, but a good hit with a torpedo can!" Finally, still frustrated that he couldn't fully explain himself, Cory finished with, "I don't know, Spence. Somehow, people have an intuition at how they can make a difference, and it seems to me that the smart ones follow their intuition." What he didn't want to say was how insecure he felt. Or how badly he wanted to succeed.

In the end, Cory's request was granted, and he received orders to transfer to advanced training school in Jacksonville, Florida, where he would learn to fly a dive-bomber.

"Wow," he said to Spencer. "I never in my life dreamed I'd get to go to Florida." But now it was real. Spencer must have been inspired by Cory's talk about the importance of dive-bombers, because he requested transfer to Texas to learn how to be a gunner/radio operator on the two-crew type of aircraft that Cory was dreaming about. It was tough to say good-bye when the time came, but the excitement was high enough to send each of them anxiously on their separate ways.

* * *

In Florida, Cory spent months learning the skills he'd need to be an effective combat weapon in battle. Not only did he have to learn how to place a bomb properly, launching it at precisely the correct point in an arc, but he also had to learn how to find his way back to the ship after a mission of several hundred miles, how to land on an aircraft carrier, and how to fly in tight three-aircraft or six-aircraft formations. By this point in the war, the Navy knew exactly how to train men to do this. First, the young pilots practiced landing on a solid-earth runway that had the outlines of a carrier flight deck painted on it. It took nearly everyone in the course numerous practice runs until they could lift off and land in the limited space. Then they had to learn the precise angle of descent and release to place the ordnance properly. Cory learned both bombs and torpedoes, although he fared a lot better on bombing runs. Then there was gunnery school. While the men like Spencer trained to shoot a rotating weapon that provided a wide arc of coverage, the pilot had to aim the aircraft in order to provide effective fire. Although not directly related to their first priority—placing the bomb or torpedo—it was extremely useful for strafing a surface ship or covering the approach of an enemy fighter.

Gunnery training started with the bare basics of shooting at clay pigeons on the ground, working up to shooting at banners trailed behind support aircraft. Each pilot's bullets were tipped in a different color of paint so they could see how effective they were. At first, almost no splatters hit the banner. By the end of training, they were all getting a good percentage.

There was so much to learn—sometimes it made Cory's head spin. For example, his first trip "under the hood" when he had to fly in a completely darkened cockpit, relying solely on instruments. It wasn't uncommon to get vertigo, and Cory was no exception. His instructor had to caution him from the back cockpit that he was descending too rapidly. Cory suppressed the instinct to call back, "I thought I was ascending, sir!" but that's exactly what it had felt like, and he broke out in a cold sweat to think that his mind could play such tricks on him. Vertigo had caused more than one pilot to crash nonchalantly into the sea, believing right up to the moment of impact that he was flying on an even trajectory thousands of feet up in the air.

Fortunately for Cory, he had an easygoing instructor, Lieutenant Stinson, who helped him get used to the instruments, and he was able to complete the entire flight, from takeoff to landing, without ever once looking out of the canopy. That was one of his best days.

Probably the most nerve-racking part of training was the first time he had to actually land on an aircraft carrier. Lieutenant Stinson worked the students through the drill before they took off for the open sea. "We'll take off at twenty-second intervals. Cory, you form up on my right. Hank, you'll be my left wing. Standard V formation. Keep your navigation board on your lap so you can keep track of your progress throughout the whole journey. You'll each have a turn leading the group, so pay attention for future reference. Once we spot the ship, I'll contact control and request permission to land. They'll turn into the wind to receive us. Remember that this is the most vulnerable moment for a carrier since they'll work to hold a steady course and speed. That makes them a sitting duck for enemy submarines, so they want us to get it right the first time.

"Once cleared, I want you to take up an echelon formation on my right. I'll lead the formation past the right side of the runway, then I'll call, 'Break.' I'll make a shallow 180-degree dive to three hundred feet, which will put me on the downwind leg, parallel to the runway. Each of you wait a few seconds before you break. Once you come out of your turn, check your interval and put wheels down. After that, watch for the landing signal officer and respond accordingly. I know you've heard it before, but if you follow the signals of the LSO, he'll get you on the ship. Don't follow his signals, and you'll either crash and burn or go in the drink. No matter what you think you should be doing, do whatever he tells you! Once your tail hook snags the arrester cable, hang on for dear life, because you're going to stop faster than your brain ever thought possible. Shut your engine down, and then your job's pretty much over. The deck crew will get you off the runway pronto. Any questions?"

Cory licked his lips, which had gone unaccountably dry. He didn't have any questions. They'd practiced this on the ground dozens and dozens of times. But in each of those practices, the runway always remained stationary. Out in the ocean, the ship would be moving, both forward and up and down with the waves. He had to consciously tell his stomach muscles to relax. It was frightening but exciting.

His leader noticed the grim look on Hank's and Cory's faces, so he added in a less authoritarian voice, "It's okay, you guys. You can do this. In another two weeks, it'll be like driving to the grocery store—you won't even think about it. So relax and stay with me. Everything will turn out fine."

As the third one to go in, Cory watched with increasing anxiety as his flight leader landed perfectly. Then he saw Hank make his approach. It looked to him like he was going too fast and too high, but Cory was so far back, he wasn't really in a position to judge. He knew something was wrong when he saw the LSO signal a wave-off to Hank. He should have applied power immediately and pulled up, but Cory watched in horror as his friend continued to settle on the deck, but too high to catch any of the cables. He'd slowed too much to maintain flight but was going way too fast to ever stop on the shortened deck of the carrier. Cory followed the LSO's direction to roll out to the right since the deck crew would be busy dealing with Hank, but even at that, he was able to see Hank's plane hit the deck hard. It must have broken one of the wheels, because suddenly the left side of the plane collapsed, snapping off the wing, and the plane careened forward and off the side of the deck out into the water. Cory was accelerating now, responding to the instruction to circle while they attempted to recover the pilot. There would be no attempt to salvage the airplane.

As he circled, he got the sickening sensation that something was wrong with his aircraft, as if the engine was running rough. When he looked down, he realized that it was his hand trembling on the control stick. His brain was racing, and he had to consciously tell himself to breathe slowly so he didn't hyperventilate. Finally, he was ordered to make his own approach. This time he had to do it alone, with no one to follow in. Fortunately, his training and practice asserted itself, and he rolled into position without trouble. As he approached the deck, he saw a signal indicating he was running hot, so he backed off a bit. Next, he was told to drop flaps to slow the aircraft even further. *I can't fly this slowly!* But, of course, that was the point. At the right moment, the LSO gave him the signal to cut it, and Cory felt the plane drop like a brick. He almost winced as the wheels hit the deck, but before he could even process what was happening, he felt the arrester cable grab, and he was thrown violently forward in his shoulder harness. It was over. He was on the deck, his aircraft was stopped, and the deck crew was signaling him to shut down the engine. Numbly he complied, and in a matter of seconds, they had manually guided his plane off the runway to a stowage area. Almost by instinct, he opened the canopy and descended the aircraft. His instructor came up to him solemnly. "Nice landing, O'Brian. It wasn't so bad, was it?"

"No, sir. It happened so fast. I almost can't believe it's over."

"Well, it is. And after a cup of coffee, we're going to do it again. Oh, right, a cup of hot chocolate."

Cory wanted to smile, but he was too concerned. "What about Hank, sir?"

"Oh, he'll get to do it again as well. But not until after a few more practices back on land."

"So he's alright?"

"Hardly had enough time to get wet before they hauled him aboard. They've taken him to the infirmary to get checked out, but he'll be fine. A hundred thousand bucks or so down the drain, but in this war, pilots are harder to come by than aircraft."

Cory felt himself release his breath, then surprised himself by letting out an involuntary war whoop. "Sorry, sir, but that was the most thrilling thing I've ever done in my life. That arrester cable just knocks the wind right out of you, doesn't it?"

Stinson laughed. "I'll tell you, O'Brian, I still get a thrill out of it. Every time. It's got to be the best job in the whole Navy. Welcome to one of the most exclusive clubs in the world."

"Thank you, sir!" Cory couldn't stop grinning as they went to the ready room to get a snack and a drink. He actually couldn't wait for the next trip up.

* * *

All in all, it took more than a year of training in California and Florida to get Ensign O'Brian ready for combat. Taking a landlocked kid who knew nothing about flying to one who could get an airplane aloft almost without thinking about it was one of the little miracles that turned the tide of war in the South Pacific to America's advantage. From suffering one defeat after another at the hands of the Japanese early in the war, to an unbroken string of victories since the momentous Battle of

Midway northwest of the Hawaiian Islands, U.S. forces had started the challenging task of moving to regain control in the region one island at a time. In mid-1943, the Japanese still had a formidable carrier fleet, fanatic pilots, and plenty of natural resources from Borneo and other conquered lands to put up a ferocious fight. It was there that Cory looked forward to playing his part.

Which is why it seemed so amazingly mundane when he received orders to transfer back to San Diego, where he would ferry new aircraft from factories in the Northeast to the various ports where they could be transported to the battle zones.

All this training to wind up as an airborne teamster. Still, it gave him lots of flight time working with the newest and best aircraft, and that would help him keep his skills sharp for when his real orders came.

Chapter Sixteen

NEW LONDON, CONNECTICUT

Boot camp in Washington State was about the same experience for Nate as it had been for Cory down in San Diego, except that Nate had no idea what he wanted to do when he completed the school. So while the six weeks of boot camp seemed interminable to Cory, they flew by for Nate. At four weeks, he was getting desperate to figure out what kind of service to request. If he didn't make a choice, he'd almost certainly be assigned to a destroyer or a PT boat, and he wasn't at all sure that's what he wanted.

That's when his drill instructor abruptly brought the group to attention and brusquely said, "Mr. Brown, fall out and report to the headquarters building!"

"Yes, sir!"

The glances from the other men confirmed his fears that he must have done something wrong. But what? It was hard not to be paranoid. It was only later that he realized he was missing the obvious. He didn't get it even when the officer of the day handed him a telephone handset.

"Second Seaman Nathan Brown!" he said crisply into the receiver.

"Nate, it's Dan."

"Dan?"

"Your father-in-law . . ."

"My father-in—" The others in the room couldn't help but laugh when they saw the change come over his face. "Oh, oh,

Dan . . . I mean, Dad . . . I mean . . . Is everything okay? Is it about the baby?" He was suddenly terrified.

Dan laughed easily, which helped calm him a bit. "No, it's not about the baby, Nate. It's about the babies!"

"The babies?"

"Yes, the babies. It turns out that you're the father of twins—a little boy and a little girl. Congratulations!"

"I have twins?"

That brought the entire room to a standstill, as everyone started listening in.

"But how can that be?"

"I'm afraid I wasn't there when it started," Dan said laconically.

Nate missed Dan's attempt at humor. "But I just don't see how . . ." And his voice trailed off.

"Kathy's doing fine . . . I know you'll be interested in that when your brain gets around to sorting all this out. We had kind of a scare with your son. He's so little, it was hard for him to catch his first breath. But it looks like he's doing okay now." There was absolute silence on the phone. At first, Dan thought he could wait it out, but eventually he had to intercede. "Nate, are you there? Are you alright?"

"I have twins . . ."

Dan laughed again. "You have twins, and this is a long-distance call. I can't afford to stay on here forever."

That had an energizing effect. "Oh, my gosh," Nate said brightening. "This is real. We have a boy and a girl." Turning to everyone in the group, "I'm a father! Hey, everybody, I have twins!" All the men in the room, including the officers, gave him a spontaneous round of applause. One of the enlisted men then put the telephone receiver back up to Nate's ear.

"How's Kathy? Is she alright?" he said anxiously.

Dan shook his head on the other end. "Kathy's doing fine. Her mother is in with her now, and the babies are in the nursery." All was quiet for another moment, then Dan said very quietly, "They're beautiful, Nate. They have Kathy's smile and your eyes. I think it would be hard for anyone to disagree with me that they're the most beautiful babies in the world. Congratulations, son."

"Oh, thank you, sir. Thank you so much. Is there any way I can talk to Kathy?"

"Not right now . . . but soon. If you'll give me over to your OOD when we're done, I'll try to arrange a time when we can call you back."

At that point the base operator intervened, since phone lines were at a premium during the war. She'd obviously been listening to the conversation, because she said, "You'll have to make that request right away, Mr. O'Brian, because we need to clear this line."

"Listen to me, Nate. You have to give the phone to your OOD right now. We'll talk again. But everything is alright. Congratulations!"

"Oh, thanks, Dan. Thank you so much!" Almost in a daze, Nate handed the phone to the OOD, who quickly scheduled a time for a follow-up call.

The OOD turned to the ensign who had accompanied Nate to headquarters. "Why don't you take Seaman Brown back to his barracks? I'm putting him on the sick report for the rest of the day. He certainly looks a little sick to me." The others in the room agreed.

"Thank you, sir," Nate said weakly. "Twins . . ."

Soon, it was the talk of the base.

* * *

In the next two weeks, a lot happened. So much so that it seemed impossible to process. First, since Nate didn't express an opinion of where he wanted to serve, the Navy put him through a battery of tests to see where his natural skills could be put to best use. The results floored him. "It turns out, Mr.

Brown, that you have the psychological profile of a submariner. It's hard to believe, since so few people do, but you scored high in virtually every category."

"Submarines?" It seemed like the normally confident Nate Brown had been reduced to responding to nearly everything with a dumb restatement lately.

"Submarines. You have three great advantages in the submarine service that you won't get anywhere else in the Navy." When Nate looked at him inquiringly the officer saw a potential sale and continued. "First, the food is fantastic—best in the service. Those guys on the subs eat better than most admirals. Second, you get better pay. Third, because a submarine has such a small crew, relative to other naval ships, a young man can advance through the ranks much faster. Within a few months, you could hold a rating on a sub that would take years to reach on a surface ship. With your college degree, you're assured a spot as an officer after you complete submarine school."

"And the disadvantages, sir?"

"The risk is proportionally higher."

Nate shook his head. He was even more confused. Since receiving Dan's phone call, it was hard not to think about the little people who had come into his life. He desperately wanted to go home and see Kathy and meet his children. But he had to make a decision as to where he wanted to serve. The chance of something in the Home Areas was virtually nonexistent at this point, with everyone in his class up for assignment to a combat role.

"My wife just gave birth to a little boy and a little girl . . ."

Captain Williams looked at him sympathetically. He leaned forward and said quietly, "Listen, son. I wish I could find a spot for you that wouldn't bring you into harm's way, but that's just not possible. We've started to enjoy some success against the Japanese, and it looks like we're holding our own in keeping the shipping lines open to Europe, but no matter where you go, there will be danger. I want to be honest with you: submarines are unusually dangerous. But they're also extremely effective. Not everyone in the old Navy thinks as I do, but I read the battle reports, and I believe that the submarines are going to prove to be our most effective weapon against the enemy. So if you want to make a difference, this is a place you can do it. You might be interested to know that a high percentage of the officer corps in the Silent Service, as it's called, are married men like you. They love their families, and yet they've chosen to serve there."

As Nate thought about it, there was something intriguing about the idea of serving on a sub. They had the latest technology and could easily be the most complex military instrument ever built. Plus, he shared the captain's view that they would prove an integral part of the country's success in battle. He had a family to support, and the extra income would be helpful. But then he thought about Kathy and knew that it would worry her to think of him in a submerged ship.

"I'm really not trying to talk you into anything, Seaman Brown, because your scores are high enough that you can choose pretty much any specialty you like. But I will tell you this—there simply aren't that many candidates for submarine service who have the aptitude that you've displayed. This could be a real opportunity for you."

Nate was surprised to hear his own voice as it said, "I'll do it, sir. If you want to recommend me for it, I'll accept an appointment."

Captain Williams wanted to smile, but the responsibility he'd just assumed was pretty daunting, talking a young father into submarines. There was a very real chance that his little babies would end up fatherless. He wished he could just send Nate home and leave him there. "I'll write the papers today and hold them till Thursday. If you change your mind, or want to talk about it some more, come see me. If not, I'll send them up Thursday, and your orders will be written for transfer to New London, Connecticut. Any questions?"

"Just one, sir. Can you arrange for me to have some time in Salt Lake City on my way to Connecticut? I simply have to see my wife and babies."

"Of course I can arrange that. And once you get to New London, you may be able to invite your wife to come live with you. It would be at least nine months before you ship out to a permanent assignment. Nine months is a long time."

For the first time in days, it was Nate who laughed. "Not as long as you think, sir. Nine months ago, I'd never even thought about a baby, and now I've got two of them!"

Williams laughed and slapped Nate's knee. "You go home and enjoy them. I'll see if I can't stretch your leave out as long as possible."

"Thank you, sir!"

As he walked back to his barracks, Nate's emotions cycled on him. But the baseline he kept coming back to was a sense of relief. At last he knew what he was going to do. Then his emotions turned joyful. "I get to see Kathy!"

* * *

Kathy looked radiant as Nate made it up the steps of the Richardses' house. Standing in the door, he thought her the most beautiful woman in the world, and when she ran out and threw her arms around him, he knew she was. Nothing had ever felt so good in his entire life. Without understanding why, he felt tears streaming down his cheeks as he whispered over and over again, "I love you so much. I love you so much." Finally, when they broke apart, he wiped his face with his sleeve and said, "I can't imagine why I've become so sentimental all of a sudden."

Expressing emotions wasn't very natural for Nate, and the fact that he had this spontaneous reaction pleased Kathy. "I can. It's because you've been gone far too long. We're a pair now, and when one of the pair is gone, things just aren't right.

Now, would you like to meet your children?" As they walked arm in arm into the living room, she whispered, "Not bad for our first attempt—a boy *and* a girl." Kathy laughed and reached up and kissed Nate.

When they reached the nursery, Nate saw two little bassinettes, as well as his mother-in-law, who had come over to help Kathy out while she helped Nate get settled. He was startled when Kathy reached down and pulled out a blanketed bundle and handed it to him. He'd never experienced this and was pretty cautious taking the baby. Kathy showed him how, and before he could fully appreciate what had happened, tears started streaming again. The little face that looked up at him was the most wonderful thing he'd ever seen. "I take it that the blue blanket signals that this is our son?"

"Very observant, Mr. Brown." Nate winced a bit, but didn't tell Kathy the different meaning *mister* had taken on in boot camp.

Carefully, he leaned over the other bassinette to see their daughter. She was asleep but looked as equally vulnerable as the boy. "Have you thought of names?"

Kathy looked at him earnestly. "What about Jonny and Meg?"

Nate nodded in surprise. "Jonny and Meg are nice names. Why those two?"

"After Grandpa and Grandma Richards—you know, Jonathon and Margaret. They've meant so much to us that I'd like to honor them. But if you have something else in mind . . ."

Nate smiled. "No, I think those names are perfect. As I look at them, they just look like a Jon and a Meg. I think you've chosen exactly right."

When Jonny started to pout a bit, Sarah stepped forward and offered to take him. "You two need time to talk. I'll be fine with the babies. If I need you, I'll call from here."

"Thank you, Mom. That would be great," Nate said, and the "Mom" seemed very natural.

* * *

Captain Williams was true to his word, and Nate was granted a four-week leave of absence. They were the best four weeks of his life. Without his mother or father in Salt Lake City and virtually all his high school friends off in the military, he and Kathy spent almost the entire time together. In his mind, he'd imagined quiet evenings together playing board games, listening to music on the radio, or just talking. The reality of two babies in the house was vastly different. Nate was amazed at how much energy it took to care for two little people—bathing and feeding them and changing diapers and rocking and walking. It seemed endless. At the end of each day, Nate and Kathy fell into bed exhausted. But happy.

Kathy was relieved to see how naturally her husband took to the role of fatherhood. As an only child, he seemed to quickly adjust to having more than one, and he was often the first to get out of bed in the middle of the night when one of the twins cried. It was a huge relief to have him home when both of them cried.

When the time came to talk about their future, Nate rather nervously told Kathy about his decision to serve in the submarine corps. He was surprised when she replied that she thought it was a good decision.

"It's exactly the kind of work that will be interesting to you and will definitely help you after the war."

Nate was left speechless. He'd mentally rehearsed all the things he could say to help her feel okay about the decision, and didn't know exactly what to say when she didn't put up a fuss. So in that odd twist, he brought up the subject of the dangers and how he'd thought about it but why it was still a good decision. He felt compelled to play out his rehearsed script, even though Kathy hadn't done her lines correctly.

Before he could finish, Kathy put her finger to his lips. "Nate, this is something that's beyond our control. I've thought about it a lot, and no matter where you go or where you serve, there's a chance of something awful happening. Since we have no choice in that reality, I'll feel better knowing that you're doing something that you want to do." She was thoughtful for a moment. "Plus, I trust the feeling you had when you decided to enlist. If we say we have faith, then we need to act like it. Don't you think?"

Nate pulled her head to his and gave her a long hug in recognition of how lucky he was to have her as a wife. Then he kissed her. And for the moment, everything was right in their world.

* * *

Eventually, the four weeks came to an end, and the family found itself back on the Union Pacific train platform, putting Nate on a transport to Cheyenne, Omaha, Chicago, New York, and Connecticut. The good-byes were poignant, but this time Kathy was actually excited, since she would be able to join him in another month herself. She hadn't been to the East, so there was an air of adventure about her. Dan promised to arrange transportation for Kathy, the babies, and Sarah, who would accompany Kathy and spend a few days helping them get settled before returning to Salt Lake City.

* * *

Nate had one more stop to make before reaching New London. He had high hopes for the outcome, as well as a lot of anxiety. When the train pulled into the Hudson River Terminal in New Jersey, he made the transfer to one of the commuter trains into Manhattan, and finally to the subway system to Brooklyn. He had only twelve hours before he had to catch a northbound train out of Grand Central Station. It would have been easier if his parents had met him in Manhattan, but he wanted to talk to his mother at her house, where the feeling of family would be strongest. As he came up the steps of the subway station, he was relieved to see his father standing on the corner. He'd never been to their new house, and it just seemed easier to meet his dad than figure out how to find them. Josh smiled broadly and came up and gave him a hug.

"Welcome back to New York!"

In a subdued way, Nate was glad he didn't say, "Welcome home."

"You look terrific, Nate. I see that basic training didn't leave you worse for the wear." Josh helped Nate put his duffel bag in the trunk of the car.

"Most of the wear took place in my brain. It's quite an adjustment learning to think as a military man. How's Mom?"

Josh grew serious. "She's fine, Nate. But she's still pretty upset about everything. I don't know what to expect when we get home. Can you be patient with her?"

Nate opened and closed his mouth before replying. "Of course I'll be patient, but I don't know what she wants from me. All I want is to have her accept Kathy and the babies so we can act like a family. Is that too much to ask?"

"It shouldn't be too much to ask, but it may be more than she can give right now." Josh smiled anxiously. "Let's hope it goes well. Now, tell me about your little boy and girl."

Just the thought of Jon and Meg brought a smile to Nate's face. "It is so exciting, Dad. I could never have imagined that it's possible to instantly love someone like I love them. They have our eyes." His eyes twinkled at the thought.

"I can't wait to see them. Are you still planning on Kathy joining you in Connecticut?"

"We are. I just have to find housing, and then she'll come out."

By now, Josh had pulled up and parked the car in front of a neat little brownstone with two trees in front. It felt a bit odd not to return to the place where he'd grown up, but that was an apartment building in Manhattan and this was much nicer. The look, smell, and slight humidity in the air brought back a wave of New York memories that washed over Nate and made him feel like a little boy again, even though this was Brooklyn. For an instant, he had an odd feeling that Salt Lake City and all that had happened there was simply an illusion. But then he thought of Kathy, and his thoughts grounded quickly in his new reality.

Walking in the front door, he saw his mother sitting on a davenport sofa in a parlor off to the left side of the entrance. "Hello, Mom," he said as cheerfully as he could. In spite of his best attempt, there was a tremble in his voice that betrayed the anxiety he felt. When she simply looked up at him, with no response, he walked over and sat down next to her and gave her a hug. She returned it stiffly. Finally, with a sigh, he realized there was likely to be a confrontation. He wasn't quite ready, though, so he made a few meaningless remarks about how lovely their new home was and how it felt great to be back on familiar furniture. She, in turn, asked him about his train ride and when he had to go. When he explained that he only had a few hours, her temper flashed.

"A few hours! Your father said that you had a month leave of absence. You could only plan a few hours with your family?"

"I was with my family, Mother. My wife and my children. I wanted to have as much time with the babies as possible."

"I see."

"Mom, please don't sound so cold. I'm a father now, and you're a grandmother. This is a happy occasion. Let me show you their pictures so we can celebrate." He unbuttoned his shirt pocket and pulled out a small stack of pictures of Kathy and the babies, which Barbara looked at quickly. "They're beautiful, don't you think? This one is Jon and this is Meg." Looking at the pictures calmed Nate's nerves.

"It looks like they have lovely eyes. How did you choose their names—usually people with twins choose rhyming names."

"We named them after Kathy's grandparents, the Richardses."

"Oh, I see," she said with another flash. "You named them after those people. Not a family name from our side of the family. Not even one from each side of the family. But after the Richardses with their big house and high ways."

"No, with their big hearts and their gracious manners and their unfailing kindness to others." Nate tried to keep his voice even. He wanted to cry out that the wonderful painting of Manhattan that hung just above his mother's head had been a gift from Margaret Richards, but he held his tongue.

"Nathan, I know I should keep still, but I can't. Why did you do this? Why did you have children when you knew there was a war on? You should have waited, until, until . . ."

That infuriated Nate, but he'd already told his father he would try to remain calm, so he inhaled slowly, then replied, "Until what, Mother? I should have waited until what?"

"Until you knew if this ill-planned marriage of yours is going to work out." Josh tried to intervene, but Barbara glowered at him and told him to stay quiet. "I know you don't want to hear this, Nathan, but you made a mistake, a big mistake, and now you've compounded it. You're not one of those people, and you shouldn't try to be. You should come back here where you belong."

"I am one of *those* people, Mother, and you know it. Not only am I married, but I joined their church. And I'm happy that I did."

"You joined because that girl pouted until you did. Why didn't she allow you to be Jewish, to investigate our ways, to learn our traditions? Why did it have to be you to make all the changes and to accept the names they give these babies and to choose the place where you live? Why have you been the one to give in to every demand?" Without even a pause to catch her breath, she answered her own questions. "Do you want to know? Well, I'll tell you even if you don't want to hear it. It's because they're selfish, that's why. They're just plain selfish. They have no sense of tradition, or they would never have asked you to do this."

Nate had never seen his mother so angry. Nor, for that matter, had he ever been so angry. Yet rather than want to storm and rage at her, he just felt an overwhelming desire to get out, to get away, to never talk to her again. And for that, he felt incredibly guilty.

Josh broke in. "Barbara, you're asking too much. We don't choose love—it simply happens. And Nate has married into a wonderful family of good and gentle people. You should calm down and look at your grandchildren and set the stage so they can come visit you."

Even Josh's anger, unusual as it was, failed to make an impression. Barbara simply ignored it. "I know you both think I'm stubborn and selfish for saying these things, but I'm not. My family has been Jewish for more than three thousand years—three thousand years! Doesn't that count for anything? And we're New Yorkers, city people, and our traditions here are important too. Perhaps you've forgotten how we were treated in Salt Lake City. How many times did people strike up a conversation and when they asked which ward we belonged to found a way to break off the discussion the instant they learned we weren't LDS, as if they were suddenly talking to someone afflicted with the plague? Or have you forgotten how many of the neighbors wouldn't let their precious sons and daughters associate with you, even play street ball with you, when they found out you were a Jew?" She was really hot now. "Or the time I went into the department store, and when I didn't have enough cash and wanted to write a check they said, 'That's alright, just show me your recommend.'" Her breath caught at that painful memory. Her eyes flashed. "You think I'm being narrow, but the truth is that they really are *those* people, and by their choice as much as ours. So while you may be able to throw away all of the traditions that have been part of our family, I can't. I simply can't turn my back on everything that matters to me as if it meant nothing. I just can't do it!"

"I'm sure that none of those people wanted to hurt you, Mother."

She looked at him earnestly. "That's just it, Nathan. I know they didn't intend to hurt us—why they'd probably be shocked to think that I was offended. But that's the whole point! They took it for granted that we belonged to their church. But when it came out that we were nonmembers, they turned away. Which is why I say that we're not part of them. They only want us if we join them. Not on our terms and not with our ways. We didn't try to convert them. Why did they insist on trying to convert us?"

"I know that what you say is true about a handful, but most of my Mormon friends were great and had no problem with me." Suddenly, Nate felt like a teenager again as he was forced to return in memory to the Salt Lake City he grew up in. It was true that he'd often been at odds with some of the guys in the public schools, which were overwhelmingly populated by Mormons. He even took pride in his difference at the time. But at a personal level, when he took time to get to know them, most of the guys were just guys. And he knew that the O'Brians and Richardses had behaved nothing like his mother had talked about. And, if his mother were honest, there was a darker side to the story. What he didn't say, but wanted to, was that he remembered all the jokes that he and his buddies had made about the Mormons and their odd ways and how they'd sometimes tried to corrupt one of their more impressionable LDS friends. He also remembered some of the conversations he overheard his mother and her friends share, which were often dripping with sarcasm and criticism.

But while it would be easy to point out that prejudice and misunderstanding often cuts both ways in a crescendo of rising bitterness, it would have done no good at this point. "Mom, I think there's some good that can be said about our time in Salt Lake City . . ."

But it was no use. Barbara shook her head from side to side, almost as if in a trance, and didn't respond.

Nate tried in a quieter voice. "I'm not asking you to abandon anything, Mother. If you want to be angry at the Mormons, then be angry. I guess that's really your business. But what I want is for you to accept that I now have a family and that I'm moving forward in my life in the way that seems best to me." He should have left it at that, but he felt compelled to continue, "And if the purpose of a church is to bring us to God, then I have to tell you that I feel closer to Him now than I ever have before. I have been on an amazing spiritual journey—"

Her eyes flashed instantly. "So there it is—you're right and we're wrong. God is only for the Mormons . . ." The last word seemed to stick in her mouth.

"You're making it hard, Mother. I'm really trying to find some common ground here. I know that God loves everyone, regardless of religion, and it's not my place to decide what is best for you. But I do know that this is what He wants for me."

Barbara didn't respond.

"All I want is for us to be a family—you, Dad, Kathy, and our babies. I'm still your son. Nothing can change that. But I'm part of my own family too, and I want you to love all of us." When she still didn't respond, he finally lost patience. "The simple fact is this, Mother. I did not make a mistake marrying Kathy, and the decision to have children was ours to make. From the moment I first held them, I knew that it was the right decision—the finest decision of my life. So I will not be coming back here without them and giving up all that has happened. This is who I am, and you need to accept that."

Barbara remained quiet for a few moments. Nate wanted to grab her and force her to turn and look at him, but he'd had his say. Finally, she turned and looked at him and said very coldly, almost in a whisper, "I don't know that I can do that,

Nathan. You've hurt me deeply, and I don't know that I can get over it. I don't know that God will let me. He has certain expectations for His chosen people, the Jewish people. All I know is that I can't decide right now." Then her anger returned. With tears streaming down her face, she looked away and said, "So if you'll excuse me, I'm not feeling at all well."

When she stood up to leave, Nate made no effort to stop her. Josh got up to go with her, but she pushed him away. Josh came and sat down next to Nate. "I'm so sorry about this, Nate. Maybe with time—"

"No, Dad. I'm afraid not. We just crossed some boundary, and I don't know how we'll get it right again."

"You've got to be willing to try."

"No, I'll be willing to put it aside, because she's my mother. But if she really thinks that my marrying Kathy and having our children was a rejection of her and a mistake, then I don't know how to ever make that right."

His father sighed. "I know. I wish it wasn't like this . . ." They sat in numbed silence for perhaps a minute. Finally, Josh said quietly, "I'd like to see your pictures, if you don't mind."

Nate turned and looked at him, and Josh noted the tremble in his son's lower lip. But Nate didn't cry. The sorrow and anger warred with each other, somehow balancing the other. Nate pulled out the pictures and followed Josh's glance down. When he saw Kathy smiling at him from the black-and-white photo, he felt his heart refill with joy.

* * *

Ensign Brown couldn't help but shiver as the gray water of the Atlantic Ocean splashed up over the metal screen at the front of the bridge of the *Tripletail,* the newest submarine with an assignment to the Pacific fleet. Winter in New England was cold enough without being exposed to the open air and salty spray of the Long Island Sound, but today was unusually bitter cold. Ice covered the cigarette deck, and long, jagged icicles streamed down from the barrel of their deck gun, looking much like stalactites from the roof of a cave. "Stalactites," he said to himself, "hold 'tight' to the ceiling." He laughed at himself for thinking of this out here. As the most junior member of the attack party, he had spent the previous seven days at sea practicing dozens of dives so that he could be relied on to clear the bridge and close the hatch before the conning tower dipped under the waves on a fast dive. This was their fourth trip out to the waters of Long Island and Block Sound, and he was amazed at how much he'd learned already.

But it wasn't enough. Captain Stahlei was driving them relentlessly to get dive time to less than thirty-five seconds from the time the order was given until the ship was underwater. Their first attempt had been pathetic, requiring nearly ninety seconds to get the three lookouts and the officer of the deck onto the ladder and down into the tower.

"Simply not acceptable," was all that Stahlei had said. "Let's do it again." While it was intimidating to be one of only two inexperienced officers who had never been to sea, he was grateful that those of higher rank were patient as he and Lieutenant Walker learned to maneuver the narrow corridors and operate the sophisticated equipment needed to secure the ship for a dive. He couldn't help but feel anxious when he thought of his responsibility as OOD when they reached the Pacific, where he'd be the first to hear a report from the lookouts about sighting an enemy ship or aircraft. It would be his responsibility to confirm the sighting and then sound the alarm to clear the deck and initiate the dive that would offer their only chance of safety. The lives of everyone on the ship would be in his hands, which is why he did his best never to mutter or complain, no matter how frequent and cold the dives were.

At first, he tried different ways to avoid getting wet, but it had proved a futile gesture—at least here in the wintry waters of the Atlantic where it seemed the wind was always whipping the waves into a gale. As the *Tripletail* plowed through the rough seas, huge waves would crash into the superstructure and flood over the railings of the bridge in great torrents that soaked everyone, no matter where they were standing. All the oilskin coats in the world couldn't keep the water out, and Nate was intrigued at how successfully the cold salty liquid could trickle its way down to the most obscure places inside his clothes. Once inside the outer garments, the fabric in his clothing slowly absorbed and distributed the moisture until every part of his body was wet and cold.

Captain Stahlei stood next to Nate on the deck. While Nate loved to watch the captain in action, it was always a bit nerve-racking to have him there to monitor the performance of the diving team.

"So, Mr. Brown, what do you think of our submarine now?" The sound of Stahlei's voice startled Nate.

"I like it, sir!" Then, when his heart slowed down a bit, "It's harder than I imagined, but I love how we work together as a team. I've never been in a situation where people are so dependent on one another." He was pleased when the captain nodded affirmatively, and so Nate added, "It certainly gets my heart pumping when the diving alarm sounds."

"Just wait till you're doing it with an enemy aircraft bearing down on you. That's when it gets really exciting."

Nate was very pleased to chat with the captain like this. Stahlei was perhaps the most capable human being he'd ever known. Already a veteran of the South Pacific War, he'd been on three combat patrols and had more than ten confirmed sinkings of enemy ships, including transport, supply, and even a destroyer. While Stahlei seldom spoke of it, except when it helped to explain a particular maneuver, the other officers and men talked about it often. Stahlei was considered one of the "lucky" captains whose skill and daring assured success in battle. Nate had quickly learned that nearly everyone in the base thought it an honor to serve with him.

"Ensign Brown, I want you to take the TDC on our next simulated attack."

Nate's heart jumped. This was the chance he'd been hoping for. While he'd done very well at the Torpedo Data Computer in the attack teacher, it was still up in the air which of the bridge officers would be permanently assigned to this post at sea. John Akers, who had similar experience to Nate's, had done well enough and was hoping to get the permanent assignment.

"Yes, sir!"

"Fine, prepare for a dive. And this time, instruct the lookouts to put a steeper incline on the dive planes. I want us to go deep at a much faster rate than we've done to this point."

While the flooding of the main tanks was the initial step required to dive, it was the angle on the forward and stern planes that determined the speed and angle of the dive. The first time they'd used the planes, the ship lurched down at a crazy angle that made Nate and the other inexperienced men struggle to find something to hold onto. Cups had come crashing down in the galley, and everything that wasn't tied down flew onto the floor. Nate had concluded that more than one of the men working deep in the bowels of the *Tripletail* must have wondered if they were in a crash dive from which there would be no recovery. But with all the practice dives since then, everything had been properly stowed, and it was now almost second nature to adjust one's own angle to stand up vertically while the ship angled its way below the waves.

When the alarm sounded with its almost deafening *Oo-gah, Oo-gah,* Nate stepped aside as the three lookouts slipped down the hatch and ladder into the conning tower. He took one last quick look around to make sure the bridge was secure, still a bit uneasy at the sight of the water coming up over the hull, then climbed in himself. In the beginning, he'd tried to take each and every step on the ladder, but like most of the others, he now simply put his feet and hands to the outside rails and quickly slid down. When he reached the deck, Nate grabbed the rope that pulled and held the hatch secure while a seaman quickly turned the wheel that made it watertight. Almost immediately, Nate felt the dive officer's order to put pressure in the boat as his ears responded with discernable discomfort to the increased air pressure.

Next, he glanced at the "Christmas tree" and saw that all the lights that were supposed to be green were, while the lights for the diving tanks were turning red. The one he always watched most closely was the main-induction valve indicator. Before the war had started, the *Squalus* had been sunk near Charleston because the crew had initiated the dive even though the main-induction valve, the source of oxygen to the ship's engines, hadn't been closed. Once the water had started in, it had flooded the engine rooms so quickly that most of the men couldn't get out. Some—who could have escaped—stayed to protect the rest of the ship from flooding by sealing the water-tight doors in front of them. Their deaths saved the rest of the crew and had led to many safety innovations, but careful attention to safety protocols was still the best protection.

Once the boat reached its assigned depth, the dive officer checked the compensation—the amount of water flooded into the ballast tanks needed to maintain a state of neutral buoyancy—and responded to the captain's order to bring the ship to sixty-five feet, the point at which the main attack periscope became functional.

"John, I want Ensign Brown on the TDC for this set."

"Yes, sir!" Nate could hear the anxiety in John Akers's voice. As a graduate of the Naval Academy in Annapolis the previous year, he had an unofficial advantage in getting the best assignment. If that were the case, it would fall to Nate to keep the plot, a manual view of the battle scene maintained on a chart table. Nate felt uncomfortable at the tension the captain's order introduced into the attack team, but he was also thrilled to think that he'd get a chance to run the TDC, to actually order the firing of torpedoes, and thus, for a moment, fill the most important position on the ship relative to their mission to destroy the enemy.

The TDC was an analog computer that was a mechanical wonder, in Nate's opinion. The estimated location and bearing of the target was displayed on a vertical piece of glass. As the captain called information from the periscope, the TDC operator continually updated information that refined the target's calculated course, speed, bearing, and range on the simulation on the glass. The various control knobs he used to enter this information also allowed him to input the estimated speed of the target. As continual readings were provided, the information on the board became ever more accurate. The captain used this data to order changes in the submarine's direction and orientation relative to the target until the point was reached that a shooting solution was achieved.

The most ingenious part of the system was that the TDC was connected by synchro-mechanisms to the torpedoes in both the forward and stern compartments, so that every change that was input by the TDC operator made instantaneous changes in the torpedo's guidance mechanism so that when it was launched, a spinning gyroscope inside the torpedo would direct it to turn in the necessary direction to execute the captain's firing command.

Captain Stahlei ordered a crisp, "Up periscope," and then quickly searched the horizon in a 360-degree field to check for hostile aircraft and other ships. Of course, there were no hostile aircraft in the Long Island Sound, but it was proper protocol, and Stahlei always observed it. "Target sighted," he said crisply, and then started calling out coordinates. Nate quickly twirled the knobs on the computer to match the captain's information. The captain then had the periscope lowered so that the target ship would not see the feather that the periscope left in the water. In a few moments, he called, "Up periscope," and quickly provided new information. Nate now had two readings and started calculating the hostile ship's estimated speed of travel. The computer supplied direction of travel as well as updating the other variables. The captain ordered the ship ahead slow, operating strictly on batteries. On the surface, they could make better than twenty-two knots, but underwater they traveled more slowly—sometimes just three or four knots if they wished to conserve energy or to minimize the sound they made while sneaking up on a target.

"The target's moving away from us, so we need to increase speed." The captain provided new instructions to the helmsmen, who maneuvered the ship with a large steering wheel located in the conning tower.

Finally, after their fifth reading, Nate called out, "We have a shooting solution, sir!"

Stahlei looked over at the TDC, grumbled that they were still farther out than he'd like to be because of the long torpedo run that would be required, but with the surface ship making fairly good speed away from them, he decided to take the shot.

"We'll fire a spread of four torpedoes. On your order, Mr. Brown."

Nate concentrated until the firing solution was as close to perfect as he could negotiate, then shouted, "Fire one. Fire two." He waited ten seconds, making a few minor adjustments, then, "Fire three. Fire four." The fire control officer pushed the appropriate buttons, and Nate felt the ship shudder as the high-speed torpedoes launched. The sonar/radio operator started tracking the torpedoes' progress through the water, while Akers tracked the time of travel through the water on a stopwatch.

Knowing the range to target, it was easy to predict when the torpedoes should strike. In combat, the accuracy would be known by all aboard the submarine if they heard the sound of a torpedo exploding when it reached the target. In these practice runs, the surface ship could track the incoming chargeless torpedoes by watching their trail of bubbles in the water.

Nate waited anxiously as the submarine surfaced and made radio contact with the target ship. The captain acknowledged their report, then said flatly, "Three out of four hits—two MOT."

In spite of himself, Nate and a number of others let out a cheer. A middle of target was considered a perfect shot. Of course, it was Stahlei who set up the shot, but it was still to Nate's credit that his action on the TDC was good enough to actually make the kill. Stahlei had them practice two more dives and simulations before calling it a day and letting them return to base. At the end of an eighteen-hour day, Nate was exhausted, but exhilarated. He found that he liked the high-stakes tension of the TDC and felt a special thrill each time he was allowed to call out the command to fire the torpedoes. It was too much to hope for, but he quietly ached for the chance to do it again.

* * *

With the war in the Pacific gaining momentum, the pressure on Electric Boat, the submarine manufacturing and training base in New London, to turn out both ships and crews was enormous. The original nine months that Nate had been promised was shortened to six months, with only three on active sea training. By this point, it was expected that the captain and experienced officers would continue the crew's training while they were transiting from New London to Honolulu.

The hardest task at school, from a logistics standpoint, had been finding an apartment that would accept babies. Still, Nate did find an apartment, owned by an elderly widow who was pleased to have Kathy and the babies live with her. It didn't provide as much privacy as they'd like, but they were together for five wonderful months. When Nate's training took place during the day, he'd spend as many evening hours at home with them as possible. When he was out on night maneuvers, he and Kathy would put the babies in strollers and take long walks together during the day. It was late in the summer of 1943 at this point, and as the days of his training drew to a close, he felt Kathy's anxiety rise.

"When do you think the orders will come?"

"Soon. We've completed all our sea trials, and they're already starting to clear our berth for the next new ship out of production. Probably a matter of weeks, maybe even days."

"I know I'm supposed to be brave, but I'm scared."

Nate walked in silence for a few moments. No one on the crew talked about their fear, both out of superstition and because no one wanted to be seen as weak. But he felt the tension in all the men—particularly the married men—as the time of departure grew close. While everyone assumed they'd be the ones to return home safely, the statistics for submariners weren't encouraging. Even though he loved being part of it, he sometimes wondered if he'd made a mistake.

"I'm a little scared too . . ." The words hung heavy in the air.

"I'll be alright, you know. I don't want you worrying about us while you're out there in the middle of the ocean. Keep your mind straight so you can come back to me."

"I'll try not to worry. But I won't try to not think about you. I'll think about you and Jon and Meg every single day."

* * *

Two days later they learned the ship was to depart in two weeks. Kathy sent a telegram to Sarah, telling her that one of the other wives they'd met had indicated she'd be happy to help Kathy back to Salt Lake City with the babies. She and her husband, an executive officer who had already been on three combat missions and had been sent back to meet a new ship and crew, didn't have any children of their own. She and Kathy had become friends during the long hours when their husbands were at sea training. Her parents lived in Seattle, so Salt Lake City was a small diversion. Kathy left three days before Nate was set to ship out. That was perhaps the saddest day of his life.

The only thing that brightened it was that later that afternoon, as the officers met at a local restaurant for a shipping-out party, Captain Stahlei announced the positions he wanted them to take during an attack sequence. "Nate, I'd like you on the TDC. John, you'll back us all up on plot." He then made the functional assignments, such as supervising communications and galley. "Any questions?" There were none. Later, when Nate happened on John while walking home, he felt uncomfortable and debated whether he should say something. He wanted to, except that he couldn't figure out what to say that wouldn't make it worse with Akers.

"Nate, I want you to know there are no hard feelings. I've thought about it a lot, because I really wanted to be there, but the fact is that you're the best man we have at the TDC. I've watched you, and you operate those controls like they were part of you. If we're going to risk our lives for this mission, then the least we can do is kill as many enemy ships as possible."

"Thank you, sir." Nate was enormously relieved at Akers's generosity.

"How did you get to be so good?" There was something of an exasperated sound to Akers's voice. "You're so darned fast!"

"How did I get to be so good?" Nate pursed his lips. "I hadn't really thought about it. Maybe it's because—and I used to get yelled at an awful lot for this—I was the pinball master of East High School! I could rack up a score so high, I almost never had to pay for more than the first round." He laughed. "Fine qualification for blowing up Japanese shipping, don't you think?"

"I think I shouldn't have listened to my mother when she told me to leave the pinballs alone." Akers put his hand on Nate's shoulder, and they walked down the road as friends.

Chapter Seventeen

SAVED BY THE USO

Cory was excited as he finished tying his tie. Looking at himself in the mirror, he couldn't help but admire the tight cut of his Navy whites. With his rank of ensign prominently displayed, he felt a thrill as he contemplated one last night in San Diego before going home for a two-week leave of absence prior to shipping out. "My, but I do look fine," he said cheerfully to himself.

"You look alright for a kid, but compared to a real man, you ain't nothing!"

Cory jumped at the sound of Jack Wilson's voice. He'd thought he was alone in the bathroom. Turning, he saw Jack step forward to an adjoining mirror where he preened himself a bit. It seemed odd that they had come back to the same point after Jack finished fighter school, but even hotshot fighter pilots were busy shuttling aircraft around.

"I can certainly see what you mean, what with your, uh, multilayered haircut and your right pant leg that's dragging the floor. With any luck, you won't trip on it."

Jack scowled as he looked down at the floor. "Darn, and I paid good money to that tailor."

Cory smiled as his friend attempted to hitch up his pants on his right hip.

"So you got plans tonight, or do you wanna come with me and some of the other fighter pilots?"

Cory struck a thoughtful pose. "Actually, I would come with you and your friends if I were a deaf-mute. That way I wouldn't have to listen to the bragging, and it wouldn't hurt my feelings that I couldn't get a word in edgewise." He pretended a rueful smile. "But since I actually like talking when I'm out with people, I think I'll go with the somewhat more humble group of bomber pilots that I hang out with. Besides, this is graduation, and those of us who can hold a steady flight while under fire need to stick together."

"Suit yourself. But you'll miss out on a great time."

"I know. But somebody's gotta drag these guys home. I guess it's up to me."

Jack laughed. "Do me a favor and drag me home too, if you see me lying in some gutter."

Cory turned and looked at Jack. In more than a year of training, their paths had crossed on a number of occasions, and on more than one of those, Cory had been jealous of Jack. He always scored at the top of the class, yet, in spite of his natural skill, he didn't have any false bravado like so many of the fighter pilots. He seemed to appreciate that it took all kinds to fight a war, and he was sincere in the praise that he'd offered Cory on more than one occasion.

"So do you know what ship you're serving on, Jack?"

"Why, the mighty *Enterprise,* of course. When the bigwigs figured out that you'd be flying on the old bird, they got desperate, so they decided they needed me to protect you and your buddies' sorry bottoms. Lucky for you, we'll see plenty of each other."

"I'm glad to hear that. While you're up there getting all the glory, shooting down the Japanese one by one, we'll go in and send 'em down by the thousands. One bomb in the ammunition locker, and it's all over."

"Man, we could go on like this for hours, O'Brian. If either one of us are half as good at flying as we are at bragging, the war will be over in no time. But frankly, I have more important things planned for tonight than talking to a bomber pilot—so go out and have some fun. I know it's hard for you, but you're all grown up now, so why not give it a try?"

"Thanks. Why don't you go out and try not to be stupid. Being grown up also means showing a little bit of restraint once in awhile."

"Restraint? Never really tried it. But it is something to think about, isn't it? Hope I see you tomorrow before you head home."

* * *

Cory didn't have any idea how hard it would be for him to be good that night. After a great meal at the Bayside on a pier out over the San Diego harbor, he and three other pilots from the unit had started walking toward some louder establishments closer into town. He felt a little overstuffed, having eaten more shrimp and scallops than he needed, but never having had seafood until coming to San Diego, he couldn't get enough of the stuff. It provided such a great contrast to the staples he'd grown up on—beef pot roast and fried chicken. The taste of seafood was more subtle and light.

Cory hadn't really been paying attention to where they were going, but some silent alarms went off as they turned off the well-lit street onto a darkened side street that had a stagnant smell that was oppressive in the humid night air. "Where are we going?" The edge to his voice was fairly obvious.

"Don't worry, O'Brian. We've planned a night you'll never forget. In fact, this is probably the most important night of your life."

Cory's stomach tightened as a sense of dread crept over him. He noticed a group of heavily rouged women standing at the next corner. Their tight skirts and blouses were far too loud and garish to be tasteful, and the cherry-red lipstick glistened in the subdued lighting streaming out the door of the cheap hotel they were standing in front of.

"You know, it's already been a good night, and I really don't need anything more to remember it."

"Come on, O'Brian. It's time to grow up. Cute little boy from Salt Lake City just isn't going to cut it anymore," Cory's least favorite classmate, "Speed" Shanigan, said. Cory would have never gone out with him in the first place, but he'd hooked up with them at the restaurant. He was a braggart and a show-off who very nearly failed out of flight school because of his constant grandstanding.

Cory desperately wanted to say something clever in retort to Speed's taunt, but his brain froze up. If he could figure a way to laugh it off, he thought the other two pilots, pretty good guys actually, would stand up for him. He opened his mouth, hoping for something good, but all that came out was, "I don't need your help, Speed."

"Ah, so you're an old hand at this. Then you'll want Candy—she's one of my favorites." With that, Speed pushed him into one of the women, who instantly wrapped her arms around Cory while planting a wet kiss on his lips.

Cory felt his face flush, particularly when she rubbed up against him, and then he pushed away. "Sorry," he stammered, "but I'm really not interested."

He heard Speed laugh in the background as the girl said, in mock hurt, "You don't like me—and we haven't even met."

"No, no, it's not you. It's just that—"

"Oh, for crying out loud, O'Brian, do you wanna stay innocent forever? Don't be such a loser!"

Cory was irritated. "Not forever—just until I get married. Call it stupid, it's what I believe."

"Well, it's not good enough. You're a Navy man, not a Navy boy—and it's time you act like one." Speed sucker punched him in the kidney, which hurt so bad that Cory collapsed to one knee.

Candy knelt down next to him and whispered, "It's not so bad, really. A lot of guys come here . . ."

"It's bad for me," he said desperately. He struggled to his feet to face Speed, resolved to do whatever it took. The fact that Speed was drunk added to the drama of the situation. Not only did it make him stupid and mean, but it also left him vulnerable, and Cory figured that he could probably hold his own if he needed to. But it would be hard against three of them. He braced as Speed made a move to shove him again, but just as the blow should have hit, one of the other pilots stepped between them.

"That's enough, Speed. O'Brian's a good man, and if he doesn't want this, then that's his business."

Cory had never felt so grateful in his life.

Speed staggered a bit, his face flushed, but when he attempted to move toward Cory again, Cory simply stepped forward as if to meet him. That stopped him. Turning angrily from Cory to the other pilot and back again, he finally muttered, "Whatever. You go home to your mommy and leave the war to us, O'Brian."

Though infuriated, Cory decided it wasn't worth getting in a fight over. "I'll see you guys later." Then, to the fellow who helped him, "Thanks, Hank."

"No problem. He's an idiot. Are you okay to find your way back to base?"

Cory had hoped that Hank would come with him, but clearly that wasn't going to happen. "I'm fine. I'll see you guys tomorrow."

"Yeah, tomorrow. Sorry to leave you, Cory." That sounded funny—no one in the Navy except Spence had ever called him by his first name.

"It's okay, really . . ." Cory turned and headed back to the main street. He wanted to turn back and look, but he figured the three would be gone. More than ever, he was grateful that he was scheduled to leave in the morning so he wouldn't have to take Speed's ridicule. He was even happier knowing that they'd been assigned to different ships. "Besides," he muttered to no one, "he's so soused he probably won't remember anyway."

Cory was angry at the hot tears that trickled down his cheeks. He shouldn't have to feel embarrassed for doing the right thing, but he was. *They're the ones who should be embarrassed,* he thought bitterly. *I'll leave all that to them!* But it didn't work. No matter how he turned it over in his mind, he was embarrassed to be called a child, embarrassed to be singled out, and embarrassed to never think of the right thing to say when people treated him like that. For the next twenty minutes, he walked without any sense of direction or purpose. His thoughts were wild and disorganized, ranging from gratitude that he was able to get out of the situation, to thoughts about what it really meant to be a man, to confusion over the sense of morality that seemed so important to him but didn't seem to matter to so many other guys. At one point, he even wondered if he was missing out on something, but instantly regretted thinking that because he knew that if he wanted to one day marry someone who had waited for him, he had to wait for her. It was miserable to ask all these questions, and he wished more than anything that the clock would hurry so he could go back to the base with some dignity. It was only 2100, and if he went back now, there really would be a lot of questions. Finally, with no idea of what else to do, he simply sat down on a bench in a small, covered bus stop.

He was aware that at least a couple of buses stopped to pick him up, but he just sat there until the doors closed and the buses rolled on. He was so lost in his self-pity that it took a moment for his brain to process the fact that a young woman was asking him a question. Looking up he saw a well-dressed girl standing in front of him, asking if he was okay. He was really miffed when his voice cracked while trying to reply, "Yeah, I'm okay." Even he could hear that what he intended to be a bright-sounding brush-off fell flat.

"You look so sad. I just thought maybe something was wrong."

Cory looked up again and tried to smile. He was sad. But happy too. It may have been a little test of his integrity, but at least he'd passed. Maybe not gracefully, but at least he passed. "I'm alright, really. But thanks for asking."

"I thought maybe something had happened in the USO."

"The USO?"

She laughed. "Yes, the USO. You have been inside, haven't you?"

It was only then that Cory realized that the music he'd been subconsciously listening to was coming out of the doors of a nearby building. When he turned and looked, he saw that there were soldiers, sailors, and marines standing around the door, many of them talking to young civilian women.

She saw his confusion. "Listen, mind if I sit down?"

"No, not at all." His cheeks flushed just a bit.

"I'm Lorraine. And you're . . ."

"Cory. Cory O'Brian."

"Pleased to meet you, Ensign O'Brian."

Cory smiled at that—it was the first time a girl had ever called him by his rank, and somehow it sounded really good.

"So if you haven't been to the USO, where have you been?"

"Oh, I just had dinner with some friends, and then they decided to, uh, to go some place that I wasn't interested in." His face flushed again as the embarrassment returned, and once again he felt like he must look and sound like a real prude. He almost didn't dare look up at the girl, but he couldn't help himself. He was pleased when he saw that she didn't look amused or skeptical.

"Out to buy their manhood, huh? That's pretty pathetic, if you ask me."

A wave of relief swept over Cory. "Well, at any rate, I was in the way, so I just somehow wound up here."

"Why don't you come in and have some fun?"

Cory must have looked confused again, because she stepped in to fill the hole in their conversation.

"If you've never been to the USO, let me tell you about it. It's a nonprofit organization created to help servicemen who are away from home. Everything inside is wholesome—with good music, lots of chances to dance, and just a nice place to spend an evening. I'm one of the local volunteers who come here to dance and talk with servicemen. It never goes further than that. So do you want to come in? You like music, don't you?"

Cory smiled. "I do like music. And I could use some fun. It hasn't been that great of a night so far."

"Good, let me introduce you to some of my friends."

As they walked into the club, Cory felt an immediate sense of belonging. He couldn't figure out why it felt so familiar and so comfortable until it struck him that it was like the Terrace Ballroom where he'd performed with his dad's band. All of a sudden, all the great feelings of being with the band came back, and he felt like he was home. Lorraine cheerfully introduced him to some beautiful girls as well as some of the other sailors from the base, and before long, Cory was laughing and talking, interspersed with an occasional dance. It felt great to let loose and show his stuff, and it turned out that he and Lorraine actually came in as first runners-up in an impromptu dance contest. As they exited the dance hall floor, they both laughed at how well they'd done.

"Can I get you a drink, sailor?" she asked in a mock sultry voice.

"Uh, some kind of juice if they have it."

"Juice?" she said in surprise. "Oh, I get it—you're a Mormon, aren't you? I should have figured that out when you said you were from Utah."

Cory braced for whatever was coming.

"Now it all makes sense—you and your stupid buddies." She turned and looked at him squarely. "Don't worry, I have a friend at San Diego State who's a Mormon. She's told me all about your Word of—what is it?"

"Word of Wisdom?"

"Yes, that's it. No coffee, tea, alcohol, or tobacco. And certainly none of that other stuff."

Cory couldn't tell if she was mocking or simply talking.

She quickly resolved the question. "I think it's great that you believe that way. Probably kind of hard while in the Navy, but I think it's great."

"Thanks." An involuntary smile of relief broke out over Cory's face.

"There is something so familiar about you." Lorraine pursed her brow. "When you said thanks, it was like I'd heard your voice before." She still looked puzzled. "Are you sure you've never been to San Diego?"

"Absolutely positive."

"That is so strange—I never forget a face—and I don't remember yours. But your voice?"

"You probably say that to all the sailors." Cory was surprised that he was actually trying to tease her. He hoped she'd laugh. But she didn't. She just kept thinking.

"O'Brian . . . O'Brian. What did you say your first name is, Ensign?"

"It's Cory—"

"Cory! That's it! You're Cory O'Brian!"

"I've told you that already."

"Hey, girls, you're not going to believe it—this is Cory O'Brian!" When her three friends looked at her with the same puzzled look, she added, "You know, Danny O'Brian and the Soldat Ordinaires!"

"Are you sure?" one of the women asked.

Lorraine turned to Cory. "You are that Cory O'Brian, aren't you? The singer?"

Cory was flabbergasted by this turn of the conversation. "Uh, yeah, I'm Cory O'Brian. But how have you heard of our band?"

"Are you kidding?" one of the girls said. "We listen every Saturday night—'And now, I'd like to turn the microphone over to Cory to sing us a ballad,'" she said, mocking Jim Chatterton's voice.

"This is unbelievable," Lorraine said. "We love your music—"

"And you're so cute," one of the others giggled. Then they all giggled—even louder when Cory's face flushed yet again.

"You'll sing for us, won't you?"

"What?"

"You've got to sing for us. I'm going to go up and tell the bandleader who you are, and I know he'll let you sing something."

"Oh, no, I couldn't. I mean, they've already got their sets, and besides, I doubt anybody else wants to hear me—"

"Oh, don't be silly. Everybody loves a good singer. It would be just really stupid to have someone like you here and not let you sing. That's what the USO is all about."

Before Cory could object, Lorraine darted for the stage, where she motioned to the bandleader. After cupping her hands over his ears, Cory watched in a bit of horror as he looked his way and smiled. Even from a distance, he could see him mouth the words, "Of course," and Cory's heart skipped a beat. Before he had time to adjust to the change of events, he heard the bandleader stop the music and ask for everyone's attention.

"Ladies and gentlemen, it turns out we have a celebrity in our midst. Not all of you may have heard of him, because his radio program's only broadcast out here in the West, but to those of us from southern California, we all know the sound of Cory O'Brian's voice. It turns out he's an ensign in the Navy and has consented to join us for a set or two. Would you all join me in welcoming Ensign Cory O'Brian?"

Cory was amazed at the gasp his name brought from many in the crowd and was overwhelmed at the cheers and applause as he made his way onto the stage. Speaking into the microphone, he said, "I had no idea my dad's program had so many fans—I'm really just the kid who followed him to work one night and wound up spending the next five years singing for my dinner." The crowd laughed. Then Cory got a bit serious. "He felt pretty bad when I had to leave, but I know he'd be happy to think that I've still got music to keep me company. So even though it's been a long time since I sang, I'd like to dedicate the next song to my dad and his band." It was only then that he realized that this new band may not even know the song he had in mind. Turning to the bandleader, he whispered, "I'll Be Seeing You?"

"Well, of course we know it." The band struck up a traditional introduction.

As Cory listened to the band, the room faded from view, and he brought the microphone up to his mouth just as he'd done a hundred times in the past. When he started singing, he heard the sound of his baritone voice amplified, and a thousand wonderful memories flooded back.

I'll be seeing you
In all the old familiar places
That this heart of mine embraces
All day through.

In that small café;
The park across the way;
The children's carousel;
The chestnut trees;
The wishin' well.

I'll be seeing you
In every lovely summer's day;
In every thing that's light and gay.
I'll always think of you that way.

I'll find you
In the morning sun
And when the night is new.
I'll be looking at the moon,
But I'll be seeing you.

As he listened during an instrumental break, he thought, *The band is good, really good.* But he was just a little pleased that they weren't as good as the Ordinaires. For one thing, the pianist wasn't nearly as smooth as his dad, and the band had more of an edge than he was used to. Still, they adapted quickly to his pace, and in no time he was one with the band. It was a feeling unlike any other.

I'll be seeing you
In every lovely summer's day;
In every thing that's light and gay.
I'll always think of you that way.

I'll find you
In the morning sun
And when the night is new.
I'll be looking at the moon,
But I'll be seeing you.

At the end, the crowd applauded enthusiastically and dragged an encore out of him. Before the night was over, he'd joined in singing at least half a dozen songs, some with the band's regular vocalists. He was also surprised at how many sailors from his unit came up to talk to him afterward and to express surprise at his hidden talent. It was an extraordinary turn of events.

"That's the great thing about jazz," Cory said to Lorraine as she walked him to the door. "it's so easy to improvise that you honestly can step right into a set and act like you're a longtime member of the band."

She smiled at his enthusiasm.

Cory glanced down at his watch and felt an electric shock go from head to toe. "Oh, no! The last bus is supposed to pull out right now, and if I miss it, I'm in big trouble!"

"It's okay, Cinderella. The bus is right there, and it's taking some time to drag some of the more 'lubricated' sailors onboard. You'll make it."

Cory felt his heart calm down, and he turned and smiled at her. "I'm really glad I met you tonight. The USO is great. Thanks."

"I'm glad we met too. You're even better live than on the radio. Who'd have thought I'd meet a celebrity?"

"It's hard for me to think of it like that. My dad's the one who really holds things together. He's this fantastic musician— and a taskmaster. I just sing because I like it. He does music like it's his life's work."

"Well, that's alright, but you're plenty good in your own right. I liked what you did with this band just fine."

Cory couldn't help but smile. "Well, I guess I've got to go. You're a really nice person, Lorraine. Thanks for a wonderful evening."

She stood there expectantly.

After a few moments, "Is it in the rules for a sailor to give a USO girl a kiss goodnight?"

"Only if she agrees." Lorraine laughed when Cory flushed and started to stammer. Rather than say any more, she simply reached up and pulled his face to hers and gave him a long kiss.

"Wow!" He staggered.

"Just a little something to help you remember San Diego, sailor boy. Wouldn't want you to forget."

"No need to worry about that." He took her hands in his, pressed them together, then turned to get onboard.

"Just a minute," she said quickly.

Cory was nervous, because he really didn't want to miss the bus.

"I know you've got to go, but just in case you ever come back here, you might want to give me a call." She pressed a note into his hands, looking a bit nervous.

"I'd like that. I really would." He turned and ran, barely getting his foot wedged in the door of the bus before it tried to slam shut. He waved from the window as the bus pulled out into traffic to take them back to the base.

* * *

Cory was nervous as the train pulled into Salt Lake's Union Station. While he couldn't wait to see his family, he also worried that they'd still treat him like a kid. After a year of living on his own, he was no longer the person they had put on the train. He needn't have worried.

As he descended the steps of the train and put his foot on the platform, he instinctively looked both right and left to see who was waiting. The squeal of his sister's voice immediately resolved that question, and he couldn't help but burst into a grin as she came running toward him, a baby bouncing on her right arm. His mother was close behind with another baby held firmly against her shoulder. But somehow the thing that pleased him most was to see his father's smile as he brought up the rear. Cory always felt good when he was able to make his dad smile. He smiled in response and ran to meet Kathy. It was a three-way hug, with the child in her arms shying away from him while she pulled his cheek toward her mouth for a warm, sisterly kiss. Very shortly it was a five-way hug as Sarah joined them.

"Oh, Cory, you look *so* handsome!"

"I bet you say that to all the guys." He smiled at Kathy.

"Actually, just two."

He looked around. "It is so good to be home. I didn't realize until this minute how much I missed it. The mountains are amazing. And look at you, Mom—a grandma!"

Sarah smiled. "I look okay in the role, don't I?"

Her smile melted his heart and unaccountably caused tears to form in his eyes. He tried to wipe them before they noticed, but Kathy laughed and Sarah teared up in response. By then, Dan had joined them, and Cory leaned into him for a long, strong hug. It felt like his dad had lost a little weight, but his hug was still as stout as it had ever been.

"We missed you, Cory. At home, at work, and in the band. It's awfully good to see you." They pulled apart, and Dan and Cory took a good look at each other. "I've got to admit that the Navy's been good for you. You're about as hard as a rock and nice and suntanned."

"It's hard work, but I think they've actually turned me into a sailor. Or is it an aviator? I never know what to say."

"Well, whatever it is, it looks good. A fellow your age should be in good shape. Do you like flying?"

"I love it, Dad. I love everything about it. Landing on an aircraft carrier was the hardest part, but once I figured that out, I've done okay. It gets scary once in awhile, particularly when you're flying in a tight formation, but I can handle it."

Dan gave him a searching look. "I'm sure you can." They started walking toward the baggage claim area where Cory could pick up his duffel bag. The light chatter and fuss that goes along with getting things collected interrupted any real conversation until they got in the car and started for home.

"How's Nate doing?"

"He's alright," Kathy said a bit too cheerfully. "He likes submarines . . ."

Cory understood. "You really should introduce me to my niece and nephew."

"Why, certainly. Cory, this is Jonny and this is Meg. Kids, this is your dashing Uncle Cory." Cory took Jonny in his arms, and after a few anxious glances at his mother, the little boy relaxed into his arms. Cory decided he liked this uncle business.

"Very nice names, Kathy. I'm sure Grandma and Grandpa Richards are pleased."

"I hope they get to come home soon," Sarah said. "The Church has told them they can come back whenever they want to, but I think they've decided to see the war out in England."

"But why? From what we hear at the base, it's getting pretty ugly over there, particularly with all the random bombing the Germans are doing."

"Your grandfather is English, and he feels like he needs to be loyal," Dan said quietly. "I think he regrets not going over there the last time . . ." A heavy silence settled in the car.

"So you obviously did well in your training. What's the life of a fighter pilot like?" Sarah never could stand silence.

"Actually, I didn't do well enough to qualify for fighters. My reflexes are good, but not good enough. You have to be something of a wild man to make it in fighters."

"I can appreciate that," Dan replied. "So what did you qualify for?"

"Dive-bombers—I get to try to blow up their aircraft carriers and their airfields." That led to a lengthy discussion that followed them into the driveway and into the house. As he walked into the house, Cory was overwhelmed by the familiar smells and the soft glow from the lamps that his mother favored over ceiling lights. "Wow, I'm really home," he said softly. In a lot of ways, it felt like he'd never left; in other ways, like he would never belong here again.

"You are home," his mother said cheerfully. "And for the next two weeks, we're going to spoil you like crazy. Then the Navy will have to start all over on their training because we'll have ruined you."

Cory laughed with Sarah but realized that she was serious. He was in for ten days of pampering, and he relished the thought.

"It will be different than when you were young," Dan added. When Cory looked up, Dan continued, "No house rules. You're a man now, and we'll respect that. Spend as much time with us as you like, but go see your friends as often as you want. This leave is for your benefit, not ours."

"Thanks, Dad." The conversation came to a comfortable silence. For just a minute, they were all together again. The two babies had fallen asleep, and the O'Brians—minus Nate—were a family.

Finally, Cory decided someone ought to say something, so he started at just the same moment as his dad. They both paused, then tried again.

"You first, son."

"What I was going to say is that I had this really crazy thing happen to me at the USO club in San Diego. I didn't really know anything about the USO until a girl invited me the last night I was in San Diego. I was talking to her and her friends when she interrupted to say that somehow I seemed familiar. We agreed that we'd never met, but she kept persisting that somehow she knew me. Then, all of a sudden, she figured out that I was in the Ordinaires. It turns out that they've listened to us for at least two or three years down there, and they love the band. About half the people in the room knew about us, and it was packed that night. It was pretty exciting to think that we're famous."

"San Diego, eh?" Dan tried to act nonchalant, but Sarah laughed at his feeble attempt at humility.

"Yeah. In fact, a lot of the people in the band had heard us, and they invited me to sing."

"You got to sing," Sarah said happily. "That must have been wonderful."

"Well, the crowd liked it, and I loved it. I'd forgotten how much I enjoyed being out there with a band."

"So tell me more about this band and about the USO," Sarah said.

"Okay." So Cory told his mother everything he knew, which wasn't that much, except that both local and national groups volunteered to help make the servicemen's lives a little more fun when they got a leave.

Sarah turned to Dan. "You ought to do that for the boys who are training out in the south valley, Dan. It sounds like this is something really worthwhile."

"What?"

Sarah started to repeat herself, but Cory interrupted, "That's not a bad idea, Dad. You could go out to their club and play for the guys. It really means a lot, believe me."

"But I've got the radio program."

"Go on Saturdays—or do the broadcast from out there on Friday."

Dan was quiet—the kind of quiet that meant he was thinking about what had been said. They all knew it was better not to push a point when he reached that stage of his thinking.

After a while, Kathy excused herself to put the babies to bed, with Sarah's help. It was then that Dan and Cory talked for perhaps an hour about all the things Cory had learned during his training. Whatever tension had existed between them about military service before the war was now gone. Cory marveled at the way his dad would accept things once it was obvious they were inevitable. It was really something to admire, and he told Dan so.

"I'm afraid it came at a price," was all Dan would say, but when Cory gave his dad a hug good night a little later, Cory felt a single tear wet his shoulder. Cory loved him more than he ever imagined possible. He liked being an adult child.

* * *

The next two weeks went by in a blur. Cory hiked up to Ensign Peak with friends, tagged along to his father's broadcast, and spent hours talking with Kathy and playing with the babies.

On Sunday, Dan was invited as a guest performer at the Tabernacle for their regular program, so the family got up and dressed. Cory looked sharp in his uniform and felt a surge of pride as he entered the Tabernacle to see dozens of others in their military dress as well. The crowd gave all the men in uniform a spontaneous round of applause. The theme of the program was patriotic, but Cory wasn't surprised when his father played a very thoughtful melody of religious hymns, accompanied by a small orchestra that had assembled for the performance. *He'll never glorify war, even when he knows the cause is just.* Somehow, even that made Cory proud.

Dan's arrangement of the hymns was unique, and the percussion of the piano mixed with the smooth refrain of the stringed instruments in such a way that the feeling in the hymns were revealed in new and interesting patterns. Cory looked at the people in the audience and saw that many of them were leaning forward in their seats in rapt attention, fully involved in the music. Perhaps the most thrilling moment came at the finale, when the medley took an unexpected turn into "The World Has Need of Willing Men" with its stirring cadence. There was an audible gasp from the audience when Dan's friend, Kyle Byland, joined in on the great Tabernacle organ while one of the tenors from the choir sang the stirring words to the hymn through the sound system. By arranging it in this way, Dan called on the voices of virtually every type of instrument to give the song its full emotional impact. It made the hair on the back of Cory's neck stand up as the long sustained tones of the huge bass pipes echoed through the hall. At the end, the crowd nearly fell forward as the music reached its conclusion. He could tell that people wanted to cheer, or stand up and march, but that wasn't the style at the Music and the Spoken Word program, so they settled back in their seats to hear the closing number by the choir. Cory reveled in the feeling of the spirit of the place, and in the Spirit that he felt in his heart.

* * *

This time, when he boarded the train, it was a very different feeling than before. Instead of feeling relief, he felt a bit sick to his stomach. The reality of combat was now on his mind, and all the brave words were just a bit hollow as the thought of facing hostile fire became real. He settled back in his seat after waving good-bye to his family on the platform and closed his eyes.

Hours later, he was tired as the train pulled out of yet another stop. It was only when they started moving that it dawned on him where they were.

"Hey, sailor. Mind if I snuggle in next to you?"

Cory rolled his eyes and slowly twisted his head in the direction of the voice. "You've got to be kidding. Of all the trains that go from Portland to Seattle, this is the one that you're assigned to. What are the odds?" Spencer Tolman, Cory's friend from basic training, grinned and flopped down in the seat next to Cory.

Chapter Eighteen

THE USS *ENTERPRISE*

By the time Cory completed his training and spent several months ferrying new aircraft across the country, it was coming up on October 1943—nearly fifteen months since training started and nearly two years since he first enlisted. It was enough time for the most celebrated ship in the Navy to have weathered four great carrier battles in the South Pacific. Most of her prewar sister carriers had been sunk or damaged beyond repair, yet the mighty *Enterprise*—the Big E—survived. Those battles had been fought in 1942. In 1943, she'd actually received no damage from the enemy but had steamed tens of thousands of miles in hostile waters, suffering the wear and tear from the constant vigilance of training and reconnaissance missions.

At long last, it was time for a much-needed overhaul and training for new air groups. Plus the experience gained in previous battles prompted many design changes that could make her an even more effective fighting weapon in the hands of her now battle-tested commanders. And so she'd been ordered back to the Bremerton, Washington, construction yard, via Pearl. On the way, she received the first Presidential Unit Citation awarded to an aircraft carrier, granted for "consistently outstanding performance and distinguished achievement during repeated action against enemy Japanese forces in the Pacific war area."

One of the consequences of success was that many of her best-trained officers and pilots were to be transferred to new ships to assume leadership roles there. More than forty percent of the total crew would be replaced on this new voyage, and two of the new crew members were Ensigns Cory O'Brian, bomber pilot, and Spencer Tolman, radio operator/gunner.

While he couldn't say how others felt on boarding, Cory's heart almost stopped as he considered the sheer size of the venerable ship. After her refit, she was 809 feet long and 109 feet wide, and displaced over 21,000 tons of water. With a crew of more than three thousand, the ship was like a small city, with multiple post offices, dining galleys segregated by rank, various places for showing movies, and crew quarters in every nook and cranny of the ship. The pilots were assigned berths forward of the hangar deck, one deck down from the flight deck. Cory's bunk actually abutted the curved bow of the ship, and at night when he heard sounds drifting down from the flight deck, he marveled that the thin steel skin he could reach out and touch extended far down and below the waterline where it kept out the water and kept them afloat. Sometimes it felt like the ship and her crew were invincible in this giant floating armory, and other times, particularly when the 40mm Oerlikon guns were practicing right on the other side of the hull, he shuddered at the thought of enemy dive-bombers releasing their payload directly into his bunk if the gunners were unsuccessful. "It's kind of crazy to think about," he said to Spencer when he came up to visit Cory's space, "but when we're the ones making a dive, I pray that the Japanese gunners will be inefficient, but when we're being attacked, I want our guys to be right on target."

The hangar deck itself was about the size of a small stadium, with room to store the fighters, bombers, and torpedo, reconnaissance, and other aircraft. In some places, aircraft were suspended from the ceiling of the hangar deck to provide more storage space. When all the aircraft were stored, it was like walking through a major air depot. When the planes were taken up to the flight deck so that the hangar deck was open, the crew had nearly 800 feet of running room, and basketball games and other sports were played regularly. A massive elevator moved the aircraft efficiently between the decks, and Cory and the other pilots marveled how efficiently the support crew could move aircraft about the various decks, refueling and repairing them, yet always seeming to get them up to the flight deck at the required moment. His role was critical, as a pilot, but without all these other men, he couldn't have done a thing. The Big E was, in reality, a big beehive of human workers who all had a part to play.

* * *

Almost immediately after leaving port, Cory and the other pilots were put on rotation to fly scouting missions to search for enemy submarines, flying the 180-degree pattern he'd drilled so many times in Florida. As frequently as conditions would permit, his group leader also drilled them on dive-bombing techniques. Flying off the carrier gave a new sense of urgency to the drills, particularly since his aircraft was loaded with depth charges each time he went on patrol, just in case they spotted an enemy submarine.

Like most of the pilots, Cory was thrilled to receive one of the newest versions of the Douglas SBD Dauntless dive-bomber rather than the faster but far more temperamental Curtis Helldiver. The Dauntless was a true workhorse, with the Curtis Wright Cyclone engine developing up to 1,200 horsepower at takeoff. Cory loved the sound of the engine when it roared to life in preparation for takeoff. He'd flown some of these aircrafts on his various shuttle trips and had learned that the controls were extremely responsive, particularly the ailerons, which provided exceptional control when making a banking maneuver. The airplane was easy to control, both in level flight and, more importantly, in the thirty seconds of a high-speed dive, recovering quickly on the pullout at 2,500 feet.

Of all the maneuvers that caused the adrenaline to flow, the two that stood out for Cory were catapult-assisted takeoffs and diving on the target. The regular reconnaissance missions were actually pretty boring as he and his gunner did their crisscross patterns to fill out their share of the grid before returning to the carrier.

The catapult-assisted launch was required on days when the headwind was too low to enable takeoff. While the carrier could add sixteen to twenty knots from the air passing over the deck from its own forward speed, an equal amount of headwind was required. On days when they were becalmed, mechanical assistance in the form of the catapult helped boost the takeoff speed in a very short distance. Extremely short, Cory discovered.

On his first assisted launch, Cory and his gunner, Joe Thompson, strapped in and then maneuvered to the proper position on the flight deck. The catapult launch was directed by the cat officer, who signaled him to cut the engine while a small brass ring was attached to the fuselage of the aircraft to hold it in place while a harness was attached to the undercarriage to link the aircraft to the hydraulic catapult. Once Cory completed a final check, he spoke into the intercom to his gunner, "Are you all set back there—completely strapped in and head secure?" When he received an affirmative, he made sure that his own head and neck were planted firmly against the headrest, then gave a signal that he was ready. He received the signal to bring the throttle all the way forward. The engine roared with a distinctive staccato sound, and the plane trembled as it pulled against the brass ring. It seemed impossible that such a small ring could hold it back against the full force of the propeller, but it did. Then he saw the officer give the signal and felt the ring release its hold on the aircraft at exactly the same moment the catapult engaged. He'd never felt anything like it in his life as his head was thrown violently against the seat, forcing him to gasp for air. In less than ten seconds they were airborne.

"Is that amazing?" Cory shouted gleefully to his gunner, who cheerfully agreed. It had to be harder on the gunner, facing backward, since he was thrown against his restraining straps with nothing to support his head.

The second most exciting experience was taking the aircraft into a dive. Typically, they would approach the target at approximately 15,000 feet. Once in the attack zone, they'd circle down to 8,000 feet, at which point the pilot would engage the dive brakes to slow the aircraft to the preferred airspeed of 180 knots at the bomb-release point. The angle of attack was critical and required the pilot to approach the target at approximately an 80-degree angle relative to the target, with the ideal release point at 2,500 feet. That angle assured that the bomb would go on a practically straight line into the target. Plus, such a steep angle of attack presented a very slim profile to enemy gunners, who would naturally do their best to shoot the aircraft out of the sky if given the chance.

On his first practice run out in the open waters of the Pacific, Cory received the signal to go straight down from 15,000 feet. At 8,000, he engaged the dive brakes and was thrown forward against his harness as the aircraft immediately lost airspeed. At 2,500 feet, still going 180 knots, he pulled the bomb release and then immediately disengaged the air brakes, since the aircraft couldn't regain level flight while the fins were deployed.

It was at this point that the feeling of being on a roller coaster hit with full force. Cory had to pull out of the dive by no lower than 1,500 feet, and the arc of the airplane as it accelerated back up to 15,000 feet put at least four to five g-forces of stress on the crew. "Tighten your stomach muscles," Cory said to himself through clenched teeth. If he didn't, the blood would be forced down from the brain and body into his legs, and it was possible for a pilot to blackout from the pooling of blood in the extremities.

"I know, I know," he heard his poor gunner say in a tight voice. At this point, they were coming out of the arc and the pressure let up immediately.

Cory laughed. "I'm sorry. I was talking to myself, not to you. I get so excited I have to remind myself of things like that."

"That's alright. Any idea how we did?"

"Wish I did, but I lost sight when we started to pull up." Later they learned that they'd had a respectable hit on that particular run. In battle, the success of a dive was measured by whether or not the target was hit. Like most of the pilots, Cory wasn't that successful at first, but with each successive practice run, he improved. By the end of the third week at sea, with daily patrol missions and occasional practice missions, Cory and Joe had turned into a good team and were gaining confidence for the day when they'd face real combat.

The ship pulled into port in Pearl Harbor on November 6. "Will you look at that," was all that Spencer could say as the ship passed Ford Island. The wreckage of the *Arizona* could still be seen above the waterline, and the harbor was still littered with debris from the aerial bombardment two years earlier.

"It's unbelievable."

Cory and Spencer weren't the only ones standing in awe at the destruction that had befallen the fleet.

"Oh, my!" This time Spence wasn't talking in the hushed tone of a few moments earlier. As they rounded the island, their attention was taken away from the defeat of two years ago to the massive armada that had replaced it. It was an awe-inspiring sight to see the harbor filled with the new *Essex*-class carriers and the cruiser-hulled light carriers that could operate at fleet speed to support the *Enterprise* and the other large carriers. The new ships included the *Essex,* the second *Yorktown, Intrepid,* the *Bunker Hill,* and the second *Wasp* and *Hornet.* The "second" ships were named after their predecessors that had been sunk in previous battles but that had earned the honor of having their name carried forward in new ships. Surrounded by the various escort destroyers that accompanied the carrier task group, it couldn't help but convey a sense of confidence to everyone who entered the harbor.

"Kind of amazing to see all this, isn't it?" Cory said.

"Yeah." Then pointing at the soot and scars that streaked one of the ships in the dry dock, Spencer observed, "But it's pretty clear that the Japanese can put up a fight."

Cory nodded. It was strange to be excited and scared at the same moment. More than anything in the world, he wanted to get out there and do his part, yet the signs of destruction all around them showed the risk.

"All I ask is that I don't get wounded and become an invalid," Cory said quietly. "I guess I'm okay with death, because it's all over. But I don't want to go through life a cripple."

"I don't want to die or get crippled," Spencer replied forcefully. "Let the Japanese die and get wounded for their country. I want to help as many of them find glory as possible."

Cory laughed but couldn't entirely shake the feeling of dread. One thing was obvious—a single person didn't matter all that much in this war. His dad had been right about that. The war would be won on the macroscale. Still, a fleet was made up of individuals, so in a way he really did matter.

His reverie was short-lived, interrupted by a call to quarters where the pilots were instructed to fly their aircraft off to land-based runways while the ship was reprovisioned. In the interim, they'd spend a couple weeks helping yet another new set of flight crews practice before heading out to the South Pacific.

* * *

Once at sea, the reconnaissance flights took on even greater urgency, since it was now fully possible that a Japanese submarine might be lying in wait for a grouping the size of a carrier task force. On the first day they were scheduled to fly, the pilots in the ready room were startled to receive the news that they'd have to fly in radio silence—no opportunity to radio the ship for directions if they were lost or to seek help if they got in trouble. Cory got a sick feeling in his gut but didn't say anything. Another pilot asked how they'd find their way back.

"You're going to have to rely on the YE," their flight commander said. "Just to make sure, let's review the procedure." He drew a large circle on the blackboard and then drew a series of lines from the center to the perimeter of the circle, so that it looked like pieces of pie. Each piece was approximately fifteen degrees. Then he wrote a different letter of the Morse code in each of the pieces of the pie. "When you're approaching the ship, you should imagine that we're in the middle of the circle. As you enter one of the zones you'll hear the homing beacon sending out one of these letters. If you keep heading straight for us, the letter won't change. But if you drift into another segment, the letter will change, which tells you that you're no longer headed straight for the ship. By looking at the YE chart, you can tell which way you've drifted and correct your course." He looked at the group and could sense their concern but decided against saying anything else other than, "You'll be fine. Just be sure you're religious about getting the new codes each time you fly. We change the YE daily so that the enemy can't figure out our code and use it to find us."

The day after leaving Pearl, Cory and his gunner took off on the first of many flights they'd make to scan the ocean for nonexistent Japanese submarines. It was tedious work that hurt their eyes as they strained to see the small feather of a periscope trail or to see the underwater shadow of the sub on sunny days. In their first of perhaps four or five flights, they didn't see anything except open ocean and the occasional dolphin. It was true for all the planes that went up. Perhaps that's why Cory and the other pilots started to relax a little bit.

While coming in at dusk one evening, Cory found the YE and was pleased to see that he was making the approach from the correct angle, which meant his knee-top navigation had been accurate enough that he could have probably found the ship by dead reckoning. As they approached the ship, he saw the huge, red flag that indicated that the *Enterprise* was turning into the wind to accept them aboard. That's when he saw Spencer's airplane off to his port side. He waved at the pilot, who pointedly ignored him. Shad Michaels was a rather arrogant guy who didn't talk much to anyone in the officer's ready room, particularly Cory. It was pretty obvious he didn't like the fact that his gunner was such good friends with another pilot. For his part, Spencer was loyal to Shad and never said anything negative about him, even when others tried to gossip a bit.

At any rate, Spencer saw Cory as the two aircraft passed each other and waved at him with a broad smile. Circling into the landing pattern, they headed toward the aft direction of the ship, well off the port beam. After entering the landing pattern, Cory was trailing Spencer's aircraft as it entered the final turn. They were cleared to land just ahead of Cory. As Cory came into position, he caught sight of the LSO and saw him give the usual set of signals. But the ocean was riding rough, with large swells that affected the timing of the landing.

"He's going in pretty high," Cory said into his headset.

"Sorry, I can't see a thing." Of course Joe couldn't, but after a couple of hours at sea, Cory just wanted to talk to someone.

"He's getting a wave-off from the LSO—he must have come in too early for the swell."

"Good. That means we'll get his spot as he does a fly around. I'm hungry!"

"Wait a minute—he's not pulling up . . . What's he doing? I can't believe what I'm seeing. I think he's going to try to land."

"You're kidding, right?"

"Pull up! For crying out loud, pull up, you idiot!"

Joe felt the backup stick that allowed him to fly the aircraft in an emergency tremble from Cory's shaking. "What's happening? Are you okay?"

"They're going to crash! They're going to crash! Please help them! Please help Spencer!"

Joe felt himself thrown to the side of his seat as Cory abruptly followed the signal to pull up and out of the landing pattern.

"Can you see what's going on?" Cory called out urgently.

"They're on fire, and the plane slid into the crash barrier."

"Oh, no . . ."

"The crews are hosing it down, and I see them dragging the guys out of the airplane." Silence for a moment. "They've got them out! They got them out, Cory!"

Cory had to force himself to breathe, but at least it was hopeful. By this time, he had completed enough of an arc that they both lost visual contact for a moment, and then the ship came back into his view just in time to see the deck crew shoving the burning plane over the side of the deck. It hit the water with a splash, which made an incredible sight as the flames of the burning aviation fuel continued to flare on the coal-black ocean even after the airplane disappeared beneath the waves. It was a haunting image.

They were now number three for landing, which was a torment unlike anything Cory had ever experienced.

"Are you okay up there?"

"Yeah, I'm okay."

"It's just that the stick is shaking . . ."

Cory looked down at his right hand and saw that he was shaking violently, at least violently enough that the aircraft was trembling ever so slightly. "Sorry. I'll use both hands. We're going to be okay. I've got to find out what happened to Tolman, so you don't need to worry."

"I'm not worried about you landing the plane—you could do that with your eyes closed." Joe wanted to sound as calm and reassuring as possible. "I'm worried about your friend too."

"Thanks, Joe. Okay, we're next." He completed the banking turn to come in line with the ship and then watched the LSO with more intensity than ever before. Even though taking off and landing had become routine, it was obvious that there really wasn't anything routine about it. "We're cleared." *Why did Michaels disobey the signals? The LSO gave him a clear wave-off—why would he ignore him?* Cory wanted to swear, and he felt a bitter bile come up in his throat. *Spencer better be okay, or I'll beat that guy to a pulp.*

As they settled on the deck and caught the second arrester cable, the fear he felt for Spencer was mingled with righteous indignation and anger at Spencer's pilot. As they screeched to a stop, Cory threw open the canopy and started to bound out of the aircraft before the propeller even stopped turning. This brought a savage remark from the flight deck officer, but he didn't care. He raced to the tower and shoved his way down the narrow staircase toward the infirmary. The adrenaline must have been flooding his system, because when he thought about it later, he realized he couldn't recall anything about his trip from the flight deck to the infirmary, several decks below amidships.

When he got there, he burst in, shouting, "Where's Ensign Tolman?" That got him dirty looks from some of the medics, but he didn't much care because about halfway in the room he saw Spencer sitting up in the middle of a bed, his body covered in grime and soot. "Spence!"

"Quiet!" one of the medics shushed him. "You can't be in here."

"But that's my best friend. Is he okay?"

The medic looked up at Spence, who gave him a sign that he'd like to talk to Cory, if he could. "He's going to be okay. If you'll be quiet, you can have a couple of minutes with him, but then you've gotta get out of here."

"Thanks." Cory jogged over to Spencer's bed. He realized that he'd probably broken a couple of dozen rules to get here, but he had to see what happened. "Are you okay?"

"Yeah, I'm okay. Burned pretty badly, but I'm okay." Spencer was very subdued.

"That Michaels didn't take the wave-off. The arrogant piece of crap thinks he's good enough to blow off an LSO. If he'd have hurt you, I'm afraid I'd have killed him."

"It's too late, Cory." Spencer's eyes watered, and he had a stricken look unlike anything Cory had ever seen in another human being.

"What do you mean?"

"I mean . . . I mean he's dead. His seat tore loose when we hit the crash barrier, and it killed him."

"Oh, I am so sorry, Spence. I'm so sorry." Now Cory wanted to crawl in a hole. No matter how much he didn't like the guy, he didn't want something like this to happen.

"We were doing fine, and then all of a sudden he acted confused and said into the intercom, 'I'm supposed to pull up, but we're going too slow. I don't think I can do it.' The next thing I know there's this tearing sound, and suddenly I'm being thrown around the cockpit like a rag doll in a dog's mouth. Then we crashed into the barrier, which pretty much knocked me senseless. But then I saw the flames start up. It was awful, Cory. I shouted to Shad, but I didn't hear anything. Then I started tearing at my restraining belts, because the heat was starting to sear my face and I was sure that the canopy was going to melt. That's when I felt somebody pulling me from the cockpit . . ." Spencer gulped hard and took a drink of water. Then calming himself down, "It was just awful . . . I was so scared . . ." He started sobbing. "And he died. He was my pilot, and he died . . ."

Cory sat down next to him and pulled Spencer to his shoulder.

"I've never had anybody die, Cory. I don't know what to do . . ."

"It's okay. It's bad, but it'll be okay. I don't know how." Now Cory felt tears on his cheeks. "I'm so sorry, Spence . . ."

* * *

Spencer was laid up for the next two weeks while his arm and burns healed. Cory and Joe continued their reconnaissance missions, always loaded with depth charges, just in case. A new wrinkle was added in the second week in that, in addition to their regular patrols, they started practicing night landings again. All the new pilots had previously qualified for night landings on land, but that was a long time ago, and it was very different out in the vast expanses of the Pacific, knowing that there was no solid earth as a backup landing spot if they got lost. On his first approach, Cory set the plane down a little harder than he liked, catching the first arrester cable and jerking to a sudden stop well short of the crash barrier. On the one hand, that meant a good landing, but in his own mind, he wondered if he were a little gun-shy because of what happened to Shad and Spencer.

Still, after a few days of flying, the accident pretty well disappeared from his thoughts, and once again he found himself passing the rather boring hours at sea with idle thoughts. To keep his mind occupied, he played mental word games or even an occasional golf game. Occasionally, he and Joe would talk, but not too often. Joe was a quiet person, fairly tall with dark hair. In some ways, he reminded Cory of his brother-in-law, but Joe was far more reserved. They'd been assigned randomly, and if he'd had his choice, he would have picked someone more talkative, but Joe was solid, and that's what mattered.

When he received the wake-up call on Friday morning at 0500, he grumbled. The early morning flights were always the worst, particularly if you had to cover the eastern horizon, because the sun was always coming straight into your eyes. Plus, sleeping in his narrow bunk was never very satisfying—he always worried that he'd fall out. Still, he was lucky to have a bunk. Down in the mess hall where more than seven hundred enlisted men slept in hammocks, it was inevitable that somebody would fall out, with the usual release of profanity before he crawled back into his net.

Grabbing his shaving pail, he made his way to the head, where he filled his pail with good, clean water. His first step was to blast the pail with the steam jet to heat it, then to brush his teeth in the clean water. Next, he lathered up and sponge bathed the vital areas. Finally, he climbed into the unheated shower to rinse off. Even though there were no restrictions on how much fresh water the men could use, everybody did their best to conserve, with the cold showers doing their part to encourage conservation. The fresh water had to be distilled from ocean water, a process which used up energy and time.

After a quick breakfast, Cory and Joe met up at the briefing, where they learned they'd be flying the eastern quadrant on the grid.

"What was that, O'Brian?"

"Nothing, sir!"

"Out with it. I heard you say something under your breath."

"I was just wondering, sir, if it was me or Ensign Thompson who aggravated the CO. Something we did in childhood, maybe?"

"Meaning?"

"Meaning, sir, that we've had the eastern quadrant four out of the last five mornings. Kind of unlikely that we've sailed over the top of the Japanese subs, so not a lot to see. Of course, the sunrise is beautiful, sir, even if it does hurt your eyes."

"Ahh, got up on the wrong side of the bed, did we, O'Brian? The thing is, O'Brian, we thought we were doing you a favor—letting you fly a little closer to home each day. I'm sure your mother would be pleased." Everybody laughed. Calling someone a mama's boy was always a good shot, and since Cory's personal habits were already suspicious, it was sure to land an extra hard blow.

"Why, thank you, sir. I hadn't realized that was your motive. I'll be sure to write to her about it in my next letter, mentioning you by name." That brought another laugh from the group and evened the score.

"Fine. Now, unless there are any other useless comments or questions, I suggest you gentlemen go look for some Japanese submarines. We're heading west where they don't want us, so chances are increasing by the hour that they're out there. Good hunting!"

Climbing the steps to the flight deck, Cory heard a familiar voice, but one that he hadn't heard for a couple of months. "Nice comeback, O'Brian. Glad to see you're still in one piece." Cory turned in astonishment to see Jack Wilson, the fighter pilot. "Jack? Where did you come from? I looked for you when I first got on board, but your name wasn't on the roster. I felt bad, because I always kind of enjoyed hearing how much better fighter pilots are than bombers. With Bob Hope off in Europe, you were the next best thing."

"Very good, O'Brian. It's a complicated story, actually. When I got to Bremerton, they changed my orders to ship out on another carrier. But apparently the *Enterprise* decided I was indispensable, because they ordered me to transfer over this week to beef up your fighter protection. Apparently they're worried about you boys."

"I'm glad to hear that—I won't have as many sleepless nights now, knowing you're on my wing. I'll bet the captain starts listening to old 78s in the evenings now, secure in the knowledge that the ship is fully protected in the capable hands of Ensign Wilson."

Jack laughed, and Cory could tell that he was genuinely happy to meet up again. That pleased Cory, somehow. While he admired all the fighter pilots, he didn't really bond with any of them. But Jack was a regular sort of guy, and it would be good to have another friend on board. Joe caught up to them at that point.

"So we're off to greet the sun, I guess," Cory said.

"Probably for the rest of the war," Joe muttered.

Cory winced. "Yes, the Big Mouth of the Big E has likely secured that prize for a long time. Sorry, Joe."

"Actually, it's not such a big deal for me, since I'm facing backward on the outbound leg and the sun is pretty much up by the time we come back. So it's you who pays the price."

"I think I like this guy," Jack said cheerfully. "Didn't really think I'd ever like a gunner, but he's alright. Oh, there was that other one, your pal. What happened to him?"

Cory explained what had happened to Spencer, which quickly sobered the discussion. They reached the flight deck and went their separate ways. Cory waved cheerfully as Jack mounted his plane, then climbed aboard his Dauntless, somehow feeling great and looking forward to getting up in the air.

* * *

After an hour outbound, it was time to turn the sweep and begin working their way back to the ship. As usual, they'd spotted nothing but whitecaps. "Your turn for squinting," Cory called back cheerfully.

"Thanks."

"Wow, you're unusually talkative this morning."

"Can it, Cory. I'm trying to figure out how to resolve general and special relativity since Einstein hasn't gotten around to figuring it out yet."

Cory burst out laughing. "Oh, my. Well, far be it from me to interrupt a genius at work."

"Thanks. Hey, wait a minute. Do you see that?"

"See what?"

"At 0800 and about two hundred yards back."

Cory turned and looked back. He didn't see anything. "My brow still hasn't unfurrowed enough from the sun to be of much use. What do you think it is?"

"I don't know, because I've never seen anything like it before. But it kind of looks like what I imagine a submarine feather would look like."

"A submarine? Okay, we've gotta be careful and do this right. If there is something there, we don't want them to see us until we're ready to drop on them. I'm going to keep flying straight for another twenty seconds, and then I'll bring her into an easy port turn. You keep sighting in on the spot and tell me if I'm heading in the right direction. I'll go off to their starboard side so you can see out of the canopy."

At the appropriate time, he brought the Dauntless around smoothly. They were now west of the target, which meant they were easier to spot through the submarine's periscope, if there was a target. Still, this was the most excitement they'd had since entering the Navy, so it was worth the time to check it out. As they approached the spot where Joe thought he saw the feather, Cory caught a brief glimpse of a small white line in the water and beneath it what looked like a large shadow, or stain, in the water.

"Do you see it?" Joe called out anxiously.

"I do see it, partner. And I believe we have ourselves an enemy sub. Prepare for attack." With that Cory applied full throttle to gain altitude so he could come down on the sub at the proper attack angle. At maximum altitude, the shadow was just a faint outline, but that made sense if they'd spotted the plane, which was very likely, and were now diving to get out of its way. Acting on sheer impulse, which had been schooled through countless practice runs, Cory started into the dive, applying the air brakes at the appropriate moment, and zoomed in on the spot at more than 180 miles per hour. He mentally calculated the forward movement of the ship to determine when to release. The question was how much depth the Japanese sub could gain in the time it took for him to make the release. "Hey, Einstein, here's what I think we should do. Care to confirm my thinking?"

"Don't need to—been doing it all along. I think you've got it perfect."

There was nothing like the feeling of a dive. The aircraft acted in sympathy with gravity instead of against it, and the combined effect of the weight of the aircraft and the power of the engine pulling them forward gave them the almost-out-of-control feeling of a fast run on the ski slopes. Cory loved it. Plus, in a dive, the engine cowling was out of the line of sight so he could actually see what was going on directly in front of him.

As the ocean zoomed up, he waited, waited, waited, then squeezed on the release and felt the depth charges drop free of the aircraft. They were programmed to splash into the water, then float down to the predetermined depth before exploding. They didn't actually have to hit the submarine to disable it, since the concussion of the displaced water caused by the explosion was often enough to rupture the hull, even from a distance. Of course, the closer the explosion, the greater the chance of damage.

As soon as he released the bombs, Cory pulled back on the stick to initiate the climb out. Suddenly, his vision started to go dark. "Squeeze the stomach," he shouted as he got up to a safe altitude and then rolled the aircraft so they could see the depth charges go off. Just in time, he saw the first of four giant waterspouts erupt from the surface of the ocean as the exploding gas of the charge made its way to the surface. All the water that boiled up and out of the ocean represented the volume of water displaced by the gas, and if there was a sub under there it was almost certain that it had been given a good tossing about. Cory watched jubilantly as the other three charges went off at intervals.

"Think we hit anything?"

"I don't know," Joe replied. "I'm pretty sure there was a sub there, and we had to hit pretty close to where it was. I wish the stupid thing would send up some debris or something."

"Let's circle for a few minutes just to make sure." At this point, Cory didn't want to use his radio since their very presence would tell the submarine commander that the *Enterprise* was in the vicinity, and he didn't want to do anything to give away the ship's position. In fact, he planned to fly in a diagonal away from the sub relative to the ship's position, just so it couldn't estimate their direction of travel in case it survived and happened to come back up as they departed.

"What do you suppose that stuff is?" Once again, Joe had been the first to spot something.

"I don't know. Let's go down and take a closer look." Cory dropped into a shallow dive and crossed over a black patch on the water.

"That's gotta be oil," he shouted cheerfully. "And since I don't think there are any oil wells out here, we must have hit something!"

"I agree. Of course, we don't know if we killed it or just hurt it. Either way, that was great shooting, Cory. Congratulations!"

"Wow—our first sub. But it's because of your eyes, Joe. You oughta get those things insured!"

"I might just do that," Joe said cheerfully.

* * *

That day turned out to be the best and worst day of Joe and Cory's partnership. When they returned to the ship and reported their action, a number of interesting things happened. First, the ship went to General Quarters, with all lookouts put on highest alert. Second, the carrier's destroyers tightened their protective outer shield while the task force picked up speed and increased their zigzag pattern. Third, the number of reconnaissance flights were increased, which was received with moans in the wardroom. And fourth, while they were congratulated for their action, their flight leader had to inform them that they couldn't be credited with a hit since the sighting was so tenuous and unconfirmed by any other boat or aircraft.

"That's alright, sir. We'll get credit when the war's over and it becomes clear that this sub never made it back."

"You're really full of yourself, aren't you, O'Brian?"

"Actually, we're not, sir. I don't know if we disabled them or not. They may have pumped the oil just to make us think they were hurt. But at least in my mind there was a sub, and we drove it down. When that's all the action you've ever seen, it makes you feel pretty good."

The lieutenant commander nodded. "You did well—both of you. At least now we know we're in range of their subs. It's been easy sailing up to now."

That was the good part of the day. The bad part came just moments later when they were descending the over-steepened stairway in the conning tower. Joe was coming down after Cory, when he slipped on a step and came tumbling down on top of Cory. Cory fell to the deck below, about to make a sarcastic remark, when Joe let out a yelp of pain. Cory looked up to see him dangling from the ladder, his arm twisted between two of the rungs and blood streaming down his sleeve.

Cory shouted for help and jumped up to help Joe extricate himself. Joe was doing his best not to cry, but the pain was obviously intense. As Cory lifted Joe's arm free of the stairwell, which required him to actually lift Joe's body to take the pressure off his arm, Joe let out a yelp of pain. Once free, he settled him onto the deck. Joe's face was white from the pain, and before he could say anything, his head dropped off to the side.

"Oh, boy. Okay, do I wait for help, or just get him to the infirmary as fast as possible?" Cory spoke out loud. Usually this stairwell was like an overcrowded highway, but now there was no one to hear him. Cory decided he had to move fast, so he gently lifted Joe up and over his shoulder and started to work his way down to the next level. It was tough enough alone, but the added weight of Joe made it even worse. Fortunately, when he reached the next landing, a couple of enlisted men came around the corner and immediately helped Cory get Joe down to the infirmary. The doctor on duty took one look at Joe and said, "Looks like he's going to be grounded for awhile." It was frustrating to think that Joe could survive all the risks of flying on and off a moving ship at sea only to be put out of action by a slippery step.

That afternoon, their flight leader came down to check on Joe, who was awake now, even if a bit drugged up from a mild dose of morphine, and wearing a new cast. He was pretty glum. Spencer was there as well, having been returned to the active duty roster two days before. After trying to cheer Joe up, without much success, Commander Mercer turned to Spencer and said, "I'm afraid I have some bad news for you too, Tolman." Spencer's face immediately clouded up.

"Sir?"

"Well, with Mr. Thompson out of commission, I'm afraid that the only spot we have for you is to fly with O'Brian." That took Spencer by surprise—a pleasant surprise. But before he could respond, Mercer continued. "I know it's a lot to ask, but unfortunately the Navy only has so many pilots and, with a war on and all, this is what it's come down to."

"Well, challenging times call for extraordinary sacrifice, sir. I guess it's the least that I could do for my country."

"Oh, no. It's the most, Mr. Tolman. The Navy is grateful." Spencer did his very best to suppress a grin, but Mercer kept a perfectly straight face.

Cory grunted. "Nice . . . really nice. If you two are done having your fun, maybe somebody would like to ask me what I think about this."

"Stand down, Ensign O'Brian. The Navy doesn't require your opinion."

"Yes, sir!" Cory said crisply.

With that, Lieutenant Commander Mercer turned on his heel and exited the room, holding his bluff perfectly to the end.

Cory did his best to continue to act wounded, particularly since Joe looked even more miserable now. It was hard to be made redundant, as the British liked to say. Still, inside Cory was happy. The reconnaissance flights wouldn't be nearly so boring now.

"Welcome aboard, Mr. Tolman. I look forward to sharing a cockpit with you." Then to Joe, "Maybe this will give you the time you need to reconcile gravity and the time-space continuum while you're laid up, Joe. Of course you'll have to take the Heisenberg Uncertainty Principle into account when contemplating the quantum physics involved."

Even in his dazed state, Joe looked up in astonishment. "Am I hallucinating or did you just describe the problems between Einstein's writings on relativity and quantum mechanics?"

"You're hallucinating. You should get some sleep."

Joe nodded, as if both his head and his arm hurt.

Once outside, Cory whispered to Spencer, "He's already in shock. Why make him consider the thought that a pilot has actually studied something serious. It could send him over the edge."

Chapter Nineteen

FRUSTRATION WITH THE MARK VI TORPEDO

The tension in the *Tripletail* control room was palpable. The crew could hear the staccato conversations taking place up in the conning tower through the loudspeaker system. After three weeks out of Pearl without a single enemy that the sub could actually engage, the captain had finally ordered the crew to battle stations as the submarine closed in on a small convoy of Japanese transport ships en route from Singapore to the Japanese home islands. From what Nate could gather, there was a large fuel tanker and several smaller ships, probably carrying food supplies. Any one of the targets would be a good kill, depriving the Japanese of much-needed supplies, but everyone knew that the tanker was the best prize. Every tanker sent to the bottom made it that much more difficult for the Japanese war effort to succeed.

"Up periscope!" Stahlei's voice—always crisp and cool—almost never betrayed the tension that he might feel. Until this moment. His next words were spoken with just the slightest hint of excitement. "Make ready the bow tubes. Estimated range, two thousand yards. Track, ninety starboard. Gyro angle, five left. Stand by!"

The tension in the room was electric. Aside from the occasional order to change the direction of the ship or to increase or decrease speed, there was very little for the crew to do during an attack, apart from the members of the attack party and the men in the forward and aft torpedo rooms. The time leading up to an attack was always filled with intense anticipation—it was, after all, the moment the whole cruise was devoted to. Too often it led to disappointment since, more often than not, an attack would be broken off before torpedoes were even launched. And even in those instances where they engaged the enemy, there was the concern that their attack might not succeed. The great scandal of the Navy in the early months of the war was the failure rate of the Mark VI magnetic exploder—the highest of any nation in the world.

"Final reading, Mr. Brown." The captain then called out the coordinates. Finally, the command they'd all been waiting for: "Fire, on your command!"

There was a brief pause as Nate locked in the final firing coordinates. It's likely that the entire crew held its collective breath at this moment, because once the fish had left the tube, they knew that the deathly silence that they had to maintain during an attack would be shattered by either the sound of the explosion on the enemy ship or by the inevitable pursuit by the escorts to drive the submarine away from the surviving ship.

"Fire one! Fire two!" The sound of Nate's voice was higher pitched than the captain's but every bit as confident. Of course, it simply masked what was really going on—fear, excitement, and exhilaration.

The chief torpedo officer clicked his stopwatch the moment the men standing by the tubes pushed the launch buttons. It would be approximately ninety seconds until the first torpedoes should arrive. It was unusual that the captain had only fired two torpedoes at such a large target. In just a moment it was clear why.

"Make ready tubes three and four, and set the depth for twenty!"

"He doesn't trust the Mark VI magnetic exploder," the navigator whispered in response to the raised eyebrow of the gunnery officer. "Too many misses on his previous cruises."

At sixty seconds, the CTO started counting down the time very quietly into the microphone so the crew could hear. At ninety seconds, they waited in anticipation but heard nothing. Stahlei cursed and had just opened his mouth to issue a new fire order, when there was a well-defined *boom* followed quickly by a second. A quiet cheer went up but was quickly cut short as Stahlei shouted, "Reset to forty feet and fire tubes three and four when ready!"

"Nice shot, Nate!" Akers said quietly from the plot table.

"Torpedoes reset. Fire three! Fire four!" Nate slumped down a bit as the tension drained from him, muttering under his breath, "That was the longest ninety seconds of my life."

Akers overheard him and laughed.

"Acquiring new target. Reload all forward tubes!" The captain intended to make as much mayhem as possible. "Scanning for escort activity," he said quietly as he rotated the periscope a full 360 degrees. Fortunately, it was a night attack, so they didn't have to worry about enemy aircraft, but it seemed certain there would be a destroyer or two that would quickly be searching for them. "Nothing sighted yet. I'm going to shoot for the lead ship and then try for the third ship if we can bring our stern tubes to bear." In short order, the captain had fed the new coordinates to the plot and TDC, and just as the third torpedo slammed into the tanker they launched three more at the next target. Then in a deft maneuver, the captain swung the ship around so that its tail was pointed at the third ship in the convoy.

Nate quickly cut in the gyro regulator for the aft torpedo room, and then used the telephone to confirm that his new settings were actually taking effect in the aft torpedo tubes. The changeover had gone perfectly, and he notified the captain that they were set for a new attack.

"The target's taking evasive maneuvers—mark position!" Nate dialed the new coordinates in, but it was difficult at this point to tell exactly its course and bearing since it was obviously in a new zigzag pattern, undoubtedly scared by the hit on the tanker. Two more readings gave them enough confidence that the captain gave permission to fire.

"Fire aft one! Fire two! Fire three!"

By this point in the battle, the sounds in the ocean were incredible. Three of their first four shots had hit the tanker, and the sound of the concussions had been ominous. But they were nothing compared to the eerie sounds of the great ship breaking up in the water. There were sounds of metal tearing loose from its fittings and the sound of high pressure steam frothing into the water when pipes were torn asunder. Approximately one minute after the last torpedo hit, there was the sound of yet another explosion.

"That would be her boilers exploding from the superheated metal being hit by the cold ocean water," the chief of the boat said quietly. The exhilaration they'd all felt just a few moments earlier was tempered by the knowledge that at this moment, men were being boiled alive in the flames of a great fuel tanker exploding on the surface.

"You should take a look at this, Nate." Captain Stahlei stepped aside so that Nate could see firsthand the effect of his work. Through the lens of the periscope, Nate saw a scene right out of Dante's *Inferno*. The night sky was aglow in red and orange sheets of flame that reached perhaps fifty or sixty feet into the sky. As the escaping fuel oil seeped out into the ocean, it created pools of flame that danced and played on the surface of the ocean, like strange specters dancing a ghostlike waltz in crimson and blue. And even though the night sky was fairly dark, it was pitch black where the great clouds of black, acrid smoke billowed up into the air, obliterating the stars in an oily mess that could have been seen for fifty or sixty miles in the daylight. But all that was nothing compared to the sight of men jumping over the sides of the sinking ship out into the inky darkness of the ocean, sometimes directly into the pools of burning oil. Although they were too far away to hear their screams, Nate imagined that he heard them screaming, and suddenly he felt very much like he wanted to throw up.

There was a brilliant flash as their torpedoes hit the lead ship and then the third ship. In a quick turn of the periscope, he saw that the entire horizon for 180 degrees was filled with burning wreckage. The sounds of the three ships breaking apart in their death throes were mingled with the cheers of the *Tripletail's* own crew for a remarkably successful attack, and it all combined to overwhelm Nate's senses.

Stepping back from the scope, Nate turned and looked at the captain, who said quietly, "I know how you feel. I never quite know what to think at a time like this."

Nate said nothing, but simply shrugged.

"Mr. Akers, care to take a look? Perhaps you can describe the scene for the rest of the crew."

Nate was surprised at how calm he actually felt. He knew that something dreadful had happened, and yet he was at peace with it. This was what was required to win the war, to bring sanity back to the world. This insane moment in which he felt close to having viewed the traditional Christian vision of hell was the very thing that was needed to bring peace once again to the world.

"You did a nice job, Mr. Brown. Congratulations."

Nate turned and saw that Captain Stahlei had been watching him.

"Are you alright?"

Nate nodded a moment, as if collecting his thoughts. "Yes, sir, I am."

"Good." The captain held his gaze for a few seconds more. This was the first time Nate had succeeded in combat, and Stahlei needed to know how he'd react. Satisfied, he said calmly, "Now, Mr. Akers, I need my periscope back."

The captain swiveled the periscope and then said quickly, "All ahead full! Enemy destroyer in pursuit, and he's got a big bone in his teeth!" He then gave the new heading.

At first, the captain attempted to get a bearing for a shot at the destroyer, but it was coming on too fast. "Dive! Depth one hundred fifty!"

The planesmen adjusted the angles of the planes, and the boat nosed its way down under full acceleration. The crew members had to hang on to whatever they could grab to avoid being thrown to the deck by the steeply angled dive. At approximately fifty feet, they heard a new sound—the swishing sound of a propeller growing louder, echoing inside the narrow hull of the ship. It didn't matter where the men were in the ship, they could hear the approach of the destroyer, knowing full well that in just a matter of moments, the price of retribution was to be paid for the three ships killed on the surface.

"We're under!" the diving officer called.

As the sound of the propellers grew to the point that it sounded like someone was about to knock on the hatch for permission to enter, they suddenly started to diminish in intensity. The swift little ship, almost exactly the same displacement as their submarine, had passed over and was now moving away from them. The change in the sound of the propeller was dramatic. There was no comfort in that fact, however, for they knew instinctively that drums of high explosive depth charges had been launched and were even now drifting lazily down in the water until they reached their preprogrammed depth.

The shock wave of a depth charge could easily crush the hull of a submarine if the enemy were lucky enough to get a direct hit, which, occasionally they did. But they didn't really need a direct hit to cause havoc. The cat-and-mouse game of depth charges was scored more like horseshoes than darts— even a near hit scored points because the concussion of the water slamming into the sub was often enough to damage its hull or wreak havoc on its instruments.

"All stop! Rig for silent running!" Captain Stahlei's orders were instantly obeyed, and the submarine became deathly quiet as all nonessential activities ceased and the electric motors were reduced to the minimum revolutions needed to maintain stability.

Click.

Nate wanted to ask someone what that sound meant. It wasn't loud, but it was very distinctive, like someone snapping their fingers.

Bang!

There was no mistaking that sound or the effect it had on the sub. Nate was knocked from his feet and would have been thrown all the way to the deck if he hadn't held onto the controls of the TDC. Pulling himself back to a standing position, he gasped for air, which was now filled with dust and cork that had been knocked loose by the force of the explosion.

Click.

Bang!

A second explosion hit with even more force than the first and knocked his breath out.

"Dive! Two hundred feet! All ahead one-third!" The captain's orders were immediately repeated by the dive officer, and almost before he could recover from the most recent blow, Nate felt the deck tilt forward as the bow planes were adjusted to take them down under power.

Click.

Bang!

Click.

Bang!

Bang!

Bang!

The force of four explosions in quick succession, the last two almost direct hits, struck with such force that the TDC was torn from the wall, throwing Nate off balance and back against John Akers's plot table. Fortunately, the apparatus only grazed his leg, but the pain was intense. Adding to his confusion, the lights went out, and for a few moments, the attack center was thrown into total darkness. Then someone turned on a flashlight, then another.

"Mr. Conrad, take us to two hundred fifty! I need damage reports! Now!"

As Nate's head cleared, he did his best to focus his thoughts, but he felt like his brain had been scrambled. Vaguely, he heard the command repeated to flood bow tanks, increasing their angle of descent.

"Flooding in the engine room. Flooding in the forward torpedo room." The reports continued to echo throughout the ship, and Nate could sense the activity that was even now taking place throughout the ship as men fought desperately to bypass broken seals that were leaking water and to brace supports that were broken or bent by the concussions. The lights in the room blinked on and off briefly, then came back at a reduced intensity. Even so, it hurt his eyes after the darkness. Just a few minutes earlier, nearly everyone on the crew had been redundant, except for the attack party. Now they were all energized into action at their emergency stations. Nate started working at clearing the wreckage of the TDC, doing his best to preserve the integrity of the wiring harness so they could make repairs once the attack was over. *If we live to make repairs.* He gulped. *Bad thing to think about—"Our thoughts are traitors."* He smiled to himself at the thought that he could think about Shakespeare at a time like this.

It was at this moment that he became aware of a rather disturbing conversation taking place in the control room below him. The ship was still sinking, even though they'd passed the 200-foot level. "Two-thirty, two-forty, two-fifty." The boat wasn't designed to go deeper than this, and Nate waited for the command to blow the ballast tanks. But then he heard the sound of the destroyer's propeller growing louder. "Oh, no!" he muttered under his breath and turned and gave John Akers a weak smile as he mouthed the words, "Here we go again!"

Nate heard Stahlei quietly curse the moon, since it was obviously creating enough light for the destroyer to track them. *Click.*

Bang!

Not as close this time.

Click.

Bang!

Further away. Nate breathed a small sigh of release.

"Three hundred twelve," came the whispered report.

"I've got to have some power, Captain, or we're going straight to the bottom."

"Ahead one-half." Stahlei's voice was quiet and calm. Even in this extreme circumstance, no one was raising his voice. By creating forward momentum, the planes—or fins—could more easily give the lift they so desperately needed right now.

"Three-fifty, three-sixty." Although quiet, the young seaman calling out the depths had a twinge of panic in his voice. Submarines were not designed to withstand the incredible pressure that was now bearing down on the *Tripletail.* New sounds began to emanate from distant recesses of the ship—a kind of deep groaning, much like the sounds of a great sea mammal in her death throes. Without warning, a bolt on one of the high-pressure tubes shot crazily across the room, as if it had been fired from a gun. The ricochet made everyone instinctively duck. Then a second shot out, and a third. Nate crouched behind the TDC, hoping to find some shelter. Then a fourth, and a groan. Not a groan from the ship—a human groan. Nate looked around desperately and saw one of the lookouts, a young seaman, with blood slowly oozing from a wound in his forehead. By the time Nate and Akers reached him, they heard an unearthly rattle from his throat, and realized that he'd actually perished the moment the bolt had penetrated his skull. It just took a few moments for his body to stop functioning.

"Blow all tanks." The voice was still controlled, but it had an urgency to it that betrayed the solemnity of their position.

Oh, Kathy, I'm so sorry. I'm just so sorry.

It was hard to tell the difference between the tears that came down Nate's cheek from the sweat that dripped off everyone's face and body. Most of the men had, by now, stripped down to their skivvies, the heat was so overpowering. There was the sound of the air blasting its way into the ballast tanks, the gurgling sound of water being forced out and into the ocean, and the incessant groaning and creaking of the hull as they approached the 400-foot mark.

"All ahead full!" Stahlei's voice was flat.

At 410 feet, the ship leveled out. The change in attitude was noticeable to everyone, and Nate imagined that he heard a collective sigh of relief. With all the water they'd taken on through seepage around the various seals in the torpedo tubes, around the hatches, and in all the other places where the exterior of the ship had to be exposed to the outside environment, it was not at all certain that even blowing the tanks could stop their descent.

As the keel started to rise, he listened in gratitude as the reading from the depth gauge started to improve. "Three-seventy, three-fifty, three-thirty . . ."

"We're going to make it." Nate was surprised to hear his own whisper. He'd intended to simply think the words, but they'd forced their way out. He looked around sheepishly, but Akers just shrugged. The noise of the ship adjusting itself to the ever-decreasing pressure was more than enough to cover his puny remark.

"Two-fifty, two-twenty."

"Reverse one-third!" There was a new urgency to Stahlei's command.

"Two hundred, one-ninety, one-eighty."

"We can't stop the ascent," Akers said quietly to Nate. "We're going to broach the surface."

By taking emergency action to stop their uncontrolled descent, they set the stage for the exact reverse to occur. At this point the ship was boiling toward the surface at an ever-increasing rate. If the diving officer, John Conrad, couldn't gain control quickly, they'd shoot out of the surface like a giant whale breaching. If their Japanese destroyer was anywhere nearby, it couldn't help but see and hear the great leviathan blowing its way up and out of the water.

Nate and the others held their breath and shifted their weight hopefully in the expectation that the angle on the deck would moderate.

"We're going to breach, Captain. I can't bring her under control in time."

"Very well, Mr. Conrad." The captain's voice sounded tired. The setup on the attack had taken nearly twelve hours while they shadowed the convoy waiting for darkness to give them the most opportune timing for the attack, plus all the maneuvering it had taken to get set up for the most efficient angle of attack. It was exhausting as they struggled to avoid detection while periodically surfacing and submerging, sometimes able to vent the ship with fresh air, other times waiting anxiously as the CO_2 content drifted up because they were under water for so long. The attack party had been on duty three hours before that, so it was now some sixteen hours since it had all started.

"When we reach the surface, I want a deck party. They'll know where we are, anyway, so let's bring some air in and perhaps set up for a surface attack if necessary."

Once again the ship sprang to life. There was no need for silence now since the sound of the ship moving at an accelerating pace through the water would easily be detectable to anyone in the vicinity.

"Brace yourselves, gentlemen!" the captain said into the public-address system. As the depth gauge got into the single digits Nate and the others held their breath. It was a natural instinct, perhaps. It was exhilarating when it happened. Nate felt the front of the ship rise up and then fall forward, his legs buckling as the bow of the ship fell forward into the water.

"All ahead, full diesels! Deck party to the bridge!"

Nate lined up as the conning tower hatch was twirled open. When it was raised, there was a great rushing sound and immediate swoosh of air as the overheated air in the ship forced its way up and out, while an equal amount of cool air was sucked back into the ship. He couldn't help but take great gulps of air in almost desperate gasps. Never had air tasted and smelled so good, and his brain seemed to clear almost immediately as his lungs and nostrils savored the smell of the sea air. But there wasn't much time to ponder. In a purely instinctual reaction, drilled in by hours of relentless practice, his feet were on the steel rungs of the wet ladder, and he was up and over the edge, moving to his position to the right and a step behind the captain. The lookouts had already climbed to the crow's nest higher up and were even now scanning the horizon.

Turning to aft, Nate saw great belches of black smoke as the diesels roared to life, three of them providing power for forward momentum while the fourth did its best to recharge the batteries that had been drained mercilessly while they'd been underwater. They'd need every stored ampere of energy possible if they had to go back under the surface. Plus, he knew that with full power, the ship's ventilation systems were even now drawing fresh air to every corner of the ship while pumps in each of the major compartments were busy forcing water out of the bilges so that essential repairs could be undertaken as quickly as possible.

"Mast at one-twenty!"

The lookout's voice was clear and strong—and frightened. Everyone on the bridge turned to the indicated position and focused their binoculars on the spot. With his higher elevation, the lookout had an advantage that took a few seconds before the enemy ship came into view for the rest of the deck party.

"He's headed away from us!" Nate said excitedly.

"Not for long," the captain replied quietly. Nate saw the enemy ship initiate a turn that meant they'd spotted the little sub.

"Shall we dive, sir?"

"Not this time. They'd have us for sure." The captain swung his glasses around the horizon to make sure it was a one-to-one duel. "Nope, this time it's us or him. All engines ahead full."

The danger was that the destroyer could fire on them using its larger surface guns. If its guns failed to connect, it could then simply ram the sub and split it right down the middle. That is, of course, unless the *Tripletail* could successfully launch torpedoes down its throat. It was now a life-or-death game of chicken, with both ships working their way up to flank speed.

"Load all forward tubes!" Nate started to move toward the hatch to move back to his position in the tower.

"Did I understand correctly that the TDC is out of action?"

"Yes, sir!"

"Then you might as well stay up here and watch the fireworks, Mr. Brown." Speaking into his intercom, the captain then said, "Mr. Akers, it's up to you on the plot! Welcome to the battle!"

Nate couldn't help but smile, knowing that Akers was right now moving into high speed, while privately grinning from ear to ear.

"All tubes loaded!"

Nate mounted the bridge attack scope, and the captain started calling coordinates to Akers in the attack room below.

"Always a tough shot," Stahlei said quietly. "The bow of a destroyer doesn't give you much to aim for. I like the big fat profile of a tanker a lot better."

Nate laughed, but no one heard. At this speed, great sprays of water were washing up and over the bridge, and it was all he could do to not get washed overboard.

A huge spout of water shot up in the air directly to port of the bridge, and the spray drenched the bridge party. "Looks like they've about found their range!" Stahlei shouted against the wind.

Another shot from the destroyer hit the water, but to their starboard side. The Japanese were bracketing the sub to increase their chance of a hit.

"We have a firing solution!" Nate heard the tension in Akers's voice.

"On my command," Stahlei responded instantly. "Fire all tubes, minimum spread! Fire at your convenience, Mr. Akers."

"Fire one! Fire two! Fire at will!"

Stahlei must have heard the tone in Akers's voice as well. "You need to lighten up, John. We're either about to kill a destroyer or meet our Maker. One or the other." Before Akers could reply, the captain added, "Of course, we can hedge our bet!" Then he shouted, "Dive! Dive! Dive!"

Thirty-five seconds later, the hatch swung closed as Nate hit the bottom of the ladder, a great torrent of water cascading down on him as he did.

"Sorry you don't get to see the destroyer go up. But just in case, I thought we ought to try to get out of the way."

There was a deafening crash on the conning tower above them.

"Looks like one of their shells found us. Let's hope they didn't tear a hole in the hull to drown us. "

"Let's hope we get down fast enough that we don't get rammed," Akers said quietly.

"Thirty seconds to impact! Fish are running true!"

Nate forced himself to breathe. It was easy to forget.

Chapter Twenty

THE FOXHOLE CIRCUIT

"What's going on with you?"

Dan looked up from the *Deseret Evening News* he'd been pretending to read. "Nothing."

"Uh-uh. You've been very secretive lately, and I want to know why." At that point it was pointless to resist. Sarah would never give up.

"Honest. I haven't done anything . . . yet." He gulped, then tried to act casual. "I've been talking to some folks in New York at Camp Shows. Today I got a call from Abe Lastfogel, the chairman of the board of the William Morris Agency."

"You get a call from the chairman of the country's largest advertising agency, and yet nothing's going on? I assume you'll tell me when something noteworthy does happen."

Dan was sheepish, because he should have talked to Sarah earlier. "I didn't want to create a stir until I knew if there was anything to even think about. Now it looks like there might be."

"Oh, Dan, why do you always wait so long to tell me things? Are you afraid I'm going to throw cold water on your plans?" This was an old discussion and probably the biggest sore point between them. Dan always thought he had tendencies toward secretiveness because of the way his mother used to try to keep things from his father. On so many occasions, she'd call him aside and whisper things to him, so that his father wouldn't overhear and get angry. When his dad did find out, it was always worse because he felt betrayed. It was a foolish pattern, but it was the way they communicated as a family. Now Dan periodically lapsed into the habit, even though there was no reason to be afraid of Sarah.

"I'm sorry. I really am." He tried to take her hand, but she pulled back. He inhaled slowly. "Let me tell you what I've been thinking about, Sarah. Camp Shows is a division of the United Service Organization, the USO that Cory talked about when he was here on leave. They're signing up tens of thousands of entertainers to go to military bases all around the world to entertain the troops. The types of shows range from bands performing in the USO clubs like the one at Wendover Air Base near here to huge outdoor events in Europe and Hawaii."

"So you're thinking that maybe you and the band ought to sign up?"

"I'm thinking about it. The really big shows are part of a tour called the Victory Circuit, which brings full-scale Broadway-level productions to large installations. Smaller groups are going out on what's called the Foxhole Circuit. That's what I was talking to them about the past few days. They think our band would be well suited to go on tour of bases here in the States."

"But why did this man from William Morris call?"

"Oh, he's the president of Camp Shows, a volunteer, and he occasionally likes to do some recruiting directly. I think he picked our name by random. He's really very passionate about what they're doing."

"So why didn't you tell me? I think it's a wonderful idea."

"Honest, honey, I wasn't cutting you out of the decision. I just wanted to study it all out before I involved other people."

Sarah decided not to press the point. She really was interested in this, and she knew that Dan was miserable right now. "Do they pay people to perform?"

"That's part of the problem. Most of it's volunteer, although they cover all the costs of moving people around, feeding, and housing them. I'd have to figure out how to make ends meet if we decided to do this."

"I can earn enough to keep things together. With the kids gone, I don't have anything better to do with my time."

"Well, that's one of the reasons I was holding off. I had to check on something, and I got a positive answer today. The truth is that I'd like you to come along as our business manager. I don't want to be gone from home without you."

She looked at him to see if he was just saying that to appease her, but she could tell that he was sincere. "Oh, Dan, why do you make it so hard for me to stay upset with you?"

His relief was immediate. "I didn't want you to be upset in the first place. I was thinking this would be a great chance for us to get out and see some of the world while helping out the war effort. It's driving me crazy to be stuck here where everything is peaceful and normal while millions of kids are out there risking their lives. I really want to do something to help."

"I thought you didn't like war."

"I don't like war. But I do like soldiers." His face darkened a bit. "Besides, this is a war worth fighting. The last one was a gigantic waste. But this time there are some really bad characters. Hitler and Mussolini are about as bad as people get, and now the Japanese and what they're doing in China." He sighed. "This one is different, and I don't mind doing what I can to help. I want to."

"I'd love to go with you, but what do I know about business management?"

He shook his head again. "Come on, dear. Who's better than you at keeping the books? You've been helping me with the band for years. Besides," he dropped his voice a bit, "I was also thinking it would be a good idea to have a nurse along."

Sarah's face fell, because she knew what that meant.

Dan saw her expression and regretted having said it that way. "It's not just me—with that many people, there are bound to be cuts and colds and such. I'll be okay. In fact it would probably be good for me to get to some humid places."

"Well, if I go, how can we afford it? We still have bills to pay, even if we're not here."

"I was going to talk to Mr. Morton tomorrow. I'm thinking the railroad might sponsor us. Lots of corporations are contributing to the USO effort, and I think we could maybe work their sponsorship into the tour somehow. Anyway, that's what I'm thinking."

Sarah smiled. "Dan, I think this is a very good idea. I hope you can work it out. And I'd love to go with you if there's enough money. What could be better than traveling together?"

He pulled her into his lap and gave her a big kiss. He loved the feeling of his arm around her waist and, once she'd settled in, pulled her head to his shoulder. She melted in and reached up her left hand to stroke his face. "We make a pretty good team, Mr. O'Brian."

"We make the best team. I love you, Sarah."

"That's what you always say."

"And I always mean it." They sat quietly for a few moments. "And as much as I meant it the last time, I mean it even more now. It's like my ability to love you just grows and grows."

"You artists are such romantics!" She gave him a devilish smile.

And so they flirted with each other as the sky darkened in the living room window.

* * *

The decision to support Dan financially had to go to the highest levels of railroad management. At first the answer was no, but somewhere along the line, one of the officers had the common sense to realize that with the economy mobilized for war, business had never been better for the Union Pacific. The thought that one of their own employees was a bandleader of some renown was seen as an excellent public relations opportunity. So the UP decided to become a sponsor. That relieved the financial worry and also gave Dan the ability to entice more than half the members of the existing band to go on the road with him. Some of the remaining band members couldn't get out of work, didn't want to go into potential battle zones, or couldn't go for other legitimate reasons. Instead, the guys who didn't sign up for the tour brought in some new players to keep doing their weekly gig, although KSL decided to drop the show for the present time. Meanwhile, Dan advertised for the appropriate sidemen and soon had the Ordinaires up to full strength.

Once the decision was made, things happened quickly. In less than six months from their initial conversation, they found themselves on their way to San Jose, California, to perform at a series of engagements at the USO club. Their reputation preceded them, and a lot of the local girls who acted as hostesses quickly spread the word that they were in town. By the second night, the house was full, and after that it was packed.

A typical USO show consisted of a comedian, singers, a couple of variety acts, and a lot of dancing. The one thing Dan learned pretty quickly was to play mostly upbeat music—this was no time for the blues. With large naval installations in San Francisco, marine training farther south, and army units getting ready to deploy, most of the young men who wandered into the club would be facing war in the very near future, and the last thing they needed was gloomy music. So even though he personally loved the rich melodies of the blues, he kept the program light and cheerful.

On their third Sunday in the area, he took Sarah out for a drive down the peninsula. As they headed south near the Palo Alto foothills, Dan grew thoughtful.

"A penny for your thoughts?" Sarah prodded.

He didn't answer.

"You've grown kind of quiet, Mr. O'Brian!"

He turned and smiled. "Sorry. It turns out there are some memories associated with this place."

"Happy memories?"

"Poignant, I'm afraid. This is the place where I first performed in public."

It suddenly struck Sarah that Trevor Richards had gone to Stanford. "Was it a good experience?"

"It was a great experience. They had an open microphone night, and some of Trevor's friends forced me on the stage. I was pretty weak on my first song, but the crowd was polite. Then I started to warm up, and before long, they couldn't pull me off the stage." He had a look of longing.

"Did they want to pull you off?"

He laughed. "No, they liked me. In fact, one of the local professors ended up offering me a scholarship. But the war came along and that didn't work out."

"I didn't know about that. Why didn't you try to renew it after the war?"

"I did, actually, but the professor who had made the offer had moved on, and the new dean wasn't interested. The reason the first one, Dr. Bramson, wanted me was because I could play both classical and contemporary." He was thoughtful again. "That's funny. I haven't thought of his name for years . . ."

Sarah waited quietly.

Dan inhaled and exhaled slowly, then forced the air through narrowed lips. "Trevor was so excited. Not to be here—he never really wanted to leave Pocatello—but to be so close to getting his engineering degree. He'd found some buddies who were talking about starting an aircraft company. He had some very wealthy friends. But then that didn't work out."

"I'm glad you got to see him down here. It sounds like it was a good time."

"It really was. We were grown and away from home." He turned and looked at Sarah. "Until you came along, Trevor was my very best supporter. He wanted me to succeed almost more than I did. He told me that I'd be a famous musician someday. I wanted to believe him."

"And now you are. And you're back here playing for some very important people. He must have been a very bright young man to spot your potential."

"He was just a great friend. You know how good Jonathon is. That's Trevor, only he was more brash and outgoing than his father."

"That's hard to believe. Jonathon is about as extroverted a person as I know."

She waited for a reply, but the moment had passed. Dan's breathing had slowed. Sarah knew that he'd move this experience back into the shell where he kept things. It was how he protected himself.

"Well, that was an interesting trip down memory lane. But now I'm here with you, and that's the best reward of all. What do you think about this USO business—is it going to be worthwhile?"

"I think it's going to be one of the most meaningful things we've ever done in our lives." Suddenly, Sarah grew serious. "You listen to me, Dan. I sometimes think you're disappointed with the way things have turned out, even that you haven't given me more things, but I want you to know that's total hogwash. I have a rich and wonderful life with you. There aren't a lot of women who get to share their life with a person who can make so many people happy. And you make me happy."

"Now you're the one getting sentimental."

"Just for a minute. No blues today—at least not for me."

Dan smiled and turned the car toward the coast. It was good to remember.

* * *

Over the course of the next twelve months, the band performed on nearly seventy stages across the country. From small clubs in Alabama to an outdoor concert in New York City where more than twenty thousand attended, they brought their talent and music to lonely young men who were facing the biggest challenge of their lives. Even though they knew they wouldn't see them, both Dan and Sarah always looked into the crowd as if expecting to see Cory or Nate.

"In a way, I guess we do see them," she said one night as they were coiling up their microphone cables.

"How so?"

"Behind every one of the faces that were looking at us tonight stands a mother and father who love those boys as much as we love ours."

"I know. It's why this is such a unique experience." The job finished, they walked easily through the cool night air back to the inexpensive hotel the USO had arranged for them.

Chapter Twenty-One

OF ISLANDS AND
AIRCRAFT CARRIERS

As Cory settled into his seat in the pilot's ready room he couldn't help but feel the electricity in the early morning air. It was November 1943, and rumors were rampant that the *Enterprise* was about to go into battle after nearly a year and a half without any major fleet action. All anyone knew for sure was that they were near a group of islands called the Gilbert Islands. The carrier had slowed considerably, and the destroyers were darting about like nervous watchdogs as they scouted for enemy submarines. Cory had to force himself to relax his stomach muscles. After their attack on the enemy submarine, all remaining patrols had been routine, with nothing sighted. If they were to go to battle stations today, it would be the first time he'd face hostile fire, and the prospect of it was a bit unnerving. And exciting.

He jumped to attention with the other pilots when the briefing officer entered the room. "At ease, gentlemen!" The pilots took their seats as a large map of the western Pacific was pulled down. Using a large pointer, the briefing officer pointed to a small island in the Gilbert Archipelago and said, "Makin Island—this is your target for the mission. The Japanese have a landing field there that is used by ground-based aircraft to provide cover for their troop convoys and supply ships, as well as protecting their fleet should it happen to be in the area, although we don't expect any fleet action in this operation. We have reason to believe we'll achieve the element of surprise in your attack on the islands. Naturally, the fighters will go out to provide protection for the bombers and to engage the enemy defenses, while the dive-bombers first site in on the landing fields then do strafing runs across the beaches to harass the Japanese defenders. Our estimates tell us they have hundreds of aircraft available, so it's likely to get pretty hot. Your flight commanders will give you your specific departure times as well as your individual attack patterns. Any questions?"

A pilot at the back of the room raised his hand. When acknowledged, he said, "If we get shot down, what are the plans for rescue?"

"We have two systems in place. First, we'll give you the direct radio call signals for a number of U.S. submarines that are in the area for life-guarding duty. You can direct a distress signal directly to them before ejecting or crash landing to let them know your location. Do your best to inflate your dinghy, then use your paddle to stay out from the island as far as possible. You want to avoid hostile shore fire that could reach you or put the sub in peril. Besides, the submarine will wait to surface until the last possible moment to reduce their exposure to both shore and aircraft based attack, so they want you in as deep of water as possible. The backup to this system is that we'll have some PBYs on station as spotter planes, in case you lose your radio and can't send your position. They'll do their best to keep track of the battle and request help in your behalf."

"Radio contact with the ship?"

"You'll be flying on the YE. With this many hostile aircraft in the area, it's more important than ever that we maintain radio silence. If your drill brings you back at night, follow stan-dard night routines to find the ship and land." He paused. "No more questions? Good luck then, and good hunting!"

Next up was the weather officer, who reported good flying conditions for the next three days. Visibility would be high and turbulence at a minimum. The only potential problem was that winds were low, so the catapult could be required for at least some of the flight groups. When that was finished, the group was dismissed, with follow-up meetings scheduled with individual flight leaders after they had a chance to review their specific orders.

Jack slapped Cory on the back. "Well, guess it's time to keep your bottoms out of the water. I'll keep a special eye out for you, O'Brian, since I assume that shiny kid face of yours will attract more than your fair share of Japanese fighters."

Cory shook his head. "I'll feel a lot better knowing you're on the case, Jack. You do your best to knock 'em out of the air, and we'll do our best to destroy them on the ground."

"Sounds fair." Then in an unusual twist, Jack stepped in close and got a serious tone to his voice. "Listen, Cory—you're going to do great up there. I've watched you, and you do an excellent job handling your aircraft. I know you haven't been in battle yet, but it does get pretty hectic up there. I really will be watching out, so you just go in and do your mission, then get the heck out of there."

Somehow, this little pep talk from Jack took Cory so much by surprise that he almost got sentimental. "Thanks, Jack. You're a good friend. I'll buy you a Coke when we get back tonight."

Jack smiled, saluted, and then turned to join his squadron.

Thirty minutes later, Cory and Spence returned to the ready room with the other bomber teams to get their individual briefing from Commander Mercer, who sat on the edge of the conference table in a relaxed fashion as he started the briefing. "Because we expect so many aircraft in the area, both friendly and hostile, we're going to fly in the nonstandard four-aircraft formations, rather than six. You're free to communicate by air-to-air radio within your groups. Once we reach the target area, our assignment is to take out the support facilities at the airstrip—hangars and repair facilities, housing units, so forth."

One of the pilots raised his hand. "Can we save their officers' club, sir? Just in case we inherit some of their beverages after we kick their sorry little carcasses off the island."

That broke the tension, and everybody laughed, including the commander.

"If you can figure out which building is which, Barnes, then you can try to save the booze. For the rest of you, who are actually here to fight a war, I suggest that your first priority is any aircraft that might be on the ground. If we achieve the surprise we're hoping for, most will be on the ground. They are your highest impact target, since every plane destroyed is one less to shoot us down or sink our ships. Any questions?" Then, with a glance at Barnes, "Any serious questions?" There were none. "Alright then, I suggest the gunners go topside and check the loading of your ammunition. Takeoff is in thirty minutes. Good luck, men. Today you get to write a piece of history."

As Cory and Spence hustled back to their lockers to get their flight gear, Spence turned to Cory and said very quietly, "Hey, I want to show you something." Reaching inside his shirt pocket, he pulled out an envelope. "This is a letter from my parents. It has their mailing address on it and everything. Just in case something happens to me, will you write to them? I want them to get something more than just a war department telegram."

Cory started to protest, because this was a clear violation of the unspoken pilot's superstition to never talk about someone not making it back, but Spence shushed him. "I don't think anything bad is going to happen. We're a great team. But this is just in case. Do you promise?"

Cory promised. Once again, his stomach did one of those uncomfortable flips that he'd experienced throughout the morning. At one moment, he felt confident and excited, the next scared and anxious. Having Spence talk like this made him anxious—like it was a bad omen. *I should do the same thing*. But there wasn't time before this flight, so he simply resolved he'd have to make it back alive.

Thirty minutes later, Cory taxied into position to be hooked up to the catapult. "All clear back there?" Spencer answered in the affirmative. Cory gave the thumbs-up to the cat officer, who indicated he should increase to full throttle. The aircraft trembled as he pushed the controls all the way forward. The roar of the engine straining against that little brass ring holding it into place was almost deafening, and when the engine achieved maximum rpms it felt like the aircraft was going to tear itself apart. Then in that heart-stopping moment when the deck crew released the ring and engaged the catapult, they shot off the deck and up into the air using less than half the space available. Cory quickly rolled to the right and pulled into the Tail-End Charlie position of the formation.

The tail-end position had both its advantages and disadvantages. The advantage was that Cory could essentially follow the leader throughout the flight, which took a little less concentration on the navigation. But he was also the most exposed aircraft in the formation, since enemy fighters could come from a number of different angles where the left and right wing aircraft couldn't provide effective cover. Spencer was really the key person in this formation, since he was the first line of defense against aircraft coming up from behind. The fighters were faster and more agile than the Dauntless. The Japanese Zero in particular was the most effective fighter aircraft in any theater of war. The American fighters were heavier and more powerful, but not as fast and as maneuverable. At any rate, Spencer could rotate a full 180 degrees in his firing harness, so his job was to force the Zero off course.

They had about a forty-five-minute flight to reach the island, and since they were to be the third wave of bombers in, Cory had to concentrate to keep his position. The various fighter aircraft flying their tight formations on the perimeter of the attack group made an impressive display of airpower. Finally, as they approached the target, Cory saw the first wave of fighters separate from the group as they started to engage the few enemy fighters that had happened to be in the air. It was an amazing sight as the various aircraft twisted and turned, gaining and surrendering altitude as they worked for a firing position on the enemy aircraft. Fortunately, the Americans had the Japanese badly outnumbered, so the initial engagement favored them.

The radio crackled. "Move into attack position!"

"Acknowledged." Cory broke out of the traditional formation and moved to the left of the left wing aircraft. They would go in as pairs, rather than four, and Cory's job was to lay his four bombs directly to the left of his leader. They dropped to 9,000 feet, the preferred altitude for land-based bombing, and made an approach on the target at a 25-degree angle, rather than the sharper angle used when attacking a ship.

"Okay, O'Brian, start your countdown to the dive."

"Acknowledged!"

Cory realized that he could almost do the countdown by counting his heartbeat and dividing by four.

The sudden firing of Spencer's gun startled him so badly that he let out an involuntary yelp.

"We've got one on our tail!" Spencer yelled. Cory could feel the effect of Spencer moving in his swivel as he shot quick bursts at the Japanese pilot.

"Starting the dive now!" he shouted into the interphones, and then he pushed forward on the steering column while simultaneously engaging the dive brakes.

"It's pretty hot back here!"

Cory looked in horror as he saw a trail of bullet holes appear in the left wing. "Gotta hold it—I need twenty seconds!"

He dropped the landing gear to slow the approach even further. Speaking to himself to confirm each step in the sequence, he repeated, "Arming switch, on. Steady at twenty-five degrees. Line up with the left side of the runway. Good heavens, look at all those Japanese fighters on the runway!"

"We've got two of them on us now!" Spencer shouted. Cory felt like he wanted to throw up, he'd never been so frightened in his life. There was no place for his adrenaline to go—he had to hold steady to get a good release, and that was absolutely counterintuitive to everything his body told him. More than anything in the world, he wanted to break out of the dive and try to get away. But he didn't. He held steady. He saw his leader release his bombs, then about three seconds later at precisely 2,000 feet, he pressed the bomb release switch and immediately started to pull out. The weight of the four bombs releasing gave an immediate jump to the aircraft.

At this point, he was pulling up so steeply that he lost visual contact with the runway he'd just attacked, but he heard Spencer let out a whistle. "Wow—it looks like all eight bombs hit. There's mayhem on the runway! We must have killed at least a couple of their fighters, maybe more!"

Cory felt a searing pain in his right side—like someone had cut him with a sharp knife. Looking down, he saw that his flight suit was torn. "I just got shot!" He'd never been so indignant in his life. He couldn't believe it.

"Are you okay?" Spencer shouted frantically.

"What?" Cory hadn't even thought about that.

"Are you okay? Do I need to fly the plane?"

Cory's senses returned, and he quickly pulled at the fabric. He could see a hash mark across his side, but there was hardly any blood, so he concluded he'd just been grazed.

"I'm okay."

"Good—you might try to get us out of here! Those two Zeros are angry now!"

Cory looked to the right and saw a Japanese Zero pass by them. He initiated standard avoidance techniques and tried to line up on the Japanese as he crossed their path, firing off a few bursts from his forward cannons. The motion was too fast for it to do any good, but the goal was to keep the enemy pilot from getting a stable firing position.

"I don't know if I can hold them off!" Cory could hear the edge of panic in Spencer's voice.

Then things happened very quickly. To the left, Cory caught sight of something in his peripheral vision, and when he turned to look, he saw a Japanese Zero heading straight for them. He saw the flashes of the enemy's machine guns as he opened fire. Cory pushed the stick down, but knew it was too late to miss the bullets. For just a moment, he heard the odd *thud* sound of bullets slamming into the airplane. The next thing he saw— kind of saw, it was too fast to fully comprehend—was an American fighter diving straight down on the Zero, his guns flashing. It was so close, and so fast, that Cory had to think about it after the fact to realize what happened. Even that was complicated by the fact that the Japanese plane burst into flames and started losing altitude on a trajectory that would have brought them into a direct collision course with Cory. Acting purely on instinct, he pulled back on the stick, pulling the aircraft into a steep ascent. He heard the sound of the Japanese aircraft breaking up as it passed just a few feet under them. He was sure that the flames would leave scorch marks on their undercarriage. And then he realized that in all the commotion, he'd actually seen Jack Wilson smiling from the cockpit of the Hellcat fighter. He tried to comprehend it while bringing the airplane back under control, but his head hurt too much.

"That was nice, Cory, but we've got another one. He's coming up from behind!"

"How are you doing on ammo?"

"I'm about Winchester!"

"Here's what I'm going to do. On three, I'm going to pull back on the throttle and engage the air brakes. We're going to drop airspeed like a brick falling to the ground. That should close the range, and then you let him have it!"

"On three!"

Cory pulled back on the throttle, pulled the flap lever, and lurched forward as the aircraft lost speed. They didn't immediately lose altitude, because there was too much momentum, but they did lose airspeed, and they lost it fast. A couple seconds later, Cory heard the machine gun fire for perhaps three seconds, then stop. *He's out! He's out of ammunition! We're sitting ducks now!*

"I got him, Cory! I got him!"

Instinctively, Cory looked to his right and saw the enemy aircraft at the extreme edge of his vision. Cranking even harder in his seat, he saw the smoke flying back from the engine past the cockpit. He also saw the pilot's face—and it shook him to the core. On it was a look of pure hatred. It was a look like nothing he had ever seen on another human being. There was no anguish, no fear, not even a sense of loss or sorrow. Just pure hatred. And then he was gone.

"We did it, Cory! We did it! There's no one following! We're in the clear!"

"You did it, you hotshot gunner! You saved our sorry skins! I owe you big!"

"Yes, you do. And the way you can pay me back is to get this thing back to the *Enterprise* in one piece."

"I can do that," Cory said with a laugh. He turned the aircraft in the direction of the ship, tuned in the YE, and started listening to the constantly repeating signal for the appropriate direction. As he did, all the anxiety drained away, and he suddenly felt tired to the marrow of his bones. It felt like his limbs were made of lead. The one-hour flight back to the ship felt like the longest of his life. He and Spencer hardly said anything to each other. It had been exhilarating, terrifying, and ultimately exhausting. His heart leaped when the *Enterprise* came into sight, just where he predicted it would be, and he was thrilled to see the giant red flag welcoming them home. He moved into position, circled to port, then made the easy sweep into the landing pattern. The signal officer gave him the signal to cut, and the now battle-christened Dauntless dropped to the deck like a shot goose. They caught the third arrester cable and careened to a stop. He sat in the seat without moving until the deck crew knocked on the cockpit cover to hurry him along. It felt great. *We did it! We survived our first battle, got a kill in the air and on the ground!* It was the most exciting adventure of his life.

* * *

As the sun settled low on the Pacific horizon, the wash of golden colors mixed in the sky and the water to give black relief to the exotic island silhouetted against the western horizon. It was a stunning sight, the kind that one dreamed of before the war. Who hadn't thought of escaping to the serenity of a tropical island? Yet now the island was filled with danger. Now that Cory and Spencer were back on the ship, the battle seemed almost unreal, as if it couldn't possibly have occurred in such a tranquil setting—except for the rash where Cory had been scraped by the bullet on his right side, a slight wound that had been painfully disinfected with iodine and wouldn't even leave a scar. There would be no physical evidence to remind them that they'd actually been at war that day.

Cory and Spencer walked out to the elevator opening in the hangar deck where they could watch the sun sink deeper into the cobalt-blue waters of the becalmed ocean.

"You did a nice job today, Spence. Your shooting saved our lives."

"And your bombing did its part to neutralize that field, at least for a few critical days. I don't know how many planes we got, but I know we got some. Who knows? Maybe the one that would have hit our ship if we hadn't taken it out."

They stood in silence as the sun quickly disappeared from view. It was always surprising how quickly it sank into the waves and how dark the world grew in just a matter of moments.

"Were you scared?"

"Scared?" Spencer replied. "Yeah. A lot. Even though we've practiced it dozens of times, it was unnerving to be stuck looking up at the sky as we went in the dive. I was sure you'd waited too long to release and that we were going to crash."

"It was scary up where I was too. But at least I had control of things. I don't think I could stand it back there—you've got to have a lot of faith."

Spencer smiled at him. "It's not so hard. I think you're a great pilot. I'll fly with you again."

"Thanks." Cory was silent for a few moments. Then very quietly, "We killed people today . . ." His words hung in the air.

"I know. We had to."

"But I don't know how to feel about it."

As Spence turned to look at Cory he could see that there was moisture in his eyes. "It's what this is all about, Cory. It's why we're here."

"But killing people—I never wanted to be a killer. Even when we were talking about all the Japanese we were going to get back in basic training, it was more like a game. But today it was real." He turned to face Spence directly. "I could see the pilot's face when he went down. He knew he was going to die, and he hated us for it!"

Spencer took a few moments to compose his thoughts. "Cory, if you saw a criminal threatening to kill a person, would you help them?"

"Of course."

"Well, that's what we did today. We acted in behalf of the millions of innocent Chinese and other Asians that the Japanese government has murdered, has allowed their troops to rape and torture. Millions, Cory, millions! We have to do this."

"I suppose you're right. But it still hurts."

"Which is why you're not one of them."

Cory looked silently out at the scene. "Thanks. I needed to talk it through." He looked up at Spence. "I'll be okay."

* * *

An experience like their first battle was something to last a lifetime. Unfortunately, fate had a lot more in store for them than that, and they returned to the skies the very next day to do it all over again. This time, the targets were shipping vessels in the small harbor that had been determined to be Japanese supply ships in disguise. There was no element of surprise this time, however, and the moment they arrived at the scene the Japanese started throwing up a barrage of antiaircraft artillery in an attempt to shoot them down—or at least to discourage them from holding firm on their target.

On this particular occasion, Cory and Spencer were given the honor of flying the lead position, in part because of their success the previous day. More importantly, it was always important to have a reserve of potential leaders who could step forward and take command of an operation if their more battle-tested commanders were killed or wounded. And since this was a relatively low-risk target, it made sense to provide some experience to one of the new guys.

At the appropriate moment, Cory radioed the specifics of the plan of attack, including dive angle and sequencing. He said this in a calm, metallic sort of voice that made it sound like he'd done it a hundred times before. In a way, he had, because he'd practiced at least two or three hundred times on his way out from the carrier. When he reached the initial point of contact, he rolled into a dive, shoved the lever to open the air brakes, and started effortlessly into the high-speed dive. Today the angle of attack was much steeper than the day before, since the bomb had to go straight into the center of the ship where it would penetrate the deck and explode inside the bowels of the ship—hopefully near the fuel tanks or boilers. At 5,000 feet, the small, mostly defenseless ship was directly in his Norden bombsight, and he saw with satisfaction that most of the crew were jumping or diving overboard. The sound of a diving bomber was pretty awesome—something like a shriek in the sky—and their approach had obviously inspired the kind of fear that they wanted it to.

Then, just as Cory was about to release the bomb, he saw one defiant sailor manning a lone machine gun on the deck, firing in their direction. He couldn't concern himself with that at the moment, but even in the fraction of an instant that he had to devote to it, he admired the Japanese sailor who was doing his job to the bitter end. Pulling the bomb release lever, Cory immediately pulled up into the climb and felt the pressure on his head and chest as the blood started to drain.

There were very few fighters in the area that day, probably because most of them were in the process of attempting an attack on the *Enterprise* and her escorts at that very moment, so Cory actually had time to roll the aircraft into position to witness the effect of their bombs. He saw the first explosion, forward of the superstructure, but still within the kill zone. That was his. Then he saw the second bomb hit the ship squarely midships. The combined explosions sent a dark and angry cloud of smoke billowing up into the air, and the flash of the explosion temporarily blinded him, even in the broad daylight. He circled just long enough to watch the ship seemingly break in half. There was no question of its complete and total destruction, and he let out a little war whoop that was echoed from the backseat by Spence and also over the radio by his wingman. "Good work!" he radioed back joyously. Two days in battle and at least three kills. This was going far better than he could have ever hoped for.

Their jubilant mood was jolted a bit as they approached their ship, however, and saw a furious air battle taking place between the *Enterprise's* fighters and the ground-based planes of the enemy. In spite of the damage they'd inflicted the previous day, the Japanese were clearly still in the game, and there were some small fires burning on the wooden landing deck of the Big E that were quickly put out. There was also no red flag out, which meant they had to enter a holding pattern until it was safe for the ship to turn into the wind to receive them.

"Hope this doesn't take too long, or we're going to have to take an unexpected swimming lesson," he called back to Spence.

"Let's not. I'd just as soon stay dry."

Fortunately, the Japanese had the same fuel situation as the bombers, having flown the same distance to get out to the ship as they had to get to the island, so the battle broke up fairly quickly, giving the ship time to make the change into the wind. Cory was relieved to see the red flag run up the halyards, and he moved into the number-eight spot in the landing pattern where everything proceeded without incident. Once safely on the deck, he tapped the fuel gauge, but it wouldn't budge off of empty.

There were no philosophical discussions this night. Cory and the other new pilots were feeling pretty good about themselves, and the atmosphere in the officer's mess was downright enjoyable. But when their heads started to droop from fatigue, someone called it a day, and then everyone drifted off to their cots to sleep. As Cory settled into his miniature bunk, he had a sense of peace come over him that he'd faced the test of battle and had proven equal to the challenge.

Chapter Twenty-Two

TOKYO BAY

"All hands brace for impact. Prepare to abandon ship on my order!"

The hope was, of course, that there would be no collision with the Japanese destroyer that was still firing on them, and hence no need to either brace or abandon. Nate found it hard to believe that the tension in the control room could be any higher than it was during their dive toward the bottom, but it was. As a second precaution, Stahlei had cleared everyone but himself and the helmsman out of the conning tower so he could quickly seal it off just in case a collision with the tower needed to be isolated from the rest of the ship. It was hopeful at best, since the force of the superstructure being torn apart would undoubtedly breach the hull anyway, but from Nate's point of view, it felt better to be with the rest of the crew, rather than isolated up in the attack center.

At this point in their encounter, the captains of both vessels were in something of an impossible position. Recognizing the approach of the *Tripletail's* torpedoes would normally call for evasive action on the part of the destroyer, just as normal protocol on a dive would be to turn the ship hard to port to get out of the way. But as close as they were to each other, either of these maneuvers would simply increase their profile to their foe. In the case of the Japanese destroyer, their only hope of survival was that the natural spread of the torpedoes would be wide enough that they'd all miss the sharp profile of the bow of the ship. Any evasive action would almost guarantee a hit as the broadside of the ship exposed itself in the turn. As for the *Tripletail,* there were only two possible positive outcomes: their torpedoes would blow a hole in the front of the destroyer that would halt its forward momentum before it reached the *Tripletail,* or they could dive sharp enough to miss a collision if the torpedoes failed. The angle on the deck was proof that Lieutenant Conrad was doing his best to assure the second positive outcome.

Time seemed to have come to a stop. Nate felt a hand touch his right hand, which caused him to turn in alarm.

"Just thought you might not want to squeeze that valve handle any harder, or the force of your grip will break either the valve or your hand." Akers gave him a wry smile.

Nate shook his head as he relaxed his grip. He was far more worried about his heart seizing up than he was about a broken hand.

"So help me, if those magnetic exploders—" Normally, the gunnery officer would have finished the phrase with, "fail to explode," but the bone-jarring explosion that rattled its way through the boat, filling the air with insulation in the process, quickly made his oath meaningless. Even though they'd been tracking the torpedo, the effect on the ship was so pronounced that their first impression was that they'd been depth charged. But, of course, that was impossible.

"I believe that was number two," their hydrophone operator said. As the weight of his statement sank in, the crew belatedly let out a cheer.

"We got a hit! We got a hit!" one of the men on the planes shouted. It was against protocol, but no one said anything.

Their excitement was short-lived, however, as the sound of the destroyer's screw grew louder. "They're not going down. They're still coming on. How is that possible?" Nate was was startled to his hear his own voice. Turning to the executive officer, "Sorry, sir."

"No, actually it's a good question."

It became obvious that time simply wasn't adequate to handle everything that could happen in a matter of moments. At least the human brain couldn't sort it all out without having to think about it later. In what seemed a simultaneous series of events, the sound of the enemy's propeller changed dramatically, indicating that something serious had happened to their ship. Another change was the sound of metal tearing itself apart, accompanied by the sound of rushing water. The third was the realization that the torpedo must have so thoroughly shredded the bow of the ship that the force of water flooding into the front was actually driving the Japanese destroyer down into the water at flank speed, sending it on a new interception course with the *Tripletail*—underwater!

Fortunately, Captain Stahlei processed it all faster than anyone else in the crew, because he barked a sharp, "Hard starboard! All ahead full!" The plane operators acted in concert with the helm to initiate a dramatic banking turn to the right on a new course that was designed to get them out of the path of the rapidly sinking destroyer. It was fast—fast enough to save the ship—but not fast enough to avoid a shearing glance across the conning tower that threw everyone to the floor. As they gained distance from the point of impact, and as the Japanese vessel inevitably slowed as it stalled in the water, Stahlei ordered, "All stop!" and the diving officer quickly brought them to neutral buoyancy, some 50 feet below the surface.

The captain called the deck party back to the attack center. "That was a little close," Stahlei said quietly. "We might try to time that a little better next time."

"There's going to be a next time?" Nate blurted out.

Even Captain Stahlei laughed. "Let's hope not. Damage control, report." The reports came into the control room, and, remarkably, there seemed to be little additional damage in any of the stations that reported. "Maintaining pressure in the hull, Captain!" was the most important report of all.

That left the question as to what had happened to the conning tower communication array. The only way to find that out would be to surface. But they were still too close to the Japanese ship for comfort. The sounds from the water made it pretty clear it was breaking up, but there was always the possibility the ship had friends in the area. "We'll proceed at half-speed for ten minutes to get some distance and to see if there are any other contacts. Then we'll surface and see what we've got. Notify me when we surface. Meanwhile, I'm going to take a tour of the boat." As the captain started to walk away, he paused for a moment and turned back to Lieutenant Akers. "Nice shooting, John."

"Thank you, sir!" The look on his face was priceless, and Nate felt an overwhelming sense of gratitude that the captain, in the middle of everything he had to worry about, would take time to acknowledge John's efforts. The executive officer acknowledged the captain's instructions, then gave the appropriate orders.

"I think that's only about ten times I thought I was going to die today," Akers whispered to Nate.

"If having your heart stop counts as dying, I think I did die a couple of times."

"What exactly happened back there?"

"The sound of the propeller?"

"Yes. It was coming on like gangbusters, and then suddenly nothing. How could it change like that?"

The chief of the boat answered. "His screw came up and out of the water. The captain blew a hole right in the chops, which allowed water to flood into the bow. With their attack speed, they must have taken on a couple of thousand tons in the first twenty or thirty seconds. The weight of the water eventually pulled the bow down, which physically lifted the stern of the ship up and out of the water." He illustrated with his fingers to mimic the action of a teeter-totter.

"I didn't know it could happen like that," Nate said. "You'd think the weight of a ship would break it in half before it could actually support the tail end out of the water."

"It couldn't hold together like that very long. But it was long enough to save our sorry hides."

"Only one of our fish hit."

"Oh, I'm not sure of that," the gunnery officer said in disgust. "We probably had two or three come close enough, but those infernal exploders—"

The executive officer interrupted the tirade with a sharp, "Belay that."

Gunnery stopped, but then added, "At least I think we can give Mr. Akers credit for getting more than one of those fish in the right place."

"And all it took was one," Nate added.

Ten minutes passed quickly, and the order was given to move to periscope depth. After a thorough search of the area, the executive officer gave the order to surface. "We can certainly call this one a confirmed kill. All that's left of that destroyer is a couple of lifeboats and a whole bunch of burning fuel."

Rather than open the hatch to the conning tower, they used the forward deck hatch to complete a visual inspection of the tower first. In keeping with Stahlei's reputation as a "lucky" captain, there were no obvious holes or tears, although there were some nasty gash marks across the port side of the bridge. "Looks like we've dodged the bullet again," Akers said to Nate as they worked their way up through the tower and out onto the bridge.

The captain came up presently and surveyed the scene. "We'll run on the surface for a couple of hours to charge the batteries and to put some distance between us and the rest of the Japanese fleet. Lookouts need to be extra alert for aircraft, since we're within the cruising range of some of their land-based scout planes." Then with a few final orders to the OOD, the captain ordered all other officers to the officers' mess for a meeting.

* * *

Chief of the Boat George Sanders completed his report on the status of the ship.

The captain took a sip of coffee before responding. "So the TDC is permanently disabled, radar is shaky, and you've got a hot bearing in the port shaft? Is that it?"

"Actually, sir, my biggest concern is the bilge pumps. We've lost two of them outright from electrical shorts on our trip down, and the others were heavily strained draining the boat. We don't really have a reliable one in the lot. If we took on much water, I'm afraid we'd have trouble with the batteries."

Stahlei pursed his lips in what was one of the few visible signs that he was unhappy. A second clue that Nate had only recently noticed was that he would tap his pencil on the table in a particular pattern. Together, it was clear that the captain didn't want to hear any of this.

"Well, gentlemen, we still have six fish in our belly and an ocean full of Japanese tankers." He was thoughtful. "Just how bad is the shaft, Mr. Sanders?" In some ways, it was a foolish question, because the racket it was making on each turn of the screw was even now making conversation difficult.

"It's warped, sir. If you put a real strain on it, there's no telling how long it would hold up or what damage it would do to the rest of the equipment."

Stahlei nodded. "Well, then, that's it. We'll make a course for Pearl. Banana splits at the Honolulu USO." Everyone stood as the captain got up from his seat. "I suppose three merchant ships plus a destroyer will ease the embarrassment about the condition of the ship." He smiled as if to acknowledge what was already obvious—this was a successful cruise by any standard. What was left unsaid was just how fortunate they'd been to recover from their trip to 400 feet. As the captain turned to exit, he looked over his shoulder and added, "May I see you in my cabin, Mr. Brown?"

"Yes, sir!" Nate's face darkened. The captain seldom called men into his cabin. Nate shot a glance at John Akers but received a shrugged shoulder in return. A few moments later, he slid into the captain's compartment. In an attempt to add dignity to it, the room was paneled in teak wood shaped to fit the curve of the hull on the outside.

"Nate, I just wanted to tell you that I'm putting you in for a promotion to full lieutenant, along with John Akers."

Nate's face flushed. "Thank you, sir, I . . . I appreciate that."

"You've earned it. You're excellent on the TDC, and I've also noticed how thoroughly you've acquainted yourself with all the other operations of the boat. Particularly the mechanical systems."

"I'm an engineer by education, sir."

"Ah. I recall that now. University of Utah, I think."

Nate was surprised. The captain had thoroughly studied his record. "Yes, sir."

"Well, it shows. Keep at it, and you may get your pin on our next cruise."

"That's what I'm hoping for, sir. At any rate, thank you."

Stahlei looked up from his papers. "Besides, you've got a family to support, and a bit of a raise may help."

"It will help a lot."

Stahlei looked down, which meant that Nate was dismissed. As he walked back toward the control room, he muttered under his breath, "$330 per month—that's a fortune!"

"What was that, sir?" one of the nonrated men asked.

"What? Oh, nothing. Just talking to myself, I'm afraid. But I don't think I've gone over the deep end or anything." He laughed, which prompted the seaman to return the laugh. Passing on down the corridor, he couldn't be faulted for whistling a bit as he pondered his good fortune. And, when he got to Pearl and it was official, he could send a telegram to Kathy telling her about it. Promotions weren't secret. *On that kind of pay, I can send her a telegram every week if I want—and get one in return.* The thought of communicating with Kathy made him even happier, and he whistled his way up to the bridge, where rough water quickly drenched him as the ship plowed into the waves. But it didn't douse his happy spirits. They were on their way to Hawaii, he'd done well on his first cruise, and they'd scored some major kills. Life was pretty good.

* * *

Banana splits were what made the Honolulu USO club famous. The federal government owned all the buildings the clubs were housed in, and Honolulu had an unusually nice venue with a balcony overlooking the street from the second-floor dance hall. The job of running the club fell to the USO nonprofit organization. Each of the clubs did their best to come up with some distinguishing feature, and Honolulu had settled on ice cream—hundreds of gallons of ice cream. Of course, it was a minor diversion for most of the men, who used the club as a stopping point on their way to the bars and taverns, but for Nate and the handful of other nondrinkers, it was the highlight. That and staying at the Royal Hawaiian Hotel. The luxury hotel had formerly been reserved for celebrities and wealthy patrons but had been commandeered by the Navy for the duration of the war. In any other setting, the bright pink Spanish columns and architecture would have been almost comical, but situated on the amazing beach at Waikiki it seemed like a fairy-tale escape for the officers on shore leave who were fortunate enough to be billeted there.

For the first two days of leave, Nate and John had simply sat in the sun and soaked in the heat. It was as if their bodies needed to absorb enough energy to wipe away the effects of hours and hours being drenched on the bridge. Of course, it was warm enough in the ship when they were on silent running, but that was different because there was no fresh air. Here in Hawaii, there was fresh air aplenty, as well as the exotic smells of plumeria, oleander, and coconut.

"I don't know if I ever want to get up again," Nate said peacefully.

"I think we may regret that decision."

Nate turned and looked at John. "What do you mean?"

"When skin looks this pink in the daylight, one can almost be certain it's going to be fire-engine red by night."

"What?" Nate looked down at his legs and stomach. Jumping up, he knocked over the latest pineapple-coconut drink that the staff had been plying him with all afternoon.

Akers laughed. "I don't think the twenty seconds it takes to get up and onto the veranda is going to make much difference now. Slow down, boy."

Nate shook his head. "I've always done this. My mother used to get so angry at me, even as a little boy. 'Come in, Nathan!' she'd shout. But I always begged for a few more minutes. Then when I did come in, I'd be burned to blisters, and she'd have to listen to me cry."

"Oh, be quiet. With your complexion, it's not going to be as bad for you as it is for me. I've got just three colors, you know."

"Three?"

"Yeah, red, white, and peeling."

Nate laughed. "Contrary to popular belief, it doesn't matter what color your skin is, it still gets burned. And I'm burned."

For the balance of their leave, Brown and Akers had to either stay out of the sun or dress in long sleeves and full-length pants. When ordered back to the docks a few days later, it was comical to see them as they moved stiffly about the boat, muttering under their breath whenever something brushed up against them. The captain and executive officer showed no sympathy and may have actually increased their load a bit in punishment for their stupidity.

Nate was glad that he'd followed through on his idea of sending a number of telegrams to Kathy. It was expensive, but getting a reply within twenty-four hours of sending a message made it seem like she was almost there with him. She couldn't say much in the telegrams, but he also had the joy of catching up on a couple months' worth of letters. That's where he discovered that Jon had learned to shove Meg, which was no end of trouble for Kathy but made Nate laugh. Laugh and cry. He'd never been sentimental, but he'd also never had children. It was a new experience, and he found himself amazed at how much he could miss them.

* * *

Nate and the others stood crisply on the deck of the refurbished *Tripletail* just four weeks after pulling in to port. Time at sea sometimes seemed to stand still; here it seemed to simply disappear.

As soon as Stahlei had reviewed the men and formally saluted the base commander and the admiral, he took the envelope that had their new orders just as the last of the dockworkers made their exit off the ship. Casting off, they slipped out of their berth and into the channel that would lead them back into the western Pacific.

* * *

A few hours later, the ship's officers assembled in the wardroom. It was a long-standing tradition extending clear back to the days of sailing ships for the captain of a ship to open his orders only after standing out to sea, well away from the shore where a casual remark or misplaced piece of paper could be picked up and used to provide intelligence to the enemy.

"Well, Captain?"

Stahlei looked up at his executive officer. "Curiosity getting the best of you, Bill?"

He regretted the look of consternation this caused, since he'd intended it as a joke. "An interesting assignment, gentlemen.

You may have noticed the unusual cases being loaded in our forward torpedo room. It looks like we're on our way to lay some mines in Sagaminada!"

The gunnery officer and exec let out a simultaneous, "No kidding? Tokyo!"

"That's what the orders tell me. Sagaminada, the navigable part of Tokyo Bay. There's a particular approach between . . ." he looked down at the paperwork, "a small island in the bay called Oshima and the Izuhanto Peninsula where they think we can nab a few fat ones before the Japanese send out minesweepers."

"I've never laid mines," the gunnery officer said a bit tentatively.

"Nor have I," the captain replied easily. "So we're going to have to do some studying in the next two thousand miles, as well as some practice. I do know that we'll do it at night using the torpedo tubes." He looked around at his officers. "And I know that we'll be doing it in the most heavily patrolled waters of the entire war. Our subs have sunk enough ships on their approach or departure from Tokyo that it's become a black eye for the Japanese naval high command."

Nate felt the muscles in his throat and stomach constrict. Like all the men there, he was thrilled at the thought of taking the battle right into the heart of the enemy's capital. But he also wanted to live to tell about it, which explained the tension that once again seeped back into his sunburned muscles.

With his promotion and the departure of two of the more senior officers for other ships, Nate had moved up the chain of command so that he was now over communications and radar. While everyone associated with the mine-laying operation began figuring out how to make it work, he busied himself learning his new responsibilities and establishing relationships with the noncommissioned officers and seamen who now reported to him.

* * *

Nate was startled when he felt a hand push down on his fingers. He looked up at Akers, who glowered back at him with a finger over his mouth. Nate must have been mentally playing the drums again, banging out the tune on the plotting table with his fingers. But in the totally silent ship, it had apparently bothered other people. He wanted to shout at John, "Sorry, but if you touch my hand like that one more time, I'm likely to strangle you," but having spent the last six hours in silent running, he didn't even dare clear his throat, yet alone yell at John or anyone else. The tension on the ship was unbelievable.

It had taken two full days to sneak into Sagaminada, since Stahlei would only let them maneuver at night, and then with only one diesel running to recharge the batteries and a second to power them when it was absolutely safe to use the diesels. In the current circumstance, the batteries had to be charged each night so the ship could lay still in the water during the day, with only minimal forward propulsion. It was agonizing to play cat-and-mouse through the night with enemy planes now flying even in the dark and patrol ships out relentlessly searching for American ships, but tonight's run was finally going to bring them into position to launch their mines and then hopefully get out of there as fast as their two propellers could take them. Of course, that wouldn't happen, since they'd have to do their sneak routine on the way out as well. Unless they had the good fortune to blow something up right away, in which case they might have to fight their way out.

"All ahead one-third," the captain whispered. After the hours of waiting, it was great to finally hear the captain speak. If you could call it speaking.

"Ahead one-third," the helmsman replied quietly in confirmation.

"Mr. Conrad, are you ready to commence your operation?"

"Yes, sir!" This was spoken a little louder. Once they started shoving mines into the torpedo tubes and launched them with compressed air, the least of their worries would be a conversation in the control room. The success of the mission lay in the chance that they could maneuver and operate in a zone not currently being patrolled.

"Up periscope!"

The main periscope slid up silently, and Stahlei quickly oriented himself to the eyepiece and took a searching glance through a 360-degree arc.

"All clear. Mr. Conrad, on your orders."

No TDC was required for this operation; once again it was up to the plot. It seemed to Nate that Akers had actually drawn the better assignment, so far. Aside from one encounter with an enemy destroyer a few days prior to their approach to the harbor, they hadn't seen a single hostile ship on their entire trip out of Pearl. And even then Stahlei had decided to pass on the chance to engage in battle so as to not alert the Japanese that they were in the area. It was a bit galling for everyone to listen to the destroyer pass overhead, completely unaware of their presence. With Stahlei's shooting skill, there was a high probability they could have killed it before they even knew what hit them. The crew of the destroyer was lucky that day but oblivious to their good fortune.

"Fire one!" The sound of the metal mines ejecting from the torpedo tube sounded like the main assembly floor of an automobile factory in contrast to the almost pure silence of the last three days. It couldn't help but startle everyone, and Nate jumped at the sound, which, to his irritation, amused Akers to no end. His glower only added to John's laughing, and before they knew it, they were both struggling to suppress a bad case of the giggles. It was unseemly, unmilitary, and unstoppable. Of course, it would have been inexcusable to laugh out loud, so they had to use their stomach muscles to stifle the sound, and before long, Nate's sides hurt. Fortunately, it all came to an abrupt end when the captain came sliding past them on his way up from the control room. It was probably impossible for him to have missed the tears on their faces, but he simply scowled, and they sobered up immediately.

"Fire two! Fire three!"

"How do we know if we're successful?" Nate wondered out loud. "There's no explosion."

"If you'd be quiet, the hydrophones can pick up the sound," the chief snarled back at them.

Nate nodded his head in acknowledgement.

It was really kind of intriguing to lay the mines, different than a torpedo attack. The mines would be forced out of the ship and then self-deploy at the correct depth. Then another batch would be sent out. Since it would be impossible to lay down a minefield that could completely block the particular approach they were interested in, the idea was to lay them in a pattern that made it close to impossible for a ship to get through the entire maze without encountering at least one of the mines. The ship might miss a dozen or two, but because of the placement, it would inevitably hit one of them.

The operation took nearly six hours of actual working time, since they had to move the ship from place to place to get the full deployment pattern. The actual time was closer to ten hours because they'd have to stop all motion whenever they got a contact, no matter how remote it was. The water in the bay was far too shallow to allow them to dive deep for cover if they came under attack, and it would be easy for the enemy destroyer to judge their depth. That assured their death if they got caught in the trap. So they had to put up with several breath-holding, silent-running episodes before their work was done. Fortunately, the night was long and cold in these northern waters on the doorstep of Japan, giving them the cover of darkness for the time needed. They could have taken two nights and been a little less pressed, but Stahlei was anxious to get it over with. The men in the torpedo room were exhausted by the end of the ordeal but had the satisfaction of knowing that virtually every mine had been deployed without a single premature explosion. There was a collective sigh of relief when word was passed up the line that the torpedo room was secured.

"All back three-quarters!" the captain said in his usual flat voice. Apparently he was going to back the boat out into more open water, like a large truck that wedged its way into an alley. They were still rigged for silent operation, although the sound of the screws could easily be picked up at this speed.

"Contact off starboard!"

"All engines stop. Silent running." The ship fell dead in the water. The sound of the propellers grew louder and, with less than a hundred feet under their keel, everybody realized that they'd be in a real bind if discovered.

The sonar operator called out very quietly, "It sounds heavy in the water, slow rate of travel. My guess is that it's a tanker or large merchant, not an enemy combatant."

"Could get exciting," Stahlei said with something of a lift in his voice.

It did get exciting. And very quickly at that. No sooner were the words out of his mouth than there was an explosion off to starboard. The shock wave told them it was fairly close, which meant it hit one of the last mines they had placed. Then there was a second explosion. And a third and a fourth and a fifth.

"Must be a very large ship," the captain said with satisfaction, concluding that the huge ship simply hit every mine in its path.

The next explosion quickly cleared up the question as to what type of ship it was. While the previous explosions had seemed substantial enough, it was now clear that they were really rather modest—*puny* would be a better word. The concussion that hit them was powerful enough to lift the entire submarine up and almost out of the water. No one maintained their footing on this one, and once again the lights faltered, the air filled with bits of insulation, and damage reports started reaching the bridge within moments.

"What in the blazes was that?" Chief Sanders said with a note of awe in his voice.

"I believe we got ourselves a high-octane tanker, Chief. I think we got him really, really hard! Up periscope!"

"Holy shmoly." The captain turned the scope over to the exec, who had a different set of terms, no less reverential, to describe what he saw. Everyone on board ached to take a look, though they obviously couldn't. But they could imagine what it must look like—a giant fireball filling the night air with enough light to be seen in Tokyo.

"That'll be good for civilian morale!" Akers said.

The captain nodded in agreement.

"New contacts, sir!"

"Bearing?"

When the captain heard the bearings, he couldn't suppress a grin. The other craft, whatever they were, would have to pass right through the minefield. Sure enough, almost as if on cue, there was a new explosion, followed quickly by two others, and then the sound of the screws stopped. A new contact was heard to be coming up behind them, but it too stopped.

"Silent running!" The ship went deathly silent again. "I want to take a look," the captain said quietly. "Let's use the attack scope so we're not as obvious." The smaller scope didn't have as broad a field of vision, but it was a mere pencil tip extending above the water. As the captain surveyed the scene, he gave an order that took everyone by surprise. "I want to surface very slowly." Surely it was madness to surface in the middle of something like this.

The diving officer called out instructions to the helm, and ever so slowly the ship nosed its way to the surface with barely a splash to betray its presence. "Limited party on the bridge." Nate stood back, not knowing if it included him. "You too, Lieutenant." Gratefully, he followed the others onto the bridge.

The scene that greeted them was astonishing. They watched the final death throes of the tanker, twisting and turning in the water like a bull wounded by matadors in a Spanish coliseum. The heat of the high-octane fuel was so intense that the metal on the superstructure was melting, and they could see it glowing in the dark even from the considerable distance that separated them from the dying ship. It was highly unlikely they'd see anyone jumping from this ship—the force of the explosion alone would have killed anyone within half a mile either by the force of the concussion or by suffocation as all the air was drawn into the fireball that had sent a massive cloud of smoke and debris up into the night sky. But that wasn't all. Off in the distance, they could see two other ships burning. "Destroyers," Stahlei said. Off the port side, they could see another destroyer nosing its way nervously toward the wreckage. "He thinks they've been torpedoed. They're listening for sounds of a submarine, maybe even trying to hit us with sonar. We're actually safer up here with our new gray paint than we would be under the water. They're not likely to look for a surface ship. Plus, with so many Japanese craft in these waters, they'll assume we're a fishing boat."

Nate couldn't help but grin at the captain. He seemed to know everything, and it was clear to Nate why he was called Lucky—three ships burning right in the mouth of Tokyo itself.

Four ships. The destroyer off their port side had just found the minefield, and two explosions made quick work of it. Unlike the others, which still had some buoyancy even though they were sinking, this one went to the bottom like the lead sinkers Nate used to put on his fishing line. With all the noise, Stahlei ordered one of the diesels to be brought online to continue their backing maneuver while using a second to charge the batteries. Before they found their way out into open waters, they were able to confirm four kills. It was doubtful there'd be any more before the Japanese swept the lanes with a minesweeper.

* * *

"Ever been to Australia, John?"

"I've hardly been out of Arkansas."

Nate loved John's drawl. "I've always imagined it looks a lot like Utah. One of the guys I went to school with in Salt Lake City had a brother who went on a mission to Australia, and he said the eastern part is quite lush and tropical near Sydney, but that the west is pretty arid."

"Guess we'll know soon enough."

Orders had been received for the *Tripletail* to work its way down to Perth for rearming, seeking out convoys along the way. They were now just two days out. It had been an exciting and productive trip—and not just because of the havoc they had created with the mines. Because they were traveling easily within range of Japanese land-based aircraft, Stahlei had instituted a regimen of three diesels on the surface at night and submerged travel during the day on half-power electrics.

It was in that way that they got the chance to try a new technique for themselves that had been piloted by some of the boats permanently assigned to Australia—the night surface attack. The Germans had used it very successfully throughout the war, but the Americans had been slow to adopt it. Unlike a submerged attack in which they sneaked up on their prey underwater, the night surface attack started by putting a tail on the enemy through the day since merchantmen didn't travel any faster than the sub when submerged. They then surfaced in the evening and outflanked them to get ahead of the convoy and into a perfect firing position somewhere around midnight. That's when the fireworks started. Some ships had reported attacking the same convoy three separate times in the course of a few days. It was making the Japanese escorts crazy, because they were still under the assumption that the subs were down, when in reality they simply withdrew at high speed and watched the mayhem from a distance.

In their own encounter with this approach, Stahlei had successfully sunk two ships at the head of the convoy and then pulled inside the formation on the surface while the escorts flirted around the outside edges, looking for them underwater. He kept enough distance that if one of the merchantmen saw them, he'd assume it was just another Japanese ship. It was daring and bold but nothing that hadn't been pioneered by other ships. It was also hugely effective and potentially disastrous if any of the merchants were armed.

Before the evening was over, they'd sunk two more ships and scared the wits out of one of the escorts. They'd finally been driven under and had braced for a night and day of depth charges, but the escorts had broken off the chase almost as soon as it began, apparently deciding it was more important to protect the ships that remained rather than hang around to torment an American sub.

"Here to relieve you, sir!" Nate smiled at the young ensign who was to take his place on the bridge. So young, so eager. Essentially him, just one cruise ago. It was amazing how inexperienced the ensign seemed and how experienced Nate felt. One cruise in combat was worth years of training otherwise.

Chapter Twenty-Three

THE MARIANAS TURKEY SHOOT

After nearly eight months at sea, Cory had the distinct impression that he belonged to his SBD-5 Dauntless, not the other way around. It was as if Cory was simply expected to adapt to its eccentricities without question or back talk—things like a tendency to flood if he gave it too rich a fuel mixture except on the coldest of days. On more than one occasion, he'd been embarrassed when he had to be pulled out of his regular spot in the takeoff queue while they flushed the cylinders for a clean start. That was infuriating. Or there was the odd vibration he'd get at 220 miles per hour, but only when heading west, not east. What could account for that?

The one quirk that caused him the most trouble, because it was always a problem, was that the aircraft's right brake tended to grab when he'd come in for a landing, which inevitably jerked him in the direction of the carrier's conning tower in such a way that it looked like he couldn't maintain control in his landings. That was the direction, of course, where the most eyes were watching. No matter how many times he reported the problem, and regardless of how many mechanics took the mechanism apart, it still did it—and always in a public way. He knew the maintenance crew thought he was crazy, at least until he took the chief up in the backseat and let him apply the brakes when they landed. After that, there were no more jokes, and instead of people thinking he was crazy or reckless, they simply thought his plane a little odd.

But then it would do something like hold together on a particularly steep dive that exceeded its design tolerances, or it would save Cory and Spencer's lives by continuing to function even when enemy shells hit the engine casing—stuff like that which made him tolerant of its other shortcomings. The truth was, he'd stick with this aircraft to the bitter end. He was getting a little superstitious—on some flights he actually caught himself counting things in a repetitive fashion, clearly a sign of stress. But at the end of the day, he liked flying, and he liked his aircraft. So he put up with her eccentricities and hoped that she'd continue to pull him through when things got hot.

He and Spencer had reached the point where they could communicate almost without words, they knew each other so well. Cory secretly believed that Spencer must have had a proverbial set of eyes in the back of his head, because even though he faced backward for the duration of the flight, he could almost always announce in advance the precise moment when they were going to go into a roll or dive down to take a look, or he'd announce to Cory, "I'll hold her steady while you stretch," just at the point that Cory thought he was going to drift off to sleep on the way back from a long patrol.

For his part, Cory had pretty much reached the point where he never even thought about Spencer's actions on the gun or radio. In their early days together, he'd sometimes hold his breath, thinking that Spence should be opening up at any moment, but inevitably Spencer would pick the perfect time to fire, and eventually Cory just stopped thinking about that part of their little two-man enterprise. It was a great partnership, both in the aircraft and back on deck.

On June 18, 1944, there was a kind of electric charge in the air. It was known that the *Enterprise* was joining up with another carrier group, and rumor had it that there would be at least seven carriers involved in the upcoming battle for the Mariana Islands and Guam. There was also talk of the enemy bringing in everything they had to repulse the landings. One look at the map immediately explained why the Japanese were so paranoid about this operation. If the Americans could take Guam, they'd be in a position to cover all of Japan's north-south trade routes with land-based aircraft, which would make Japan's commercial shipping sitting ducks for both aircraft attacks as well as increased submarine activity since the American aircraft could provide cover for the subs.

That was bad enough, all by itself, to draw out the fleet. But completely unacceptable was the fact that long-range heavy bombers could also fly round-trip from Guam to the Japanese home islands. After Jimmy Doolittle's famous raid on Tokyo, Osaka, Nagoya, and Kobe early in the war, the Japanese government knew firsthand the devastating effect that land-based bombers would have on civilian morale. Plus, with American aircraft positioned at such a forward point, it would significantly reduce their leverage in getting the Americans to back out of the war. The shock of Japan's early successes on American public opinion was now threatened in reverse, and they had to stop it at all costs. So the anticipation was very high that the next few days would see the greatest battle in the past year and a half. Perhaps the biggest of the entire war.

When orders came the morning of June 11, Cory and Spencer took off without catapult assistance, since there was a good strong headwind blowing across the bow of the ship. Once airborne, they talked in amazement at what they'd learned in their preflight briefing early that morning.

"Can you believe it? Seven heavy carriers and eight light carriers! There are over nine hundred aircraft scheduled to take part in this thing! This has got to be the greatest show on earth!"

"Kind of incredible."

Kind of incredible? Cory reflected on the fact that Spencer was so understated. He shook his head and smiled. In spite of Spencer's calm outward appearance, Cory had learned that there was a fire burning under the surface. More than once,

Spencer had cursed under his breath when he missed a shot or failed to spot an enemy as quickly as he thought he should have. Still, this understated response to the biggest battle they had ever faced was typical.

Cory calmed his voice down as much as he possibly could, taking out all of the emotion, until he could reply in a totally flat voice, "Yes, it's kind of incredible—in the same way that a volcano exploding or a hurricane tearing trees out by their roots is incredible." He heard Spencer groan, which broadened his smile.

The truth was, this was scary. There was no telling how many Japanese aircraft would be in the sky, but it was bound to be everything they could put up—probably hundreds—so the risk was greater than anything they'd ever faced.

Their initial objective was to soften up the beaches in preparation for Allied troops, who were set to force a landing. This consisted of strafing runs by the fighters to push the Japanese troops off the beach and up into cover, followed by the bombers who would lay their bombs down in a successive pattern inside the line of trees where they could effect the greatest actual and psychological damage. Their efforts would be supplemented by heavy artillery fire from the destroyers and battleships once the aircraft cleared the area. The goal was to stun the defenders so there'd be an opportunity for the marines to make it ashore without excessive enemy fire. Of course, this worked better in the European theater of the war—the Japanese were such tenacious fighters, with such little regard for their own lives, that it was always a fierce fight, no matter how much advance bombardment took place.

"38 Viper to all bombers. The first division will lead with their incendiaries set to explode just past the large creek inlet into the bay. Second division will attack the pillbox located on the short hill to the east of the initial target. Out."

"Looks like we get to blow up some cement!"

"Looks like we're going to have company going in."

"Roger that. See if you can't give him a bloody nose if he gets too close."

"Aye, aye, sir—one bloody Japanese, coming up!"

They started into a fairly shallow dive, although with the hill rising up, Cory would have to release at approximately 3,000 feet. Once again, he found himself counting the seconds while Spencer called out their altitude. He felt, more than heard, Spencer's weapon start to fire, which meant that the Zero had decided to follow them down. They were now about four seconds away from the release. At home, four seconds would have been nothing—a passage of time so trivial that it wouldn't have even been noticed. But when being fired on by armor piercing shells . . . well, four seconds seemed like an eternity. It made Cory want to count faster, to make the seconds go by more quickly, but of course that didn't work. Finally, he reached the drop point, pulled the bomb release, and felt it fly loose on its own.

This time, instead of pulling straight up, he pulled back on the stick and to the right, which sent them into something of a crazy ascent that threw the Zero off their trail for a moment. Even in the heat of the moment, he heard Spencer laugh and was pleased to feel the concussions of his guns firing off to the port side of the aircraft. As he climbed back up to 5,000 feet, he saw a couple Hellcats come racing by, and in something like the blink of an eye, he saw a flash off to his left and realized that the Zero was now heading into the trees in flames. "With any luck, he took out a couple of his infantry friends in the crash!" he shouted back to Spence.

With a full load of ammunition in their forward cannons, Cory turned in the direction of the beach and got in line to do a quick strafing run before heading back to the ship. As they were tearing down the beach, kicking up little splashes in the sand and water while the Japanese defenders scattered, he saw something amazing—an American fighter chasing a Japanese Zero at treetop level. The Japanese fighter burst into flames, and then just a moment later the American aircraft exploded. So intent had the pilot been on getting his target that he'd allowed another Japanese aircraft to turn him into the prey. It was sickening to watch the American plane crash into the trees.

"I guess that's enough for now," he said to Spencer. "Did you see if we hit the pillbox?"

"I think so, but I can't be sure. Your little turn took me by surprise, and I spent most of the climb out trying to pull my face off the canopy."

"Hope I didn't damage those soft little cheeks of yours—it would be a great disappointment to the women in your life if I did!"

"It would take a lot more than what you've got to make me unattractive to women!"

They laughed and pulled free of the melee on their way back to the *Enterprise*.

* * *

The next two days were pretty much a repeat of their first engagement in the Marianas. It was always hard to know if attacks on the beaches really made a difference. The bomb descended into the lush tropical undergrowth and pretty much disappeared from sight. Cory had always imagined what it would be like to attack a ship, where you could see immediately if you'd been successful. Other than the ship they'd hit in the harbor nearly five months earlier, they hadn't had any obvious targets to shoot at. Still, it was part of the routine, and he'd come to figure that every one of the enemy that their bombs took out in the bush was that many more GIs who could land without getting killed. It was an insidious kind of math.

June 19 turned out to be one of the most important days in the air war. Cory and the other bomber pilots took off in the afternoon and approached the islands for yet another round of interior bombing to expand the perimeter of the beachhead established by the marines on June 15. As they approached the target area, Cory's eyes grew wide in astonishment. "I wish you could see this, Spence. There must be at least two or three hundred fighters engaging each other. I've never seen anything like it!"

In fact, there were more than 400 Japanese aircraft in the air that day and nearly twice that number of American planes. The Japanese were desperate to turn back the landings and to hold on to their bases. Usually, the Japanese could hold their own or better, but it was clear from this battle scene that the Americans had finally figured out how to offset the inherent advantages of the Zero by using team assaults, and the results were clearly devastating to the Japanese.

"There are fighters everywhere, and the Japanese are falling out of the air like wounded birds. There goes another one in flames!"

"I see it too. This really is unbelievable!" Then in a hushed voice, "Unbelievable . . ." Even Spencer couldn't maintain his usual feigned indifference.

When they had time to think about it later that night and to learn the details of what had happened, it was both thrilling and humbling. With a two-to-one advantage in the number of Allied aircraft engaged in combat, and with the Japanese pilots being unusually clumsy, probably from fatigue and lack of training, it was turning into a rout that was nothing short of an out-and-out slaughter. In fact, before the day was over, more than three hundred Japanese aircraft and pilots were destroyed. The aviators who witnessed it almost immediately started calling it a turkey shoot, and the images of burning Japanese airplanes being chased down and into the water or shot at while trying to land made a macabre, but somehow elegant scene—like ballet dancers pirouetting and twisting in the air, but with deadly results.

The bomber strike force was told to hold off at the outside of the battle scene since the initial assault was one for the fighters, so Cory and the others withdrew to a position approximately twenty miles back toward Guam. Finally, after about four hours of watching this incredible engagement, they were ordered to drop their ordnance on the Orote Peninsula to damage the field so that whatever Japanese aircrews survived would have to ditch their aircraft rather than risk a landing.

That night, there was a festive atmosphere in the wardroom, but Cory felt that everyone talked just a little too loud to mask the terror they'd felt in the greatest air battle in history.

* * *

June 20 dawned bright and clear. The fighters took off immediately in search of enemy aircraft that might be launching against the Allied carriers and in search of the Japanese fleet. All the strike group bomber and torpedo pilots spent the morning in the ready room, waiting for the order to scramble, but nothing was heard. Occasionally, reports of air combat would come in, but nothing like the day before. Finally, the steward brought out lunch, and the pilots munched down a stack of sandwiches. Some tried to play cards, others reread magazines for the fifth or sixth time, and some engaged in the ever-popular activity of telling raunchy stories and jokes. Cory couldn't understand how they could laugh at the same idiotic jokes over and over, but they did. When Cory went to check up on Spencer, he found that a number of the radiomen had started up a basketball game on the hangar deck. He joined in to take his mind off the waiting.

In the early afternoon, the klaxon sounded, and they scrambled to the briefing room. One of their pilots, Stu Nelson, had contacted the Japanese fleet in a VT-10. Within moments, they'd adjusted the plans they'd made earlier that day, with a particular emphasis on how to conserve fuel since the distance to the enemy was at their extreme range. There was a huge buzz in the room, since they were finally coming head-to-head with the Japanese fleet for the first time in more than eighteen months. For a lot of the pilots, it would be the first time ever.

Still, the waiting wasn't over, as their leaders decided to close the gap a bit. Finally, word was received to launch at 1620. Twelve SBD dive-bombers, five torpedo planes, and twelve fighters would launch from the *Enterprise*. With fourteen other carriers involved in the action, the total strike force was truly awesome. As Cory and Spencer mounted their airplane, Cory gave Spence a thumbs-up, then climbed into the cockpit and started strapping himself in. There was so much tension in the air that he was tempted to take shortcuts with the preflight checklist, but Spencer would have none of it. Cory went through each step methodically—but quickly—with Spencer confirming the sequence. Then Spencer did a check of his area and called out that he was clear. Cory gave a visual signal to the deck officer, who ordered them into the takeoff pattern. In just a few moments, he had the engine run up to full throttle, the big plane trembling against the brakes. The flagman waved him off, and he released the brakes and felt the surge of forward momentum as the aircraft, freed from its constraints, leaped forward on the deck in a great cloud of smoke. They easily lifted off the deck and up into the sky.

Cory quickly took up position as the flight leader in their "fluid four" formation. They were flying off to the west on a heading of 290 degrees, with their throttles set for maximum fuel efficiency. There were more than 250 miles of ocean between them and the Japanese fleet—250 miles of anticipation. Each pilot dreamed of being the one to put a bomb or torpedo square in the heart of an aircraft carrier, because that, more than any other action, would damage the ability of the enemy to wage war. Cory repeated the attack protocol over and over in his mind. Finally, he decided to review it with Spence, who patiently listened to him repeat it three times.

When he started through it the fourth time, Spencer called forward, "For crying out loud, O'Brian, you've done this before. You know what to do. Now shut up and think about golf or something. You're going to have this so well rehearsed that if things don't line up perfectly, you won't be able to adjust. So knock it off."

"Golf? A gentleman's game. I'm afraid I had but a casual acquaintance with it."

"Well, you should take it up, because it gives you plenty of time to think, and you seem to like that. I can just see you practicing the eighteenth hole while lining up on the second. You've got to take things as they come, Cory."

"You're one to talk. I saw you studying the charts all afternoon. You probably know the islands in this area better than the natives." He heard a sigh.

"Okay—so we're both a little over the top. What did you do for fun, if not golf?"

"Skiing—I like skiing. Nice and quiet and nobody giving you trouble from the backseat."

Spencer laughed. "So for fun, you started at the top of a steep, icy slope and tore downhill on two greased pieces of wood. Now, for employment, you start at the top of a steep dive and hurl yourself down toward the ocean. You must have a death wish."

"Never thought of it like that, but I guess I do like going down really fast. Gravity feels pretty good when you let it have its way. It's even better with twelve hundred horsepower pulling you even faster."

This light banter was just what was needed, and Spencer managed to keep Cory distracted right up until the moment that the order was received to prepare for battle.

At 1900, they were 225 miles out from the *Enterprise*, flying at 15,000 feet, when someone in the group shouted into their air-to-air radio, "Tallyho!" The Japanese force was in sight, fifteen miles to port. The first group they saw was six fleet tankers and half a dozen destroyers. Normally, these would be tempting targets, but their flight leader told them to keep it steady. To waste their bombs on these targets when at least seven carriers were within range would be like shooting squirrels when your objective was elephants.

"Alright, Cory," Spencer called into the interphone, "now it's okay to do your attack checklist."

"What? We're going into battle? I didn't know that."

Spencer rolled his eyes.

"Fine . . . Engine blower, on. Gas tanks, balanced. Bomb release, set. Gun switches, on. Bombsight, activated. I think we're ready, Mr. Tolman."

"Good luck, then. I'll keep the bad guys away. You just hit a bull's-eye and then get us out of here!"

"38 Viper to strike group. First division will dive on the largest CV carrier. Other sections will dive on the small guys, unless the big one is still not hit. Good hunting!"

Cory was in the second division, so he followed his leader into a banking turn to port. As they looked down at the ocean, they saw a sight never to be forgotten. Stretched out across the horizon, as far as they could see, was an armada of Japanese naval battleships, destroyers, cruisers, and—bless 'em—aircraft carriers. The Japanese organized their strike force very differently than the Americans. Whereas the U.S. destroyers kept a very tight formation around the carriers, with concentric rings of support ships arranged to put up an increasingly fierce barrage of antiaircraft artillery as the enemy planes attempted to reach the aircraft carrier in the center, the Japanese had their support ships widely dispersed from the carrier, arranged in rings but much farther apart than the Americans. At first glance, it seemed crazy in that it made it much easier for the bombers and torpedo planes to get into the carrier.

Word was passed that Cory's group was to attack the *Hiyo*. They'd be joined in their attack by pilots from the C.V. *Belleau Woods*.

"Okay, Spence, here we go!" After nearly two years of preparation, they were now ready to engage the enemy in vital waters.

Cory started his dive from 15,000 feet as the carriers started heading for cloud cover. At 13,000 feet, small white puffs of flak started appearing, but Cory held his formation and concentration. At 10,000 feet, the carrier was starting to loom ever bigger in his bombsight, and Cory pushed the actuator to engage his air flaps to slow his airspeed. The aircraft immediately responded, and the view in his bombsight steadied. Out the corner of his eye, he saw a bright explosion, which surely indicated one of the fighters had knocked down an intruder. Hopefully it was a Japanese aircraft that exploded, not one of their American fighters.

There was a lot of radio chatter going on, which usually didn't bother Cory. But something was really strange this time, and for just a moment, he diverted his attention to it. "It's Japanese!" he said in indignation. There were so many aircraft in the area that the Japanese were using the same frequencies as the Americans, adding to the sense of mayhem. "Hope they're saying their prayers," he called back to Spence, but there was no reply.

Spencer was now facing almost straight up into the sky, since the dive was as close to vertical as possible to present the smallest target to the Triple A guns and to give maximum control of the bomb release. In spite of the angle, he was scanning the horizon in all directions that were available to his view for any hostile aircraft that might attack them from the side.

"I've got the target in the sites," Cory called out to him. "I'll release at twenty-five hundred feet!"

Spencer started calling out the altitude so Cory could keep his eye steady in the bombsite. "Six thousand . . . five thousand . . . forty-five hundred . . . four thousand . . ." The pitch of his voice started rising. "Thirty-five hundred . . . three thousand . . . twenty-five hundred!"

"Bombs away!" Cory shouted exultantly. At this point the aircraft carrier filled not only the bombsight, but the front of his canopy as well. And they were approaching it at nearly 200 miles per hour. Cory started his pullout at 1,800 feet—way too low, really—and he had the distinct feeling that he might not be able to pull out in time. In spite of his pullback, the ship continued to grow larger for a few moments—long enough to make it feel like he'd never take a breath again—and then they suddenly flattened out and started up in a banking turn away from the ship. At the bottom of the dive, he could actually see the faces of men on the deck of the ship.

On the rebound up, he checked his engine and was grateful to hear and see that it was running perfectly. With the dive flaps back in neutral position, they were already climbing at 280 knots. Their steep ascent took his breath away, but he was still able to look out and see a gaping hole in the forward deck of the *Hiyo*—probably from his release. There was very little smoke, which seemed discouraging, until he remembered that it was an armor-piercing bomb that had undoubtedly passed through at least a couple of decks before exploding. Even at this moment, it was probably the cause of a firestorm in the forward compartments of the ship. *If they have the same sleeping arrangements as we do, my bomb would have passed right through my bunk!* A sobering thought, to say the least.

"We did it, Spence! We did it! We hit an aircraft carrier!"

"Good shooting, Cory. Enjoy this moment! 'Cause in about ten seconds, we're in for it."

Cory looked off to his left side and saw a Japanese Zero approaching at high speed. Acting on pure instinct, he pulled them into a hard dive to starboard.

Fortunately, Spencer knew Cory well enough by now that he anticipated this move, and as the plane turned on its side, he let out a couple of bursts of machine gun fire, swiveling in his turret to hold his bead steady. He could see the tracers find their way into the cowling of the Japanese fighter. As they recovered from the turn he swiveled to the other side to continue the attack but had to search the sky for a few moments to find the Japanese fighter. He was on fire and losing altitude quickly. He watched in fascination as the aircraft dove into the water at high speed, throwing up an enormous waterspout where the collision took place. "Wow. I didn't expect it to be that easy," he said breathlessly into the microphone.

"Is it just me, or does it seem that the Japanese pilots aren't flying as well as usual."

"It's not just you. They're clearly inexperienced compared to others we've met. They must be scraping the bottom of the barrel. And they're paying a heavy price for it!"

Cory did a quick survey around the horizon, where it looked very much like the day before, with American fighters successfully engaging the Japanese in every area of activity. It was sickening, really, to see so many young pilots losing their lives. But it was exhilarating to think that the battle was decisively in the hands of the Americans. As he scanned back across the horizon, Cory could see at least two or three of the great carriers in smoke, as well as numerous other ships on fire.

As they retired from the battle scene on a heading of 90 degrees, it quickly became obvious why the Japanese had spread out their ship formation. It meant that an exiting aircraft had to pass through a far larger distance where they could be attacked. As they flew past ship after ship, Cory saw countless orange flashes signaling the firing of yet another round of flak that would momentarily burst into either a large black or a small white puff in front of them. It was as frightening as anything Cory had ever encountered. At first, his group tried flying low, right above the ocean, because it was much harder for the ships to lower their elevation and maintain any accuracy in firing. As they cleared the first ring of resistance, Cory let out a sigh of relief, only to be nearly blinded by a bright flash two or three hundred yards in front of him, which meant they'd come into range of one of the ships in the second ring. He immediately took evasive action. As they came into line with ever more of the enemies' guns from this ring, they were caught in a crossfire. At least two of the shells burst close enough that the concussion of their blast buffeted them, and Cory could see some holes appear at the outer end of his port wing.

"Are you okay back there?" he called out to Spencer. He'd heard of more than one occasion where a pilot became so involved in his flying that he didn't realize his gunner had been killed until much later in the flight when he finally tried to reestablish communication.

"I'm alright, but it's pretty darn hot out there. Have you thought of going for altitude?"

"I've thought of everything, but I think it's more a matter of luck than skill right now." There was a blinding flash off to their left side, and Cory instinctively turned to see an American torpedo plane burst into flames. It must have been a direct hit, because the aircraft exploded in midair. "I think I'll take up your suggestion for more altitude." Cory pulled back on the stick and added full power, even though it was crucial now that they conserve fuel. As they gained altitude, the flak diminished, but the risk of enemy fighters increased.

Cory wanted to call back to Spencer to keep his eyes sharp for fighters, but that would have been a tremendous insult. Spencer knew exactly what to do and was far better at it than Cory. So instead, he called into the interphone, "Do you see anything I should be worried about?"

"Not at present. I have this feeling that the Japanese fighters are pretty desperate to protect what carriers they have left. And it looks like you've outrun the flak. I'll keep you posted if I see anything."

At that, Cory finally allowed his muscles to relax a little. He had a habit of bracing his feet against the curved surface of the cockpit and pushing back against his seat to stretch his leg and back muscles. It felt good to stretch. He then checked his engine and found that he had 32 inches of manifold pressure and was flying along at approximately 2,000 rpms. That was the most fuel-efficient setting. The drone of the engine operating at this easy pace started to lull him.

One of the things they hadn't anticipated when they took off was that it would be dark on the way back. Since everyone was night certified, that shouldn't have been a problem, but with fuel stocks running as low as they were, it soon became obvious that there would be no room for error when they got back to the fleet or people would run out of fuel before they could land. And with seven carriers in the vicinity, it was going to be particularly difficult to identify their own ship in a timely fashion.

After approximately an hour of flying time away from the battle scene, Cory started to hear traffic that was heart wrenching. One by one, aircraft started to run out of fuel, and the pilots had to ditch. He watched out his starboard side and saw the propeller of a torpedo plane suddenly stop turning and then watched as the aircraft started down. He was grateful to see three chutes appear but could only wonder what it would be like to hit the water in the dark. A few minutes later, he overheard radio chatter from an entire squadron who decided to ditch together to increase their chance of being found and rescued. It was eerie to listen to them talking away and then disappear into sudden silence. As Cory approached the spot where he thought the fleet should be, he grew increasingly anxious at the thought that if he was at all off in his navigation, it would be almost impossible to correct course in time.

"Among your many accomplishments, did you learn to be a swimmer?" he called back to Spence.

"I told you earlier that I hate getting wet, O'Brian, so you just fly this blasted thing onto our carrier."

"It would help if I knew where it was. Wish they'd turn on the lights so we could see them."

"Right, they're going to turn on the lights so that we—and the entire Japanese Naval Air Force—can find them."

"I know, but they should be coming into sight any moment, and I don't see a thing!"

Then the sky burst into semidaylight, and Cory had to squint for a moment to see anything. First, one, then a second, and then a trio of star shells burst into the night sky, lighting up the entire area with an eerie blue light that was brighter than a full moon. There, below them, was the American fleet. All of a sudden, as if somebody turned one giant switch, the ocean began to flame into light as every ship in the fleet turned on their lights.

"I can't believe it, Spence. Do you see that? They've turned on the lights for us. They've turned on every darn light in the fleet! We might make it after all!"

It was the single most thrilling thing ever to happen to him. It was against all military protocol to turn on the lights in the midst of a battle, particularly since the enemy had already started launching night attacks, but there they were. The admiral had decided it was worth the risk to recover his aircraft. Word came on the radio that each aircraft should find whatever carrier was available and move into the landing pattern as quickly as possible. There was to be no preference given—each aircraft carrier would take onboard anybody they could.

It was now something of a free-for-all, one that was patently open to anyone who wanted to land, and Cory started searching desperately for a carrier. At first, it was great to see all the ships in the fleet illuminated, particularly with the spotlights blazing up into the sky to serve as a beacon for aircraft that might be off course, but now he wished that they would have only illuminated the decks of the carriers, since it was difficult to sort out which ship was which. Finally, he spied the distinctive runway lights that indicated a potential safe haven, and he quickly moved into the landing pattern to make his turn into the stern.

"None too soon," he called back to Spencer. "I'd be surprised if we have twenty gallons in all the tanks combined."

As he approached the deck, he finally caught sight of the LSO, who was illuminated off to the port side of the runway, and was dismayed to see him doing a wave-off.

"What do you mean, a wave-off?" he shouted furiously to no one in particular.

Of course, Spence heard it, and as they pulled off to the side, he called up, "Aircraft burning on the deck."

That explained it, but it didn't help their situation. As he flew through the mass of ships searching for a new host, he was dismayed to see yet another aircraft settle into the water with a great splash and was then relieved when the searchlight of a destroyer immediately settled on the spot so they could effect a rescue.

"Got another one in sight—let's hope they're available!" Once again he did a fly around, and this time the deck looked clear. Moving into the pattern, he silently prayed that their engines would hold out long enough. As he completed the turn, he saw the LSO and was relieved to see him waving him in. At that moment, he heard the engine sputter, and he quickly switched tanks yet again. The engine caught, and they were quickly under power. As he made the approach in the darkness, his eyes were fixed on the LSO. It was hard enough to land in the daylight, but at night, there was an increase in his natural anxiety. Plus, the LSO looked very unnatural in his reflective paint—each of his motions were jerky, like those of a marionette. Cory caught himself counting, and at just the last moment, the LSO gave him the cut signal. He pulled the throttle back and felt them drop to the deck with a thud. *Where's the arrester cable?* His heart raced, but then they were thrown forward in their harness, indicating they were safe. He moved to shut down the engine, but found that it had done that already.

"We did that with about ten seconds to spare," he shouted to Spencer as they lurched out of the cockpit so the deck crew could move their aircraft out of the way for the next landing.

"What ship is this?" he asked the crewman at the base of the wing.

"*Yorktown.* You're from the *Enterprise?*"

"We are, indeed! Thanks for the use of your flight deck!" Once clear of the aircraft, they moved toward the island, but found themselves a little lost. A sympathetic crewman waved them over and told them how to find the wardroom. That night, they slept on a bedroll on the hangar deck. But at least they were warm and dry—not like the more than a hundred crewmen who had ditched all across the ocean clear out to the Japanese fleet. Cory was asleep and dreaming in no time.

* * *

As the reports started coming in the next morning, they learned that ninety-seven aircraft had been lost in the battle and on the way back to the ships. Fortunately, more than eighty percent of the crews were rescued. It had been far more devastating for the Japanese, with more than 450 aircraft lost in the battle so far. Apparently, the aircraft carrier that Cory and Spencer had bombed had indeed sunk, although credit for the decisive wound went to the pilots of the C.V. *Belleau Woods.* A little after lunch, they received permission to fly back to the Big E, where they were relieved to learn that virtually all the Dauntless crews had made it, although one had gone into the drink. Cory was also pleased beyond measure to see Jack Wilson, who gave him a thumbs-up, and then started telling everyone how the fighters had saved the bombers' tails. Cory laughed along with the rest, although Spencer was a little irritated. The one group that never got mentioned in Jack's story were the gunners.

The next day, Cory's group was called in for a special briefing.

"We're going to try something new tonight. We want to hit some of the Japanese land-based facilities using radar. You'll follow a lead aircraft equipped with radar out to the drop and then follow his instructions when you get there. It should give you an interesting vantage point. Any questions?"

There were none.

"Good! Dismissed!"

"How you holding up, Cory?"

"What? Oh, I'm fine."

"It was pretty rough the past few days. Are your nerves okay?"

Spencer always took time to ask questions like this. Running the gauntlet of Triple A after the drop had been extremely frightening, and Cory sometimes found his hands trembling. At one point during the briefing, he'd actually put them under his legs so nobody would notice them shaking. All the pilots talked big, like they were invincible, but the strain showed on all their faces.

"I really am okay, Spence. I didn't like the Triple A, but we made it through. I'm glad I had you back there, particularly keeping track of our navigation. You brought us home right to the spot."

"You did some great flying. We're not a bad team, are we?"

Cory felt a wave of appreciation flood over him. The one thing he worried about most as a pilot was his crew. If he made a mistake that cost him his own life, well, he deserved it. But it bothered him that Spence had to sit back there, effectively helpless to make up for any error Cory made.

Their flight commander ordered them to take a nap—which was a very unusual order. But since they'd be leaving the ship at 2100, he wanted them to be as well rested as possible. Cory didn't think he could sleep, but he figured out that he was wrong when he felt himself being shook in his berth. It took a few moments to clear his head, then he rolled out to the floor and tried to straighten his clothing. He'd been sleeping in them for the past three days, and he couldn't wait for a lull in the action so he could actually take a quick shower and change.

They took off in absolute darkness, the blue and orange flames of the aircraft in front of them being their primary source of light. Cory made a clean takeoff and quickly joined the leader. They only had a forty-five minute flight to the target. As they came up through the clouds, he was startled to see a full moon shining brightly on the fluffy layer beneath them. They flew over in silence, the sky a deep indigo blue above them, the clouds a silvery ghost beneath them. Cory marveled at the beauty of creation. It seemed impossible in such a serene and timeless setting that in just a few minutes they'd be the subject of enemy fire and that their ordnance would set the jungle on fire beneath them. "What is man, that thou art mindful of him?"

"What did you say?"

"Oh, sorry. I guess I was just caught up in the scene. It's beautiful, don't you think?"

Spencer was quiet for a few moments. "It is beautiful. And, as to man, you have to wonder what God is thinking at times like this, when millions are engaged in mortal combat. Maybe He gives us quiet moments like this to remember what it's all about."

"It makes me think of eternity."

Their reverie was interrupted by a crackle of static and then the voice of the lead aircraft. "Approaching target area. We'll start the dive in sixty seconds." He then continued with the specifics of the approach. Cory was mentally rehearsing his role in the project when he saw a flash of orange down on the horizon.

"Looks like they're on to us. I just spotted a Triple A flash down there."

"Well, just get us in and out. I'm looking forward to a hot shower."

Cory started the roll at the moment indicated, and once again they were in a shallow dive to knock out enemy docks. As they approached the ground, the jungle floor started pulsing with staccato bursts of yellow and orange, indicating that in addition to Triple A, the Japanese defenders were firing their small arms. Spencer started calling out the altitude, and at the assigned spot, Cory leveled out and released the bomb. He felt like it had to be pretty good and started their roll up. "How did we do?" he shouted to Spencer, who was now in a better position to see.

"I think we were off a little—too far in. You probably hit some trucks or something, but I don't think you got the docks."

That was disappointing. Maddening, actually. To come this far and to be off by a few critical feet. Cory was busy replaying the scene in his mind to figure out how his aim could have been off when suddenly there was a blinding light in his eyes and the sound of a concussion that left him temporarily dazed. He shook his head to clear it, but was startled to discover that he couldn't hear anything. In almost the same instant, he was aware of a searing pain in his left leg—very much, he imagined, like it would feel if someone heated up a butcher knife and stabbed it right into the calf. It was eerie that he couldn't hear himself screaming.

His training asserted itself, and he quickly checked all the dials. In spite of a terrific ringing sound, he started to hear the noise of the engine again, and then more sounds. When his hearing cleared enough, he realized that *what* he was hearing wasn't good. The engine was running unevenly, and there was the sound of escaping air, which probably meant a leak in their hydraulics. Suddenly, he felt a terrible pang of fear in his stomach as he heard Spencer shouting, "Cory! Are you okay?"

Even though it was hard to concentrate, he called back, "I'm alive. That's something. What about you?"

"I'm okay. I may have been hit, but I'm okay. We're not going to make it, are we?" The fear in Spencer's voice was palpable, even though it was obvious that he was forcing himself to speak evenly.

"I'm losing power steadily. We've got to go into the drink. Can you radio our position?"

There was a maddening silence for a few moments, and then, "I think our radio's working. I can't be sure." He waited to hear Spence call out their coordinates. "I think I've got it. Can you confirm my calculations?" That was unusual. Spencer was a far better navigator than Cory and usually made him run the calculations only when they were in open flight as an exercise to help Cory keep his skills up.

It registered with Cory that something must be wrong, but he didn't have time to think of it just now. He wanted more than anything to just reach down and stroke his injured leg to try to find some relief, but that was impossible. So in spite of everything he was doing to try to maintain flight, Cory furiously calculated where they were and shouted it back to him. He was so relieved when he heard Spencer start calling, "Mayday, mayday, aircraft hit. We're going down." Then Spencer called out the numbers. He did this repeatedly, even as his voice grew hoarse.

"Okay, Spence, you can stop now! Listen to me. Something is really wrong with my leg. I can barely hold my concentration, it hurts so badly. I don't think I can bail out, but you should. You'll need to fire your ejection seat fast. I'll ride the plane in and get out as soon as I hit the water. Do you understand?"

"I understand, but you're nuts if you think I'm going to leave you. You can just forget that."

Cory winced as the plane was buffeted by some piece of one of the wings flying off. "Spencer, I'm ordering you to bail out. I've never had to give you an order, so don't give me trouble on this one."

"Cory, I'm not leaving. So tell me how you want to proceed with both of us riding it in."

It was exasperating, but Cory felt enormously relieved to think that Spencer would be with him. "Okay, then. Here's what we're going to do. I'm going to set her down on the ocean. As soon as you feel us hit and we stabilize, fire your canopy and get the lifeboat out. I'll try to pull myself onto the wing, although I don't know what's going on with my leg. It may be caught for all I know." He tried tugging it again but couldn't feel anything other than the pain. "Once we're both out, we'll just let the plane sink below us and then climb into the boat. Hopefully they'll have somebody out here in no time to rescue us. Is that clear?"

"Roger." Then Spencer called back the steps to Cory.

"Okay, we're about twenty seconds from impact. Do your best to relax so that you'll be flexible when we hit the water. Do you understand?"

There was silence for a moment, then Spencer said quietly, "I understand." He sounded so tired and so scared.

Once again, Cory felt unnerved, so he started concentrating on the crash landing. If he muffed that, nothing else would matter. The aircraft was losing altitude naturally, but now Cory took control of the situation and used what little power he had to level off the descent into as smooth a glide path as possible. Slowly but surely, they drifted toward the water. The clouds had broken apart now and the sheen of the moon illuminated the surface to show a practically smooth ocean with very few waves. *That's good. It'll make it easier to spot us.* He wished that Spencer could get off one more message, but he wasn't hearing anything from the backseat, so he concentrated on doing his job. He had to stay focused, even though his heart was racing with fear.

As they got closer to the surface, everything seemed to speed up, and he saw that there were actually more waves than he originally thought. The pain in his leg was gone, and he realized, almost dreamily, that he felt warm all over his body. He could hear his heart pounding in his ears, and he felt sleepy. That seemed so odd, given the urgency of their situation. Finally, with a start, he realized that they were just about to hit, and at the last possible moment, he pulled up on the nose, only to be thrown forward against his restraints as the water cascaded up and over the fuselage. The last thing he remembered was hearing the engine sputter to a stop as they settled dead in the water.

* * *

Cory was in the backyard of his house playing in his sandbox. It was a warm summer day, and he felt happy. He could hear his mother singing in the garden, and it sounded like his dad was hammering on something. The hammering bothered him and he wished it would go away, but instead it just got louder and more irritating. Then he felt water on his legs, which didn't make sense.

"Oh, no," he shouted, and he came to consciousness with a jerk. Doing his best to recall what had happened, he looked up in the direction of the pounding and saw Spencer hammering away on his canopy. The water in the cockpit was almost covering his thighs by this point, and he felt a surge of adrenaline flood his body as he was mobilized by terror into throwing the canopy open.

"About time!" Spencer cried out. "I hope you had a good nap, but you've got to get out right now, Cory. This thing is going down fast!"

Cory tried to free his leg, but it was too painful. "I can't get out! I can't make my legs work!" he cried out helplessly.

Spencer reached in and got his arms under Cory's armpits. "Cory, no matter how bad your leg hurts, you've got to push with everything you've got. We've got to get you out of there right now!"

Cory pushed. Even with all the salt water that had splashed on him, he could still feel the taste of the tears that rolled down his cheek from the effort. While Spencer pulled from above, Cory pushed with both his arms and legs and finally broke loose from whatever was tethering him down. He floated up and out of the cockpit as the top of the aircraft started to sink below the waves.

For some reason, it panicked him to be in the water, but Spencer quickly calmed him. "It's okay. Everything is going just like you said it would. We're going to let the airplane sink below us, and then we'll crawl into the raft."

At that point, Cory remembered that he knew how to swim, and it actually felt good to have the buoyancy of the water hold up his injured leg. He listened as Spencer inflated the raft and then did his best to come back up to the surface as the aircraft sucked both of them under when it finally slipped beneath the waves. For a moment, he thought he might not break free, but there was a sudden burst of bubbles as air trapped in the airplane broke free and shot up to the surface. Like a cork, he and Spencer popped up and out onto the glassy surface of the dark Pacific Ocean. Spencer found the raft and held it in the water as Cory pulled himself in. Then Cory reached over the side and helped Spencer pull himself in. It seemed very difficult for Spence to find the energy to get in, but he finally crawled in.

"We made it," Cory said jubilantly. "I can't believe we made it!"

Spencer simply sighed. "What about your leg?"

Cory looked down and, in the moonlight, saw that his left foot was twisted at a crazy angle. Clearly the bone was broken. He tugged at his pant leg to see if there was blood and was surprised to see the jagged fragment of a bone protruding out of the skin approximately six inches above his ankle. It frightened him so badly that he let out a yelp. Spencer looked down at the leg and quickly tore a piece of material from his own shirt and wrapped a tourniquet just below Cory's knee.

"How did you learn to do that?" Cory asked indignantly.

Spencer rolled his eyes. "Oh, for heaven's sake, I learned how to do that in basic first aid. Just like you did." Spencer laid his head back against the side of the boat.

"You saved my life."

"I know. I'll have to live with it, I guess."

"Do you think they heard us?"

"I don't know." Spencer sounded so tired.

"Are you okay, Spence?'

"I don't think so, Cory." His voice was weak. Very weak.

Suddenly, it struck Cory that something was wrong with Spencer. Sliding closer to him, he saw that Spencer's eyes were closed.

"Spencer? What's wrong? Tell me what's happened!" But there was nothing. Frantically, Cory started tearing at Spencer's shirt. He hadn't noticed it before, because there was so much water in the boat from their climbing in, but the front of Spencer's shirt was wet with a darker color.

Cory tore furiously at the shirt. "Oh, Spencer! Wake up, buddy! You've got to wake up! We've got to get you fixed up now. Spencer!" At this point, Cory had Spencer's shirt open, and he could see that the wound to his belly was severe enough that he'd been slowly bleeding to death. Aside from the blood Cory could see on the outside of Spencer's body, it was likely there was even more internally.

"Oh, Spencer. Why did this have to happen?"

"It's cold, Cory. It's so cold . . ."

"I know it's cold—and you hate getting wet!"

He heard Spencer mutter something, but it was so weak as to be incoherent. "Say it again, buddy, say it again." Leaning his ear right up against Spencer's mouth, he heard him whisper that he was thirsty.

"So thirsty!"

Cory broke out the water supply and let Spencer take great gulps.

When nearly all the water was gone, he whispered, "Thank you," and then started talking about how thirsty he was again. Cory knew that there wasn't enough water in the ocean to take care of what he needed right then.

When Spencer's head flopped to the side, Cory slid over and pulled his head into his lap. "Hang, in there, buddy. Hang in there. Someone should be by to rescue us soon. Can you hang in there?" Cory was crying, so it was hard to get the words out. But he wanted to keep talking.

"Cory—" Spencer's body went limp.

Frantically, Cory tried to shake him, but it was over. Cory sat there in stunned silence. Then it felt like his own life was draining from him. The surge of adrenaline was replaced by a wave of despair.

"Oh, Spencer, you hated getting wet. Why did you have to get wet?"

* * *

As he looked out on the great expanse of the Pacific Ocean, illuminated as far as he could see by the reflection of the moon on the horizon, Cory felt numb. Emotionally and physically. He was all alone. Alone with the person he had come to consider a partner and a friend, but whose shell was all that remained. He lay back in the boat, determined not to sleep. He had a flare he could fire, if the opportunity presented itself. But all was quiet. He knew it was irresponsible, but he too was more thirsty than he'd ever been in his life, so he gulped greedily at the remaining fresh water until it was gone.

After that, he lay back against the side of the small boat and listened to the sounds of the ocean. But he had lost a fair amount of blood, and in time, he started to feel warm and comfortable.

Chapter Twenty-Four

ATTACK ON A JAPANESE CARRIER

"You didn't enjoy Perth much, did you Nate?" John asked.

"It was alright." The sub bucked over the largest wave they'd encountered yet that day.

"So what's bothering you?"

Nate kept his gaze on the horizon. The sea was running fairly smooth, and he'd actually spent the whole watch without getting wet from so much as a single splash. That was about the best thing to happen to him in the last few months.

Shortly before reaching Australia, the *Tripletail* had pursued a Japanese convoy into some shallow waters where, as irony would have it, they hit a mine. Fortunately, they only sheared the side of the mine in such a way that most of the force of the explosion was dissipated in the surrounding water. Still, it had made a mess of the forward torpedo room, killing two men there, and they had to limp their way into Australia.

With the limited repair facilities at the dock, it had taken what seemed like forever to get the ship repaired, particularly when they had to wait for parts from the U.S. mainland. Most of the men were thrilled with the unplanned leave, since it kept them out of the battle zone. But part of the crew had been reassigned as replacements on other boats that were ready to go out, and Nate had pretty much lost all the men under his command. He had to start retraining almost from the moment the new men got onboard. Plus, the extended shore leave had been bad on discipline, at least from his point of view. Most of the officers had transferred to an elegant hotel inland, leaving the enlisted men in the rowdier sections of town, where they became known as troublemakers.

"I'm just in a bad mood, I guess."

"But why? We're finally back in the action. This is what you've wanted, and now you're unhappy here too."

"I miss Kathy. I miss her really bad."

Akers softened. "I know it's hard being away. I just hate to see you so miserable."

Nate remained silent.

"I think Captain Stahlei feels the same way you do, so I suspect we'll have plenty of action to keep us occupied."

"I hope so." Then Nate tried to force the thoughts of home from his mind so he could concentrate on the tasks at hand.

* * *

"What is it, sir?" The men around the table looked at Stahlei expectantly. He'd just decoded new orders and was busy reading through them for details. The speed with which his eyes darted back and forth across the page told them that whatever was in there was exciting.

The captain looked up and flashed a quick grin. Nate was tempted to think that he was enjoying their anticipation. Finally, "It looks like we get to join the biggest party of the war in the last year and a half!" After a pause to let that sink in, "The Japanese fleet has been discovered near the Marianas. Our aircraft have been harassing their land-based fields, and it looks like there's going to be major fleet action tomorrow or, at the latest, the next day. The good news is they've decided to let the subs see what they can do to stir things up. So we're to proceed at best possible speed, if it looks like we can get there in time. If not, we're to try to bottle up any shipping that may be working its way north." He let the second part sink in for a moment. "I definitely don't want to be waiting for tramp steamers while there are aircraft carriers out there. So . . ."

Almost instantly, the navigator was up at his table finding the Marianas. He pulled out his protractor and compass. The conversation came to a standstill while they awaited his verdict. "Twenty-six hours at twenty knots. Maybe a little better if the seas stay this calm."

No one said anything. Clearly, there would be no problem if this was peacetime and they could sail at maximum speed on the surface. But it wasn't, and the great unknown was how much time they'd have to spend diving to avoid detection. The prudent course would be to lie low until the battle resolved itself and then move in to pick off the remnants. All eyes turned to the captain, who had taken on his impassive look. There was no sense trying to guess his intentions.

"We'll surface and proceed at flank speed. Maintain an extra lookout and prepare the crew for a long day and night." He then fixed everyone with his gaze. "I want a capital ship, gentlemen. I want to bring this war to Japan, and the Marianas allows us to reach Tokyo from land-based airfields. This is a chance to make a big difference. We will make it to the battle. Is that understood?"

"Yes, sir!" The feeling in the room was so heady that the only thing Nate could compare it to was the football game he played in high school between East and West. The captain stood and moved to the microphone to tell the crew what was happening. His effect on the broad group was even more electric, and Nate could hear a cheer go up in every compartment. Having just completed a watch, it was his turn to hot bunk it for four hours. As he stripped down, he felt the four diesels winding up to maximum power and found himself thrilled as the ship started bucking its way at flank speed.

* * *

They'd only had to dive three times in the previous twenty-four hours. It seemed as though all the Japanese had gone missing in action. Even the usually ubiquitous air reconnaissance patrols were absent. When asked about it, Stahlei replied, "I suspect they've all been ordered to the battle. Our last report tells me that they've suffered a terrible loss of aircraft, something like three hundred in the last twenty-four hours." That drew an appreciative response from the men in the control room.

Now they had submerged and taken up position west of the Japanese fleet. Stahlei had decided to move through the screen of destroyers just before sunrise so he could get a shot at one of the carriers. It was risky, but in all his cruises, he'd never had the chance to take on a carrier, and he made it clear that was exactly what he wanted to do. Even though it didn't really matter what they thought, everyone in the wardroom was in agreement.

Six hours later—and after two rounds of depth charges and an encounter with a Japanese bomber—the captain ordered the periscope up for the last time. Even the normally unflappable Stahlei couldn't help but whistle when he reported on the battle scene. Japanese ships were in flames all around them, and the carrier that they'd picked out was under attack by dive-bombers. Even as he watched, a huge explosion sent up a cloud of smoke at the aft end of the deck.

"Alright, gentlemen, we're not going to get an exclusive on this, but we're in position to speed the carrier's demise. Load all forward torpedo tubes. I want a standard spread and will launch all the fish. Next, I want an immediate reload in case defensive action is needed or another target presents itself."

Stahlei started calling out the coordinates to Nate. As he dialed the controls on the TDC, the scene resolved itself in his mind. "We have a shooting solution, Captain!"

"Then fire at will, Mr. Brown."

Nate dialed the final correction. "Fire one! Fire two! Fire three! Fire four!" A pause of sixty seconds. "Fire five, Fire six!"

"Ahead two-thirds, port thirty degrees!"

The ship accelerated under their feet. As they moved closer to the target, but on a shearing course that would put them in front of it, Stahlei made his intention clear. He was going to turn around and use his stern tubes if other shots were needed.

"Thirty seconds," John called out solemnly. "Fifteen, fourteen, thirteen . . ." As the countdown reached zero, Akers took an unusual risk. "Up periscope!" He wanted to see what happened, which is why he was the first to register the hits from the *Tripletail*. He saw two great waterspouts and then a third and a fourth toward the bow. They waited, but no others appeared. It was impossible to know if they'd missed with the last two torpedoes or if they were duds, but they'd put four torpedoes below the waterline of the great carrier, and in no time at all, there was a noticeable list to starboard as the huge ship took on water.

"I want four fish from the stern tubes. Make ready stern tubes!"

Nate had already shifted the TDC to the stern so was in position to start an immediate plot. This time Stahlei wanted a closer aim directed specifically at the stern of the carrier. "Let's see if we can hit their propellers." Of course, at 2,000 yards, conventional wisdom was that any hit was a good hit. But with the beating the ship was taking from overhead and four in her side, it was worth the attempt. He called out very specific coordinates.

"Shooting solution obtained!"

"Then fire."

"Fire one! Fire two!" A pause. "Fire three! Fire four!" With the fish off and running, Stahlei ordered the ship ahead full-speed to put some distance between them. There were so many propellers in the water it was difficult to sort them out, but Nate's staff detected one growing louder, which prompted them to take immediate evasive action. They should have dived immediately, but at the last moment Stahlei ordered the periscope up—just in time to see a great waterspout at the tail end of the carrier—undoubtedly a direct hit on the propeller or steering mechanism.

"Only one, but that's enough. Now, let's get out of here. Take us to two hundred feet, Mr. Conrad." Then, "Good shooting, Nate."

Nate couldn't help but grin. "Thank you, sir!"

Akers stood and slapped him on the back and then handed him a rag to wipe the sweat from his face.

* * *

Later that night, the captain glanced at a new order. He handed it to the executive officer, who gave new coordinates to the helm. "Surface. All ahead full!" The crew gave each other a puzzled look, but no explanation was forthcoming.

Chapter Twenty-Five

IN THE WATER

Cory licked his lips and tasted salt. He awoke with a start, disoriented and thirsty. More thirsty than he could ever remember. He felt the sun beating down on him, and he had to squint when he tried to look east. Spencer's head still rested on his lap, but his body was cold and stiff. Normally, Cory would have been horrified, but this was Spencer, and Cory wasn't ready to let go of him yet. Assuming help didn't come shortly, which seemed very unlikely now, he'd have to roll Spencer's body into the sea, just as had been done for sailors since ancient times. It didn't seem unnatural or even unkind, but when the time came, he would irrevocably be alone. That was the part he dreaded.

He looked down at his leg. "Looks like I'll be joining you soon enough."

After they were hit, he had tried to put as much distance as possible between them and the island because the last thing he wanted was to be taken prisoner by the Japanese. Stories of the abuse suffered in the Philippines were sickening, and he knew that the Japanese would show little compassion for one of the pilots involved in the battles of the past week.

He didn't blame them. In the end, it was kind of a business transaction—two sides fighting it out, with winners and losers on both sides. The day before yesterday, he was among the winners, those who had made it back to their ship. Today, he was part of the losers, one among millions who would die in this war. In that regard, it didn't really matter which country won the war—it was an entirely personal war when one was in a lifeboat in the middle of a great ocean.

After this battle, it was inevitable that America would win the war. With the Japanese fleet in flames and land bases secured within a day's flight from Tokyo, the end was rapidly becoming a foregone conclusion. But how many more would have to die before that end was realized?

He looked around at the great expanse of nothingness. "We're out here where it's almost impossible to find us. So I get to die alone." He'd been on a couple of search and rescue flights and knew how difficult it was. "Just look how hard it is to find an entire Japanese fleet! It takes weeks sometimes, with hundreds of airplanes looking for dozens of capital-sized ships!" His tiny little dinghy would hardly be a speck on the vastness of the ocean. And, if another battle were to erupt, there would be far more pressing issues occupying the pilots than doing an extensive search pattern. So the most practical thing was to let go of hope so the remaining hours would not be passed in frustration and despair.

He looked down at Spencer. "You said it was a noble thing to help others gain their freedom." He shook his head as he thought about their many conversations again. Then he nodded. "I will miss you, Spencer Tolman." Tears welled again. "But I will not mourn you. It would dishonor what you have done." He rubbed his friend's hair. It was still soft. "And, maybe I'll see you soon.

"It isn't fair! I was the one who was going to drown in the cockpit until you saved me. Meanwhile, you were dying from a wound I didn't even know you had! How is it fair that you had to die instead of me?" Cory was surprised that he could still have enough moisture to muster yet another round of tears. "Why did you have to die, Spence? Why?"

He gently lifted the body off his lap and to his side so he could stretch his legs. He couldn't stand up, so he lifted them in turn, stretching as hard as he could. His left leg was as mangled in the daylight as he thought it was at night. *What was it they said about bone fragments? "If there is a bone fragment, the onset of infection is inevitable."*

"In other words, Mr. O'Brian, the leg will have to be amputated." He used his most authoritarian voice to complete the mental picture of the doctor telling him that. But there were no doctors out here, and he suddenly laughed at the thought of a shark performing the surgery.

Okay, that's a little weird. Let's try to focus on something a little less macabre. Skiing. With the sun baking down on him, the thought of the ski slopes seemed refreshing. He closed his eyes and rested his head on the side of the boat.

Just as he was about to make the final turn on his favorite course at Alta, he was almost knocked out of the boat by what at first seemed like a tremendous explosion, except that there was no concussion, just the sound of rushing water and escaping gas. The noise had come off his port side, so he turned anxiously to see what was happening. Suddenly—and it was very sudden—where moments earlier there had been nothing but flat ocean, a huge shape was boiling up and out of the water. It was like some giant sea monster, and for a moment he imagined that a whale was breaching. But it was much larger than a whale, and it finally dawned on him that it was a submarine.

"A submarine, Spencer, a submarine! We're being rescued!" His joy turned to horror. "What if it's a Japanese sub? What will we do?" He fumbled to see if he had his pistol in his pant leg, but it had been in the pant leg of his injured leg and had been blown away by the flak.

Fortunately, there wasn't much time to worry, because as the monster heaved into view, not ten feet from his position, he was relieved to see a United States flag and the enormous white numbers of the sub painted on the side of the conning tower. He watched in fascination as a hatch popped open in the forward part of the ship and a sailor came up and out of the hole.

"Hey, buddy. Are you hitching a ride?"

In spite of the seriousness of his condition, the absurdity of the question caused Cory to laugh. "Only if you promise you won't stop until we dock in Salt Lake City!"

"Salt Lake City, huh? I assume they have water there . . ."

Cory laid his head back and said a prayer of thanks. If ever there was a miracle, this was it. To be found in the open water of the Pacific Ocean by one of their own subs. He wiped his eyes with his hands, but immediately regretted it since the salt caked on his fingers started to burn immediately.

"Can you row over to us?"

Cory looked frantically for an oar, but in the hurry of getting out of the aircraft, it must have fallen out. "I don't have a paddle, but I'll try with my hands," he called back.

"No problem. We'll fire a line across you. Lay down until it drops on top of the boat."

Cory settled down, heard a loud pop, and listened as the air was disturbed by the line flying at high-speed overhead. The rope settled on him, and he lifted his head above the side. "It's here. I've got it!"

"Alright, we're going to haul you in. Hold on tight!"

With that, the crew started reeling him in like a fish. When the raft bumped up against the submarine, a couple of men came to help lift him out.

"My gunner is dead. Can you get him out first?"

The one sailor looked at the other. "Sure, no problem. Can you lift him up to us?"

Carefully, Cory wedged himself under the body again, and then lifted with what strength he could muster. Four strong arms took over and pulled Spencer's body up and out of the dinghy. Then they reached in and grabbed Cory's outstretched arms. When he was on the deck, one of the sailors pushed the dinghy away and then took out a handgun and shot it. The noise startled Cory, and he couldn't help but wince at the sound.

"Sorry, but we don't want anything left on the surface to tell enemy aircraft that we were here."

"That's alright." Cory was doing his best to balance on his good leg.

"We've got to get you below for some medical attention. Let me help you to the hatch."

"What about Spencer?"

The sailors turned and looked at the lieutenant who had come up to supervise. "I'm afraid we're going to have to bury him at sea. I'll send down for a body bag. We're too far out to bring him with us." He braced for Cory's response.

"I understand. Do you mind if I wait up here so I can say good-bye?"

The sailors looked relieved, and the lieutenant went over to the hatch, where he sent a message down to someone in the ship. A few moments later, another officer came up through the opening carrying a canvas bag. He introduced himself as the captain and expressed his sympathy. They removed Spencer's dog tags, then allowed Cory to put his hand on his shoulder one last time.

This time there were no tears. "I'll miss you, buddy. Watch out for me over there."

Just as they were about to close the bag, Cory let out a yelp. "Wait! I need to get something out of his pocket. It'll just take a second." He reached down inside the bag and fished around until he found the envelope. He whispered to Spencer, "A promise is a promise—and I'll keep this one." Then he stepped back and let them finish closing the bag.

The captain started to say a few words in tribute when one of the lookouts shouted, "Aircraft at 0900!"

The captain shouted, "Clear for diving!" People started moving faster than anything Cory had ever seen in his life. The captain grabbed him and said, "Sorry, but we've got to let him go so we can get out of here!"

"I understand."

Two sailors gently shoved the bag over the side. Another guy was forcing Cory toward the open hatch, but he still managed to catch a glimpse of the bag as it slipped under the waves. The next thing he knew, he was being lowered into the bowels of the ship, supported by two hands in his armpits. As he started to fall, he was caught by some others, who quickly moved him out of the way into a narrow passageway. All the jostling hurt his leg, but he realized that that was the least of their problems right then. He felt the ship moving in an odd, disorienting way that made him nauseous. Not that that was too unusual, given the amount of seawater he'd ingested and the fact that the whole sub reeked of diesel fuel and human body odor. But he watched in amazement as the entire deck party came sliding down the ladder—no one seemed to use the rungs—and the shaft of sunlight suddenly disappeared as he heard the distinct metallic thud of the hatch being closed.

The sickening motion increased, and he became disoriented. He knew that they were diving, which was becoming very obvious as the ship came under power and the deck tilted forward, but there was no reference point to help him judge the angle of descent. There was some kind of crashing sound, and then everything went quiet. Before he could fully comprehend what was happening, the ship started to level off and things grew very quiet.

A voice down the hall called out, "Damage control, report!"

"It appears they hit our communications array. The radio operator is assessing the damage, but it may be out of commission."

There was silence again for a few moments. Cory's heart beat faster than usual—not just from the news about getting hit, which seemed ominous enough, but there was something in the voice of the officer who called for the damage report. It was so familiar.

The captain responded, "Thank you, Mr. Brown. Let's stay down awhile, just in case, and then we'll surface to inspect the damage topside."

Chapter Twenty-Six

INCOMMUNICADO

Once he'd gotten past the shock of picking up Cory, Nate quickly compiled the damage control report for the captain. The enemy aircraft had done more serious damage than the initial report suggested. In an unusually lucky hit, it had destroyed their ability to communicate with Pearl or even with other ships in the area. With all but four fish fired, Captain Stahlei decided they should return directly to Pearl for repair. When Nate inquired about what they'd do with Cory, the captain said that he'd have to come along since it was too dangerous to try to find the fleet and communicate their intentions without a functioning radio.

"Looks like you get to be a submariner," Nate said cheerfully. "It'll do you good to see how the bottom dwellers live."

Cory tried to smile, but he was clearly concerned.

"You don't want our hospitality?"

"It's not that, Nate. I'm extremely glad to have your hospitality, particularly since the alternative is a rubber raft. It's just that they're going to list me as MIA, which means they'll send a telegram to Mom and Dad. You can imagine what that will do to them."

"Of course. I should have thought about that. Kathy will be frantic too." Nate's mind started racing, but he couldn't come up with any alternatives. "I know it will be terrible on them, but we really don't have any choice."

"So if you drive this thing well, how long before we get to Pearl?"

"About three weeks. At least they won't have to be left in the dark too long. In the old days, we stood a pretty good chance of seeing some action, but the Japanese are getting harder and harder to find as you head east. So it may be a pretty boring voyage."

"Sounds fine to me. I saw enough enemy to keep me for a day or two. And one of them had my number. How is it you came to rescue me?"

Nate was puzzled by the leisurely pace of Cory's conversation, given the injuries he'd suffered and the stress he was going through. Then, when Cory's head started to nod, Nate shouted for immediate medical assistance.

* * *

Cory heard Nate's shout, but he jerked awake at the sound of Hospital Apprentice Jones's voice. Something was wrong. He wasn't in the corridor. He was in a bed, and when he felt down for his leg, he realized that it had been set. "What happened?" he asked groggily.

"You took a little nap," Nate said quietly. "Seaman Jones did his best to set the leg immediately after the ship stabilized."

"How long has it been?"

"A couple of hours."

It was difficult for Cory to concentrate. Then he felt a stab of pain and realized that he must have been given morphine. When he touched the wound, the sharpness of the pain told him that his leg was still in trouble.

Nate introduced him to Jones and asked, "How's he doing?"

Jones looked a little pale. "If the ensign will pull up his blanket, you'll see some nasty red streaks starting to radiate out from the wound. We have to do something fast, or he'll be in serious trouble."

This was the conversation that Cory had dreaded. He knew what had to happen. There was no sense making Jones say it. "So how much of the leg do I have to lose?"

The relief in the young man's face was immediate.

"About midcalf. That's very good, because it will make it easy to attach an artificial limb, and you'll have mobility at the knee."

Nate spoke up, "When should we do the surgery, Mr. Jones?"

"We should do it right now, Lieutenant Brown. Now that I see how fast it's spreading, we should have done it the second he came on board."

"Alright, tell me what you need, and we'll get started." Nate turned and smiled at Cory.

"Have you ever done an amputation?" Cory asked quietly.

"I'm sorry to say that I have. With all this equipment on board, it's almost inevitable that somebody will get a bone or a limb crushed. Infection is sure to follow. Unfortunately, I'm not a surgeon, so about the only thing I can do is cut and sew and then wait for a hospital at port."

Cory laid his head back and swallowed hard. He was frightened—extremely frightened. "Well, let's go to it then. Is there anyway you can be here with me, Lieutenant Brown?"

"I'll be here the whole time. Somebody's got to hand John the instruments." The puzzled look on Jones's face prompted a follow-up. "I guess you haven't heard that Ensign O'Brian here is my brother-in-law. My wife will have my hide if we don't do this right."

"Oh, I thought there must be something special about him, the way everybody was treating him."

"Not only that, but he's my friend and a very good man."

"You don't need to worry, sir. We'll make it right."

"I'll be back as quick as I can, Cory. I'm going to report to the captain. He'll take us down so we can remain nice and steady during the surgery."

"Thanks, Nate."

It was hard to hear Cory, his voice was so quiet. Nate saw the sheet trembling on his hammock and knew it wasn't from the cold.

Forty minutes later, the submarine was submerged and holding at neutral buoyancy. The captain had shut down all nonessential functions so there would be no distractions for Seaman Jones.

"I'm going to give you some more morphine, sir, to numb you up."

"Okay."

"Now, Lieutenant, if you were to come up here at the head of the table and hold Mr. O'Brian's shoulders while Mr. Akers there holds his leg above the knee, we'll get started." Having previously sliced off Cory's pant leg at midcalf, Jones poured some whiskey over the open wound, which, even with the morphine, caused Cory to wince. Then he pulled out a saw and a scalpel. He drew a line around Cory's skin above the highest break and then made an incision to separate the skin. Bleeding was controlled by a new tourniquet. "This is going to hurt, Ensign, so if you want to scream, just go ahead and let it out. Everybody on the ship will understand."

Nate looked sympathetically at Cory's heaving chest. He was taking great deep breaths to try to calm himself. "It's going to be okay, Cory. You need to slow your breathing. It will be alright."

And then the cutting began. Cory let out an involuntary sob, and then bit down as hard as he could on the cloth-wrapped stick they'd given him to hold between his teeth. His whole body trembled at the exercise, and he made strangled, gurgling sounds as he fought to control himself. Tears streamed down both his cheeks. Mercifully, when the blade hit the marrow of his bone, he let out a shriek, and then passed out from the pain.

"That will be better then," Jones said. "Now he can rest while we do this bloody job."

* * *

When Cory awoke the next morning, he felt like his left foot was on fire, and he gasped in pain as he struggled against the restraints to reach down and rub it.

"Call Lieutenant Brown and tell him that Ensign O'Brian is waking up." The chief of the boat had taken his turn waiting for Cory and wanted to make sure that Nate was there when he gained consciousness. Nate came running.

"I've got to touch my foot. Please, let me touch my foot. It's burning up!" Cory struggled to reach down to where his left foot should have been.

Jones had joined them and said, "It's called phantom-limb pain, sir. Your brain doesn't realize that your foot is gone, and so it creates a sense of pain from the nerves that are no longer communicating with it."

"How long will it last?"

"It can last forever, I'm afraid. From what I understand, it usually goes away eventually, but for the next few days you're likely to feel a lot of pain from a leg that has now been flushed out to sea." Jones was not known for his delicate manner of speech.

"Nate, help me with my foot. It's killing me!"

Nate turned to Jones. "Can you give him something for it?"

"I've got morphine, but he's already had a lot."

"I think you better give him some more." It took only a few moments after the injection before Cory started to calm down. In just a matter of minutes, he'd fallen asleep again. Nate raised the sheet and looked at the stump. Jones had done a very credible job of drawing the skin together and stitching it. More importantly, the red streaks above the incision had disappeared. Nate could see the yellow stains of the sulfa powder that had been poured liberally in the wound to try to stem the spread of the infection. Even with all of that, it was still a gruesome sight, with the dark stitches holding the inflamed skin together in an unsightly bundle.

"Are you alright, Mr. Brown?"

"What? Oh, yes, I'm alright. Why?"

"You're very pale, sir. I take it this is your first surgery to observe?"

The comment irritated Nate. But then, when he thought about it, he backed off. "It's not that. It's that for the first time in the war, I know all the people who care about the patient, and I can just picture what he's going to have to go through as he deals with this kind of loss. He's a nice kid, the kind who seldom complains, so he won't even have the relief that comes from getting angry. Is he going to be alright, Jones?"

"I didn't do as well as I should have. There was a crack in the bone that went above the point of amputation. That's going to cause him trouble. And I'm afraid that I left some of his nerve endings more ragged than I'd have liked. That's going to cause him unnecessary pain." When he saw the look in Nate's face, he hastened to add, "It's not that I didn't try, sir. But the tools I have to work with are just too crude. So I did all this in such a way that they can fix it up when we get back to Pearl. It's not unusual to have more than one surgery, you know."

Nate calmed down. "I know, John. I appreciate what you did."

* * *

The next three weeks were discouraging. Cory's leg hurt almost constantly, and there were a few occasions when the tissue around the stitches flared up, giving rise to fears of infection. The sulfa did a fairly good job of holding it down, but it meant that Cory was always in pain. HA Jones did his best to strike a balance between giving him the medication he needed to live with the pain without giving so much that it would create addiction problems for him.

Fortunately, other than having to dive on two occasions because of fear that they'd encountered an enemy sub on the surface, the trip went without incident. Even though it frustrated

Captain Stahlei to return home with fish still in inventory, he held a steady course.

As word of Cory's relationship to Nate circulated through the ship, people went out of their way to be nice to him. One by one they stopped by and introduced themselves, told him what a great officer Nate was, and then offered to do anything they could to help. Many offered him cigarettes before they put two and two together. Then they made it clear that there were no cigarettes for him, even if he wanted one. It was obvious that Nate had gained their respect even in that regard.

About a week after the surgery, Cory asked if he could get out of the bed and stretch his good leg.

It bothered Nate that he started calling his right leg *good,* which implied that the left leg was *bad.* "It's just shorter than the other one," Nate tried to tease, but Cory simply shrugged.

When the time came to swing his legs over the edge of the bed, Cory gasped in pain as the stump fell lower than his torso. The increased flow of blood caused an immediate stinging sensation, and he reported that it felt like the end was going to blow right off.

"Perfectly normal, sir," Jones assured him. "But it will ease up as the wound continues to heal."

"I hope so," he said breathlessly, "because this is pretty hard to deal with." With Nate's help, he stood down on his good leg and used his arms to brace against the narrow walls of the passage so he could hop back and forth a few steps before asking for help back into bed. He lay back exhausted. "At least it's a start," he said through clenched lips.

"It's a good start, Cory. A very good start."

* * *

"Ensign O'Brian!"

Cory looked up, and then sat up, as Captain Stahlei saluted him. He immediately returned the salute, from the sitting position.

"Yes, sir!"

"I wanted you to know that we're about two hours from Pearl. I've asked the crew to rummage among their things to get you a new set of clothes. Mr. Jones is going to help you take a shower. The crew has been saving water so you can take a long enough shower to get really clean. That's actually quite a big deal on a submarine."

"Yes, sir. I know. Thank you. Thanks to all of you."

"When you get dressed, we'll carry you to the forward escape hatch. I think that will be the easiest one for you to navigate. Of course, we'll have someone assigned to help you out. We're going to surface as we make the approach to Pearl and will indicate by flags that we've lost our radio. As soon as we get a confirmation, we'll send a semaphore requesting medical assistance at the dock."

"You've all been so good to me, Captain. I can't thank you enough for rescuing me." He dropped his gaze. "I'm sorry it cost you your communications tower."

"Not to worry. That's the hazards of war. We were about finished with our cruise, anyway."

"Yes, sir."

"At any rate, O'Brian, I want to wish you luck and a good recovery. I've read your report, and I'm recommending both you and Ensign Tolman for a citation. You should be proud of your service."

Cory had actually managed to spend the previous twenty-four hours without thinking about Spencer, and the mention of his name caused his throat to tighten. But this was a great honor to be spoken to in this way by a ship's captain, so he swallowed hard and thanked Captain Stahlei again for his kind words.

"One more thing. Nate's going to be busy while we're in port, but I'll make sure he has as much time as he needs to come see you at the base hospital. Good luck, son."

By the time he hobbled out of the shower and into a good, clean towel, he felt better than he'd felt in weeks. Pulling on his skivvies, then a clean pair of Navy blues, he had a sense of himself again. His mind was always a little bit hazy because he continued to need pain medication, but even that couldn't subdue the excitement he felt at finally getting out of the sub and into the fresh air. He'd decided weeks earlier that he was made for the sky, not for the deep.

Two hours later, Cory stood at the base of the forward hatch. "We made it!" he said brightly. "Thanks for the lift, Nate."

Nate returned the smile. "Right now, I'm just glad to get you to Pearl so we can send that telegram to your folks."

Chapter Twenty-Seven

REHAB AT PEARL

It was always a grand event when a ship returned to Pearl Harbor from combat. Occasionally, there would be a band at the pier to greet her, particularly after an unusually successful cruise. But since the *Tripletail* hadn't been able to communicate her return, there was little of the usual pageantry. Still, as she pulled through the aquiline waters of the harbor, other ships mustered sailors to stand at attention and salute, merchant marine vessels sounded their horns, and dockworkers at her assigned berth stood at attention. The men of the *Tripletail* did their part by assembling on deck in their dress whites, held in reserve for this occasion as there weren't a lot of formal dinners at sea. Since it was too painful for Cory to stand, they'd brought up a chair that they placed near the conning tower. As the lines were thrown overboard to tie them up, Nate came back to assist Cory off the boat.

"The machinists made a present for you, Cory. This used to be a chair." He held out a nicely turned crutch.

Cory laughed. "This is probably the most useful present I've ever received." Holding himself in position with his right hand braced against the conning tower, he held up the crutch in his other hand and waved to the crew. "Thank you!" he shouted. Everyone applauded to wish him well. At a more practical level, the medical party from the hospital came onboard with a wheelchair and helped Cory get settled. "I guess this is good-bye, Nate. At least for awhile."

"Actually, it isn't. Captain Stahlei wants me to accompany you to the hospital. I think the crew has come to think of you as one of us, and so he wants one of our officers to go with you."

Cory smiled. It was just another one of the small things he'd observed Stahlei do that made his men so loyal. "I'll be glad to have you. For some reason, I'm kind of scared again. But you've got to admit, it feels great to have the sun on your face!"

As they proceeded toward Diamondhead, there was a lot of congestion on the road. "What's up?" Nate asked the driver.

"They're staging a variety show. Jimmy Durante is here, along with a bunch of other performers, so they had to plan for the whole island to attend."

Nate laughed. "That would be some show. How long are they here?"

"Just a couple of days, I think."

"Who's the band?"

"I haven't heard of them before—some French name—but a lot of guys from the West Coast say they're really good."

Cory went weak. "It's Dad, Nate. He's here. We have to see him. Can we pull over, driver?"

"I can't do that, Ensign. I'm under orders."

Nate intervened. "He's made it this far without the services of a hospital, he can certainly make it a few more minutes while we check it out."

"Oh, this is bad. I'm going to get in trouble. I just can't. You can check it out later—"

"I'll take full responsibility."

The driver didn't say anything, but suddenly the car lurched and they heard the siren sound from under the hood. "If I'm going to do this, we might as well do it in style!" The driver turned and flashed them a toothy grin.

The crowd was miffed as the ambulance pulled up behind the stage. Fortunately, the driver turned off the siren before they got too close. As they rolled to a stop, Cory smiled and said, "That's them alright—nobody plays 'Mood Indigo' like that. I just can't believe it. What are we going to do?"

"I'm going to go up on stage and pull him away to come see you."

"No, wait, Nate. Can you help me on stage? If you can catch Jim Chatterton's eye, I think I can pay Dad back for something he did for me a long time ago."

Nate looked at him suspiciously, but helped him out of the car and up onto the stage.

As they stumbled behind the backdrop, the sound of the band playing on the other side, Cory looked over at a table and saw his mother. When she looked up, it was just too much emotion and he slumped to the floor.

"Cory!" she shouted, but the noise of the band was too much for her to be heard. She ran across the back of the stage and slumped to his side, where she started laughing and sobbing and caressing him. After a few moments, she glanced at his leg. "You're hurt. Oh, my dear boy, you're hurt."

"It's okay, Mom. I've had some trouble with my leg, but everything's fine. Nate helped me a lot."

"Nate?" It was the only word she could get out as she looked up at her son-in-law.

He laughed. "It's way too complicated—just one of those miracles I've come to expect with your family."

"Oh, Nate. We've been so worried. Your ship has been incommunicado, and Cory's been missing in action. It's been the hardest thing in the world to keep our sanity. Dan has been frantic. But now you're both here." She started crying again.

Cory pulled her close and rested his head on her shoulder.

Recovering, Sarah stroked his face and said, "Oh, my beautiful boy, are you in a lot of pain?"

"It hurts. Sometimes really bad. But I'm okay." The words were hard to get out, but as she wiped his tears, he remembered the smell of her hand, and it filled him with warmth and comfort.

"Mom, can I surprise Dad?"

"I'm sure you will—you about surprised me into an early grave."

"No, I want to do something special. I need Jim's help."

He then whispered his plan to his mother. She got up and went to the edge of the backdrop.

A few moments later Jim Chatterton came off the stage to see what was wrong. When he saw Cory, his jaw dropped open, then he kneeled down on the plywood floor and vigorously shook his hand. Jim was not one to show his emotions, so the most he could say was, "Looks like you've done alright by yourself, Cory. Looks like you've done fine."

Cory smiled at the sound of his voice, thinking back on all the times that Jim had chased Cory and a friend off the stage for causing some kind of trouble. The Terrace Ballroom came into his mind and a whole new set of emotions swept over him—things that couldn't be said. He just shook Jim's hand in return and told him how glad he was to see him.

Sarah told Jim what they had in mind, and Jim told her he'd arrange it. A few moments later, he handed a microphone to Cory and helped him hop to a place just out of sight of the stage where he could rest against the backdrop. When the song ended, Jim stepped out on the stage. One of the entertainers started telling a couple of jokes, which gave Jim time to move around the stage, whispering to the band members. Dan was busy looking over an arrangement, so he didn't suspect anything. Finally, when they turned the show back over to the band, Dan looked at everyone, raised his hand, and brought it down.

But they didn't respond as he suggested.

Instead, without any accompaniment, the words to an old, familiar song emerged from the loudspeaker system.

God be with you till we meet again;
By his counsels guide, uphold you;
With his sheep securely fold you.
God be with you till we meet again.

At that, Cory's words faded, but the band picked up the chorus. The initial look of irritation on Dan's faced was replaced by shock and then recognition, and he bolted off the piano bench and went racing to the back of the stage where Cory stepped out into the sunlight. He swept his son into his arms. If Dan noticed his missing leg, he didn't make mention of it. He just hugged Cory as hard as he could until Cory laughed and squeaked out the words, "I surrender, Dad!" Only then did Dan release his grip and step back to look Cory squarely in the face. Dan pursed his lips and then gave him another, more gentle hug.

As the song drew to an end, Jim Chatterton stepped forward and announced, "Ladies and gentlemen, we've just had a little reunion on stage. It seems that our bandleader's son, Ensign Cory O'Brian, has just returned by way of submarine from the Marianas where his Dauntless dive-bomber was shot down by hostile ground fire. Ensign O'Brian was on his way to the hospital when they realized we were here. So perhaps you'd join me in welcoming him home! He's been listed as MIA for the past three weeks."

As Cory and Dan stepped out into full view, the crowd went crazy. When they realized that Cory had lost his leg, everyone rose in a standing ovation. Dan motioned for Nate and Sarah to join them, and together they celebrated their reunion with a thousand men in uniform from all branches of the military.

"Welcome back, Cory," Dan whispered. "And if you ever do something like this again, I'll beat you silly!"

Cory laughed and waved to the crowd.

"You four get out of here!" Jim Chatterton yelled in Dan's ear. "If you hang around, you'll ruin all this. Go with your boys. We'll be fine."

"Thanks, Jim."

Jim gave Cory a thumbs-up, then signaled for the band to play "Strike Up the Band." With everybody already on their feet, they needed something exciting, and that was just the ticket to keep things revved up. Jim had a sense about such things.

Chapter Twenty-Eight

A DIFFERENT KIND
OF BATTLE

"Mr. and Mrs. O'Brian, may I speak with you for a moment?"

Dan and Sarah looked up at Cory's doctor.

"Of course. Is this a good place?" Dan responded.

"Better in my office. It's just down the hall."

Naturally, that raised some alarms in their minds. All indications to this point were that Cory's surgery had gone well and that his leg was healing in a satisfactory way.

Once they were again seated, the doctor cleared his throat. "Your son's leg is healing very well. As I probably told you before, we were able to save enough bone beneath the knee that he should be able to wear a prosthesis that allows him a great deal of flexibility. I'm pleased with the results."

"But?"

The doctor looked uncomfortable. He wasn't used to dealing with parents here in Hawaii. "By this point in his recovery, we would expect his pain management to be further along than it apparently is."

This didn't have any significance to Dan, until he turned and looked at his wife, who had gone noticeably pale. "What does that mean?" he asked.

"It means that usually we'd expect the patient to be either completely off morphine, or at least at a much smaller dosage than Ensign O'Brian continues to request."

"Are you saying he's addicted?" Dan asked in alarm.

"No, I'm not saying that at all. But apparently he was using the drug quite heavily during his time on the submarine. Given the condition of the wound when he got here, I can under- stand why. But now, with an additional two weeks, it's time he learns to manage this better."

"What do you suggest we do?" Sarah asked.

"You're a nurse, aren't you, Mrs. O'Brian?"

"I am."

"Have you ever had experience with this?"

Sarah sighed. "I'm afraid I have. It can be quite a trial for the patient."

"Well, that's why I invited you in. We can take control of the situation, if you like. But I thought it might be easier if one or both of you talked with him. I don't know if your travel plans permit you to stay, but I'm sure it would help your son if someone remained with him throughout the ordeal, assuming he has developed some kind of dependency."

"So you don't know that he's dependent?"

"No, Mr. O'Brian, I don't. I do know that he's been known to badger the nurses for more and that he's even tried decep- tion on at least two occasions to get more drugs than he should. But that could all be due to legitimate pain. We'll find out soon enough once we begin to reduce the dosage and then withdraw it."

"Sarah?" Dan looked to his wife.

"I've worried that Cory has a problem, Dan, just by the way he gets when the drug starts to wear off. It's a fairly stark personality change. In fact, I was going to approach Dr. Linder about it myself."

"So do you want to be involved?" the doctor asked.

"I'll talk with him," Sarah said quietly.

"No, it should be me."

Sarah looked at Dan with surprise. Usually he'd withdraw from something like this. The haunted look in his eye certainly made it appear that he'd want to avoid it. "There's more going on here than pain in his amputated limb. Perhaps it's time we talk." When Sarah looked doubtful, he continued, "It turns out that in this case, I'm the one with the relevant experience." Dan inhaled slowly, and released his breath through pursed lips. "My war meets Cory's war."

"I'm glad, Dan. I think you're right."

Dr. Linder's inquiring look prompted Dan to quickly explain that he'd been wounded in the First World War and knew what it was like to live with the pain and loss. "When's the best time to start, Doctor?"

"The sooner the better, actually. I'm sure your wife can fill you in on what to expect, but I'd be glad to answer any questions either of you have." When Dan didn't say anything, the doctor added quietly, "He may require restraints, particularly to protect his leg. That can be pretty hard to deal with, and he may say things that are hard to hear . . ."

Dan smiled wanly. "As I said, I think I'm the one who has the relevant experience."

* * *

Cory looked up and smiled at his father. "Got a little time off from rehearsal?"

"I've got all afternoon."

"Good. It's getting kind of boring around here. Maybe we could play a board game or something."

"I'd like that. How are you feeling?"

"I'm feeling pretty good, but my leg is hurting a lot. I was hoping maybe they could give me something for it."

"Haven't you already received your dose of medication?"

"I guess—but it doesn't last as long as it needs to. I keep trying to tell them that, but they don't listen. Maybe you could say something?" Cory smiled again.

"Actually, that's why I'm here."

Cory's smile faded. "What do you mean?" There was an instant edge to his voice.

"I mean that maybe it's time for you to move to the next level in pain control. Perhaps it's time for you to start managing it on your own, without the aid of drugs."

Cory's face hardened into a look that Dan had never seen before. It unnerved him, but he did his level best to keep his expression neutral.

"Dad, it's about the morphine, isn't it? I knew something was up by the way the nursing staff was acting. This isn't a problem. I just need it to take the edge off. I'm not addicted."

"That's why it's important that you start to taper off now. I'm sure you don't want to become addicted."

Cory's face flushed. "Listen, Dad, this really isn't something for you to decide. This is a medical problem, and I don't think you know just how bad this thing feels. I think you should leave this with the doctors."

"They're the ones who asked me to talk with you, Cory. They wanted to cut you off immediately, but your mother has talked them into a more gradual reduction if that will help ease you through the transition."

Now there was cold fury in Cory's voice. "So everybody's been talking about me! Behind my back, no less! Well, I don't need any of you people to tell me whether my leg hurts or not. I can't believe you'd think this about me."

Dan sat quietly, even though his heart was pounding in his chest and his stomach was churning. His heart beat even harder so that he could feel it in his temples, but he knew that if he tried to convince Cory, it would only provoke a counter-argument. He had to stay quiet—not an easy thing to do.

After a good minute, which felt like an hour, Cory finally said, "Well, aren't you going to say anything?"

Dan pursed his lips and reached out and rested his hand on Cory's. At first, Cory started to pull away, but then he left his hand in contact with his father's. Dan was relieved.

Tears dripped down Cory's cheeks. Now he whispered, with a desperate edge to his voice, "I don't know if I can do it, Dad. I'm terrified of what will happen if I don't get the drug. The pain can be excruciating."

"That's why your mother and I will be here the whole time."

"Does the doctor really think I'm addicted?" There was a sound of panic in his voice.

Dan knew that his thoughts were racing, undoubtedly caused by Cory trying to picture the future as a lifetime of yearning and addiction. It was a bleak picture for those who fell into the trap. "He doesn't think so. But you're definitely to the point that you have to deal with it. I think it's going to be really difficult."

Cory was silent for at least another minute, his eyes clenched. Dan saw him squeezing his hands in a rhythmic pattern. Dan wanted to reach out and take him in his arms and just give him what he wanted—what his body may actually have needed. But this was a battle that had to be fought, and only Cory could fight it. On top of everything else his son had gone through, he now had to face this ordeal and win it by himself.

"It really does hurt." Cory smiled through his tears. His statement was a reflection of the fact that he wanted to save at least some of his dignity. For a boy who had never broken the Word of Wisdom, this had to be a humiliating and embarrassing experience—and very frightening.

"I know it hurts, son. And so does your leg, doesn't it?"

Cory shook his head as he tried to process this unusual turn of the phrase. Then it hit him what his dad had said. "Yes—even my leg." He started crying more freely. "Oh, Dad, what am I going to do? What's going to happen to me? How can I go through life like this, without a leg?"

Dan leaned over and embraced him. They hugged for the longest time, and Dan's heart seemed to melt.

Finally, Cory sighed and let his chest heave a few times before he caught his breath. "Oh, boy, am I scared."

"I know you are, and I know that you have good reason to be. But I also know that this battle will be fought with your heart and soul, and because they are so good and so strong, I know that you will win. I have absolutely no doubt of that, Cory. No doubt whatsoever." Dan felt Cory relax a little.

"I just don't see the future right now. It's not that I'm mad at anybody, and it's not that I feel sorry for myself. This happened—it happens to lots of guys. I'm lucky to be alive, but I don't know what to do with that life. The future isn't black. It's just blank."

Dan shook his head in amazement. "You are a thousand times ahead of where I was when I was wounded, Cory. I surely wasn't able to see things from such a generous perspective. I was angry, and I felt betrayed. I didn't want anything to do with anybody. If I could have crawled in a cave and stayed there until I died, I would have."

Cory was quiet. "I get angry, and I get scared. But it doesn't do me any good. So I try to be strong." He pondered a moment. "But for all my brave words, I haven't done it without the help of medication. So maybe I'd feel just like you did without it."

"No, I don't think so. What you told me is that you're not going to play the role of a victim, even though you have a dozen good reasons to do so. The drug thing can be fixed. The harder task is to heal emotionally—something I'm not sure I've ever done. But I think you will." He smiled. "That shows remarkable maturity."

"It doesn't answer my questions."

"Then let's talk about them." Dan's anxiety had subsided, as it always did after facing a problem. "Have you thought about a singing career? You could join the band—I'm sure the Navy would love to send you on tour with us. And I honestly believe you have the talent to make it commercially." Though he tried to remain calm and dispassionate, the hopefulness in Dan's voice betrayed him.

Cory's face flushed, and he stammered a bit before responding. "Dad, making music is your dream. You love it and you're so good at it. You touch people's lives in ways that are wonderful. But it just isn't my dream. I like singing. I think I'll always do it at church and maybe even in community theatre. But not as my life's work. I just don't want that kind of life, always on the road, always under pressure to come out with a new hit. And being famous doesn't matter to me. It's just not for me." He looked at his father anxiously. "I didn't hurt your feelings, did I?"

Dan quietly took a deep breath. He needed his voice to be steady for this response. He had always nurtured the hope that Cory would choose music, would choose to follow in his footsteps. But now it was time to release those dreams. So he smiled. "No—it doesn't hurt my feelings. I guess I've known all along. You have a natural talent, to be sure, but it's just music to you. To me it's the innermost feelings of a person's heart, it's the majesty of God and His creations. To me, music is life itself. But I know it doesn't mean all that to most people. And that's alright." He smiled again, as if reassuring both of them. "So what we need to do is find out what your dream is. Or what it can be."

"You're not sad? I've dreaded the day we'd have this conversation."

Dan laughed. "Sad? Not in the least. If you felt about music as I do, I'd be happy. But I've lived long enough to know that there's something out there for everybody, something that matters to you as much as music does to me. You have to find that."

"Thanks, Dad."

"I'm sorry if I made you think I'd be unhappy. I probably pushed you too hard—but I never wanted it to come at your expense."

"I'm glad we got to make music together. I hope we can do it again—often. But for pleasure, not for work. For pleasure and for joy. If nothing else, to make you and Mom happy, because I know you love it so much."

Dan swallowed his disappointment, doing his best to cover it with a look of interested concern. "Now back to my question. What about you? Have you thought about what you're going to do in the Navy until your enlistment runs out?"

Cory sighed. "Not really. I can't imagine doing anything but flying. A desk job would kill me. And I'd miss the other pilots."

"Isn't there someplace where you could work with the pilots? Perhaps training?"

Cory was thoughtful again. "Probably not on a ship. But maybe I could teach at ground school. That's the perfect place for former pilots, because they can speak from experience. The Navy might go for that."

Dan sat silently at his son's side. This conversation could have gone so badly, but now it seemed to have taken the kind of turn he'd hoped for. Far better, in fact. *Thank you, Heavenly Father . . .*

The thoughtfulness in Cory's expression toughened up a bit, and he said with something resembling resolve, "If I'm going to do this, I've got to wean myself from the morphine. It may be the only thing standing between me and the kind of life I want to have. You'll help me?" The resolve was mingled with a tinge of panic that had crept back into his voice.

"Even better, your mom and I will help you. And God. With your doctors and the nursing staff, I think that's a pretty good support team."

"Whew." Cory blew the air through his teeth slowly and deliberately. "Maybe you better give me one last hug before I go crazy for a few days. I'm not sure what it's like, but from what I've heard, I may not be nice again for quite awhile."

Dan sat on the edge of the bed and pulled his boy to close to him. Just then, Sarah walked in. The poignant expression on Dan's face told her what she needed to know, and she came over and sat next to the two men in her life.

* * *

It was much harder than anyone expected, even for Sarah and the medical staff. The thing that wasn't obvious until they started to taper off the dosage was just how much the drug had asserted itself. It soon became clear that Cory was both physically and psychologically dependent on morphine, and the next three days and nights were the longest in any of their lives. Between the three of them, Dan, Sarah, and Nate, they kept a twenty-four-hour vigil at Cory's side. Sometimes they'd read to him, sometimes they'd hold him while his body trembled and convulsed, sometimes they'd have to just sit and watch as he twisted and turned, crying out with something of an animal sound. At times, tears would flow as he tried to cope with the pain and the unspeakable desire. Like the siren song of ancient Greek mythology, the pull of the drug was enough to make him mad with yearning, and his body ached for relief.

The changes in his mood were so profound as to almost be unbelievable. Sometimes he'd be subdued and withdrawn, others angry and hurtful, and still others grateful and fawning. Sometimes the latter was sincere, yet other times it was an attempt to manipulate their emotions to get just a bit more than the medical staff prescribed. It was wrenching to watch and terrible to experience. At one point, he whispered to his dad that he wished he had died on the ocean. For the first time in their lives, Cory and Dan truly understood each other. Now Cory knew why his father had been so adamant against the war. The boy felt a wave of empathy for the man who had been a boy in an earlier war, and he took comfort that his father understood what he was going through.

On the second day, the worst of the three, an unexpected ally joined the battle. The *Enterprise* had returned to port, and Jack Wilson made his way to the hospital. At first, Dan and Sarah had tried to keep him away, fearing that Cory would be embarrassed. Jack was not the type to be easily dissuaded, however, and eventually intuited what was going on. In his usual way, he was very direct. "Is Cory having some trouble getting off the morphine?"

Dan and Sarah turned and looked at each, trying to decide what to say. But of course that act alone confirmed Jack's suspicion.

"Listen, it's great that you are here to help him. But don't you think he really needs someone who was out there with him?"

"That would be very nice," Sarah replied. "Let me tell him you're here."

Far from being embarrassed, Cory sat straight up in bed and shouted for Jack to come in. For the next three hours, the two of them talked nonstop while Dan and Sarah stayed out in the waiting room. Although they didn't consciously try to listen in, occasionally they'd hear phrases, including the names of people they served with, even the young man who had been Cory's gunner. When Jack finally emerged from the room, Cory was asleep. One of the first times he'd been able to sleep since the ordeal had started.

"He's a great kid, you know that?"

"We know. Thank you for helping him."

"He had a lot on his mind. It's scary out there. And losing your gunner is about the hardest thing that can happen to a guy."

Dan nodded. "I'm glad he has a Navy colleague to talk to. I know I needed someone from the infantry when I was wounded."

"Actually, Cory talked to me about that once. I was almost in the same spot he is, and he pulled me through a tough night. I'm glad I could help him." Jack looked down at his watch. "Listen, I've got to go, but I'll be back. How long is he going to be like this?"

"It should start to break tomorrow," Sarah replied. "Another twenty-four hours, and the chemical addiction will start to abate."

"Then I'll be here as much as I can."

* * *

While Dan hadn't told the band what was going on, they knew that something intense was happening at the hospital, so Jim Chatterton had taken over at the keyboard and told Dan to take as much time as he needed. As the week drew to a close Dan approached them, because it was time for the band to head back to the States.

"I don't know what to do, Jim. I need to go with you guys, but I'm not sure Cory is out of the woods yet."

"You should stay, of course. We can cover the gigs in San Francisco, and you'll join up with us when we get back to Salt Lake City."

Dan hesitated.

"I know you think you're indispensable, Dan, and you are. But at this moment you're indispensable here too. Just relax and trust us. You know I can't replace you on the keyboard since our ratings are going down by the minute. And we won't hire a replacement. So take it easy and come home when you can."

"Thanks, Jim. I appreciate all of you watching out for me. Will you say good-bye to the guys for me? It would be kind of hard—"

"Of course I will."

The two embraced, and Dan returned to the hospital.

* * *

At the end of the second week, Cory was starting to act more like himself again. His leg was stitched properly, which caused him no end of itching, and the doctors had him up and moving around to maintain his strength. With the physical pull of the drug gone, the battle was much easier to fight, although there were times he found himself reaching for the bell to request some pain medication before he realized what he was doing.

Dan was helping him exercise his leg when Dr. Linder stopped by to check on him.

"Can I ask you a question, Dr. Linder?"

"Anything you like, Ensign."

"I know I'm supposed to be over the physical addiction, but sometimes I find myself still wanting it. Is that natural?"

"Chances are it's a psychological yearning. You won't have an actual physical need for morphine again. But your mind may give you a little more trouble."

That frightened Cory. "So is this something that will bother me the rest of my life?"

"I don't think so. You've beaten it. You'll have to watch yourself if you get in a particularly tense situation, but it will go away, and before long, you'll think of this as a bad memory. I don't think I'd ever let anyone prescribe morphine again, if I were in your shoes. Tell them you're allergic to it so you don't have to go into all this. But I can honestly tell you that you'll be fine." Dr. Linder could see that something was still bothering him. "What else, Ensign?"

"I was just wondering if this is going to go in my permanent record. Will I be put in a category of abusers?"

The doctor sighed. "What will go in your report is that you took morphine under doctor's orders. It seems to me that if anyone is responsible, it's your medical staff. It's unfortunate that you developed this fundamental attachment to the drug. But if I were to go back, I don't think I'd change anything, given the time it took you to get back from the scene of the battle."

Cory still didn't look reassured.

"Let me be clear—there will be nothing in your permanent record, because you did nothing wrong. What I'd like to put in your record is that you deserve far more than the Purple Heart you're going to get, because you fought an even tougher battle and won. In my mind, you're a hero twice over."

Finally, Cory looked relieved. "Thank you, sir. It was tough." Cory shuddered as some of the memories of the worst days of his ordeal came back. Thankfully, he'd forgotten a lot of them.

The doctor was thoughtful. "You're a good person, Ensign O'Brian. You're lucky to have people who care about you so much. Maybe you could stop in and look me up if you come back through Pearl again. I'd like to see how you're doing."

"I promise, sir. Thank you. I'll never forget what you did—never."

As the doctor walked away, Cory was very quiet. Almost instinctively, he reached out and grabbed his father's hand.

"Are you alright?" Dan asked.

Cory had a distressed look on his face. "I'm just thinking about how bad I want the drug sometimes. I know the doctor said I beat it, but I worry that it will always have a pull."

Dan replied, "I have a friend who quit smoking cigarettes more than forty years ago and yet, when he gets in a tight situation, he still find himself reaching to his shirt pocket for a smoke."

"That's not very encouraging."

"No," Dan said, "but the point is that he doesn't smoke. He did beat it, and so can you."

Cory sighed and closed his eyes. "It's kind of hard not to be bitter."

"Belicve me, I know."

"How did you get over it, Dad? How did you stop being bitter about your lungs and everything?"

"Who says I got over it?" Dan tried to smile, but there was too much truth in the statement to be a joke. "I don't know that I've ever entirely gotten over it. I doubt you will either. There are times when it hurt, like when I wanted to run and play baseball with my son but I had to stand on the sidelines and tell myself it was just as good to be a coach." The words caught in Dan's throat.

"But that was okay—you were a good coach. I didn't ever mind."

Dan nodded. "And that's how you get over the bitterness. You ultimately realize that you can either let it ruin your life or you can get on with life. I tried it both ways." They sat quietly for a few moments. Cory suspected that Dan had more to say, but he had learned that it took time for him to put his thoughts into words. Finally, "A couple of other things have helped me. For one, I stopped blaming the German soldiers who launched the gas attack. I almost hated them for it. But they were just following orders, like I was. I still hold the political leaders responsible, for whatever good that does me, but not the soldiers. Second, I remind myself that things simply happen—not for any purpose, not because I did something right or something wrong, but just as a consequence of living and being part of society. So whether I like it or not, that's just the way it is."

"Kind of fatalistic, isn't it?"

"Yes, but not in a helpless way. It's more of an attitude that I might as well accept it and move on. That way I have wrested control from the old useless memories. It's all about writing your own script, not letting bitterness or hate do it for you."

Cory nodded. "I think I see that. I remember the first Japanese pilot we shot down. I actually saw his face, and it scared me to see how much he hated us. But I wasn't fighting him because I hated him. I didn't even know him. I was doing what I had to do."

"That's the best way to look at it. In the end, there's more than enough hurt to go around, so we have to just move on with our lives. I hope you can do a better job of it than I did."

* * *

Fortunately, Dr. Linder didn't forget Cory. In fact, he wired ahead to a friend of his in the chain of command recommending that Cory's request for transfer to ground school be approved. Accompanied with the recommendation of his flight commander from the *Enterprise,* he received orders to transfer back to San Francisco for a fitting with a new prosthesis and whatever rehabilitation was required to adapt to it and to then present himself at the naval training academy in San Diego where he'd learn to become an instructor. It was one of the happy moments that betrayed the deceit of depression that whispered it would never get better.

Nate approached the family in Cory's room that same afternoon to tell them about his new orders. "They're sending me back to New London to bring out a new sub."

"What does that mean?" Sarah asked. "Is there something wrong with the ship you were on?"

"It's a boat, actually. And, no, there's nothing wrong with it. It's just that when a new sub is getting close to completion at Electric Boat, they need to assign a crew to it. And they always need to put a good mix of experienced people with new people. Last time, I was the green guy. Now, I'll go back there as one of the seasoned ones. It's our job to train and drill the crew as we transit from Connecticut to Hawaii."

"So this is a compliment to you?"

He laughed. "It's pretty usual. But I am excited about one thing. My commanding officer recommended that I meet with some of the engineers at Electric Boat to talk about some of my ideas on some minor design changes that could really improve efficiency. Command here in Hawaii passed his note along, and it looks like I'll get to spend at least a week doing that. I'm pretty excited."

"Good for you, Nate," Dan said. "You're a natural at engineering, so this will give you a chance to have an impact. When do you leave?"

"I'm afraid they want me on an aircraft tomorrow afternoon, sir."

"Will you get to see Kathy?"

"Yes, I will, Mom. I'll take a train from San Francisco and
spend a couple of weeks in Salt Lake City. Then, she can travel
with me to New London. We should have at least three months
together. I can't wait to see the kids."

"Well, I hope we get home before you all leave. I miss my
grandchildren desperately."

Sarah gave Nate a hug, and Dan and Cory promised to
come to see him off.

* * *

Two days later, Dan and Sarah had to say good-bye to
Cory. He was off to San Francisco for rehabilitation. They
decided to take an extra week to relax on the beaches in Oahu
and to visit the LDS temple in Laie.

"Can we call you when we get to San Francisco?" Sarah said
tearfully.

"I don't know. But I'm going to be okay, Mom. I'll find a
way to let you know how things are going. I promise."

With that, there were more hugs and farewells, and Sarah
and Dan stood by each other as they watched Cory be taken to
the naval aircraft in a wheelchair. He turned and waved good-
bye, and then they were alone.

Chapter Twenty-Nine

ALL IS WELL

After their short vacation in Laie, Dan asked Sarah if she'd like him to arrange to fly back to the mainland rather than taking a boat. "But you hate airplanes," she replied incredulously.

"Yes, but I think we should try to see Nate, Kathy, and the grandchildren before they leave for New London." Sarah protested once more but was happy when Dan persisted. The USO was sympathetic and arranged for transport in the back of an old cargo plane.

The trip was very rough on them, particularly on Dan, since the aircraft wasn't pressurized. Sarah was relieved when they made it to Los Angeles, where they transferred to a train for the trip home to Salt Lake City. They arrived home just a week before the kids were scheduled to leave. Jonny and Meg were a bit tentative at first, having been separated from their grandparents for nearly six months, but it didn't take long before they warmed up and started playing and chattering. Kathy marveled at how happy her parents seemed.

On their third day home, a telegram was delivered to the door. Dan read it to himself, then burst into a big grin.

"What is it?" Kathy asked anxiously. "What does it say?"

"Oh, nothing of too much interest," Dan teased.

"Daniel!"

"Oh, alright. It's just that Jonathon and Margaret are coming home and should get here this Friday. That will give them two days before you guys leave for Connecticut!"

Kathy let out a squeal, which startled the children. The family spent the rest of the day cleaning the Richardses' house in anticipation of the reunion.

At about seven that evening, Sarah looked up at Dan and was startled at how gray he looked. "We'd better go home and get some rest," she said quietly, trying to mask her anxiety. When Dan didn't protest, as he usually did, she hurried him out to the car.

After a light dinner, he really didn't look any better. Sarah was alarmed but did her best to remain steady. "Are you alright, Danny? You look like you're having some trouble."

"I've been coughing all day."

"Maybe we should go to the hospital . . ."

"I'll be alright. I think I should just go to bed and get some rest. Of course, I hate to leave you alone."

"I'll be fine. I have a book to finish. You go to bed." She helped him get undressed, even though it was only eight o'clock. About an hour later, just as she was getting to the most exciting part of her book, she heard him cough. Then he coughed more violently, and she heard a desperate gasping sound.

Dropping the book to the floor, she rushed into the bedroom. Dan was sitting up in bed, heaving violently. The sheets and bedding were covered in blood; he was gasping for air, but it was impossible for him to use what breath he managed to take. She rushed over and sat beside him. "We've got to get you to the hospital!"

He grasped her hand. "Just hold me," he managed to rasp. "I'm so sorry . . ." Finally, he weakly whispered, "I love you."

* * *

The Salt Lake City Cemetery sits high on the north bench with a magnificent view of the Salt Lake Valley to the south, the Wasatch Mountains to the east, and the more rounded

Oquirrh Mountains to the west. At the conclusion of the dedi-
cation of the grave site and the three-rifle military salute
provided by the Veterans of Foreign Wars from the Ft. Douglas
Post, Jonathon and Cory moved away from the crowd and
stood side by side, looking at the view. It was a splendid day,
and the smell of flowers filled the air. The sound of "Taps"
played by two bugles, one acting as an echo, provided a
poignant ending to the service.

Cory struggled to balance on his crutch, so Jonathon
moved closer to steady him. "I'm so sorry we didn't get here a
few days earlier so I could have seen him."

Cory didn't turn, but he could hear Jonathon's voice
tighten as he suppressed a sob. Not knowing how to deal with
his grandfather's emotions, Cory said, "I'm glad you're here to
be with Mom, since I have to go to San Diego and Nate has to
go back to sea."

"Margaret had a feeling we should come home, but I kept
putting it off." Jonathon's voice broke again.

Cory swallowed hard. "Dad would love this view. It's going
to be beautiful in all seasons of the year."

That steadied Jonathon. "I think you're right, Cory. The
artist in him would appreciate the mix of colors and distinctive
lines of the mountains. It's the perfect spot, really."

"Was he always like that—so artistic?"

"It's what brought him into our family in the first place,
you know." For a moment, Jonathon gazed off, opening his
mind to another time and place. "The first time Dan came to
our house, his friends trapped him into singing a song. It was
'Danny Boy,' his mother's favorite. He accompanied himself.
Oh, how beautiful his voice was—so strong and confident and
clear. Margaret was taken by him immediately. At any rate,
after the breakfast we'd scheduled with the young men, she
asked if he would like her to teach him piano—not at the basic
level he already knew, but formal training. He was so shy, he
almost said no."

"What changed his mind?"

Jonathon laughed. "The Steinway, I think. That piano was like a magnet to him. So he started taking lessons, and that brought him over regularly. Then he and Trevor became best friends, and soon it was like we had two sons . . ." Jonathon's voice trailed off. "They were the best years of our lives . . ."

"I didn't mean to open painful memories, Grandpa. I'm sorry."

Jonathon turned, and even though his eyes glistened, he said firmly, "Don't be sorry, Cory. Those memories have blessed me a thousand times—a million times. It's the time you spend as a father that makes your life worth living. Someday you'll have that opportunity." A moment passed in silence. "Still, it somehow isn't right that a man should outlive his sons. I don't think nature intended it that way." Very slowly he continued, "God was so kind to me the day that He sent that fifteen-year-old boy into our home and into our lives. Now both of my boys have gone home."

"I miss him, Grandpa!" There was a desperate sound to Cory's voice. "He's only been gone a few days, and I miss him already. I can't imagine what it will be like as the time goes on."

"You'll never stop missing him—but it won't hurt as much. Time doesn't necessarily heal all wounds, but it makes them bearable."

Just then, Jonny came bounding up to Jonathon, nearly knocking him to the ground with the collision. At least that's how Jonathon pretended it happened. Nate came running over and scooped up his son, and then he walked with Cory and Jonathon back toward the casket.

Soon, Jonathon was engaged in conversation with an old friend, leaving Cory alone for a moment. He looked around at the huge crowd—his mother was talking with some of Dan's friends from the railroad, Margaret was talking with the music director from Temple Square, and Kathy and Nate were talking quietly with members of the band. There had been nearly a thousand people at the funeral, many of whom Cory didn't recognize. It was natural, he guessed, that through his music and his work, his father had touched so many people. Looking at the black-and-white photograph of Dan that Sarah had placed on an easel by the casket, he smiled again and said quietly to himself, "And God was kind to send me into this family. Thank you, Dad! I hope your lungs don't hurt now and that you are singing for all those people in heaven." He looked up and saw his mother smile at him through her tears, and he moved to join her as she was presented with the flag of the United States of America that had covered Dan's casket during the service.

Chapter Thirty

A BROOKLYN TRANSITION

Dear Kathy and Nate,

It's hard to believe that I've been here a month now. After the three-month ordeal in San Francisco, getting fitted for my prosthesis, it's a relief to be out. I still use a crutch most of the time, but for short distances. I can actually walk on my own. After getting shot down and going through my incident in Hawaii, I didn't think anything could scare me again. But then I had to face a class of twenty year olds who want to be pilots, and I was terrified. I was embarrassed by my leg until I got this bit of inspiration to turn it into an object lesson. I held it up the first day of class and told them that no matter how good they were, this could be in their future. That sobered them up pretty quickly. At the very least, I gained some respect. The real turning point came when my friend Jack Wilson showed up. He's a hotshot fighter pilot, and he told them the most amazing stories from our days on the Enterprise. *The class loved him. The thing Jack did was to help me learn to lighten up and have fun with the group. Even though it's military, you can still tell stories and make the subject interesting. I'm finding that I like teaching and could easily see making a career out of it.*

Jack's coming was a mixed blessing. There was a girl I'd met in San Diego before shipping out who I'd started dating, but when she and Jack met, it was like Kismet. Now he has my girl. Fighter pilots! But it's okay. She and Jack really do go together. So, now I'm single, footloose— single on the foot—and fancy free. If I meet the right girl, I'll start dating again.

I've found a ward I go to on Sunday, and I've learned how to get myself out there without help using city buses, so, all in all, I think things are going to be alright.

I still miss Dad so much, but I'm sure you know how I feel. I hope everything goes good on Nate's next cruise. You'll all be in my prayers.

Love you,
Cory

* * *

A week before his departure, Kathy asked Nate if he was going to go to Brooklyn to see his mother.

"Why? You know she'll make some excuse not to see us. We'll just sit there in the living room talking to Dad while she pouts in her bedroom. The kids will be nervous because they'll feel the tension, and then they'll break something—"

"You're writing a pretty good story, Nate."

"I'm simply reading from a well-worn script. We've tried this before."

"I'm sorry that it's so hard. She's missing out on so much. I wish she could forgive us."

Nate's face clouded up.

Kathy sighed and relented. "We don't need to go. The last thing I want to do is ruin our last days together." She smiled, hoping to divert his attention. "I'm sorry I said anything."

"No, you were right. I believe I'll be fine on this cruise, but you never know. I think I should make one more effort at reconciliation, just in case something happens to me." He looked up with a wry smile. "At the very least, if I do get killed out there and she's mean to us, she'll have a good reason to feel guilty." He tried to make his grin look conspiratorial.

Kathy didn't buy it. "I don't like it when you talk that way."

"I'm sorry. It's just that in some ways, it's easier to think about going into battle against the Japanese than against my mother."

At two o'clock the next day, they pulled up in front of Nate's parents' house in a car that Nate had borrowed from one of the officers on the boat. It was hard moving around with two babies, particularly since the twins were toddlers now and into everything they came into contact with. When his knock on the door went unanswered, Nate went around back and used his key to open the house.

Once inside, he let Kathy in, and then wandered around looking for his parents. Kathy saw him tense up when he found a pile of unopened letters on the hall table. She stole up beside him and started reading the handwritten note that was lying on top of the stack of the letters. It said, *Please forward to Mr. Joshua Brown at 1185 Kensington Place, Brooklyn.* It was in Nate's mother's handwriting. Nate felt a terror rise up in his breast that he'd never experienced before.

"Gather up the kids and let's go!"

"Where, Nate?"

"To 1185 Kensington Place. I've got to find out what's going on." His voice was tense and his face drawn. Kathy quickly took Jon and Meg to the bathroom, then joined Nate at the front of the house, where he already had the motor running. Ten minutes later, they pulled up in front of an apartment building. This time, when they rang the bell there was a delayed answer. When Nate heard Josh's voice, his heart skipped a beat again. "Dad, it's Nate. Can we come up?"

"Nate? Do you have Kathy with you?"

"And the kids. Can we come up?"

"Of course you can." The tone in his father's voice had brightened immeasurably.

Once up the stairs, they walked down a darkened, grimy corridor until they reached the apartment. Before they could knock, Josh opened the door and held his arms open in a welcoming gesture. "Oh, Nate. It's so good to see you. How did you know that I needed to see you today?"

"I didn't know, Dad," Nate stammered. "I just . . . I'm shipping out next week, and I wanted to see you and Mother."

Without any pretense, Josh said, "I prayed for you to come. God heard my prayers, and He sent you. Come in. Please, come in."

They entered a small but very clean apartment. Josh was dressed well, and he immediately found some things for the children to play with. They remembered their grandpa and snuggled up in his lap while he read them their favorite "Grandpa Brown" story from an old book that had been Nate's when he was a baby. Finally, he sent them into the one bedroom to do some coloring.

"Dad, what are you doing here? Where's Mother?" Both Kathy and Nate had frightened looks on their faces.

"I'm afraid that it's just what it looks like, Nate. We've separated."

"How can that be?"

"It's the natural thing—we haven't been close for years. We haven't been intimate for even longer than that." Josh had never talked like that before, always maintaining strict privacy about his relationship with Barbara.

"It's because of us, isn't it?" Kathy said nervously.

Josh could see tears forming in her eyes. "Of course it's not you. You're the best thing ever to happen to Nate, Kathy. How could something so good be responsible for something like this?"

"Because Mother has never forgiven me, that's how." Nate had a dark look on his face. "I left the faith, and now I'm dead to her."

"Nate, the problems between your mother and me started long before you and Kathy fell in love. The way she's treating you is just a symptom. She's not a bad person. She just has a very rigid view of how the world should be. And, unfortunately, I never measured up to her vision. She never really blamed you for what happened. She always blamed me for taking us to Salt Lake City."

"But that's exactly the thing that has made me happy, Dad! Why can't she see that?"

"Maybe she does. But it doesn't match the way she thinks the world should be, so it's out."

Nate sighed and laid his head back in the rocking chair. "So what are you going to do?"

Josh looked up and smiled. "I'm going to move back to Salt Lake City. I've called KSL, and they'd like me to come back as an engineer. The Richardses said I can live with them until I find a place, so that's what I'm going to do."

"You talked to my grandparents?"

"Just yesterday."

"But why Salt Lake, Dad? You've got a great job here in New York."

"I guess I like it there. I don't think I'm Mormon material, but I like living with LDS people. It was the happiest time in my life, and I hope to recapture a bit of it."

"This is such a shock," Nate said. "It's hard to believe it's happening. What about Mother? What happens to her?"

"I think she's going to sell the house and move in with her sister. That's where she's staying right now. Since your uncle died, she's been there every day anyway. She'll be alright. Plus, I'll see that she has plenty to live on. I won't abandon her, even if we follow through with a divorce." He smiled at Nate weakly. "After all, she gave me the most important thing in my life."

"Dad . . ." Nate dropped his gaze.

After that there wasn't a lot to say, so Josh took them out to his favorite Italian restaurant, and then they loaded up the kids for the lonesome trip back to Connecticut.

As they prepared to say good-bye, Josh leaned into the car. "Nate, keep sending your mother the letters and the pictures. I know she never answers, but I also know that she's pasted every picture of you and the children into a scrapbook. I honestly believe that someday she'll come around and want to be part of your lives."

"Pictures? What pictures? I haven't sent her any—" He turned with a look of indignation at Kathy. "You've been communicating with my mother?"

"Communication is too strong a word. It implies that both parties participate. I've been sending her things. Don't be angry, please."

Nate took a couple of deep breaths. "It's alright that you've sent pictures. You can send more." Then he looked at both his father and his wife. "But you've both got to understand that there are two sides to this. I have feelings too, and my mother has done nothing to help me since this started. No matter how hard Kathy and I try, she continues to insult the people I love—even you, Dad. So it's going to take time for me to deal with this. I understand the whole 'he's dead to me' syndrome in Jewish lore, but it doesn't have to be that way. Mother can make a different choice."

Josh nodded. "I understand. But you need to know something too, Nate. I continue to love your mother. I want her to be happy, and I'm sorry that I can't live with her. So in spite of what's happened, I can't simply write her out of my life. You'll need to be tolerant of that."

Nate was pale, and Kathy noticed a slight tremble in his hands. "I know the right thing to say at this moment is that I'll be fine and that I'll continue to keep the door open for her. But I don't know that I can do that. I'm sorry for what's happened to you, Dad. Are you going to be okay?"

"I will. I'll have my challenges, but I'll be alright."

Nate shook his head, as if he had to try to make sense of it one last time. "I love the traditions I grew up with, Dad, and I love the people who were part of my life. They are great people. But I have accepted a different way, one that I believe is more complete. I wish Mom could accept that." Nate tried to smile but couldn't quite manage it. Anger, disappointment, sorrow, and a sense of betrayal made a toxic brew. He tried to say something more, but the words couldn't come out because of the painful lump in his throat.

He clasped his father's hands one last time and then released them as he pushed the clutch in and shoved the gear stick into first gear. As they pulled away, Kathy and the twins turned and waved good-bye to Josh.

They drove in silence. Kathy wanted to scoot closer on the seat to comfort him, but she noticed that his hands were clenched tight and knew that he needed time to sort out his feelings.

Chapter Thirty-One

RETURN TO THE SEA OF JAPAN

May 15, 1945

The new boat was interesting. It was essentially the same as the *Tripletail* from a design and performance point of view, but it wasn't the same. "It needs to develop its own personality," the executive officer, Dave Morgan, said. "Each boat takes on the personality of its crew until it has its own unique sound and smell and rhythm."

"The USS *Silverfin*. It's certainly a good name." In truth, Nate was having a grand time with the new ship. While all the functions were the same, the engineering was state of the art and included some of the suggestions he'd submitted. It was gratifying to know that things would function more efficiently because of some very simple design changes. Nate enjoyed talking with Morgan, an affable man who, though very efficient, was relaxed around the men both on and off the bridge. "Captain Emmett is a lot more outgoing than Captain Stahlei."

"I've served under a lot of captains, both on surface ships and in submarines, and he's the best I've ever worked with. He senses the dynamics of a situation and somehow gets inside the head of the enemy. More than once, I've seen him make an impossible shot just because he seemed to intuit how the enemy was going to make a turn." Morgan turned to Nate. "He seems to trust you on the TDC, which is something of a compliment."

Nate was pleased to hear that. Even though Captain Emmett had told him he was doing a good job on a number of occasions, he tended to speak positively to everyone in the crew, so Nate couldn't really tell the depth of his remarks. Hearing it from the exec probably indicated that he was on solid ground.

"It seems strange that we're on our way to a battle zone when the war in Europe came to an end just last week." Nate relished the sound of V-E day, May 8, 1945. The only thing left on the agenda was V-J day, which would hopefully occur before he got killed. The country was so excited, the celebrations were overwhelming. For about two-thirds of the active duty troops, it meant their conflict was over.

Morgan laughed. "That had to be one of the best days in the history of the world. Even though we knew it was coming, it was still a shock to hear that the fighting was finally over. What a huge relief. Unfortunately, I don't remember a lot, because the first thing I did was head for the bar, and I didn't come out until the next morning."

Nate laughed.

At this point, they were in the middle of the Pacific, just two days from Pearl Harbor, where they would spend a couple of weeks getting refitted to correct the minor problems they'd encountered on their maiden voyage. Fortunately, the ship had functioned very well, so there was little to worry about. That meant the officers might actually get to enjoy a bit of shore leave.

"You've gone to some other place, Mr. Brown. Where have your dreams taken you?"

Nate jumped at the interruption. "What? Oh, I was back in New London thinking about my wife and kids. It was frustrating that the boat was two months late coming out of dry dock, but it was great for our family."

"You've got a terrific wife. She's a bundle of energy and manages your children very well. I'm a little jealous, you know." Morgan was divorced—a casualty of his full-time military career. He and Nate had talked about his children, all grown, and how he'd missed most of their growing up years because he was at sea.

"Well, I can understand why. I'm jealous of all the shipyard workers right now who get to be with their families while I'm out here with a bunch of smelly men—present company excluded, of course." They laughed.

The sound of the klaxon horn blasted overhead, with an intensity that would have scared Nate silly before the war. Now, it seemed as natural as hearing a train whistle, and he simply reacted out of habit to the alarm. The fact that no one panicked was testimony to the daily drills they'd conducted on their way out from New London. In less than thirty seconds, he was down in the tower while the ship was in a steep dive to drill the planesmen yet another time before they reached Pearl.

Two weeks later, the *Silverfin* pulled out of port to the tune of "Anchors Aweigh," played by the shipyard brass band. With the war in Europe over, the huge industrial output of America was already starting to be felt in this theater, and the port was crowded beyond belief. It actually felt good to get out to sea where, except for the sounds of the ship, it was quiet again. From the gossip he had heard on the beaches from boats that were back on leave, it was getting harder and harder to find any targets. That was a good sign. "But if I had it my way, we'd find and shoot every single enemy ship out of the water, just so we could get this thing over with."

"Japan doesn't seem to see it your way, Mr. Brown."

"What, sir?"

"Getting it over with. You were mumbling, and I overheard you."

Nate's face flushed. The last thing he needed was for the captain to hear him talking to himself.

"I agree with your sentiment, though. You have a fighter's heart, which is just what we're going to need when we do find our targets." Turning to look straight at Nate, the captain continued, "And we will find targets, Nate. You can count on that. I'm not burning through thousands of gallons of fuel for a pleasure cruise."

Nate laughed. It was probably at that moment that the bond between them was sealed. No matter what else happened now, the captain knew he could count on his third officer, and Nate knew that he could trust his captain's instincts.

* * *

"This is a tough one. But it can't be helped." Nate held his gaze steady on the TDC plot. The captain had sighted a Japanese troop ship in the process of loading Japanese prisoners off one of the islands that was being evacuated. Their boat had sneaked into the harbor under cover of darkness, and it was just now twilight when the sky would start to lighten in the east. They were on the surface, which meant that the moment they were spotted, they'd become sitting ducks for any shore batteries or guns on the troopship. But the water was shallow enough that they could barely have submerged anyway, plus this gave them the best chance to make a getaway once they'd disposed of the ship. It was always disheartening to take down a ship loaded with men, but every single Japanese soldier taken out of action here was one less to fight the Americans when they finally reached the Japanese homeland. There had been so many reports of Japanese atrocities as the various islands of the South Pacific were retaken that it was clearly their duty to protect the infantry as much as possible. By now, they'd heard of the sheer infamy of what had happened to the American prisoners of war who had been taken in the Bataan Peninsula at the outbreak of the war. It was horrific, and everybody knew that even worse was waiting once troops landed in Japan. So this was the perfect opportunity to improve the odds.

"Final bearing. Mark!" Nate confirmed the setting on the periscope, fed the coordinates into the TDC, and quietly announced that they had a firing solution. "Fire at will, Mr. Brown."

"Fire one! Fire two! Fire three!" His voice was calm and steady, but his heart was racing. There was absolutely no way they could miss the shot, because the troopship was dead in the water. But the moment the enemy saw what was coming, they'd try to fire on the sub, if for no other reason than to gain their last-minute revenge. Plus, Emmett suspected that there was a destroyer prowling around a point of land off to the south and that the explosion would bring them rushing in pell-mell.

"Torpedoes running true!" the captain said with a hint of excitement in his voice. Stahlei would have been deadpan at this point, and Nate decided he liked Emmett's way better. "Why don't you get us out of here, Mr. Morgan?"

"Aye, aye, sir. All back, two-thirds." Their escape route had been carefully plotted and laid in before the first salvo was even set up on the board. While the ship shuddered to life, with a mountain of foam thrown up and over the stern by the wash of the propeller, Nate watched his stopwatch to calculate the moment of impact. Exactly seventy seconds after his command, they heard the first explosion. It sounded very different on the surface than it would have if they were submerged. The captain and the lookouts came sliding down the rail as the ship reversed engines and started forward on all four diesels. In quick succession, the two other torpedoes struck, and the fate of the ship was sealed.

"Prepare to dive in five minutes, unless I see something earlier." Captain Emmett had positioned himself at the periscope, where he constantly surveyed both the horizon and the sky. At this point, enemy aircraft were so scarce that they were seldom a problem.

"Dive, dive, dive!" the captain shouted. "Aircraft overhead!" For the next hour, things were pretty hot, but Captain Emmett expertly nursed the boat out to the open sea.

* * *

That was the last chance the *Silverfin* ever had to shoot at an enemy ship—there weren't enough of them to go around. But as the fleet continued its pattern of leapfrogging toward the islands of Japan, there were multiple opportunities to rescue downed pilots. Because of Cory, Nate felt a special affinity for each of the pilots they were able to rescue and mourned those who were lost. The worst was when they'd get word of a downed pilot, go to the coordinates, but not find anything. It wasn't hard to imagine the hopelessness one would feel to be lost at sea and die alone.

The rescue operation took a dangerous turn when the captain assembled the leadership team in the crowded officers' mess at noon on a Tuesday in June. "We've just received word of a downed pilot on a medium-sized atoll some two hours from here."

"Standard operation?" the executive officer asked.

"Unfortunately, no. Apparently, he crashed in the lagoon within range of shore fire and had to swim for the island. He's hiding in the underbrush in severe danger of being found by the Japanese. They've taken a terrific pounding from our aircraft and aren't likely to be too gentle on one of the guys that's been bombing them. The report also indicates that he might be wounded."

The wardroom was quiet. This meant that there'd have to be a shore party to go on the island, find, and rescue him. Probably in full sight of the enemy.

"I should lead the party," Morgan said.

The captain looked up with no expression on his face. This would usually fall to the third officer, not the exec. But Nate had a small family . . .

"With all due respect to Mr. Morgan, I'm the one who should go," Nate said evenly.

"Mr. Brown, you'll lead the party. Take five men and the motorized launch. We'll surface just out of range of their guns, wait for a signal from the pilot, and then send you in. Keep everybody's head down. My guess is that on an island this small, our deck gun will have a longer range than whatever shore artillery they have. If so, we'll keep things pretty lively for the Japanese so they can't harass you too much. Once on land, find the pilot and drag him out of there pronto. Any questions?"

"No, sir!" Nate said confidently. But inside, he felt anything but confident. What limited training he'd had in this area had been nearly two years ago, and he'd never faced the prospect of hand-to-hand combat. Still, it was his duty.

Approximately two and a half hours later, the captain gave a crisp, "Periscope down. Prepare to surface!" and the ship moved into position for the launch. Nate and the four enlisted men who had volunteered to go with him had changed into all-weather gear, secure in the knowledge that they'd be getting wet. They also each carried a pistol and a rifle with the maximum number of rounds in their ammunition belts. Once topside, Nate looked anxiously for the signal, which would be sunlight reflected off the pilot's pocket mirror. Slowly scanning the horizon, he didn't see anything on the first pass with his binoculars, nor the second. Then on the third, he caught a glance of a brief flash, moved the glasses back to the spot and pulled a mirror out of his own pocket. He caught the sun and flashed it in the direction he'd seen. A few seconds later, he saw another series of flashes that confirmed they'd found their man.

"Alright, everybody, let's go." If his voice sounded strained, it was more from excitement than anxiety. This was vintage Navy—the kind of warfare that had been practiced clear back to the days of sailing ships, before the marines had taken over landing duties.

Gauging the current, Nate ordered the helm to aim for a spot slightly to the east of their landing spot and then started paying attention to the massive waves crashing on the coral reef that surrounded the island. If they didn't time their approach to the reef almost perfectly, the razor sharp coral would tear the bottom out of their little wooden hull like a chainsaw cutting through a two-by-four.

As they approached the coral, the sound of the surf was ominous, to say the least, and Nate was tensed at the front of the boat like a cheetah ready to spring. He couldn't imagine anything more dangerous or frightening than this and was holding his hand up as a signal to the helm to hold off until he dropped his hand, when something more frightening and dangerous shot up the water next to them—a shore-based battery that had managed to find both their range and position.

"Now!" Nate shouted at the top of his lungs, dropping his hand savagely. He was pleased to hear the little engine roar to life and was almost knocked back into the boat by the forward thrust of both the engine and the wave that was lifting them up and over the coral into the aquamarine blue of the lagoon. Even in this circumstance, he was struck by the incredible beauty of the place, with colors that blended together into a most serene setting. "Kathy would love this," he found himself saying, then shook his head to focus on the more immediate threat. "Hard starboard," he shouted as another shell landed perhaps twenty feet to port. After twenty seconds, "Now, hard port! Full ahead!" The boat responded quickly, and, fortunately, just in time to avoid another shell.

"It's going to be cat-and-mouse from here on in," he shouted gleefully. "Us against them. Are you up to it, Mr. Mason?"

"Yes, sir!" he heard from the back of the boat.

"Alright, everybody else, they're way out of range, but every so often I want you to fire with your muzzle elevated so they can see the flash of your rifle. We'll keep 'em guessing when one of our shells is going to come down on their heads." Nate's confidence was shaken just a little by the shower he got at this point from a shell that landed just four feet to port. "Ahead full!" he shouted, figuring that the Japanese would expect him to deviate either left or right.

"Sure could use some help from the *Silverfin*," one of the men said. He had excellent timing, because a split second later, they heard the most incredible whining sound as a projectile from the sub screamed through the air over their heads. Instinctively, all heads turned in the direction of shore, and they watched with satisfaction as a small explosion lit up the jungle within a few inches from their vantage point of where the enemy gun had been firing. When three shells followed in quick succession, each hammering the spot, a cheer went up from the men in the boat. That was the last long-range fire that came at them.

Nate's heart slowed a little, and he settled down for the rest of the ride in. The next danger would be from small ground fire when they came in range. At least they could shoot back at that point. Sure enough, at approximately 500 yards out, they started hearing the pinging sound that indicated bullets hitting the water. "Return fire, but don't waste too many rounds—just enough to keep their heads down."

As a deep wave approached the shallow waters of a shore, the speed of water at the top of the wave increased, and the little boat seemed to accelerate ferociously as they got near the island. Nate was struck by the smell of the place—that wonderful combination of fresh vegetation mixed with salt water and even the decay of all the luxuriant undergrowth.

"Once on shore, I want you to create a perimeter until we find out if the Japanese are on top of us. If they're on the beach, we'll go to immediate hand-to-hand combat. If not, we'll form up and move to the pilot. He's supposed to fire a flare so we can find him. Of course, that means the enemy can find him, as well, so we have to move fast. Any questions?" There were none. "Fix bayonets!" Then Nate leaped out of the boat shouting as he went. Four of the five went after him, the helmsman staying with the boat so they could make a quick escape when the time came.

The first sound that registered when he hit the dry sand was the sickening thud of a bullet slamming into the bodies of one of his men, who let out an involuntary scream. Instinctively, Nate and the others dropped to the deck, and he turned to see that it was a young seaman named Williamson. The nature of the wound to his head made it clear that he was dead. The next sound was that of a number of bullets slamming into the sand near him, and he tucked his head even closer to the ground to avoid sand in his eyes. Glancing up, he fired a couple of rounds in the direction he thought the hostile fire was coming from. The tree line was twenty-five feet away, so he and the others starting crabbing their way toward the cover of the brush, firing off rounds as fast as they could to keep the enemy down. There was a slight rise in the ground, which would have made them a sitting target, so they crawled their way behind it.

"What are we going to do now? We're pinned down!"

The sound of terror in Seaman Coleman's voice was palpable.

"You're going to create covering fire, and I'm going to go for the tree line. When I'm close enough, I'll throw a hand grenade and take those guys out."

"But what if there are too many of them?"

Just then, a flare went up from approximately a hundred yards to the right, perhaps ten yards inside the tree line.

"There aren't too many of them or they would have found the pilot before now. Jones, you and Hurst have the automatic weapons, so give me cover. Coleman, you follow as soon as I make it to the tree line. If I determine that the Japanese are too far to reach with a grenade, I'll call in fire from the ship. Any questions?" He could see that the very fact of his decisiveness had given the men resolve, so he gave them the sign, they started firing, and he started running in a crouch.

It clearly took the Japanese by surprise, because he was at least halfway to the trees before he heard opposing fire. He did a quick zigzag and kept running, diving into the underbrush just as he heard a bullet pass overhead. He was amazed that he could actually hear the bullets. *So this is what the marines have been doing on every darned island in the Pacific.* He wondered which was worse—depth charges or this? He heard another bullet slam into the tree next to him.

Reaching in his backpack, he pulled out a grenade and watched down along the perimeter of the trees to see where the fire was coming from. He turned and caught Hurst's eye and was pleased when he understood and fired off a few rounds to draw return fire. He could see that the enemy gun was perhaps thirty feet to his left. Crawling through the underbrush, which he quickly found was sharp and stickery and bug-infested, he worked into position. "If I ever had the chance to throw a strike, please let it be now!"

In his mind, he pictured one of those weekend baseball games with Cory when he had first moved to Salt Lake City. He pulled the pin, pulled himself up to his knees, and threw with all his might. Less than two seconds later, the forest flared in fire, at which he stood up in a crouch and started running toward the spot. He must have hit something, because at first there was no enemy fire. Then from off to his right, he heard a noise, spun in the direction, and was startled to have a Japanese soldier come screaming at him through the undergrowth.

He screamed in return and was knocked backward by his opponent's forward momentum, losing his gun in the fall. Nate found himself in a wrestling match with a knife-wielding, wild-eyed attacker who was trying to maneuver Nate into position to stab him. Nate jerked and twisted again, this time gaining some leverage on his much smaller opponent. There was a lot of grunting and groaning as the two twisted back and forth. When Nate felt the blade slip into his left arm, he couldn't help but cry out. The pain was so intense, that he rolled off his attacker, leaving him completely exposed to a fatal blow.

There was the concussion of a rifle inches above his head, and blood splattered out from a wound in the Japanese soldier's chest. The body fell on top of Nate, which prompted him to scream even more as he struggled to push it off, and, when he did, he was so startled by this turn of events that he instinctively rolled into a ball to protect himself. It took a few moments to register that it was Seaman Jones who had fired.

"Are you alright, sir?"

Nate shook his head to clear it. "I am now that you're here. Are there others?"

"It doesn't look like it, although we heard rustling off in the distance. You threw that grenade about perfectly. I think you killed at least three of them!"

Nate felt a wave of relief flood over him.

"You've been cut, sir!"

Nate looked down at his arm and quickly tore a piece of fabric from his shirt to wrap around it. It hurt, but it didn't feel like it had been cut through too far.

"We've got to go get that pilot. Help me up!"

With that, the little group started working their way through the thick growth, Jones at the front, slicing through the undergrowth with the dead Japanese soldier's machete, while Nate and Hurst provided cover in case they were ambushed. As they neared the spot where the pilot should be, Nate whistled a popular American tune. They all stopped and listened in silence, but could only hear the sounds of the jungle. They moved forward perhaps another dozen yards, and he tried it again. This time he faintly heard a humming sound, but it was their song, all right. He pushed on ahead and found a pilot cowering under a clump of bushes.

"Why didn't you whistle so we could hear you?" he asked indignantly.

"I can't whistle, sir!"

"What kind of person deserves to be rescued who can't whistle?" Hurst said under his breath.

Nate added, "Maybe we ought to leave him and go find somebody who knows the routine."

The rescue team laughed, just in case the pilot thought they were serious.

"I'm Lieutenant Brown—Nate Brown."

"Gary Thomas, sir. Boy, am I glad to see you."

"Are you hurt?"

"I think my left leg is broken. I can't put any weight on it."

"Pilots and broken legs . . . The bane of our existence." Thomas looked at him, but Nate didn't take time to explain.

"The Japanese are bound to know where we're at, so we've got to move fast. My left arm is pretty useless, so I'll help Thomas here. You guys have got to keep the way clear."

With that, the little group started back on a slightly different angle that would bring them out closer to their boat. Hopefully it was still there.

When they reached the boat, they couldn't see Mason, but as they started out across the sand, constantly surveying all directions, they saw him pop his head above the gunwale and point his rifle in case it was needed. Luckily, it wasn't, and in no time they were back in the boat, shoving it out into open water for the return trip across the reef.

Chapter Thirty-Two

AN INVITATION TO TOKYO

The Germans called it a *Milchkuh*—a huge oversized submarine that carried everything needed to restock a combat submarine at sea. The Americans used "sub tenders," large surface ships that carried fuel, food, mail, tools to make simple repairs, and the thousands of other items needed to fully restock a submarine in the middle of the ocean so they could avoid the time and cost of returning to base. Of course, the crew wasn't always happy to meet a tender, since it meant one less leave of absence, but it always reduced anxiety to once again have plenty of fuel and supplies.

One of the services they provided was medical attention to Nate's arm. After making it across the reef and back to the *Silverfin,* their medical assistant had cleaned the wound thoroughly, put some twenty stitches in, and doused it in sulfa powder to knock down any infection. But the knife had been so sharp that it was difficult for the wound to heal. Perhaps because of Cory's experience, Nate had been obsessive about scrubbing and cleaning it each day to the point that he probably interfered with the skin's natural ability to stitch itself. When the tender arrived, they had a doctor onboard who took a personal interest in Nate by performing a minor surgery to get the skin to lay flat and to improve the chances of it healing. The improvement was almost immediate, and now, as their rendezvous was coming to an end, Nate felt the tight, clean bandage with gratitude. His arm still hurt, but at least it was clear that it would heal with nothing more than a rather substantial scar and some mild nerve damage that left his fingers tingling on occasion.

As Nate and the others on the deck party watched their tender pull away, they chatted quietly about the next step in the war. With few major fleet surface battles in the previous months, it was clear that the Navy was gearing up for the ultimate objective of the war with Japan—invasion of the Home Islands. The first firebombing of Tokyo had taken place several months earlier, and from what they could gather, it was a horrific spectacle. So many bombs were dropped in a concentrated area that great howling, rolling waves of fire sucked up all the oxygen in the area, incinerating thousands, suffocating thousands more. Yet, there was no sign of yielding even an inch. Everyone sensed that the actual invasion when American troops landed would be a grueling ordeal, since the Japanese placed loyalty to country far above their own personal lives—as witnessed by the increasingly frequent kamikaze attacks on American ships. Some actually believed that they'd prefer to commit national suicide than to ever yield to an outside enemy. It was expected that millions of U.S. troops would have to be landed, with casualties expected in the hundreds of thousands.

The role of submarines in the conflict would be to choke off all traffic in and out of Japan in order to completely starve the islands into an early submission. It was a grim task that awaited the men of the *Silverfin,* and they were mentally gearing up for yet another round of combat, following the relative calm of the previous two months.

Which is why the order that Captain Emmett received on August 10, 1945, was so puzzling. In a rather cryptic way, it said that a new type of explosive device had been dropped on the Japanese cities of Hiroshima and Nagasaki on August 6 and August 9 that had the potential to alter invasion plans and that all subs in the Pacific should temporarily stand down from combat activities until further word was received. It also indicated that Russia, America's ally in the European theater, but never in the Pacific theater, had declared war on Japan on August 8.

"That has to terrify the Japanese, since they know how the Russians are likely to treat them if there's an invasion from the West," Morgan said.

"What do you suppose they mean by a new type of explosive device?" Nate asked.

"I don't know—but did you notice that they said only one per city?"

That sent chills up Nate's spine. They'd heard rumors for a long time that both the Germans and the Allies had been working on some sort of doomsday device that would completely devastate an enemy. Hitler had been promising his beleaguered citizens and military that such a bomb was nearly complete and that it could wipe out the entire city of London in a single blow. Was it possible that America had actually succeeded in creating such a monster?

"All I can say is that if it brings this war to an end without our guys having to go into the Home Islands, I say use it until they cry uncle," Morgan said decisively. "I mean, they know we're going to beat them, there's really no question about that anymore. Yet, they keep fighting, keep killing, keep committing suicide in order to kill our guys. I say use whatever it takes."

It was a sobering thought, but Nate decided he agreed.

On August 14, 1945, a special message was broadcast throughout the entire ship announcing that the United States and its Allies had accepted the Japanese offer of surrender. The cheering onboard the *Silverfin* was amazing, and the cook broke out steaks and eggs, and anything else anybody wanted.

It was only later, when they were in Tokyo, that the crew learned that the decisive moment came when the emperor, who was held as a god by the Japanese people, overrode the advice of his military advisers telling him to stay in the war even if it meant total annihilation. The broadcast was played live over the radio, with huge public-address speakers playing the message in the open air so that everyone would hear it, and when they heard the emperor's voice, they all fell to the ground in astonishment. It was the first time that the citizenry had ever heard the emperor's voice, and the effect on public morale had been stunning. Soldiers, guards, and others simply walked off whatever job they were performing and went home.

"So what do we do now?" someone asked Captain Emmett.

"We wait for orders. There are a couple of things that are certain. First, we'll need a large occupying force to enter all the islands while we help the Japanese set up a new government. Second, there will be pockets of resistance out on some of the thousands of Pacific islands where Japanese soldiers don't get the message of surrender—or refuse to accept it—so things will still be pretty dangerous for awhile. Third, while we'd all like to go home right this minute, there's no way Pearl or the other bases could handle all the ships coming back at once. So I'm afraid we just have to wait for orders and see where they want us."

That was a little frustrating. But the relief of no longer having to worry about combat was so overwhelming that it was really impossible to stay unhappy about anything for very long. Finally, on August 20, Captain Emmett received orders to take up position in the heart of Tokyo Bay. He was to be accorded the great honor of being present at the formal signing of the Articles of Surrender when General Douglas MacArthur and other leaders from each of the services would assume responsibility for the future of Japan.

* * *

"Can you see anything, Mr. Brown?" The young ensign who was standing next to him had an anxious, excited sound in his voice.

"Take a look yourself." Nate handed him his binoculars.

"That is a mighty big ship, sir!"

Nate couldn't help but smile.

"I think I see General MacArthur!"

"Alright, Eaves, I need my glasses back."

Reluctantly the ensign handed him his binoculars.

"Oh, for heavens sake, there's another pair down in the tower."

Gratefully, Eaves descended the stairwell.

Nate then spoke into the public-address system, "All hands, assemble on deck." On this occasion, Nate was the officer in charge of the entire ship. Captain Emmett had been taken to the USS *Missouri* earlier that morning by the boat's launch, and First Officer Morgan had been invited to one of the nearby subs where one of his former captains was in charge.

He listened with satisfaction at the sound of the men hustling up and out onto the deck. He didn't really see himself as one who would ever desire command, but on occasion, it felt satisfying to give an order and watch it be obeyed. Of course, in this instance, the men were all glad to get the order, because everybody wanted to be part of the historic moment. Once assembled, Nate gave the order to stand at ease, then walked amiably along the ranks of the men talking with each of them in turn. As he looked up and down the line, he didn't see anyone that he thought he would naturally form a friendship with, and yet at this moment, he cared for each of them almost more than words could express.

At the appointed moment a signal was fired up to the various ships in the harbor, and Nate turned to look at the platform at the front of the mighty *Missouri* where the various military leaders of Japan had finally assembled, awaiting the moment when they would accept total and unconditional surrender.

The *Missouri* itself was an amazing sight. With its huge, sixteen-inch guns, it had served with distinction. Now there were sailors and dignitaries crowded on every deck of the ship.

Above the platform where the ceremony was taking place, men sat with their legs dangling from the decks, while others leaned on the rails above them.

Everybody in harbor that day knew that this was a grand moment—hopefully one that signaled an end to tyranny once and for all. Although they hadn't heard a great deal about it, the knowledge of just how devastating the atomic bomb had been also cast something of a pall over the jubilation of victory—once you let a genie of that type out of the proverbial bottle, how do you ever get it back in?

At the appointed moment, the signal indicating that the documents had been signed was given, and a great cheer went up on every ship in the harbor, along with the sound of horns and everything else that could make noise. Chills ran up and down Nate's spine as he realized that finally, the most destructive war in human history had come to an end.

* * *

Two days later, they received orders to return to New London. Nate used his allotment of cigarettes to bribe the radio operator into adding an extra destination to his cable back to Kathy. By typing in the address for the naval training academy, his simple message was received simultaneously in Salt Lake City and San Diego.

I'M COMING HOME.

SYMBOL OF GRATITUDE ENGRAVED IN METAL

Written by Jerry Borrowman, reprinted with permission of the
Church News where it originally appeared on August 18, 1990.

As World War II broke out in the Pacific, Elder Carl Ned
Allen was serving his mission in Scranton, Pennsylvania. Shortly
thereafter, he and all the other missionaries went to register with
the local draft board in their assigned areas. With a full year left to
serve, Elder Allen worried he wouldn't be allowed to complete his
mission, but the government honored his ministry and allowed
those already in the field to complete their scheduled term.

Ned returned to his father's farm in Hyrum, Utah, in
March 1943, where he helped on the family farm until being
drafted the following September. Upon reporting to duty at
Camp Fannin, Texas, he was issued a set of army dog tags.
When asked what religious preference he wanted stamped on
the tags, he said, "LDS."

"Sorry," was the reply. "You'll have to be Jewish, Protestant,
or Catholic."

"Well," he thought to himself. "I'm not Jewish or Catholic,
so I'll have to settle for Protestant." A large "P" was stamped in
the bottom corner of his tags.

In March 1944, he filed aboard the USS *Hermitage* in San
Francisco to transfer to Goodenough Island at the lower end of
New Guinea in the South Pacific. It wasn't long before he was

wading through the jungle swamps in what turned out to be some of the most intense fighting of the war. He was reported missing in action for four days. On one occasion, he spent 32 consecutive days in the muddy, insect-infested swamp. During one battle he was knocked to the ground by the impact of a bullet smashing into his body. When he looked for the wound, however, he found the bullet had smashed into the shells on the bandoleer across his chest, stopping less than an inch short of his heart.

During a much needed break, he attended a memorial service for his companions who had lost their lives. During the service he was struck with gratitude for the Lord's hand in protecting his life. He decided that his dog tags didn't pay proper respect to his religious feelings. Because so many of his friends had been killed, he determined that if he died, he wanted people to know that he belonged to the restored Church of Jesus Christ.

With this resolve in mind, he undertook a plan to correct his dog tags while working his way through the fetid swamps of the South Pacific one oppressive spring morning. Using a stiff needle from his survival pack, he started very carefully to punch a pattern of dots in the hard metal of his dog tags to form the letters, "LDS." In time, he had altered both tags to show his true religion.

Ned served in many campaigns throughout the balance of the war, including the assault on the infamous Villa Verde trail in the Philippines. He was one of just a handful from his division that survived the campaign. Ultimately, he ended up in Japan as part of the occupation force.

Ned Allen never had occasion for his dog tags to identify him during the war. But today, 45 years later (and eight years since his death in McCammon, Idaho), those dog tags are a cherished reminder to his posterity that their grandfather loved the Lord and his Church. Of all the testimonies borne of the gospel, this is perhaps the simplest, yet most persuasive. In just three short letters—LDS—etched in metal like the plates of old, he told the world what he believed in.